THE MOONSHINE WOMEN

Michelle Collins Anderson

John Scognamiglio Books
Kensington Publishing Corp.
kensingtonbooks.com

JOHN SCOGNAMIGLIO BOOKS are published by

Kensington Publishing Corp.
900 Third Avenue
New York, NY 10022

All Kensington titles, imprints, and distributed lines are available at special quantity discounts for bulk purchases for sales promotion, premiums, fund-raising, and educational or institutional use.

Special book excerpts or customized printings can also be created to fit specific needs. For details, write or phone the office of the Kensington Sales Manager: Kensington Publishing Corp., 900 Third Avenue, New York, NY 10022. Attn. Sales Department. Phone: 1-800-221-2647.

The JS and John Scognamiglio Books logo is a trademark of Kensington Publishing Corp.

ISBN: 978-1-4967-4830-0
ISBN: 978-1-4967-4831-7 (ebook)

First Kensington Trade Paperback Edition: April 2026

10 9 8 7 6 5 4 3 2 1

Printed in the United States of America

The authorized representative in the EU for product safety and compliance
is eucomply OU, Parnu mnt 139b-14, Apt 123
Tallinn, Berlin 11317, hello@eucompliancepartner.com

Praise for *The Moonshine Women*

"Three extraordinary sisters fight against their hardscrabble life during Prohibition by selling the best moonshine in the Ozark Mountains. This captivating story of family secrets, vengeance, run-ins with the lawn and even gangsters such as Al Capone are impeccably crafted. The descriptive prose will have you breathing in the Ozark mountain air as the determined Strong sisters do whatever it takes to keep their family together, and they'll leave you thinking about them long after closing the book."
—Loretta Ellsworth, author of *The French Winemaker's Daughter*

"A feminine odyssey of legendary proportions, *The Moonshine Women* absolutely brims with hope, heat, and heart. When a murder in the mountains threatens the Strong family's way of life, their legacy and sisterhood both hang in the balance. Tender and gripping, this story is juicy all the way down to the last drop." —Amy Jo Burns, author of *Shiner*

"Michelle Collins Anderson has given us four distinctly different, yet similarly fierce protagonists to cheer for in *The Moonshine Women*. Set in the Ozarks during Prohibition, the Strong women have to fend for themselves and protect the family legacy of the best moonshine west of the Mississippi. From the Missouri hills to the flashy resort town of Hot Springs (where even Al Capone enjoys the nightlife), these women find their own places in this turbulent world but never break the bonds of love and respect that tie them together. This is a rip-roaring family saga that proves a man can't hold a candle to a woman when it comes to protecting—and avenging—the ones you love."
—Melanie Benjamin, *New York Times* bestselling author

"Transportive and deeply immersive, *The Moonshine Women* is a big-hearted homage not only to the hardscrabble Ozarks and the three formidable sisters whose stories Michelle Collins Anderson deftly depicts, but to a survival instinct encoded in the American experience. I especially enjoyed the collision of fact and fiction and the vivid evocation of the story's geographical and emotional terrain." —Christopher Castellani, author of *Last Seen*

And praise for *The Flower Sisters*

"Anderson weaves a rich and poignant tale of a small Ozarks town's factual tragedy, its generational secrets and the juxtapose of searching and belonging. Vivid and evocative, this is a debut to savor."
—Kim Michele Richardson, *New York Times* bestselling author of *The Book Woman of Troublesome Creek*

Books by Michelle Collins Anderson

THE FLOWER SISTERS

THE MOONSHINE WOMEN

Published by Kensington Publishing Corp.

For Benjamin, Levi & Vivian . . .
my "hearts."

As you gain confidence in
smelling the difference between
the point where the heads stop and the hearts begin,
the better flavor you'll be able to produce.

—Jennifer Poindexter,
"How to Make Moonshine the
Old-Fashioned Way in 6 Easy Steps"

THE MOONSHINE WOMEN

Prologue

October 1912

Lidy

She waited impatiently for the cedars.

The dry summer heat had held all through September, finally breaking in October with soaking rains and chilly nights that had the Strong family hauling out their quilts. The hills surrounding the cabin and fields turned colors, beginning with the bright red pops of leggy sassafras trees, bushy sumac and Virginia creeper vines that gave way to golden hickory, river birch and—near the creek—stately yellow cottonwoods. The oaks stubbornly held their leaves, yielding only a buttery brown before turning the color of old soil.

Likewise, the scrubby evergreens began to take on an orange cast as the fall wore on. And the cedar berries, which first appeared as clusters of green in compact cones, began ripening to the dusty deep hue of a blueberry. Every morning, after Lidy finished cooking for Hiram and the girls, cleaning up the dishes and sweeping the cabin clean, she wrapped up in a woolen shawl and walked the woods and fencerows with a tin pail.

Lidy's thoughts were a jumble. She alternated between worry for the baby and a low boiling anger at her daughter-in-law. How could she be so selfish? So stupid? These thoughts gave her a brief pang—but then she felt righteous. Who was here fixing things, after all? And who was suffering? Not Alta, of that she was sure. And meanwhile, Lidy battled bone-deep exhaustion from doing the work of a much younger woman every day.

She had known something was terribly wrong when Rebecca showed up at dusk two months ago on a field mule which could scarce be spared during harvest time to visit an old widow lady three hollers over. The thin switch of a girl wore dusty dungarees and a baggy cotton work shirt cinched with a piece of twine, her sun-bronzed face shaded by a large straw hat. If she hadn't known better, Lidy might have thought a young man had arrived in her patch of the Ozark Mountains, looking for work or selling something out of his saddle bag.

"Ma fell out the barn loft and she won't wake up." No greeting, no preamble. Lidy knew it took every ounce of bravery the girl possessed to report this to her. Because Lidy was not just the girl's grandmother, she was the closest thing there was to a doctor in these parts. She was the first one summoned if a birth looked worrisome, a broken leg needed setting or a child spiked a fever that wouldn't break. Lidy was full of what folks around called "granny cures," part training, part tinctures and herbal expertise, part common sense—topped with a goodly dollop of superstition. Fetching Lidy meant admitting things were serious.

Lidy had peered up at the girl's countenance, hidden beneath the brim of her hat. Her large brown eyes were full of fear, and her dirty face showed the evidence of tear tracks, the only clean spots on the child. Lidy kept her own face expressionless, not wanting to further frighten the girl. But if Alta wouldn't wake up . . . well, it didn't bode well.

After Lidy arrived at the cabin to assess the damage Alta had suffered in her fall—certainly no accident, she surmised, although she didn't say that out loud—Alta was as good as gone. The question was whether the baby was alive. She put her hand on the mound of Alta's stomach, estimating her at six or seven months along. She was carrying low, which meant a boy. And hadn't Lidy confirmed it, a few months back, cajoling her reluctant daughter-in-law until she was allowed to fasten Alta's wedding band to a strand of her long, dark hair? Dangling it over the mound of Alta's belly, she held her breath as the ring began to move. Back and forth, back and forth. Not in circles. She couldn't hide her pleasure: Hiram would have a son at last. Yet Alta hadn't even smiled. As if Lidy had said "Looks like rain" instead of "Looks like you'll be having a son."

It took nearly twenty minutes. Rebecca and Elsie, ten and six, crowded around Alta, petting her arm and smoothing the hair away from her brow. Hiram sat beside her, too, his head resting despondently in his hands. The truth was, Lidy had just about given up when she felt it: a burst like a bubble at the surface of a pond, followed by a writhing elbow jutting out as it turned.

"Thatta boy," Lidy said. Her granddaughters' eyes grew large.

"He's all right?" Elsie, the nurturer, could not hide the hope in her voice. Rebecca, as silent as she was sensitive, looked to her gran for the truth. But Lidy was impenetrable metal in looks and demeanor: steel-colored eyes set in a face burnished by decades of sun into the mottled copper of a well-used penny, framed by hair the silvery gray of pure iron. The hard line of her mouth gave nothing away.

"He's alive," Lidy said. "That's good enough for now."

So had begun the race against time. How long could Alta hang on, a body without benefit of a mind? How much time before the baby could survive in the outside world?

Lidy stopped dead in her tracks at a unique, piercing cry that could only mean one thing: the cedar waxwings were back. After a summer in cooler climes, the chubby birds had returned, with their black robber's masks and tails that looked to have been dipped in gold. And sure enough, just as Lidy came upon a stand of ten-year-old cedars at the edge of the woods, she startled one of the titular birds. The creature squeaked and fluttered its way out of a tree's thick middle before taking to the sky.

"If they are ripe enough for you, sir, they are good enough for me."

Lidy put her pail on the ground and reached into her apron pocket for a tin of salve made from beeswax and rubbed it into her dry, large-knuckled hands. Then she reached for one of the evergreen's branches, slightly bowed from the weight of the berry-filled cones. Cedars were scratchy by nature. Just poking around in the thick swaths of needles could bring blood and the cedar oil could cause a rash. The salve gave Lidy some protection, but she avoided the spiky sprays as best she could in her quest to fill her bucket.

But the smell . . . that sure didn't hurt anything. Lidy inhaled the sharp green odor and decided it alone could heal a world of wrongs.

Around her, there was the bustle of birds and squirrels in the wooded thicket. Living creatures were getting ready for winter, fattening up on fruits, berries, nuts and seeds, finding shelters, lining nests. Alta should be doing the same for her own family: putting up the rest of the vegetables, salting and curing the pork from the slaughtered pig, filling the cellar full of root vegetables—carrots, potatoes, yams, beets, radishes—and drying herbs. She should be lining the top dresser drawer with a hand-knit blanket, making a bed for the baby, crocheting a sweater and booties to keep him warm in the coming months.

But not a hat. Everyone knew making a cap for a baby before it was born was bad luck.

Maybe Alta did not know that superstition, being a town girl. Perhaps she had unwittingly crocheted herself into this mess. Lidy shook her head at her own ridiculous thoughts. Even a cursory look around the cabin showed there was no planning for this child. No knitting or sewing of tiny frocks or blankets, socks or mittens.

Because Alta had no intention of having a baby. She knew when she threw herself from that barn loft what would happen. What she hoped would happen, anyway. That the child would come early. Too early. And die.

And now, by God, it *would* happen. The baby would still come before his time.

But now, at least, he had a chance to live.

Lidy returned to the cabin, glancing at Alta, who remained exactly as she had left her that morning. She did a quick check of Alta's belly, warm beneath her hand, before setting about the business of making the tea: a cup of cedar berries boiled with twice as much water. After the mixture steeped, Lidy removed the berries and added a touch of honey to taste.

"Ooh, it's so pretty! Can I try some, Gran?" said Elsie, upon returning from her morning chores and finding Lidy's concoction cooling on the windowsill.

"No, that's your mama's," Lidy said. "It's time for the baby to be born and she needs all the help she can get."

Over the next three days, Lidy managed to dribble most of the tea into Alta's mouth and throat without choking her. But nothing happened. It was discouraging, but all the same, Lidy admired the child's stubborn will to remain in the perceived safe space of Alta's womb. It was a doggedness that had served him well thus far.

"It's high time you come out and meet us," Lidy said to her unborn grandson, one crisp October morning that left a velvety frost over the corn stubble and the remaining brown leaves on the trees. "The people who will love on you and keep you safe. And that damn sure doesn't include your mother."

As if on cue, Alta's belly tightened, a firm high knot hardening and holding itself stiffly before releasing. Lidy watched, amazed, as—a few minutes later—the whole routine started again.

"Why, I'll be good and goddamned," said Lidy. "It's time."

She rushed to the front porch and rang the dinner bell, even though it was only nine thirty in the morning. As usual, Elsie was first to show up, eager for the more social parts of the day over the solitude and drudgery of chores.

"Tell your daddy the baby is coming," Lidy yelled. "Then I need you and Rebecca."

Lidy had thought this through. Chatty Elsie would be asking questions as fast as they popped into her head, but she was quick and sympathetic to suffering. Rebecca was quiet, hardworking and had all the experience of birthing calves and foals. It had been a while since Lidy herself had shepherded a birth, and she knew her strength—if it was needed to pull or help push—wasn't what it used to be. But Rebecca was solid and strong as an ox, preferring to do rather than say. She was the calm to Elsie's storm, and together they'd make a fine team to bring their brother into the world.

The cabin took on a bustling, almost festive atmosphere. Rebecca brought in two large pails of water; Elsie put them on the wood stove to boil.

Hiram poked his head in the cabin door exactly once and had it nearly bitten clean off by the womenfolk. One woman anyway.

"Out! Busy yourself in the barn, Hiram," Lidy ordered. He did not have it in him to see his wife in additional pain, let alone blood or any of the other unmentionables involved in birthing. "Go chop some firewood."

"But . . ."

"But nothing." Lidy was stern. "*Scram!*"

"Please." Hiram fumbled in his pants pocket for his prized folding knife. "Put this under her mattress, won't you?"

Lidy smiled despite herself. She knew good and well he had not placed a skillet under the bed to guarantee a girl the previous two times he had awaited a birth. But her only son wanted to do everything in his power to ensure this would be a boy. Men were funny about sons. Even though Hiram had not gotten along with his own father—or perhaps because of that—he seemed desperate for this chance for a different relationship. Or maybe it was the relief another pair of broad shoulders could provide that appealed to him after so many years of overwork.

Lidy slid the knife into her apron pocket. "It will be all right, Hiram," she said, shooing him out the door. "You'll see."

"Gran, come quick," Elsie called. She held a pocket watch in her hand that had belonged to Alta's father, a rare treasure from her mother's prior life. "Her belly turns rock solid every two minutes now."

Had she overdone the cedar berry tea? If things happened too fast there could be tearing or hemorrhaging. Too much pressure on the child.

"Well, we better get ready to catch your baby brother." Lidy pushed up Alta's skirt and positioned her legs apart with the knees up, feet resting on the bottom of the mattress. Then she pulled down the old flour sack that was serving as a diaper.

In that instant, Lidy regretted her decision to involve the girls. What must it feel like, seeing their mother as helpless as a babe, soiled and oblivious of her ripe stench? But there was no use worrying about that now.

Elsie's eyes were fixated on the patch of the purply-pink skin between her mother's legs, growing larger with each tensing and release of Alta's body. She moved to her mother's side—out of sight of her sibling's determined struggle—and took her mother's limp hand.

"Mama, he's coming," she whispered. Lidy knew she didn't like this one bit, the painful-looking stretching, the body doing what it would without her mother's permission. Her modest mother, who would not tolerate this indignity were she awake.

Lidy's worry grew as the baby crowned and then lost steam.

"Stuck shoulder," Lidy said, under her breath. Alta was no help. No additional pushing or contorting, standing or squatting, was possible. To the silent granddaughter sitting between her mother's legs, she said: "Go wash your hands with the lye soap. Every inch of skin and under the nails."

Quick as a barn cat, Rebecca did her bidding. When she returned, slender hands red and raw, she looked expectantly at her grandmother.

"Slip your hand inside there until you feel that shoulder and push it in gently. Then when you feel your mama pushing, try helping if you can find anywhere to take hold."

Lidy cursed her own knobby arthritic hands that made her worthless. But Rebecca didn't need her help. A quick motion and she had turned the child, and in the next instant, with the aid of a strong contraction, Rebecca caught the slippery, blood-and-goop-covered babe in her lap.

Lidy snatched it up, vigorously rubbing and drying the purply body. Where was the breath? There needed to be crying. She had brought the fragile being into the world too soon.

Just as hopelessness set in, the baby opened its mouth and cut loose the highest-pitched, most awful noise Lidy ever heard. Yet even with her whole body set on edge by that yowl, she was jubilant. The child would live.

In the next breath, Lidy saw what she—in her panic—had missed: this was no baby boy.

She didn't trust her experienced eyes to be telling the truth. She turned the squalling child in her hands, spread the skinny legs in a vain search for the equipment a boy should have. Instead, she found creases upon creases, which she cleaned with care and no shortage of awe.

She had just delivered her third granddaughter.

With a jolt, she felt the sudden weight in her pocket. Hiram's knife. Not under Alta's mattress, ensuring there would finally be a male heir, but still nestled safely in her apron. Harmless. *No sharp object here.* Her face flushed. Yes, it was superstition, she knew this on some level. But *yet* . . .

"Gran?" The sisters stood stock still, awaiting her pronouncement on this writhing, wriggling being making herself known with her voice and the strength of her will.

"Meet your little sister," Lidy said. She swaddled the baby in a blanket made of quilt scraps and offered the bundle to Rebecca. But Elsie's outstretched hands intercepted the petite package, and she settled the baby into her arms as though she had mothered all her short life.

"Welcome to the family," Elsie whispered, her mouth by the shell-shaped ear. And then, to the perspiring heap on the nearby cot: "She is plumb perfect, Mama."

Rebecca nodded her solemn agreement, reaching out a tentative hand to touch the body that she had so recently dislodged.

"Well, don't just stand there," Lidy said. "Get your daddy."

He had waited long enough.

But when Hiram met his third and final daughter, he broke down.

"No!" He threw himself across Alta's body. The sounds he made were not human, somewhere between a guttural growl and animal keening. Lidy looked away. She did not approve of her son being so soft. Weak.

But Lidy knew Hiram held plenty of hard-earned grief for this wife he had adored and treasured like the most precious of pearls, laid out with a broken body and—most devastatingly—a broken mind. And now this shameful sadness, this disappointment. Hiram had been so certain that a son would be his lot. *Their* lot. He had chosen the name: Jason. *The Lord is salvation.*

So, Lidy did what she knew how to do: she kept going. And she would keep Hiram and the girls—all three of them—going, too. She took the swaddled babe, noiseless now, and handed her to her father. Hiram stared in bafflement and wonder at this girl child with the full head of hair that had dried into a halo of brilliant orange. And she stared back, unblinking.

He held the infant in the palm of his left hand, where she fit in all her miniature perfection. With his right index finger, he traced a cross on her forehead. Seeming satisfied with what he saw there, he nodded.

"Jace," he pronounced. "*The Lord is salvation.* But you, little one: you will save this family."

So Jace it was. Or, in the sternest of situations, Jace Alta Strong, when the flame-haired child needed her full-on, God-given Jesus name to fall into line. Or as an accompaniment to a whack on the back of those chubby legs with Gran's willow switch.

But everyone called her Shine.

Foreshots

July 1929

Hiram

The day was gloriously clear and still. As if the yellow-white ball of the sun burned in the Missouri sky just for him and his little girl—the perfect kind of morning for making shine. Not too hot. And no wind to carry the scent of mash or burning wood, raising the suspicions of any passing prohi or nosy neighbor.

The hardest part was getting out of bed.

"Daddy, rise and *shine*!" She laughed briefly at her own wit—but then she was jabbing him in the ribs. Hard. She had waited long enough. With her brown work overalls and thicket of orange-red hair in a high ponytail, she resembled nothing so much as a lit matchstick. And as usual, her pants were on fire to get up and at 'em. Where had she come from, this fireball of a girl? Hiram had thought long and hard on the mystery of her: not only different in looks from him and her ma and sisters, but that temperament! Woe unto the person who crossed the youngest Strong. Nope. Best stay on her good side. Even if she was irritating the hell out of you, like she was right about now.

He tried to sling an arm across his eyes to keep out the light, but it was too late. The slant of the sun through a chink high in the cabin wall told him all he needed to know: it was already mid-morning. There would be no more sleeping. His daughter would see to that.

"You can grab a biscuit and piece of fried ham on the way out the door," she went on. "Beck's got the chores nearly done and Elsie's churning butter. Gran's in the garden, and she's brought in one bushel of pole beans already. If we don't get to making moonshine, I'm scared of what we might be asked to do round here."

Of course, his little girl was not so little. Nearly seventeen. She was supposed to have been a boy. His only son, after two daughters. Hiram spent years breaking his back on this piece of Ozark mountain so hard you practically had to shoot the corn seeds into the hillside to get them in the dirt. He'd *needed* that boy.

But God knew better. Her mama died not long after she was born. But while the Lord took Hiram's heart, He saw fit to give him a light. Because in the darkness of those days after losing Alta, that baby girl managed to charm him. Pull him out of his funk. Give him purpose again. Even though she was an infant, he saw her spit and vinegar, that spirit that would soon be lighting a fire under them all. His ma said he took a shine to her right away—and that settled it.

Shine.

It was time to check the mash. Hiram and Shine had shoved the barrel full of fermenting grain into the limestone cave exactly two weeks ago and the temperatures since had been steady; not too hot. And if everything looked good, why, they'd light a fire under a kettle-full and get some quality hooch dripping.

"Daddy, get a move on," Shine said, poking her father's bare foot hanging out from beneath the thin quilt on his cot. He had built a slant-roofed room off the back of the house so Lidy and the girls could have more room in the cabin. He didn't need much space with Alta gone.

"Early bird gets the worm. Isn't that what you told me?"

Hiram grunted, pulling the feather pillow from beneath his head and placing it squarely on top of his face. There was a downside to living with a man who knew how to make good moonshine: he was typically good at drinking it, too. Maybe that wasn't the right way to put it. Because while Hiram was skilled at socking away the white lightning, he was not that gifted at dealing with the consequences. Sometimes, he didn't move too quick the next day. Or he woke up on the wrong side of the bed, as Lidy put it. Grouchy. Short with everyone and everything. Bloodshot eyes and breath that smelled like kerosene and was probably about as flammable.

In his younger days, he was quarrelsome when drunk or hungover, ready to pick a fight with his words or finish one with his fists. But these days, the battles he fought were mostly on the inside. He drank when he was sad. Or lonely. Or angry. But he also drank when he felt a glimmer of happy, sitting in the afternoon shade of his cabin, looking over his rough patch of land and watching his girls at work or play. He drank for no good reason. And every bad one.

He missed his woman. Hiram loved his three girls. He was even fond of his hard-as-nails mother. But Alta . . . just the sound of her name made him feel as if he were up in the clouds or on a mountaintop somewhere. And without her, he felt the lows. Dark crevices and hollers, the eddying, swirling deeps of a slow-moving river. A moonless Ozark night without a lantern to find one's way out of the shadows.

Alta had brought a much-needed softness to his life, with her delicate hands and her book learning. And her quiet faith. While being a preacher's daughter hadn't made her rich or above hard work, she had been unfamiliar with the punishing physical labor and loneliness that came with life in these hills. It can eat away at you, that lonesomeness. Especially when there is no respite from the work.

He knew she suffered. Alta went about her chores like a faithful workhorse, caring for the girls, tending the garden, feeding the hens and gathering eggs, cooking three meals a day, preserving, pickling, mending, sewing, washing. But she lost her smile those last few years. And in their narrow bed, she turned her back. She never refused him, but then, Hiram didn't ask. He kept hoping for an invitation that never came. So he reached for a bottle instead.

Hiram would have loved to treat Alta like the queen he saw her to be, bringing her plump blackberries and bouquets of wildflowers. Letting her dedicate herself to motherhood, instead of taking it on fearfully, reluctantly. Another chore. She should have been delighted by that third pregnancy. Hadn't he believed it a miracle? Instead, the baby sucked the remaining joy out of her like an opossum draining the contents of a chicken egg—leaving nothing but the near-perfect shell behind.

He didn't like to think on the shell that had housed her sweet soul . . . until it didn't. Those long months of staring nothingness from a body that had warmed his heart and his bed for nigh on twenty years. Alta had quietly slipped away one morning, utterly alone, while he had been out hunting.

He didn't even get to say goodbye.

Sometimes, when he drank, Hiram could feel Alta arrive at the edge of his consciousness. He would get this gnawing feeling in his gut and only the burn of moonshine down his gullet could make it stop, replace it with a glowing, spreading warmth from his belly to the tips of his fingers and toes. That felt like Alta; the old Alta. Warming him, stilling his mind. Helping him forget his pain. Alta, who would never betray him.

But she had been gone close to seventeen years. Shine was living proof of that. And it took more drinking—more often—to find that burning ember inside him that was his love. That made him want to carry on.

God, his head hurt something awful.

The girl put her freckly face right up next to his.

"Damn you, girl, and your endless bouncing and bossing," Hiram sighed. "And God bless you, too." He knew he wouldn't have had the motivation to get out of bed without her pushing and prodding, her constant questions, that burning need to know this and that and every kind of thing. She'd had no patience for sewing and mending like Elsie, hunting and tracking like Rebecca or gardening and gathering like her gran. But Shine loved the still.

She yanked off the pillow. "Let's go. Time's wasting!"

They grabbed their hats from a row of five hooks on the front porch and took off for their secret still, a good half mile away as the crow flies. Hiram never used the same route twice, starting along the cow path by the fencerow and doubling back now and again. Shine followed behind, carrying a fresh-cut oak limb Hiram had fashioned into something like a broom, removing the side limbs but keeping the bottom ones, with their full fans of fresh green leaves. She dragged the makeshift sweeper in front of her, back and forth and occasionally to the side, varying the designs in the dry dirt of any game trails they used. Her own specially soled boots covered her tracks handily, but she made sure to erase his, too. Just in case.

Meanwhile, Hiram had the knapsack with the big glass jug and clean mason jars. And a Winchester slung over his shoulder. One couldn't be too careful out there, what with Prohibition agents and snooping sheriffs and jealous or territorial neighbors. Besides, you never knew when you might come across supper—whether on four legs or on the wing. A man needed to be prepared.

Danger was everywhere. Greed, too. Hadn't he just warned off Elsie's beau after he appeared a mite more interested in what the Strongs might be cooking up top of their mountain than in warming the tender heart of his lovesick middle daughter?

At a stand of cedars, Hiram veered off from the fencerow into the woods. A few hundred yards farther and he could hear Kinney Creek, burbling a greeting. And smell it, that clean cool scent that follows a spring rain. Like a speckled trout, fresh out of the water, or mossy green rocks. There was a steep slope that led to the creek, and they soundlessly picked their way among the rocks and roots until they could see the entrance to the cave where the spring came up from deep underground.

Hiram motioned for Shine to hang back, making his way to the cave with caution. He checked the entrance for disturbances, both on the ground and in the screen of brush and limbs they had placed in front of the narrow opening for cover two weeks ago. His back to the cave, Hiram scanned their surroundings, his Winchester at the ready. Satisfied, he put down his knapsack, leaned his gun against the limestone ledge of the cave and motioned to his daughter.

All clear.

Shine

Shine ducked into the slender entrance of the cave tucked back into the limestone karst of the hard Ozark hillside. She loved this secret spot. Shine had been coming here as long as she could remember—playing house with Elsie or hide-'n-seek with Becks. They had knelt for great gulping mouthfuls of icy water from the little grotto, collecting in a crystalline pool before it spilled over to form the head of Kinney Creek. The narrow ledge around the cave offered purchase for those who were slim and nimble. And inside? A hiding place like no other for a slip of a girl.

Or a mash barrel.

Because the cave wasn't for fun anymore. Her daddy had claimed the girls' hidey-hole for his own, long before Shine and her sisters had outgrown their games. Said it was perfect for hiding his fermenting mash from prying eyes for the two weeks it took to come together. Before distilling time.

Prohibition had come to Missouri—as it did officially across the entire nation—in January of 1920. But some of the bordering states had gotten a serious head start going dry, like Arkansas in 1915. And since Kinney Creek was a stone's throw from the state line, more than a few Arkansawyers had slaked their considerable thirst with spirits from their northern neighbors. Like the Strongs.

But now the entire country was parched—and had been for nearly a decade.

Shine squeezed herself in behind the mash barrel tucked a few feet back so she could push while her daddy pulled. Once they had the barrel on flat, dry ground, Hiram pried open the lid. The pungent air set free from the mess of fermenting corn smelled exactly like pineapples.

Shine couldn't fill her lungs up fast enough. She had only ever savored one of the strange, spiky-headed fruits—for Christmas one year, a rare treat in these parts—but she had declared it "divine." That sweetness in the escaping air was a good sign. A sour odor could mean the mash had gotten some sort of contaminant, maybe even gone bad.

"Smells perfect," she said.

"And what do you see in there, girl?"

"No bubbles," said Shine. "So I believe we're ready to get cooking."

"I do most heartily agree," Hiram said. "Pretty soon you won't need your old man for nothing."

Shine laughed. But they both knew it was true. She had a knack for this moonshine business. There was a true pleasure in measuring out the corn and sugar, the yeast and barley; in cooking and titrating until you knew with every sense—sight, smell, touch, taste and even the sound and rhythm of the condensing, dripping shine—that you had achieved perfection. Her daddy said he felt it in his very marrow. And she understood because she did, too.

"Awww, now. I'll always need you, Daddy. You know I can't stand the stuff," Shine said. "Someone's gotta do the hard work of tasting the goods."

It was Hiram's turn to smile. "I reckon I'll keep doing it. Makes me feel useful. Now, get that fire burning, girl."

Shine hauled out a jumble of nice-sized rocks to the creek bank and placed them in a near-perfect ring for the fire. Then she started gathering wood, venturing around their outdoor distillery in ever larger circles until she had a decent pile of sticks. Shine busted a few of the larger limbs over her knee and made a teepee of kindling and leaves. Only the dry stuff would do. Green wood or wet leaves would make visible smoke, and the last thing they needed was a neighbor or worse—the sheriff or a fed—getting curious.

Before Prohibition, her daddy had made modest batches of hooch, as did most every farm family across the Ozark hills. It wasn't unusual. Just as each farm wife made her own blackberry preserves, persimmon jam and apple pies and canned the excess harvest of home-grown green beans, tomatoes, pickles, peaches and peas, every man made his own spirits. No self-respecting farmer would buy moonshine from a neighbor or—worse—a bar or saloon. What a waste of money!

And there was pride involved. Moonshine might not be bought and sold between neighbors, but it was surely offered as hospitality—and some men simply made it better than others. Recipes, routines and methodologies were handed down from generation to generation as reverently as a family Bible. Secret ingredients or tricks were guarded jealously, like a pious church lady unwilling to part with her prune cake recipe. Even if she did, you could bet she "forgot" to write down a key component or altered an amount here and there.

In the Strongs' case, Lidy taught Hiram everything he knew about making shine. A medicine woman of sorts, she often turned to tinctures for those seeking relief. Made with their homemade liquor, the elixirs could offer a much-needed calming effect at a certain dosage or serve as a painkiller in larger ones.

As for special ingredients, she rarely made the same recipe twice. Lidy loved nothing more than tossing a bucketful of over-ripe peaches or the innards of a mushy melon into the corn mash. Or fermenting some fresh fruit in a batch of shine to make her hooch something special—and giving those peaches or pawpaws a kick. Shine's daddy had followed suit. But they didn't speak of that extra "somethin'-somethin'" outside the family. You went to your grave with that shit. Or you might get put in it early.

But these days, moonshine was more than a hobby. Farming—

never a get-rich-quick scheme by any means—had become even harder since the Great War, as debt for machinery and equipment skyrocketed and crop prices plummeted. The Strongs turned their near-worthless corn into alcohol. Sending a few jugs on the sly to Springfield or Joplin or down to northern Arkansas was much more lucrative than selling their extra grain or bartering eggs, fruits and vegetables. Make something illegal and suddenly everyone wants what they can't have. Human nature, her daddy said. All that secretive stuff, the making and the hiding, the seeking and the finding. Plus the higher price tag. It made that hooch all the more satisfying when it finally bolted down your gullet and warmed your innards.

Shine didn't care much for that part. But she relished everything else about distilling day: the way the sun warmed her scalp through her hair on a midsummer's morning, the sweet scent of delicate Carolina roses, the breeze full of birdsong—bluebirds and orioles, crows and cardinals—warning each other of the Strongs' intrusion.

But mostly she loved being with her father. Out here in the woods, he walked upright, moving with a freedom and purpose he lacked out in the field or in the barnyard. In those places, he seemed bent, bowed. Not like this tall, long-striding daddy who whistled the birds' songs back to them, who taught her how to perfectly imitate their calls. It made Shine wish she favored him more—but Elsie was blond and blue-eyed like Hiram and Rebecca got his length along with her mother's dark hair and eyes.

But I got his magic. She loved their secret, almost mystical spot and the idea that no one knew exactly where they were. Shine and her daddy were in their own world.

With her sticks set just so, Shine reached into the pocket of her father's bag and grabbed the rusty metal match box, removing a single stick. She prided herself on never wasting a match. With a quick flick of her wrist, she had light—and almost instantaneously, a vivid flame which she set to the base of her tented kindling. The satisfying crackle and pop made Shine sit back on her haunches and enjoy the interplay of blue and orange and yellow-white flames.

Maybe *this* was why she loved making shine. The fire mesmerized her, made her feel as if it was heating and purifying every last thing inside her, making way for something painstakingly polished and new. There was something incredible to her about burning things up to create an entirely different substance. From solids to liquids to gas . . . and back to liquid again. A clear and colorless liquid that looked exactly like water. But did it ever pack a punch!

"Well done, daughter."

The fire was dancing blue blazes, and she and Hiram hoisted the copper pot on the grate. It took a while to get the mash boiling, but soon the vapors rose in the lyne arm and made their way to the worm box, where the cold spring water cooled the condensate. Shine waited for the first drop to emerge from the last copper coil and plink into the mason jar, which took forever. The second wasn't much faster. But then the drops started to come, quicker and heavier. It was a rhythm to a song that Shine knew in her bones: *drip, drip, drip* . . . when it was about three to five drops every second, she would get up and poke the fire so that the embers spread. Time to turn down the heat.

After a while, the drip from the still slowed and eventually stopped. Shine counted nearly two dozen pints, in two neat rows like soldiers. Hiram brought over the big jug made of bluish flint glass, placing a tin funnel on its open mouth.

"Now for the fun part." Hiram settled onto the large fallen hickory that served as their bench and rested his large, work-worn hands on his knees, pointy even through the thick canvas work pants. "Help me out, Shine."

She took the first jar and breathed in its aroma. This was the "foreshots," the beginning stuff not fit for human consumption. It might be good for stripping the paint off the side of your barn, but it wasn't something you'd willingly put in your body. If it didn't kill you outright, it would make you go blind and *wish* you were dead.

Ick. The delicate skin inside Shine's nose burned. She unceremoniously dumped the entire jar on the ground.

"That's right," Hiram said, nodding his approval. "But that's the easy part."

The next half dozen jars were the "heads"—also not good for drinking. But they would keep the last third or so of this portion and run it through the still once more for some heavy-duty alcohol. Shine knew that as she made her way along the continuum there would be a point where the bad smell began to turn slightly sweet. She took the briefest of whiffs from each open jar, passing by the ones that offended her young but experienced nose. When she had gone through about a half dozen or so, she smelled it: the sweet, almost floral scent of the "hearts."

"Here, Pa," Shine said, handing Hiram the pint jar that finally pleased her. He thrust his sharp nose down below the rim and inhaled.

"Heaven on earth, right here in this jar," he declared. Then he tipped his head back and took a deep gulp of the clear liquid, his Adam's apple bobbing in his throat. Wiping his mouth with the back of his hand, he set the jar down with a thump. "Perfect."

"Hmph." Shine shook her head. "You told me yourself that you only need to smell the hearts to know they've arrived. No need for swigging. By my calculations, you just drank a whole silver dollar."

"All I know is it went down smoother than silver and makes me feel shinier than a gold piece," Hiram laughed. "But our work here isn't done."

"Never said it was. You're the one taking a drink break," Shine huffed. She grabbed the next jar in line and the next and next, all duly sniffed and approved for funneling into the large take-home jug.

An oily film formed a layer on the last few jars of liquid. The smell shifted from flowery to something more like a brownish husk. She splashed some into the palm of her hand and rubbed it around. It felt greasy. The "tails." Shine overturned the jars, the discarded liquid running in muddy rivulets down toward the creek.

Shine sighed. "All that work for less than two gallons of moonshine," she said, joining her father on the hickory log at last.

"But this is God's work we're doing here, Shine," Hiram said, and belched. "Don't you forget it."

Then: a sharp sudden crack of a tree limb, followed by a rustle deep in the woods.

Both Strongs stood, scrambling for cover. Shine made it behind a shingle oak, breathing hard.

Who's there?

Shine peered from behind her tree trunk in time to see the flag of a massive white-tail buck zigzagging through the trees before stopping short at the creek, not ten yards from where she stood.

The majestic creature raised his head, sniffing the air with suspicion before taking a drink. Deer were not plentiful anymore in these parts thanks to overzealous hunters, so Shine took a moment to commit him to memory. The buck paused, raising his heavy rack again—she counted a dozen antlers—and stared back precisely where Shine stood hidden, as if he sensed her there.

He was probably looking out for his family. Checking things out ahead, blazing a trail, keeping them safe from harm. Just like her own daddy. She imagined a doe, and three spotted fawns, curled up right this minute, nose tucked to haunch, in a makeshift bed of leaves and scrub. Invisible until they emerged at dusk to stretch their spindly legs and find a dinner of tender greens and a drink from the burbling creek.

"Damn," said Hiram, emitting a low whistle somewhere behind her. "And me without my Winchester."

Her daddy's voice broke the spell, sending the buck bolting into the undergrowth, flag flying. Shine had to smile. Venison would have been a treat, but she felt light, almost giddy with relief that the bounding buck had been spared. And that she and Hiram were safe, too. After all, the animal wasn't the only one with reason to be skittish. The woods weren't the haven they once were for humans, either, with lawmen of every stripe crawling the mountains in search of moonshine.

And its makers.

Rebecca

Sugar, please, and plenty of it!

Rebecca had gotten her marching orders from Shine and Hiram this morning as she saddled up Marge and pointed the old mare's nose toward town. Now she fidgeted near the counter, biding her time until Mr. Hanson could wait on her. There was a line at the store this morning, and at the front of it was Nan Giddings, who invariably wasted the proprietor's time (and that of the people in line behind her) by insisting on being shown needles in every size, threads in every color, fabric of every shade, before making the tiniest of purchases, her examined but discarded items piled high on one end of Mr. Hanson's gleaming wooden countertop.

"I suppose I'll take three and a quarter yards of your muslin," Nan finally said with a sigh. Mr. Hanson, without a twitch of impatience, unfolded the plain coarse fabric from the bolt with a practiced turn of his wrist. Pressing the fold up against the measuring stick he had affixed to the edge of the counter, he brought the open scissors toward the fabric just as Nan said, "Better make it three and a half . . . if you don't mind, Charles."

"Not at all, Mrs. Giddings," he said. He calmly unrolled a fresh swath of material, setting aside the ruined piece he had just nicked. But Rebecca saw the large purply vein at his temple shift back and forth.

It was a good four miles by trail and dirt road from the Strong cabin to the small town of Kinney and Hanson's General Store. The large, two-story building's front room contained a cash register on the counter, behind which stood the owner of the place, Charles Hanson. And behind him, shelves of essentials, from elixirs and pipe tobacco to soap and sewing needles, plus various types of twine and rope, wire and chain, hammers and saws. Even a large glass jar of shiny black, four-hole buttons, the kind a rag doll might sport for eyes.

A glass-front display case next to the counter held every manner of penny candy, which a much younger Rebecca and her sisters had coveted every Saturday morning when the family trekked in for staples and socializing. When Rebecca did get to choose a piece of hard candy—horehound and licorice were her favorites—she wouldn't eat it right away like her younger sisters. She wanted to savor the special treat as long as she could. Which is why, when she excavated it from the depths of her pants pocket a week later, she found it sticky and covered with lint . . . but beneath, every bit as delicious as she dreamed it would be.

The aisles had barrels of cornmeal, flour, sugar, sorghum, molasses, walnuts and a variety of other basics in bulk that needed to be precisely measured out, weighed and wrapped by Mr. Hanson. There were also bolts of fabric, mostly durable wools and canvases in grays and browns, but the occasional delicate cotton floral print that had the ladies *ooh*ing and *aah*ing until every female within twenty miles of the holler had pretty much the same dress—Rebecca being the exception: she didn't care for dresses. Give her a pair of dungarees any day.

In the back was a storeroom where Mr. Hanson kept his extra stock and out-of-season goods. There was a water closet, a wood stove and a several three-legged stools for the men to sit and pass the time while the women gawked at the finer things they couldn't afford and bargained for the things they *almost* could. Here, gossip and fish stories were passed back and forth with as much enjoyment as the flasks the men shared, even if it wasn't yet ten o'clock in the morning.

Hanson's was where Alta had traded her precious hens' eggs in their delicate hues of blue and tan—and now Rebecca or Elsie did the same. But today was not about eggs. Rebecca had brought two squarish burlap bags for Mr. Hanson to fill to bursting with sugar—fifty pounds, to be exact. If Marge could handle a bigger load, Rebecca would ask for even more.

It took lot of sugar to make moonshine.

When it was finally Rebecca's turn, she froze. She was not a good conversationalist, with the exception of one-sided talks she had with her farm animals. In those instances, she felt both witty and completely understood. With people, especially those she didn't know well, her tongue seemed suddenly too large for her mouth, her thoughts racing around the inside of her head like a bunch of wild horses in a corral. She couldn't capture them, skittish and slippery creatures that they were.

"Good morning, Rebecca." Mr. Hanson bailed her out, amused, it seemed, by her silence. "What will the Strongs be needing today?"

"Morning, sir," she managed. "My gran is needing some sugar. I brought some bags to fill."

Mr. Hanson raised an eyebrow. "Mighty big bags."

This was the part she had practiced with her sisters at home. Otherwise, she might have turned and fled.

"You know my gran," Rebecca said, shrugging. "When she gets to making her jellies and jams and pies, there ain't no stopping her. Fifty pounds, please."

Mr. Hanson gave a doubtful smile, but rang her up. "Take your sacks round back," he said. "Jedediah will fill them from the shipping barrels and load your mare."

Rebecca released her breath. She had made it. Again. It was becoming increasingly difficult to buy what they needed to keep the still going and not bring their operation under scrutiny. Especially since it had grown. They were making ten times the money on moonshine as they did selling their corn for feed. Her father had gone from making a few gallons for himself—and he drank a sight more than he should—to making dozens for the thirsty hordes that lived beyond their mountain.

But it wasn't legal. Not by a country mile. And Rebecca faltered in that knowledge. *We gotta make a living, don't we?* Before moonshining, they had barely scraped by, year after year. And God made corn and rain and sunshine and the human desire to drink and be merry . . . surely, He understood how those things went together and approved.

She walked Marge around to the back of the store. The midsummer sun was already high in the sky and the mare left horseshoe prints in the fine gray silt. There had been no relief in the form of rain for a few days.

"Sugar again, huh?" Jedediah's voice was overly sweet, as if laden with sugar itself. But Rebecca heard an edge in it. He took the flat sacks and stood for a moment, scratching his blond, unkempt hair. Handsome, somehow, a face of fine angles, like a statue. Blue eyes as cold and light as a winter sky and about as empty. She didn't know how Mr. Hanson allowed his only son to look like such a ruffian, with his rumpled clothes and unshaven face. It didn't seem good for business. Maybe that was why he was here in the back.

"Pretty sure what you all are up to," he said. "I'm thinking you could use a helper?"

Rebecca kept her mouth closed. Conversation with Jed wasn't necessary to the procurement process and she damn well wasn't making any with the likes of him. But her taciturn nature didn't deter him.

"Alrighty then." Jed sulked. "You Strongs think your shit don't stink. Might want me on your side is all I'm saying."

"The sugar?"

"Speaking of sweetness, how is Elsie, that fine sister of yours?"

Rebecca did not like the way her name sounded in his mouth, like a bite of savory stew meat, greasy and tender at once. "We are all well, thank you. You'd know that if you'd been to church with her of late."

He frowned at the obvious coolness in her tone. "Hmmm. Might ask your daddy about that. Anyways, I been busy here at the store, it being summer and all. But please tell her I said 'howdy do.'"

That was curious. She wanted to know what her daddy had said or done to keep Jed from church and—by extension—Elsie. But that would require conversation. Rebecca let it pass.

Marge switched her tail impatiently as Jed loaded the two sacks behind her saddle with a grunt and gave an overfamiliar slap to the mare's rump.

"There you go, ladies," he said.

Marge responded by lifting her tail and relieving herself with a few steaming plops. Rebecca swung up into the saddle, leaned forward over Marge's right ear and gave her the half an apple she had in her shirt pocket. *My feelings exactly, girl.*

She'd started to kick the mare's sides with her heels and head toward home when she heard the screech of brakes, car wheels spinning gravel. Doors slammed and a man shouted. Something was happening out in front of the store. And against her better judgment, she turned the horse around to find out what it was.

John

"Step right up, ladies and gentlemen!" R. J. McConnell stood fat and sweating in his ill-fitting suit in the middle of Kinney's main street. The town's only street, in fact. He mopped his brow with a folded handkerchief before giving John the signal to unload the hooch.

"You're about to see what happens when you get on the wrong side of the law in these parts," he bellowed. "Flanagan?"

John Flanagan despised alcohol and everything that went along with it. He had grown up in Ohio in an Irish family in the righteous shadow of Carrie Nation and the temperance movement that evolved—finally—into the Volstead Act. *Prohibition.*

He was a "prohi," a federal agent charged with enforcing the Volstead Act and searching out offenders, small and large, who saw fit to break the law. His motivation derived from years of watching his father squander his meager paycheck on drinking at a corner bar after work, leaving nothing for his family of seven to buy food or clothing. Or pay the rent.

At age nine, John had marched. His ma had sent her raggedy clutch of children—barefoot and in patched, outgrown clothing—into the streets of Westerville, Ohio, to protest drunkenness in general. But more specifically in the person of Patrick Flanagan. She felt corroded by Catholic shame, baring her troubles with her husband like so much dirty laundry hung out to dry. She had married him, after all. Made her bed and all of that. But that shame foundered in the face of a starving toddler. The way the kids would cry because their empty stomachs hurt—and worse, when they stopped crying and huddled together for comfort and warmth in a quiet, shivering heap.

Miraculously, the marching and protesting worked. John didn't know about the rest of Ohio or the U.S. as a whole, but Patrick Flanagan had straightened up and been a man about it. He didn't like his children in the street and, even more humiliating, sent to fetch him, drunk on his barstool with his snockered drinking buddies looking on in amusement or pity. It wasn't what the Lord had intended for a man and wife, a family. So: no more drinking. At least, no drinking in saloons. And that was enough to get his family fed and sheltered. Nothing else should matter.

Except . . . it *did* matter to John. It wasn't enough for his father to see the error of his ways. He wanted this happy ending reenacted in other homes and in other families. Which was how he found himself heaving a pickup truck full of confiscated mash and shine—in barrels, glass growlers and even buckets—onto the rutted clay road under a molten midday sun.

Kinney was barely a wide spot in the road, but it was bustling on a Saturday with last-minute customers at the dry goods store and others trading gossip and eggs and jams on the corner near the run-down church. McConnell had made a point of revving his engines, clearing the pedestrians and parking right in the center of the skinny street, blocking any potential traffic—whether horse, wagon or the rare automobile—from getting through.

With a showman's flourish, McConnell took every bottle, bucket and barrel and emptied them one after another into the dusty street—amid gasps and groans from the crowd that had gathered. Sheriff Burkett stood off to the side, not really endorsing the performance, but not stopping it, either. It was a fine line to walk in these parts, staying on the right side of the law and the citizens at the same time.

"Lemme grab a cupful if you're gonna waste it!" yelled someone in the back, creating a wave of sniggering.

"The only waste around here is those who throw away their lives by imbibing," McConnell thundered. "And your government will not abide it."

McConnell's show was over-the-top—not quite up to his New York City antics, thank God—but John had to admit it made the point. There was something like a massive group sigh from the spectators as they watched the prodigious puddles of moonshine spread into tinier and tinier tributaries until soaking into the clay dirt for good.

But McConnell was just getting started. He took the glass containers and held them overhead briefly before smashing them into shards in the street. The shocked crowd took several steps back, afraid of flying debris. Meanwhile, John chopped up any remaining wooden buckets or barrels with an axe until they were fit for nothing but the fire. McConnell would have loved to perform that part of the spectacle, but he wasn't a young man anymore. His soft, well-upholstered body and a heart prone to palpitations made him afraid of hard labor, even for show.

John had rolled up his shirtsleeves by then, and not a few females in the crowd took notice of the broad shoulders and well-muscled arms as he hacked away at the contraband containers. In these moments, he channeled Carrie Nation, with the devastating "hatchetations" she waged on bars and saloons across the Midwest. Sweaty work, to be sure, but so satisfying. And on the right side of the Lord and the law.

Sometimes at these displays there was clapping, mostly from the churchgoing and mainly women. Occasionally, the prohis were shouted down or threatened. But today, there was only pained silence, with heads shaking. Helpless shrugs. It wasn't their hooch, after all. But still, it hurt to see it squandered.

He had started his career in New York City, the place where everyone knew illegal spirits ran like rivers through the boroughs, tunnels and streets of the city. Might as well start at the top! Or the bottom, as it were. Because to this fresh-faced Ohio-born-and-bred Catholic boy, New York appeared a haven for a bunch of low-lifes, scoundrels and full-on criminals.

He was paired up with R. J. McConnell ostensibly because the senior prohi had much to teach a rookie like John. His statistics were unparalleled in the city—and even the country. He often bragged that he had a couple dozen arrests under his sizable belt before breakfast. He wasn't the typical thin, lanky fed who spoke in clipped, economical sentences and looked good in a suit. He was rumpled, rotund and extremely loquacious. The man loved to eat. And drink. And, John would find out, fornicate.

Early in his career, McConnell would knock on the door of a speakeasy or a "blind tiger"—a storefront that posed as a pharmacy or fruit store but sold illegal booze under the counter—and demand a drink. The unassuming-looking prohi would slam down the shot he was given and promptly arrest the surprised bartender. But charges didn't stick without evidence. And the evidence was busy warming that big belly of his. That was when McConnell craftily devised a funnel that perched in his vest's pencil pocket. A tube attached to the bottom of the funnel drained behind the vest and into a small glass bottle in his pants pocket. Once he was served, he sipped the drink, and surreptitiously tipped the rest into the funnel. Then he excused himself to the bathroom, where he corked the bottle with the contraband, marking it with the time and place of violation.

He was proud of that.

"Using the old noggin, I tell ya," McConnell boasted, pointing to his round balding head. "But I still got to taste the wares."

For several years, McConnell made an incredible number of collars, solely by being a squat, middle-aged man in a pair of grungy coveralls—with a badge in his pocket. McConnell would regale anyone at headquarters who would listen about his success stories. Lord knew Flanagan suffered through the telling and re-telling of his partner's grandiose tales often enough.

"I'd knock on a door and ask if anyone had a drink for a thirsty Prohibition agent," he bragged. "The bartenders would take one look at me, laugh and serve me up . . . and clap me on the back for being such a comedian. When I'd take out my badge, they thought it was a joke. Until it wasn't."

After his early years of success, his unconventional looks became an alarm bell rather than a welcome mat. Bartenders, bootleggers and speakeasy proprietors had pictures of R. J. McConnell thumbtacked behind their bars or taped to an office wall. His face and figure were infamous. And his arrest numbers plummeted.

Flanagan had only been around a few weeks when he understood that he was partnered with McConnell because no one else with any rank would agree to work with him. He was a big blowhard. And worse than that, McConnell was going to greater extremes and schemes to bust the bartenders and establishments selling hooch. He was driven. Obsessed. And maybe slightly unhinged.

He started using props to get himself in the door of a suspected speakeasy or purported bar. One day he showed up with a fishing pole, the next a jug of cream or some home-canned cucumbers.

"Who would picture a prohi as a fat guy with a jar of sour dills?" McConnell would say, laughing uproariously, slapping his thigh. "I put those boys in a pickle, all right!"

At first Flanagan was told to "stay back and watch a pro at work," as McConnell picked up the prop or donned the outfit of the day. John stepped in to provide backup if McConnell needed it, accepting his assignment with both reluctance—he wanted to be in on the action!—but also a goodly amount of relief. He wasn't sure he was cut out for McConnell's brand of bar-busting. Like the time he took a trumpet to a bar known to be a musician hangout, tooted out a squeaky but heartfelt rendition of "How Dry I Am," and was rewarded with enthusiastic applause and a free round of drinks by the waitstaff and bartenders. He and Flanagan arrested the lot of them.

But as the underbelly of New York City became wise to McConnell's ploys, he had to go even further. And he expected Flanagan to follow suit.

Literally.

The first time McConnell insisted that he and Flanagan put on disguises together to bust a bar, he had them dress as fruit vendors, complete with a loaded cart of waxy red apples and bumpy navel oranges. Who wouldn't give this hardworking pair a shot of the hard stuff?

Then it was coal delivery men. Ice vendors. Cigar salesmen. Lawyers in suits with reams of documents bulging from their black briefcases. They even put on white lab coats to pass for doctors in a speakeasy near Mt. Sinai Hospital frequented by off-duty physicians. Nothing was off-limits. And their arrest record was unprecedented.

"Son, we're cuffing a couple dozen bad eggs before breakfast," McConnell would chuckle, punching Flanagan playfully in the arm. "That's *unbeatable*!"

The New York press was in love with McConnell—and by extension, his sidekick, Flanagan. They were the Mutt and Jeff of Prohibition enforcement. And their antics made great fodder for readers. Although Flanagan would never choose to talk to a reporter, the blustery McConnell was a media darling, with his everyman looks, clever schemes to outsmart the outlaws and an endless stream of quotable quips.

That didn't mean Flanagan had to like it. The arrests and bringing the criminals to justice? That was what kept him going, day in and day out. Cleaning up the wettest spots of New York City by pouring out illegal liquor in the streets. But he hated the vaudevillian aspect of McConnell's approach: the costumes, the adopted personas, the showmanship of it all. It wasn't him. And, truth be told, he felt like a laughingstock among his peers.

The end came when McConnell put Flanagan in a wig and bride's dress—John refused the lipstick on principle; he had some pride, after all—with himself outfitted as the lucky groom. They busted a ring of priests selling sacramental wine to thirty-five congregants in the basement of a Catholic church.

That was a bit *too* much success—even by New York standards.

McConnell and Flanagan were making the other prohis look bad. And the higher-ups in D.C. didn't like their popularity. Or the fact that the duo didn't adhere to their prescribed ideas for how a fed should look and behave.

They could turn in their badges. McConnell could retire or—as more likely in the case of the younger Flanagan—try another career. Or they could head to the middle of nowhere and dry up the ever-increasing flow of Ozarks moonshine.

Thank God. Flanagan knew he disappointed his partner when he didn't act heartbroken to take on the new unglamorous assignment in a place that was by all accounts uncivilized. But he was a serious young man—and he was more than ready to get serious about his work. Which was why he ended up tramping through the heart of the Ozark Mountains with a crazy man, on a mission to destroy every moonshine still they could find.

ELSIE

Elsie chose a square cotton cloth with simple yellow daisies embroidered by her own hand, even though tablecloths were typically only for Sunday dinner. Then she placed the five tin plates and forks on top and filled the five tin cups to the brim from the water bucket. Hands on hips, Elsie surveyed her work and, dissatisfied, grabbed her gran's sewing shears and slid them into her apron pocket.

Flowers.

She didn't need to go far. A few short steps out the door and behind the cabin and she was in the garden. Below it, the woods, and to the west, pasture. A fencerow of barbed wire and wooden posts allowed tangles of high grasses and wildflowers that weren't easily accessed by curving scythes and grasping cow tongues. Besides, both her gran and her older sister liked a little wild at their edges—it made for good medicines and comfortable nesting places for quail and rabbits.

With a pang, she remembered playing "rabbit" in that very fencerow, making herself small amidst the stems of scarlet bee balm and coneflowers. She had been six then, hiding from a hungry coyote or a hunter. Elsie had put her arms down in front of her on the ground—her forelegs!—and waited for her mother rabbit to return safely to their home of thick green fescue and flower stalks.

Elsie should have been in the cornfield alongside her big sister and daddy. But she got so tired! The worn wooden handle of the hoe she used for weeding around the green fountain-like corn plants was taller than she was and her tender hands filled with red weepy blisters. She regularly found excuses to get out of hard labor. An outhouse break. A trip to the creek to fetch some drinking water. That day, she said Mama wanted her early to help get dinner on the table.

Only, she hadn't. Which was why Elsie was pretending to be a bunny, passing the time until she could reasonably appear at home and do something for her mama before the other two showed up. From where she crouched, she could see the barn loft open, way up high. The hay they had cut in early summer piled high in the center, cured and keeping dry in the August heat. Elsie loved that smell, golden and dusty, and spent many hours with Rebecca, playing "barn cat" or burrowing into the haystack for hide-'n-seek.

But that day, she had seen something strange: her mother was at the door of the loft. Alta never went up there. Her precious chickens—her "girls"—had a coop and the feeding and watering of the larger barn animals—horses, mules, cows and hogs—were Rebecca's responsibility. Her beautiful mama put a hand on her bump of a belly and leaned against the edge of the opening. They were going to have a baby; a brother, her gran had said, rubbing her hands together in a rare show of delight.

At first, Elsie thought her mother was shaking out a calico blanket or a rug and letting it go. But then she realized her mother was trying to fly from the loft, pushing herself into the air. There was a sliver of time—a split second, really—when Elsie thought Alta had achieved the impossible: flight. A homespun, dark-haired angel, reaching for the heavens where she belonged. But then falling instead, terrifyingly fast, landing on the hard grassless earth of the barnyard.

A sound she would never forget: her mother's head meeting a

limestone rock, half exposed in a wheel rut and covered with a pile of manure. Like a soft, ripe cantaloupe splitting open.

Later, she would ask questions. Not of her father, whose grief made him unreachable to anything other than moonshine. But of her practical gran. "*Why?* Why did Mama jump?"

"Hush, now, child." Lidy put a stiff finger to Elsie's tender lips. "Your mama fell. It was an accident. No one's fault. Plain bad luck."

Elsie said nothing. But she knew what she saw.

Reflexively, she touched her own belly, there among the blooms and weeds. Said a silent prayer. *Forgive me, Mama. But I don't want to feel sad today.*

She gathered a wild and winsome bouquet, beginning with brilliant black-eyed Susans, gold halos ringing their single dark orbs, finely textured with seed bumps. She snipped a dozen stems, leaving some for future enjoyment and reseeding. Gran would skin her if she cleared out the patch. Farther down, the purple coneflowers stood on taller stems, orangey centers like suns. Elsie clipped a couple for height. On the way back to the kitchen, she stopped by Gran's herb patch for two nice sprigs of lavender.

Festive.

Elsie was in the mood to celebrate. Put on a frock, do a jig, sing at the top of her lungs. Something. But on this crusty old farm, she was short on fancy. This felt like the next best thing. Inside, she arranged every blossom just so in one of Lidy's glass canning jars and placed the flowers on the center of the table. *There.*

"What's this?" Gran's voice accompanied the slamming of the door. She had been on a gathering expedition of her own, the basket on her arm full of gooseberries. "Who are we expecting for dinner? The Queen of England? Better put on my Sunday dress."

Elsie's cheeks reddened. Before she could say anything, the door creaked open again and Rebecca was setting down her Winchester in the corner and hanging her flat, brown-brimmed hat on the wall.

"Rebecca, ring that bell!" Lidy said. "Better bring in Shine and your pa for the hoity-toity dinner we're having."

Rebecca obliged, leaning out the door and grabbing the twine attached to the dinner bell. She gave it three quick jerks in succession, which was family code for "suppertime." Here of late, they'd had to adopt another code. A nonstop clanging that could only mean one thing: John Law was here and you best hide anything that needs hiding—including your own damn self—until it was safe to come out. The "all clear" was a single note rung on the old copper bell.

After Hiram and Shine washed up and slid into their seats, Lidy ladled a steaming serving of rabbit stew onto each plate while Elsie started around a bowl of greens boiled with hambone. Everyone helped themselves to the basket with thick slabs of fresh-baked wheat bread for "soppin'."

Every head bowed. Usually Hiram made do with a perfunctory "Lord God, Heavenly Father, bless us and these Thy gifts which we receive from Thy bountiful goodness, through Jesus Christ, our Lord."

But not today. Hiram appeared duty bound to mention the beauteous summer weather and hopeful start to the corn crop; to send up a plea for a good soaking rain and give gratitude for gifts like greens and ham, wheat and butter. Entreaties for the less fortunate, the hungry and sick and poor, whether in body or spirit.

When would it end? Elsie noted a gelatinous skin had formed on her stew with her daddy's "pontificating," as Gran called it.

A sudden sharp pain in her shin. Elsie raised her head to Shine—that devil—pulling a face and Rebecca suppressing a smile. Everyone was ganging up on her! But Gran, with the terrifying arch of single brow, returned the girls to their pious poses.

"Amen." Hiram raised his head and winked at Elsie.

"*Amen!*" Forks flashed and exclamations were made over the first satisfying bites of stew and bread.

"Daddy, I swear," Elsie pouted. "My meal's practically cold."

"But you wouldn't short the Lord his due, would you now, daughter?" Hiram took a mouthful of stew meat. "There's plenty of time for hearing about the day's goings-on. Fine dish, Ma."

"Thank you, son. Rebecca brought me a young rabbit and that does make tender meat a hair easier, pardon the pun."

Elsie took her opening. "Speaking of Rebecca, how was your trip to town?" She aimed for a casual tone. But she was dying to hear all about it, every last bit!

Hiram held up a hand. "Don't you want to hear what Shine and I were up to today? Why, we had that still a thumping like a thunderstorm today, right in the middle of a sunny summer day. Didn't we now, gal?"

Shine bobbed her orange-red head. "Another day, another five dollars, I'd say. And another gallon or two for Gran to do her magic. I was wondering: Will she steep this batch with blackberries or something I haven't even thought of yet?"

Lidy laughed. "You all are tormenting Elsie. Let the girl hear about town now."

Elsie fumed silently. She hated everyone teasing her this way, but she craved the details of any trip to Kinney. How did they do it, living out here on a lonesome mountain, seeing only each other and a bunch of brainless chickens, cows and corn all day long? Plus the occasional seeker of Gran's tinctures or advice. She was sick to death of wearing the same work clothes, eating the same meals—Lidy was a good cook, but it was a limited rotation—talking endlessly about the weather, the season, the crops. Her whole life, she'd been no different, content to play with her sisters, hold conversations with the laying hens, help Gran with the mending or a batch of lye soap.

But lately there was something inside her that was yearning to get out. Like she had been hibernating, a dark animal slumber, and now the rich, verdant smells of warmer weather were beckoning her to wake up, to skip across the hillsides and hollers, smell some new exotic blooms, break off a piece of fresh honeycomb, lick it clean and chew the waxy cells until there was nothing left.

She settled for glimmers. And today those would be provided, willingly or not, by her oldest sister.

"Well . . ." Rebecca was uncomfortable with all eyes on her but knew the adventure was hers alone to tell. "Marge and I got started around sunup. We hadn't made it but a half mile when she pulled up lame and wouldn't go any further.

"I hopped down and quick as you please, Marge held up her front hoof for me to take out a rock stuck up in the tender spot."

"Right or left hoof?" Shine's eyes danced wickedly. "I've pondered whether an animal favors one over another, like us."

Elsie couldn't help herself; tears came to the corners of her eyes. "Please, Beck. Get me to town already."

The entire table burst out laughing. They were maddening, the whole lot of them!

Rebecca looked hurt. "I was getting there, Else." She was as methodical and dependable as sunrise and sunset, and she wouldn't be rushed. "When we pulled up to Hanson's, there was already a line—and I had to wait while Nan Giddings ran Mr. Hanson ragged for a bit of muslin in the end."

Everyone bobbed their heads. The woman was a notorious prattler and time waster.

"Then Mr. Hanson rang me up for the sugar," she continued. "But it was so much, he sent me out back to get our sacks loaded up."

"Did he have any black licorice?" Her younger sister wore what might pass as an earnest expression, if Elsie hadn't known it as another ploy to get Rebecca off track.

"No one cares about licorice, Shine! Especially you! You hate the stuff and you know it." Elsie's heart was pounding. *Please. Tell me about* him.

"Jedediah loaded old Marge," Rebecca said and at last Elsie relaxed into her chair, like a child ready for her favorite chapter of a well-loved bedtime story. "But . . ."

"But *what*?" Elsie wanted more. More details of Rebecca's interaction with her crush, her *love*. More "ands" and no "buts."

"I don't know. He went on about how much sugar it was for a family our size, Daddy. His pa mentioned it, too. Jed's aiming to find out what we're up to. Figure out how he can get a piece of it somehow."

"Why, I'd like to give that cake eater a piece of my fist!" Hiram pounded on the table and the tin cups jumped, sloshing water. "The boy must be thick between the ears."

"Hiram, calm yourself," said Lidy. She was used to his rash displays; impulsive from the time he wore short pants. But fortunately, his flare-ups were easily quelled and his memory for transgressions momentary. A knock-down, drag-out with a fellow over some perceived slight could end, ten minutes later, in laughter with the same man over a glass of whiskey.

"But did Jed ask about *me*?" Elsie finally blurted, sick to death of her family and their distractions. And their maligning of her love.

"Speaking of *sugar*," said Shine.

"Jedediah did ask after you, sis," Rebecca said. "Told me to say 'howdy do.' But I'd rather you howdy *didn't*."

Everyone roared; Rebecca rarely joked.

"I also saw a couple of prohis in the middle of Main. Dumping shine, splintering kegs and shattering a few stills." Rebecca employed the same steady drone that might disinterestedly report an inch of rainfall or mention that fruit had set on the peach trees.

"Daughter!" Hiram was purple-faced. "We ask about town and *this* is what gets told last? Jesus Christ on a cracker!"

The dinner-table discussion dissolved in gasps and shouts, Shine riled up and ready to wage war against a perceived threat while Hiram and Lidy peppered Rebecca with questions:

"Who did they bust?"

"How *much* hooch?"

"Where was the sheriff in all this?"

"Do we know where they're headed next?"

But Elsie missed all of that. She didn't hear anything beyond the fact that Jedediah asked about her. It was the only thing she needed to hear this whole dang night. She would take that hope, polish it to a high shine, put it under her pillow and dream.

John

"God*damn* it."

John was not one to take the Lord's name in vain, but he found himself doing so halfway up this Ozark mountain, following a game trail through a forested slope. He was sweating like a horse and getting hung up on low-hanging blackjack branches. Maybe the deer didn't mind getting scratched on their thick hides, but John's own pale freckled skin looked as if he'd been raked from stem to stern—or attacked by a switch-wielding hillbilly. Which, he had to concede, was better than a gun-wielding one.

A month ago, he and McConnell had taken some buckshot from a farmer over in Taney County. He had not relished tweezing the cylindrical gray pellets out of his burly buddy's behind, but this fed job was not glamorous even on the best days. That McConnell had howled like a baby—bringing the boardinghouse matron to their door to remind them in no uncertain terms that she ran a "clean" establishment—had made it memorable, but not more enjoyable.

Neither he nor McConnell carried a weapon. They were not sanctioned to do so by the government, which made John anxious—especially in the face of an angry, possibly drunk and definitely armed mountain man guarding his beloved still. Their mandate was to find those making or selling moonshine or other alcohols, arrest them if possible and, most importantly, destroy the offending product and the equipment it was made in.

Which is how John came to be on this forested nightmare of an Ozark hillside, full of brambles and thickets, low-limbed trees and ropy vines of poison ivy, a place where you couldn't safely set one foot in front of another without stepping on a treacherous hunk of limestone rock. In fact, one could argue that rocks were a cover crop in these parts.

McConnell had made the prudent decision to walk the lowermost portion of this hilly land cut through by Kinney Creek and bordered by the gravel road into Kinney on the south. Using the rough landmarks he'd been given for the Strong property lines, McConnell had assigned John the uphill job—walking the woods on the west side until he couldn't go any higher, then heading east across the creek until he hit a fence going north and south. The Prohibition officers had split up to make a sweep of the land on foot and would meet back at the truck.

John came upon the cold spring gurgling and pooling on its way down the side of the rocky hill. He knelt and put his face in the stream, taking a long drink with its shocking chill and clean, mineral taste. There were too many places to hide here, too many nooks and crannies and a formidable crop of leafy, woody vegetation in, around and on top of them. And any self-respecting moonshiner would be especially wary about drawing attention to his operation after the big display in front of Hanson's a few days ago. John didn't expect to find any telltale columns of smoke or the loud pounding beat of a thump keg in use today. But it depended on how much of the fear of God he and McConnell had put in the populace, didn't it?

John stopped to lean against an old hickory, felt its hard crackled surface through the thin damp of his dress shirt. His thigh muscles burned from the uphill climb and his feet were sore in the cheap, stiff brown shoes that—while they looked professional—were not meant for picking his way around loose rocks and tree roots. This had been an exercise in futility, no doubt. He wondered, not for the first time that day, why he and McConnell had seen fit to follow this wild goose chase.

Their tipster declared the only thing he wanted for his invaluable information was a half gallon of hooch from the Strongs' hidden stills. But why not bribe or threaten the Strongs himself? No need for a prohi as a middleman, although John had to believe it was infinitely less dangerous.

Something else must be at play here, although John could not fathom what it might be. And he had given up trying to figure out the intricate mix of grudge holding, family loyalty, fear, neighborliness, jealousy, desperation and revenge that drove these hard Ozark people to both tattle on each other and, conversely, fight for one another to the death against a common threat—whether real or imagined. All he knew was that he was exhausted, with nothing to show for it but rank sweat and scores of red scrapes, some edged with blood.

Just then, a branch snapped, echoing across the forested swath of hillside. John instinctively held his breath, waiting for a follow-up noise or perhaps some wild thing to burst out of a thicket and into his path. A couple hundred yards away, a flash of brilliant orange disappeared behind a large tree trunk, reemerging a few seconds later farther down the hill—only to vanish again. Too large and tall for a fox, too vivid for a deer or bear. John strained to focus.

He left the hickory tree in haste, trying to keep an eye on the place he had last seen the creature. But when he arrived, he was disappointed: it was only a game trail along a low crooked fencerow, not much more than twin strands of barbed wire nailed to whatever tree was closest to a straight line. And clearly used by the Strongs' cattle as well, judging by the hoofprints in a variety of sizes. John headed south down the worn path, certain that while he may have missed the animal he was trailing, he had reached the eastern boundary of the Strong land.

A trill of unfamiliar birdsong. Not the "pretty boy" call of a cardinal, a whippoorwill echoing its own name or the eternal questioning of a red-eyed vireo—but a tuneful whistling, cheerful and unafraid, not a warning to fellow birds or forest dwellers.

And not a bird at all!

John quickened his pace, sure now that the flash of color and the whistling belonged to a human being—possibly even a person on the wrong side of the law—and he was intent on catching up. Stealth was key, and John had lots of experience being quiet and blending into his surroundings. It wasn't just part of the job; it was his personality.

The whistling grew louder as John closed in on its source. He took his eyes off the uneven ground to catch a glimpse of his target and caught the toe of his left shoe on the exposed root of a large cedar. John went sprawling, outstretched hands scraping the scrub-and-gravel-pitted ground. He gave a sharp grunt on impact and rolled a few yards downhill before stopping.

He rose and dusted off his hands, the flesh of his palms dented by sharp rocks. One finger was bleeding. But the whistling had stopped abruptly with his fall, and now ahead of him, he heard running.

John ran, too, ignoring the pain in his feet as they slapped in the flat soles against the hard red dirt. The slope steepened, forcing him to run faster, almost out of control. He leaned back to slow his pace and avoid another fall, which would have been decidedly worse at full clip.

But he didn't want to lose this creature that he was pursuing, a someone who clearly didn't want to be caught—which meant he or she had something to hide or a reason to hide themselves. In these hills, that something was likely a still. All of John's discomfort and irritation from the morning search diminished in the potential of its discovery.

I've almost got you.

He stopped abruptly where the woods ended, opening out onto a luminous hillside pasture. Shading his eyes, John scanned for movement and saw that he had come to the farmstead, with its cozy cabin and barnyard in the front. He could see the dazzling rows of young corn plants, green sprays set in the dark brown dirt. The only sound was his breathing above the low hum of bees on the red clover scattered throughout the field of green fescue. There wasn't anything moving, running or otherwise. He noted one brown milk cow in the pasture, eyeing him with a look of boredom as she chewed her cud, swishing at her back with her tail to keep the horseflies from biting. A thin-legged calf nursed beneath her back legs, bumping its mother impatiently so her milk would let down.

Disappointed, John continued down the fencerow. He was supposed to meet McConnell at the dirt road bordering the farm, and he imagined his partner sitting against a shady oak, fedora pulled low over his eyes for a quick snooze. Waiting for John to show up after doing the bulk of the work, as usual. But today, despite his best efforts, he would return with nothing. Zero. Zilch.

He had only gone a few hundred feet toward the road when his eye landed on a bizarre sight: a single brown toeless boot, laces loose and tongue spread open, as if its owner had stepped right out of it and kept going.

John picked up the boot, the leather warm in his hands—from the beating July sun or a recently departed human foot? But this was no ordinary boot. Turning it over in his hands, he nearly dropped it in surprise when he discovered the sole with strange multiple heels. Hooves. A smaller one in front, a larger behind. Both cloven. Cow hooves. Detached in gruesome fashion from their original owner.

What the hell?

He looked up from the strange footwear to consider the solitary cow, guarding the calf who had curled up to doze in a patch of clover. She glared at him from a large, lazy brown eye, as if he were the culprit who had taken the hooves from one of her own—a sister? Her own mother?

If only she could talk.

When John reached the road at last, he was unsurprised to find

McConnell napping behind the wheel of their flatbed truck, head tilted back and drool leaking slowly out one side of his mouth. He was parked in a gated drive and shaded on either side by clutches of Osage orange trees.

"Up and at 'em." John reached through the open window to shake McConnell, who startled before grumpily unfolding himself from the driver's seat.

"Took you long enough," McConnell groused, removing his hat to slick back his few thin hairs before replacing it squarely on his head.

"Yeah, sorry you had to take a nap," John said. "The going was tougher than expected. But here, take a gander at this."

John tossed his partner the boot and McConnell squinted hard at the contraption before his eyes lit up.

"Holy Mother Mary and the baby Jesus, too," he chortled. "Why, that's amazing. I've heard about these babies but never set eyes on any myself."

"Wait. What *is* it exactly?"

"A boot—one of a pair, I'm certain—that is fashioned exclusively to throw us feds off the trail, if you get my drift. Genius!"

The two of them quickened their pace, making their way along the road to the worn path to the farmstead. John told McConnell what he had seen, how he'd lost the trail when he emerged from the woods, where he found the strange boot.

"I got me a real good feeling about this." McConnell hit the heels of the boot against one meaty thigh. "You done a nice job, Flannie. I believe we're about to find some hot hooch. Ever heard that saying about waiting till the cows come home?"

John nodded, finding himself strangely warmed by the older man's praise. And encouraged by his partner's enthusiasm for something—anything—outside of the showmanship of destruction, drinking or a dalliance.

"I hear me some cowbells," McConnell laughed, and slapped John on the back.

Shine

The door screeched then slammed as she burst into the cabin, chest heaving and eyes wild. Her cotton dress was covered in burs and she was short one boot. The tangled mass of her orange-red curls and the crimson spots on her cheeks made her look as though she were on fire. Her heart thumped so hard she thought surely Lidy could hear it, too, the red throbbing noise filling her own ears to bursting. But her unflappable grandmother stood stock still in the kitchen, sleeves rolled up and forearms covered in flour.

"Gran!"

Lidy looked up from her pie crust, rolled flat on the floured table into a buttery golden round. Assessing her granddaughter for blood or a severed limb and seeing nothing but a hot mess missing a boot, she resumed her work, peeling up the pie crust and pressing it into a metal pan, fluting the rim of the dough along the edge with her practiced fingers.

"Yes, Shine?" She picked up a fork and poked the tines randomly around the bottom and sides of her crust, leaving a set of four perfectly aligned holes with each punch.

"The feds are coming!"

Lidy set the fork down. "Now?"

"I think so. I had one hot on my tail about halfway down the mountain coming back from the still. One minute I'm whistling away, minding my own beeswax, and the next I'm a deer in the crosshairs." Shine still panted, tugging off her remaining boot without unlacing it and heaving it into the wood box.

"Whistling?" Lidy sucked her teeth and shook her head. "What've I told you, Shine? 'A whistling girl and a crowing hen/ always come to a sad end.' "

But Shine paid no attention. Something even more alarming had crossed her mind. "Daddy's up there yet! We were getting ready to stir the mash when I realized we didn't have enough yeast. He'll be wondering where I'm at . . . Oh, Lord."

Shine's shoulders fell. "I can't go back up there to tell him, either. I saw my fed heading toward the road. Likely as not getting his partner, that big fat windbag Becks was talking about, pouring shine in the street and whipping everyone into a frenzy the other day. They'll be here any minute!"

"Settle down, child." Lidy dusted her hands as though she wished to be rid of more than the flour that clung there. "I haven't met a lawman yet who can match wits with a Strong and come out a winner."

Wiping her hands on her apron, Lidy stepped out onto the front porch and reached for the rope of the dinner bell, creating a nonstop clanging that had Shine—who had followed her outside in sock feet—holding her ears for a good long minute.

Gran knew how to get Hiram the message.

At that moment, two men emerged from the woods below the house, following the footpath to the cabin. Shine felt she knew them already. Everyone within fifty miles had heard about their stunts in Kinney from someone who had been there or someone who knew someone who had: There was the overweight, older fed clutching his fedora in one hand, his sandy hair slicked back into something resembling duck wings on either side of his head and leaving only a scant, oily strand or two across the top. And his counterpart, striding up to where Shine and her grandma stood, a black-haired young man with intense blue eyes and a dusting of freckles across his nose and cheeks.

He was surely the one who had run after her, tracking her

through the woods. Shine took in the stiff dress shoes covered with dust and decided she had them to thank for his being unable to catch up. That—and her natural speed and wits.

Meanwhile, Elsie nearly ran into him at the bottom of the steps as she hurried from the direction of the chicken coop, clutching the bottom of her apron to her belly, making a safe carrier for the dozen or so warm brown eggs she had gathered.

"Oh dear!" She stopped short in front of the young man, eyes wide, and instinctively put her other hand around her improvised basket to protect her precious load.

The heavy *clip, clop* of Marge's hooves could be heard approaching from the cornfield beyond the barn with more urgency than the stubborn, plodding mare usually displayed. Before long, Rebecca arrived. She pulled up alongside the porch and swung down from the mare's back, grabbing her rifle and the reins in one fluid motion.

"Tad early for lunch, wouldn't you agree?" The huffing, heavyset man had caught up to his partner at the porch, smiling with his mouth but not his eyes. "By my watch, it's just past ten in the morning."

"When you get up as early as we do, you get hungry well before noon," Lidy said sharply. "You probably aren't familiar with real work that requires sweat, long hours and lots of elbow grease."

All three of her granddaughters had joined Lidy on the front porch, making a formidable-looking line, especially with Rebecca's Winchester in her hands.

"Looks like you got quite a hungry crew," chuckled the large man darkly. He patted his substantial stomach. "I don't miss many meals myself," he said. "But as an expert in the eating department, I don't smell much in the way of vittles around here.

"Are you sure you're cooking up dinner and not a big batch of shine?"

Elsie promptly let go of her apron and a dozen eggs hit the wood slats of the porch, splatting wetly as they cracked and released their viscous insides. A lone survivor rolled slowly to the edge of the porch and hesitated briefly before throwing itself over the edge, as if life were not worth living without its fellows.

"Oh dear." Elsie was on her knees, untying her apron and swiping at the devastated eggs.

But the other Strong women held their nerve. Lidy didn't even bat an eyelash at McConnell's accusation.

"It's none of your damn business what I'm cooking, for lunch or otherwise," she said, chin held high. "Isn't that right, girls?"

Shine crossed her arms in what she hoped was a menacing manner. *Damn, Gran is cold.* She admired it. Her own natural coloring made it much harder to hide what she was feeling—try as she might. Her cheeks lit up the instant she was angry or embarrassed. Or even if she as much as *thought* something she knew she shouldn't.

Like why was that handsome prohi looking at her legs?

Right on cue, her face turned pink. And as she lowered her gaze from the young man's face, Shine noticed something else, too: he was holding her other boot!

Holy cow . . . shit.

Rebecca had given them to her last year on her sixteenth birthday, shyly pulling out a lumpy package loosely wrapped in a stained oilcloth, devoid of even a bow.

"I made it myself," she had said.

"What in the world?" Shine's curiosity had been piqued. If Rebecca made it, there would be no pretty buttons or embroidered pink roses like those on the dress from Gran or the handkerchief from Elsie. That certainty had both thrilled and frightened her. She had hoped it wasn't a rabbit or squirrel skin. Or a skinned rabbit or squirrel for that matter!

Unrolling the contents of the package from its cloth, Shine still hadn't been sure what she was seeing. A pair of . . . *boots*? That looked, in fact, much like the boots she had outgrown a few months back. But Rebecca had cut out the toe of each boot, like a sandal. And when Shine turned one worn boot over, she had gasped.

Attached to the sole were a pair of cloven cow hooves, one on the front part of the shoe, the other on the heel.

"Uhm . . ." Shine had been at a loss for words. She was not Elsie—Shine didn't give a fig if she had stylish dresses or shoes. Or even *clean* dresses and shoes. But she wasn't sure she would deign to wear hand-me-down footwear from a dead cow.

"I guess I'll be hoofin' it in style," Shine had finally said, smiling uncertainly.

Rebecca had clapped her hands, beaming. "I knew you'd understand!"

She had reached for the boots, loosening the laces and motioning for Shine to slip her feet in. With a yank, she tied up each foot in turn. Shine's bare toes peeked out over the tops of the shoes, but Rebecca's genius had made even these too-small boots of Shine's fit again. Or fit well enough.

"You can wear them up to the still and back," Rebecca had explained. "You won't need to cover your tracks anymore because you won't make any. At least"—she shrugged—"not any human-looking ones. This will keep the law off your trail. Or any busybody poking around where they shouldn't."

Shine had thrown her head back in laughter. Then, crossing her arms and squatting, she performed a jig on the dirt floor of the cabin. Clattering her cloven-footed clogs, she alternated kicking out a leg, reducing all the Strong women to tears and shrieks of hilarity.

"Catch me if you can, prohis!" Shine had crowed, lifting the hem of her skirt and stomping for good measure. "And Becks, please: I don't ever want to know who originally wore these hooves."

And now, here was one of those boots, being held out in the palm of the young prohi as though it were the most delicate of slippers.

"Agent Flanagan," he introduced himself. "This is my partner, Agent McConnell. Does this happen to belong to one of you ladies?"

Which of the three sisters was his Cinderella? Not Rebecca, with her bony feet as big as her father's and typically outfitted in a pair of his castoffs. Or Elsie, whose feet were so dainty she wore a child-sized shoe.

No, Shine had a feeling the answer was as obvious as she felt there in her stockinged feet, one pristine, the other dirty and halfway down her calf. Vertical runs and snags striped the sad sock, chock-full of burs and bagged loosely at the ankle. When her special boot had come off in the chase, she had felt it was more important to keep going than risk getting caught.

"Why, if it isn't Prince Charming himself," Lidy guffawed. "And no, it isn't mine, not that you were including me in your group of 'ladies.' I'll try not to have hurt feelings."

Now it was the young man's turn to color. "Pardon me, ma'am. I'm sure appreciative of anyone owning up to it."

"To be honest, it looks like some fancy heifer has taken to dressing to the nines," Lidy said. "Our cattle tend to stick to regular hooves on the legs they were born with."

"Well, since I found it in on your property, you could understand my confusion." His amusement showed in the slightly upturned corners of his mouth.

Shine casually crossed the calf with the shredded stocking behind the other. But she knew Flanagan was onto her.

Lidy was having none of it. "People trespass all the time," she said, with a pointed look at the two Prohibition officers. "We can't be responsible for their belongings. We're running a farm, not a lost and found."

Elsie giggled, a habit she had when she was nervous. Or in the presence of a good-looking young man. Or both. Meanwhile, Rebecca seemed the only one unmoved by the appearance of the two lawmen—not visibly frightened or charmed, either one. But Shine noticed her firm grip on her rifle.

"What I wanna know is if I followed them hoofprints back up the hill, would I find a still?" McConnell said. "And maybe someone operating it. Like the man of the house."

"Your partner didn't find anything," Shine said, bolstered by her gran's bold stance and unable to keep her own trap shut for five minutes. She knew she shouldn't egg them on; this moonshine business was the Strong family's livelihood now. Shine needed the feds snooping around like she needed a hole in the head.

McConnell looked at Shine as if he were full up on impudence. "Yeah? Well, we've found that sometimes the best hiding places are in plain sight. Let's take a look in that barn of yours."

Lidy led the way, diminutive but fierce. Her obvious disgust for the goings-on had her stomping more forcefully than normal, raising dust in her wake. Shine peeled off her stockings and fell in behind her—popping up and down like kettle corn to see what would happen next. Then came the two prohis, Flanagan first and then slow-going McConnell. Elsie and Rebecca brought up the rear, the former trying for an unobstructed view of Flanagan from the backside and the latter holding her rifle as though she were marching a group of POWs.

Lidy threw open the barn door and the sunshine cut a swath of gold into the semidarkness. Farther inside, it was cool and dim, with occasional strips of light showing through the wooden planks of the walls and streaking the dirt and straw on the floor. Shine heard Cowboy stamping in his stall, along with the horse's strong yellow teeth working a chunk of alfalfa. And . . . *snoring*?

At the sound, McConnell shoved his way in front of Lidy to reach the stalls first. Cowboy eyed him suspiciously—smart boy—and kicked a back hoof against the wall in greeting or warning, Shine wasn't sure. Next to him was an empty stall where the Guernsey cow spent her nights and a larger one for the two plow horses, Cain and Abel, brothers named by Lidy for their opposite dispositions. Despite their differences, they nestled head to rump, a single round two-headed beast. Cain perked up his ears as the entourage passed, but neither animal rose. They had already put in a good morning's work under Rebecca's supervision, hauling the wagon full of quartz and limestone rocks she had cleared from a patch of land to make another cornfield.

"What in the Sam Hill is going on in here?" McConnell said, peering into the final stall. No farm beast to be seen, but instead, there was Hiram, snoring to beat the band. He was stretched out horizontally on the hay, hands clasped over his chest, hat pulled low over his eyes.

"Who is this?"

Hiram reached out a hand to push up his hat brim. "Well, I might ask the same of you. This here is my barn last time I checked. Can't a man escape the womenfolk in his life without getting harangued from here to high noon?"

Shine stifled a laugh, tickling her in the gut, like someone had taken a feather duster to her insides. Now was not the time for levity. But *dang.* Daddy was quite convincing in his role as the honest farmer falsely persecuted. By both the law and the opposite gender.

All the air seemed to go out of McConnell. He had geared himself up for a big bust—and ended up looking foolish, holding an empty bag. The Strongs seemed happily off the hook.

But Flanagan wasn't finished yet.

The young prohi reached into the stall to give Hiram a hand up. "John Flanagan," he said. "This is Agent McConnell. We're following up on a tip that there might be a still on this property. We can see there may have been a misunderstanding."

Hiram nodded sagely. This greenhorn was falling for his act. By Shine's estimation, they would have both officers back in their truck and off on another fool's errand by noon.

"But since you all have nothing to hide, I'm sure you won't mind showing us around." Here, Flanagan flashed a winning smile at the group lined up in the barn aisle. "Maybe it's because we're getting close to lunchtime, but I'd really like to see the inside of that smokehouse and your cellar, please."

"How about a tour of the outhouse while we're at it?" Shine had had about enough of these prohis and their pointless posturing. "No shine there but it's seen more than a fair share of moons."

Lidy yelped in amusement. What would Shine say next? Not even her youngest granddaughter knew.

Flanagan smiled. "My mother taught me it was best not to—pardon the expression—shit where I eat. And I'd bet my last dollar that you people who live closer to the land and the creatures who fertilize it likely take that to heart, too."

Shine shrugged. "Suit yourself."

"Shine, show these gentlemen what they want to see," Hiram said. "Now that they've ruined my favorite hiding spot, I best get to work before one of you women tans my hide."

Rebecca stayed back with Hiram and the animals, fed up with this prohi nonsense.

Lidy was worried; Shine felt it. Her gran's expression showed nothing but irritation, but Lidy made a move to join the tour. This was like watching a train wreck in slow motion. Nothing any of them could do to stop it. Yet Lidy had to see what Shine would do when the Strongs were caught red-handed with enough moonshine to get the entire population of Kinney drunk as skunks. As for Elsie, she didn't want to miss the rare chance for excitement, even if it held an element of danger for the family. She followed closely behind the two feds, practically skipping from a strange combination of nerves and delight.

Shine led the way toward the wooden smokehouse used for curing and flavoring their ham and bacon. She pulled open the creaking door to a deliciously salty, smoky scent that hit their noses all at once. Shine's stomach rumbled. These men were starting to come between her and her dinner—and that was ill-advised.

"Nothing to see here." She'd started to close the door when McConnell put up a large hand.

"Hold up," he said. "I'll be the judge of that."

He jostled his generous girth up near the front of the smokehouse and stuck his arms and meaty shoulders through the opening, twisting slowly from side to side as he peered upward. The Strongs didn't slaughter and smoke until fall, so the four large iron hooks—one centered on each wall near the top—were empty. Shine would love nothing better than to hang that man's lardy self from one of those menacing beauties. Instead, she settled for enjoying McConnell's discomfort as he pushed in a few more inches to complete his inspection and found himself completely wedged in the doorframe by his midsection.

Elsie broke out in another fit of nervous giggling, made worse when Shine reared back, raising one leg as if she was going to kick McConnell in his big behind with one of her bare feet.

"Why, Jace Alta Strong," barked Lidy, employing her youngest granddaughter's full name in a false show of reprimand. "I declare! Show some respect." Her indignant tone was clearly a thin veneer for underlying mirth.

But Shine was just warming up. She loved making her gran proud. Lidy wasn't one for a pat on the back or words of praise or encouragement. But Shine could sense it sometimes, as though she were channeling Lidy's own seditious thoughts, simply the vessel through which Lidy could act out, young and carefree and ornery once more.

Shine was so caught up in her own rascality she had forgotten about Flanagan.

"I believe my boss needs a hand, not a foot," interjected the handsome prohi. *Oops.*

"Flanagan, get me the hell out of this thing!" It took the young agent a tremendous tug on McConnell's trunk-like legs to dislodge him.

The older man pulled himself up to his full height—a mere five foot six—and dusted himself off as if nothing had happened, though soot ringed his white shirt and his face was an angry crimson.

"Which way to the root cellar?"

Shine was fully in charge now, leading the way past the cabin. About a hundred feet away, Hiram had dug into the slight hill edging the woods—much easier than making a hole in the rocky Ozarks ground. It took several years and more than as many shovels, but eventually, he carved out a room about eight feet long and tall enough to stand in. Over time, he braced the ceiling and added wooden shelving for the canned goods, along with built-in bins on the packed dirt floor for heaping potatoes, onions, beets and carrots for winter storage.

When Shine threw open the door, the cool air escaping from the earthy enclosure smelled dark and musty but not entirely unpleasant. There was a hint of mellowing onion sweetened with the scent of bright carrot; upside-down bunches of dried rosemary added a sharp astringent woodiness. Once her eyes adjusted, she could see a rainbow of potatoes in their bins, ranging from dirty brown and russet to golden yellow and even reddish pink, alongside piles of purply red beets and orange carrots, and crisp apples the size of fists in brilliant reds and golds.

But the most remarkable display was all Lidy: rows and rows of glass jars on the shelves, gleaming in the sunlight the open door allowed. Quart after quart of sun-ripened peaches, skinned and smooth as a baby's behind, floating in clear syrup—there must have been ten dozen! Plus pint-sized mason jars filled with jewel-tone jellies and jams: blackberry, raspberry, strawberry, peach, apricot, cherry, gooseberry, persimmon and mulberry.

Shine led the two feds into the root cellar, but the cramped space forced the rest of the Strongs to stay outside, forming a quiet but anxious ring around the door. Shine was nervous, too. She didn't want to say or do anything to arouse the suspicions of the prohis, who were already on high alert. She wanted to be casual, offhand, but also exude an unshakable confidence in who she was and what the Strongs were all about. It was like breaking a horse or sneaking a warm egg from the underside of a fussy hen: you couldn't let them smell or sense your fear. Or you were done for.

"Gran's outdone herself these last few years," Shine said, gesturing at the jars of shiny golden peach halves. "You heard of making hay while the sun shines, but she bottles up the actual *sunshine* for us to enjoy all year round. And a few lucky customers in Kinney when we have extra."

McConnell and Flanagan surveyed the bounty of the earthen hideaway, clearly impressed.

Shine could feel them deflate, their hopes for hijinks evaporating in the July heat. She felt an itch in her throat, a need to release a victory whoop. They were so close to pulling one over on these men. Yet she knew she wouldn't be able to relax until she had them out of the root cellar and off their land. Back on the red dirt road and on the trail of some other unfortunate squealed on by a grudge-holding neighbor or a competitor trying to take the heat off their own illicit operation.

Shine stole a sideways glance at the prohis, hands on hips, defeated. They had worked hard—well, at least Flanagan had—and they were about to leave with nothing. It gave Shine great satisfaction to basically have rubbed one of her cow-heeled boots in McConnell's fat face. But something about the other one gave her pause, as if Flanagan knew what she was up to—inside and out. It made her uncomfortable to be sized up like that. To be seen. And if he left without making an arrest or two (or five!), busting up a still or hauling away a batch of moonshine, it was only because he knew he could if he wanted to.

And she knew it, too.

"Hate for you two to leave without something for your trouble," Shine said. She reached for a jar of Lidy's peach preserves and another of blackberry jam. "This stuff's more addictive than spirits. Don't say I didn't warn you."

McConnell reached greedily for both jars, hands outstretched, but Shine allowed him one, making sure her favorite—peach—remained for Flanagan. But the young fed surprised her by reaching toward one of the shelves for a quart-sized jar of peach halves, shiny as egg yolks.

"I do love peaches," he said. Did Shine imagine it, or did he raise his eyebrow ever so slightly? There was also a mischievous smirk at the corner of his mouth. Shine nearly dropped the jar of preserves.

"But this lasts longer," she said, finding her mental footing. She swapped out his jar for the one in her own hand.

"I suppose it would be too much to hope for both," he said, beaming at her. Shine blushed furiously, unused to this strange, unsettled feeling, like she was backed into a corner and yet didn't wish to be anywhere else.

"Greed and gluttony are two of the deadly sins," Shine retorted. "But maybe next time you're in town."

"Much thanks, miss," Flanagan said gallantly, as Shine replaced the peaches on an upper shelf. "I do have a feeling we will cross paths again. Hopefully on the right side of the law."

"Where I have always been and pledge to remain," Shine said, turning to face him, fingers crossed behind her back.

No need for him to know which side of the law she considered "right."

Outside the root cellar, McConnell grunted a disgusted goodbye, while Flanagan tipped his hat to Lidy, Elsie and Shine in turn. "And Miss Strong," he added, with a pointed look at Shine, "I do hope this year's crops are bountiful enough for you to procure a new pair of shoes."

For once in her life, Shine had absolutely nothing to say.

She walked them as far as the cabin, then watched the two feds make their way down the long, steep path that led through the woods to the gravel road. McConnell stopped twice to hitch his pants as he tried to keep up with Flanagan, whose faster pace left puffs of dust in his wake before he disappeared into the trees. A minute later, McConnell was gone, too.

She felt rather than heard Lidy join her on one side, Elsie on the other. There was no sound but the lazy buzz of satiated insects until, finally, the women heard the cough and sputter of the prohi truck. There was a slow crunch of tires on gravel accompanied by the *rat-a-tat-tat* of a motor on its last leg.

Shine took a deep breath and released it. *Good riddance.*

Elsie, though, burst into tears, all her nerves from the unexpected visit liquifying and squeezing out of her eyes. "I thought for sure we were going to jail," she sobbed. "Good job, Shine. I don't know how you talked to those men like that. I swear, I would have wet my drawers."

Rebecca and Hiram joined them; she with her Winchester slung casually back around her shoulder now that the feds were gone, and he with a quart jar of golden peaches.

"This definitely calls for a celebration," he said, unscrewing the ring of the lid and popping the top off the sealed canning jar. He tipped the mouth of the jar to his own, and took a large swallow, wiping his mouth afterward with the back of his hand. "Who's next?"

None of the women typically drank, but today was different. Everyone passed the jar and took at least a sip or—in Shine's case—a bite of an extremely inebriated peach half.

Shine chewed the fruit thoughtfully and sighed. "Best peach I've ever tasted. With a kick like a Missouri mule. Wasn't it the fat one that said 'the best hiding places are in plain sight'?"

Rebecca scoffed. "I've skinned squirrels with bigger brains than that one."

"Nonetheless," said Lidy. "That was a bit close for comfort. We got lucky that moonshine was in a soaking phase. But who knows when someone else might tip off another fed about our special brand of shine—and he might know better what he's looking at when he's staring at a wall of hooch-sopped fruit."

Elsie

Her earliest memories of her mother were of the reading and telling of bedtime stories. Alta would gather both girls in her lap after supper and read a page of one of her precious books—*Little Women* was Elsie's preference and, she suspected, Rebecca's, too. Winter meant the glow of the kerosene lantern on her mother's serious face as she read, the flickers of flame like characters themselves playing across the cabin walls. In summer, the fading rays of a vivid sunset, the colors of ripe watermelons and plums, provided the light for the stage of the front porch, where tales were told—until the fireflies took over, providing a finale of flashes in the inky dark.

Alta often chose Bible stories, which she told from memory and embellished as she saw fit to drive home a lesson. Cain and Abel. Samson and Delilah. Jonah inside the whale. Joseph in his multicolored coat. Moses was a popular choice, whether as an abandoned baby in a basket among the river rushes or a fierce man of God, parting the Red Sea. And Joseph and Mary, desperately in search of a place she could give birth to their first child.

But Elsie's favorite stories weren't from the Bible or her mother's meager shelf. She preferred when Alta meandered into make-believe: breathtaking princesses in need of saving and the princes who galloped atop white steeds, climbed ladders made of gloriously long golden hair to a tower window or bestowed a delicate kiss on a slumbering beauty.

She loved happily ever after.

After Alta died, she missed so much about her mother. Things she couldn't put words to, being only six years old. Safety. Certainty. Softness. Someone who shared her penchant for pretty things, even if having them was rarely possible. Elsie began telling stories to herself. Sometimes to Rebecca, and later, Shine. Musings about mothers who tried to fly and failed. Sisters who stuck together. Mostly tales of hardship and suffering and rescue, of fairy godmothers, Rumpelstiltskins and, of course, handsome princes.

A tiny but tenacious part of her believed them. Which is probably why she didn't worry when she found herself in a tough spot.

It started about a year ago. Elsie had felt Jed's eyes on her the entire time she was at Hanson's. He was on a break, smoking a cigarette near the large front porch of the general store.

She had worn her favorite dress, a cornflower blue dotted with butter-yellow flowers, which she knew perfectly accented her eyes and hair. She carried two dozen of her hens' fresh eggs in a basket on one arm, ready to barter with Charles Hanson for the items on the Strong family's shopping list.

Elsie had begged Hiram to let her ride to town with him. She wasn't comfortable on a mule or a horse by herself; it frightened her to feel all that animal strength and will beneath her. Rebecca's mare sensed her fear when Elsie rode her and did what she could get away with, stopping every few yards to graze at a shock of green grass or grab a low-hanging persimmon. The horse had tossed her to the ground as casually as if shaking off a horsefly or some rainwater.

"Get back in the saddle," Rebecca ordered, giving her a hand up from the ground and dusting her off. Her older sister didn't understand physical failures or limitations; how could anyone be unable to ride a horse? Rebecca loved harnessing the power of her own body to do her will and any animal connected to it felt like graceful extra limbs. How could exquisite Elsie be so clumsy and fearful? Animals were waiting their master's commands, wanting desperately to please and know their place in the world. But Rebecca gave up when it became clear that being thrown off a horse repeatedly—and with increasing violence—could cause regrettable injury to Elsie and the horse's understanding of who was boss.

Everyone in the Strong family decided it was best for Elsie to be squired about, like the princess she was.

That day, her job was supposedly bartering her eggs. But in truth, Elsie was there to see who was out and about, peruse the latest fabrics, buttons and lace at Hanson's and trade some idle gossip. She'd learned that an old classmate, Agnes, had given birth to her third child, another girl. And Molly Kerns, who was Shine's age, was getting married next month to a nice farm boy a few hollers over.

Each piece of news about a baby or a wedding wormed its way into her heart like a splinter under a fingernail, painful and hard to ignore. But not enough to keep her from asking. It was like throwing water on a grease fire, hearing about these domestic happinesses that she had thus far been denied.

Elsie was twenty-three years old. Old maid territory. It wasn't that there hadn't been interest. She was stunning. And smart enough. Kindhearted. But she was waiting for something she hadn't yet been able to find: a better, more thrilling life than what she had on the farm. She wanted to spend her days dolled up in fancy dresses, sewing for the pleasure of handwork instead of mending, gardening for the fragrance and flash of glorious blooms, not for utility or to feed a growling belly. She *wanted.*

"Morning, Miss Strong." Jedediah tipped his hat. "The Strongs see fit to let you off the farm for a change?"

"I reckon I get to town as often as I like," Elsie said. She felt an ache at being seen as she saw herself: trapped and stunted by the place and people she came from. A songbird in a cage.

"Besides, anyone who wants to see more of me knows where to look," she continued. "I'm at church most Sunday mornings. And Wednesday nights. Not that you'd be familiar with that."

"I'd like to see more of you," Jed said. Elsie blushed, partly from the pleasure of his obvious interest, but mostly from his boldness. Taken a certain way—a manner in which no proper lady should be spoken to in town on a Saturday morning—the words made her tingle all over. She liked it, but felt the need to look over her shoulder, making sure no one else had heard.

"Sundays and Wednesdays." With a toss of her head, Elsie made her way toward the farrier's two blocks away without so much as a backward glance. She was to meet her father there after they saw to all their errands; the horse needed a new shoe. It was only when she reached for the latch on the gate that she saw her basket, still filled with brown freckled eggs. Her one task and she had failed!

She turned around and headed back to Hanson's, walking slower than before, hoping Jedediah had returned to his post at the back so he wouldn't see how foolish she was. And yet, if she were being honest, she was disappointed when she reached the store's front porch and Jed was nowhere to be seen.

But—miracle of miracles—he began showing up at church. Freshly slicked hair and shoes polished, he slipped into the back row on Sundays, sliding onto one of those golden oak pews worn to a shine from the backsides of the penitent and the prayerful—plus the primly righteous and those there to see and be seen. The scent of Saturday night clung to him like a jealous lover: smoke and perspiration laced with hard liquor. But there he sat, singing, praying and occasionally shouting a fervent "*Amen!*"

What had brought this notorious sinner into the fold? Brother Aiken liked to believe it was his inspired preaching. Several of the older women in the congregation felt—individually—that it was her trademark monkey bread or pawpaw pie served up with a warm hello at the hospitality table after Wednesday night service.

The men of the church—from those who were barely old

enough to shave to the ones sporting a few thin hairs stretched across their bald pates—knew the truth: Jed had his eye on Elsie, sure, but his hopes were pinned on the promise of the Strong family still. They shook their heads at his obvious transparency and some people's inability to see it. Yet if Elsie were to give any of them even the slightest encouragement, they would trample the life out of each other to get near her.

The young girls and women knew the reason Jed was there. More than one had been the object of Jed's fleeting affections before, but none had inspired him to turn to Jesus. The girls stared at Jed ogling Elsie and wondered what they could do to incite that kind of passion. The women—some married, some not—looked at Elsie and tallied their shortcomings. Were they too tall? Too curvy? Brown-eyed or brown-haired? Too shy or loud? Or was it (more than one blushed and squirmed at the memory) that they had carelessly given away the proverbial milk without forcing Jed to buy the cow?

It didn't matter. The rakish Jed was not someone their parents would welcome as a son-in-law. But reek as he did of alcohol and cigarettes, there was also the whiff of money in his wake. Even if his daddy had him working out back, the store surely was to be his someday. And, for all Jed's flaws, what girl wouldn't want to yoke herself to that?

Elsie was oblivious to the ripples of speculation, sitting straight and still in a front-row pew with whichever Strong had provided the transportation. A hungover Hiram. A skeptical Shine. Or a resigned Rebecca, who preferred the God she encountered in a chapel of solemn hardwood trees and cedars to one with walls and a ceiling. Pragmatic Lidy wasn't the praying type: Why sit with hands folded when you could busy them doing all manner of good? She reserved her rare church appearances for weddings and funerals.

Elsie, though, felt pulled toward belief in a higher power. How else to explain the heartbreaking beauty of this world? Someone must be in charge of it, of all of this. A kindly Father looking down on the chaos and pain of human striving and wanting the best for them. For *her*. Faith made her feel closer to her mama, the daughter of a preacher and the one who had gotten the Strongs to church in the first place—whether or not it stuck. Elsie had long ago claimed her mother's Bible; the miniature gold cross on a delicate chain that once encircled her mother's throat now rested around her own.

Neither Shine nor Rebecca was interested in either.

But while Elsie didn't notice that she was the object of interest to everyone in attendance, there was one pair of eyes that she felt without fail. She knew without turning around when Jed made his appearance, always late, during the opening hymn, "To God Be the Glory" or "How Great Thou Art." It took every ounce of her will not to turn around and meet those eyes. She knew what she saw there would unnerve her. And embolden him.

After the service, Jed waited for her outside. Elsie had never felt particularly powerful or lucky, but now it seemed she was both. Hadn't she single-handedly brought a notorious sinner to Jesus? And won the heart of a dashing young man—the closest thing to a prince in these parts—who would make money without breaking his back? Or hers?

"Miss Strong," he would say with a wry smile, offering his arm. "Fancy meeting you here."

It didn't take long, maybe a month or two, for Jed to assume responsibility for seeing Elsie to and from church. The other Strongs were frankly relieved not to have to sit through Brother Aiken's sermons and the repeated exhortations to give themselves to Jesus. Were they convinced of Jedediah Hanson's conversion? Hardly.

Shine didn't care a speck for Jed and said so; Rebecca shared her sentiments—though she kept them to herself. But Hiram, like Elsie, tended to see the best in people. And what he first saw in Jed was devotion to his daughter and—although he wouldn't have admitted it—the things money could buy. A solid house.

Provisions that didn't require working a field sunup to sundown. A car! And not just any car, but a nice late-model Ford at that. Elsie could do worse around here; much worse.

And in fact, she *did* do something worse than allow Jedediah Hanson to escort her to and from church on bluebird Sunday mornings and those warm Wednesday twilights of early spring, filled with the lemony scent of evening primrose. Like the delicate yellow blooms that opened only at night, awaiting their nocturnal visitors—moths and bats—to do the necessary work of pollination, Elsie opened herself one evening, too.

But she kept that secret to herself. Until she couldn't.

Lidy

She had first felt it in the spring, when the dazzling white blooms of dogwoods, serviceberry, wild plum and hawthorn trees became a welcome sight against the gray and brown trunks of the overstory trees. Here and there, deep pink blooms clung to the redbud branches; blood-red spikes accented the tips of buckeye trees. The boughs of their own apple trees swelled with luscious white blooms, the dozen trees of their orchard decked out like brides.

What Lidy felt then was a presence more than anything else. Something other than the usual circle of human beings that made up her family. At first, she dismissed it out of hand, her mind playing tricks on her. But as the weeks went by, the presence had grown stronger, more insistent. Lidy had a thought that Alta was back to check on her girls—or to haunt Lidy for the way she had gone out of this world. But Lidy banished that idea and Alta from her mind. No good came of dwelling on the past. She knew that better than anyone.

But then it all came clear as the laundry she was scrubbing this July morning. Wash day. Hiram and Shine were headed to the still, ready to turn their latest batch of mash into clear, sweet moonshine. She had warned them to take extra care. It had been nearly two weeks since those damn prohis had given them a scare. Not long enough—in her opinion, at least.

"A good mash waits for no man," Hiram said. "It's now or never, Ma. It would be sinful to waste."

"Good luck avoiding sin in this situation," Lidy replied. "You're damned if you do or if you don't," she said. But Hiram had only winked.

Lidy, uneasy, watched them go. Meanwhile, Rebecca lit a fire in the front yard before she took off hunting, filling the big cast-iron pot with water from the creek. That left Lidy and Elsie to boil the water, soak and then scrub the clothes—eventually hanging them up to dry on the clothesline rigged from one corner post of the house out back to a pole in the garden, away from the dust of the barnyard.

Elsie sat with a tin washtub in front of her and a wooden washboard between her knees, scrubbing the Strong bed linens while Lidy handled the more personal whites: handkerchiefs, petticoats, underthings. She knew her granddaughters intimately through this chore, the assortment of rags from their monthly cycles as regular as the seasons.

And they cycled together, too, like the cows and mares on the farm came into heat at the same time. Maybe it had to do with the moon; maybe it was living in close quarters that put them on the same schedule. Not her, though. She had gone through the change decades ago and didn't miss it one whit.

But this wash day there were not nearly so many rags needing her attention. Lidy frowned. She turned her eagle eye to the jumble of underwear at her feet. A quick sorting gave her the information she needed—while simultaneously filling her with dread. The larger pairs showed dribs and drabs of blood, or, in one unfortunate case, what appeared to be wholesale hemorrhaging. Rebecca. While Shine might get caught unprepared for her monthly, that oldest girl didn't care to be bothered. If it weren't for complaints from the laundry department—her and Elsie—she might not try at all.

The smallest sizes were hardly in need of washing. Elsie was fastidious anyway, but not a single drop of blood? And where were all the rags? That was when the presence that Lidy felt so keenly solidified into a being. A *human being.* A baby.

Lidy dropped her scrub brush into the washtub with a clatter. A startled Elsie looked up from her own tub.

Why hadn't she seen it before? Elsie's porcelain skin, paler than usual, even in the heat and ruthless summer sun. Circles under her eyes. And there: slightly more buxom, belly pooched out beneath the empire waist of her dress. Lord, how far gone was she? Lidy's brain scrabbled for something to catch hold of. When had she first felt it? A month ago? *Three?*

Immediately, she was calculating the best way to get rid of it. The longer they delayed, the more difficult it could be. Lidy—caught up in formulating plans to relieve Elsie of this intruder, this burden—realized with a jolt that she hadn't given a thought to how this situation had come to be.

Jedediah Hanson.

The scoundrel! Presenting himself as a changed man, showing up at church twice a week. Such a complete overhaul of his low-life leanings—a denouncing of the drinking and carousing and Lord-knows-what-all-else that he had been up to before courting Elsie. But there had not been a wedding, nor even talk of a wedding. The only questions popped were about where and what the Strongs might be up to on their mountainside. Hiram had put a stop to that. To all of it. But too late, it seemed. Lidy felt a twinge of guilt. She had failed to be vigilant and keep her granddaughter safe, this girl so eager to have her head turned. To be adored and amused. To have a life other than the hard, relentless one offered by the farm.

Just like her mother. Except Alta had lived that other life once upon a time, so she had known exactly what she was missing.

But Elsie would only dream of that life. Because now she had gone and ensured that she would have nothing but hardship. Lidy made sure the girls had gotten some schooling, whether at the one-room schoolhouse near Kinney or at their kitchen table. It was her way of honoring Alta, who wanted her girls to be able to read, write and do their sums. Elsie was a reader but didn't have other skills beyond the basics. She was good with a needle and thread, handwork of all types, laundry, cooking, tending the hens. In short: she would make a good farmwife.

"Gran, are you all right?" Elsie was talking to her. How many times had she been asked the question? "Here. You dropped your brush."

Lidy stared at the bristle-haired brush in Elsie's outstretched hand.

"You mustn't keep it," Lidy said. She took the brush and began scrubbing fiercely at the unfortunate piece of laundry on her washboard.

"Keep what?"

Treacherous girl! The innocence in her voice could not shield the truth of what she had done. Lidy felt fury clawing inside her chest. She forced herself to take a deep breath. Anger would not be useful to achieve the right outcome here.

"The child."

Elsie's face fell. "But . . . how . . . ?"

"Nothing gets by your gran," Lidy sighed. "But I'd like to know why you didn't come to me when you knew you were in trouble. Like every other woman within shoutin' of this holler."

Elsie's look was nothing short of beatific. *For the love of God, the girl actually* glows.

"Gran, I'm not in *trouble*," Elsie said, resting a hand on the round of her belly. "I'm going to be a mama, that's all. Won't you love being a great-gran?"

"You're putting the cart before the horse, Elsie," Lidy said, exasperated. "You need to be a wife before you are a mother. The way the good Lord intended."

Elsie blushed at this, lowering her eyes. *Good. Show some shame.* Then she whispered something Lidy couldn't hear. "Speak up, for heaven's sake!"

"I said he loves me, Gran," Elsie said, pulling back and making eye contact with her grandmother at last. "And we are getting married."

"When, exactly, is this blessed event taking place?"

Elsie shrugged. "Soon as Jedediah and I talk about it."

"Is this the same young man who hasn't been to church in the last . . ." Lidy thought hard, her mind reaching back. Everyone knew Jed had much rather tie one on than tie the knot. But he had made such an astounding transformation to secure what he wanted! When had Hiram discerned that Jed's intentions weren't entirely pure? That Elsie was only the young man's means of getting in on some "easy" money and quenching his bottomless thirst in the process? "I'm going to say three months?"

Elsie's blue eyes clouded. "He's busy at the store. His pa gave him more responsibility, so he can't be running off to church twice a week. And he was right sick a few weeks, he said, last time I brought in our eggs. I couldn't find him anywhere and had to ask his daddy where he might be. He found Jed behind a stack of feed sacks in the tack room, and I said, 'Now, Jedediah Hanson, are you trying to hide from me?' And he said, 'Nah, sneaking in a lunch break,' even though it was nine thirty in the morning. . . ."

Her voice trailed off. "My word, but I'm slow. Aren't I, Gran?"

She threw herself into Lidy's arms, nearly knocking over the wash bucket. Lidy was not good at this sort of thing, but she shaped her embrace around her diminutive granddaughter and brought her close. When the sobs slowed, she pushed Elsie back to look her in the face.

"You're not stupid," said Lidy, "and you're about to prove it. I've got ways to take care of things like this."

"So you'll talk to Jed?"

"What? No! Make that a 'hell no,'" spat Lidy. "You'll have no more to do with that no-good, lazy—"

Lidy took a breath. She needed to calm down. "What I mean is . . . I can give you something for the womb. To cleanse it." Lidy tiptoed around the word "baby." She didn't want Elsie to think of what was inside her as a someone or something to get attached to.

Elsie's lashes still held tears. "I don't need it, Gran," she said simply. "I just need to talk to Jed. God brought him to church. And to me. He won't take him away now."

Lidy sighed. She stood up, making her way around the washtubs and toward the cabin door. "Well, then. You'll need to take good care of yourself. Eat better and more than usual. Sleep when you feel the urge. And take something to keep your insides strong."

Elsie seemed pleased. "All right, Gran." Grabbing a bucket, she added hot water to her tub before getting back to the laundry.

Inside the cabin, Lidy rummaged through the vials and bottles she kept in a wooden cupboard in the far corner. A pie safe, to cool and store all manner of delectable creations until eating time. Far better than a risky windowsill or the kitchen table, where a pie could be plundered by a squirrel or a hungry husband or youngster. It had been a wedding present from her to Alta and Hiram. She converted it when she moved in; a place to keep her cures and potions. Plus her coffee can of incidental cash and change. Besides, the critters—animals and humans alike—were too scared of her to bother her pies, wherever they cooled.

She pulled open both doors, scanning the shelves for the dried tansy leaves. Lidy crushed them with the mortar and pestle she kept nestled in the cabinet.

A few moments later, she returned to where her granddaughter sat humming and scrubbing as if she hadn't a care in the world. Soon—God willing—she wouldn't.

"A glass of buttermilk for your strength, Elsie," Lidy said. "And your child."

Elsie set it on the stump beside her. "Thank you, Gran. We are both much obliged."

Lidy flushed with pleasure. *That was almost too easy.*

That glass of tansy buttermilk was the first of many she would serve her granddaughter in the name of prenatal and maternal health—along with copious cups of cedar berry tea. Lidy calibrated the ingredients for effectiveness, trying not to overwhelm the elixirs with strong smells or unpleasant textures. She didn't want to raise Elsie's suspicions.

Or Jed's child.

Alta hadn't wanted to raise another child. That much had been clear.

It had confounded Lidy when her daughter-in-law threw herself out of the barn loft. Alta—unlike Elsie—was a married woman, with a good-hearted husband and two healthy girls. And this baby (wrongly, it turned out) was expected to be a boy. Maybe Alta had been bone-weary, exhausted by the prospect of caring for an infant again a half dozen years after Elsie's birth.

Sometimes pregnant women did peculiar things. Lidy understood better than anyone the way a fetus changed not only the body, but the very essence of its mother. She was no longer herself, but two selves, and sometimes that shared blood—nourishing to the growing baby—turned against her, troubled her mind. Dark thoughts disturbed the placid waters of her soul, roiling them up, until they became unrecognizable as her own.

Lidy knew Alta had no business in the upstairs of a barn. She told her granddaughters that what happened was an accident. And, in a way, it was: Alta performed a calculated act to end her baby's life—inadvertently cutting short her own. But Lidy had to wait nearly two years to find out what sent her daughter-in-law over that edge.

"Spring has sprung, child," she said. "Finally."

Lidy surveyed the land, eighteen-month-old Shine balanced on one sharp hip. The yellow-white sun warming the earth also heated her bones, dulling the aches and pains of old age exacerbated by bitter cold.

Shine clapped her hands, sensing her gran's mood. "Down! Down, *peas*!"

Lidy set the child on the porch. The sunshine energized her

as she set to work, squatting on the wooden planks and collecting what she found there: acorns separated from their caps, a twig, a piece of twine, a smooth rock. There was no shortage of interesting things to look at outside after a winter of being cooped up, limited to the four walls of the cabin.

Time to get the corn in the ground. Hiram and the girls were in the farthest of the two cornfields, turning the dark dirt and dislodging any rocks they found before making the miniature hills of seed that would become their corn crop. Six kernels of corn in every mound: *"One for the cutworm, one for the crow, one for the blackbird and three to grow."*

Lidy knew all the ways of planting: how to ensure a good crop. Or mitigate a potentially bad one. She had time-tested means of predicting which way it might go. Some called them superstitions, or worse, nonsense. But Lidy considered them essential. Like when she pried open a seed from one of last year's persimmons, saving it back from one of the largest and best of the fruits, a dusty orange orb with nearly translucent skin. If the halved seed contained a perfect white spoon shape, it meant a bumper crop; if a knife or fork, a bad one.

Spoon.

Lidy smiled now at the memory. How they needed a good year! The last few, they had barely scratched a living out of that rocky hillside, like a bunch of lean chickens pecking for insects or grain in the hard-packed earth of the barnyard. But as difficult as it had been for growing things, it had been even harder on the human beings doing the farming. The loss of Alta had taken a toll on everyone, and a gorgeous spring coupled with the promise of an abundant yield would go far to pull them out of their funk.

It was midmorning, several hours before she would ring the bell, calling the laborers to dinner. Lidy had already made a sugar pie and left it cooling. Soon she would fry some fatback and open a jar each of green beans and peaches from last year, then fashion a few fresh buttermilk biscuits for soaking up the leftover goodness on their plates.

She took a deep breath of the fresh Missouri morning, a crisp edge of cool to the air that made her lungs feel cleaned out. There were a million things that needed doing. But Shine was chattering happily, lining her treasures on the porch in an order that only made sense to her, so Lidy took a moment to sit. Heaven knew she needed it. She had thought her child-rearing days were long behind her, and—Lord Jesus!—they were long days.

She heard singing then, a cheerful baritone coming up the path behind the house. Before she could discern the source, a man in worn black pants and jacket and a black wide-brim fedora on his head appeared at the corner of the porch. Lidy scrambled to her feet.

"Pardon me, ma'am. I didn't mean to frighten you," he said. He carried a worn Bible in his hands, but tucked it into his front pocket to extend a hand to her in greeting. Lidy ignored it, staring at him. They didn't get many strangers around here. Visitors, yes. Especially neighbors needing a piece of medical advice or one of Lidy's tinctures. Or someone sent to fetch her to set a bone or help birth a troublesome babe.

"Can I help you?" she finally managed.

"Name's Robert Smythe," he said, putting his hand down by his side. "I'm looking for Miz Alta."

"I'm sorry, she doesn't live here anymore," Lidy said. The fine hairs on the back of her neck stood at attention. Who was this man, asking around after a dead woman? He didn't look like kin. No sign of her dark hair and eyes, too young to be her daddy.

The man removed his hat, holding it along the brim. He had the reddest hair she had ever seen on a grown man. Not an auburn that comes with age to most redheads, but a fiery orange color only found in sunsets. Or a spectacular sugar maple in the fall.

"Any idea where I could find her?" Smythe's voice and gaze were steady, his eyes as green as bottle glass. But she could tell by the way he turned the hat in his hands that he was anxious for her answer.

"She's out yonder." Lidy swept her arm toward a patch of green near the woods bordering the cornfield. He turned, as if expecting Alta to emerge from the dull brown woods now laced with dogwood and serviceberry. "Dead and buried. Died after giving birth. I'm sorry, but that's the long and short of it."

The man's shoulders sagged and he clutched his hat to his heart, as if he was experiencing a sharp pain, a wound that needed covering in this probing May light.

"I'm sorry for your loss, Ms. . . ."

"Strong. Lidy Strong. I was her mother-in-law. She married my son, Hiram. He's up at the cornfield with his girls."

She wanted him to know she wasn't alone, in case he had more on his mind than saying how-do to her dead daughter-in-law. Not that they had much to offer a thief or even a shyster selling some miracle cure for what ailed them. But he didn't look like either.

Smythe replaced his hat on his head; it was like snuffing out a candle.

"I met Miz Alta about two years ago on my way to a revival meeting west of Kinney. I'm a preacher," he added, pulling the smooth leather-covered Bible from his pocket. "I been all the way to Arizona since and now I'm making my way back to my people in Kentucky. It's been a long road, but I can't complain. God has blessed me with His abundance."

"Aren't you lucky," Lidy said. Not a question.

"Fortunate, yes," he agreed. "But the path of righteousness is rocky. I been sustained by the kindness of strangers and the protection of the Father. 'For I was an hungred and ye gave me meat; I was thirsty and ye gave me drink; I was a stranger and ye took me in . . .' "

"Forgive me if I stop you right there," Lidy said. "We don't need to go into the naked part. Breakfast is done and gone and lunch a long ways off. Besides, I don't hold with everything in the Bible."

"That's a shame, sister. But would you mind terribly if I said a prayer? Alta and I prayed together that time we met. She offered me a meal and unburdened herself while we shared table. She suffered some in this place, I know. But she was a godly woman, wanting to gracefully bear the cross she was given. Would you pray with me?"

Lidy scrutinized her visitor. There was something about him. Familiar.

A tug at her skirt.

"Firsty, Gwan." Shine was beside her, looking up at her with those wise eyes, round-cut emeralds in her peachy cream face. *Green as midsummer grass.*

Startled, she looked up Smythe. Their eyes locked briefly and then they were both staring down at the child, mesmerized.

"Is she Alta's?"

"I think you need to get off our land," Lidy said. She felt light-headed, as if she were in a dream and knew it, but couldn't shake herself awake.

"And don't never come back."

Lidy had watched until the man had disappeared back down the path and into the woods. Then she grabbed up Shine and went inside the cabin, her hands shaking. Then she proceeded to tear the cabin apart; looking for what, she did not know.

Until she found it. A letter, worn with repeated reading, folded once and flattened to fit beneath the false bottom of Alta's jewelry box, which contained her gold cross necklace and her father's pocket watch.

God and time.

Lidy only needed to read the letter once to understand that Alta had run out of both.

She slipped the damning envelope inside her Bible for safekeeping. Until she could decide what to do with it.

But what to do about the child? Until an hour ago, she had cared for her without thought. And now, she felt a reluctance, an ugly tug inside her: Why should she?

Shine had sat on the dirt floor, stretching up her arms to her gran. "Up? Up, peas."

Lidy flashed on the yellow warbler's nest she had found in the lower fork of a dogwood the day before, the dainty cup woven from dry grass, bark and nettles. Inside, two delicate grayish-white speckled eggs lay beside each other in the shadow of a much larger green egg, mottled with brown spots: a brown-headed cowbird had deposited her egg in the nest, too, abandoning it for the more dutiful warbler to warm, hatch and feed. The foreign chick would emerge more quickly, take up more room in the nest and stretch above its adopted siblings for the lion's share of the insects brought by the warbler parents. It might even smother its warbler brethren to death in the bottom of the nest.

"Up, Gwan!" Shine reached toward Lidy, impatient for the arms that typically lifted and carried her at her whim.

Lidy considered this odd creature who had already taken over their home—and the hearts of everyone in it—over the short span of her life. Parasite? Or protector?

She scooped Shine up, shifted her onto her hip once more. Where she belonged.

Hiram

They sat on their favorite log together, watching for the first drops of alcohol to emerge from the coil stretching from the worm box and begin to fill the first jug. Hiram and Shine had been in the woods for several hours and it was way past lunchtime, the sun having slid from straight overhead toward the west. She got out the tin pail and popped open the lid. Inside were two thick slices of Lidy's wheat bread slathered with butter and sprinkled with white sugar. Plus two blood-red apples from last year's crop, cool and crisp from the cellar. Shine set her meal on the log bench and handed Hiram his in the lunch bucket.

"Here, Daddy."

They both bit and chewed and swallowed in a rhythm punctuated by the first slow drips from the coil hitting the bottom of the glass jug. The late summer sun broke through the trees overhead, warming their backs and beating through their hats. The only sounds accompanying the tinkling creek and steady drip of the still were intermittent bursts of birdsong—a thrush, a jay, a cardinal—with the occasional *rat-a-tat-tat* of a pileated woodpecker.

"Need yourself a drink?" Shine asked, but it was only politeness. She already knew the answer.

"Naw, I reckon I'm about to get my fill of firewater here in a short while," he said, winking.

"Remember, your job is to 'taste,' not guzzle," Shine said. "No going overboard. Cuts into the profits."

Hiram grimaced. That stung. Shine didn't pull punches. She didn't like him drinking. Hell, he didn't like himself drinking. Mostly the morning after, when getting out of bed was near impossible. Like this morning. He had been the reason for their slow start.

She made her way the few yards down to the creek, kneeling near one of the pools formed by a ledge of limestone. Cupping her hands, she filled them with the icy cold water and splashed it over her face and neck, the shock of it making her laugh out loud. Hiram, watching, smiled at the sound, the way her exuberant laughter echoed in the trees, coming back to reverberate in his breastbone, making his own heart sing.

That laughter was her mother's. Alta's. A clear tinkling sound, shallow creek water over slick, smooth stones. It was a sound he dearly missed, had missed, even before she died. The music of her laughter stilled by life's difficulties, his drinking not least among them. Her joy leaking away slowly, a last docile note dissipating in an airless parlor.

But Shine! Her laughter, her delight in life was abundant. She didn't reserve it, miserly, meting it out in dribs and drabs. And she didn't rein in that temper, either. He was glad she deigned not to drink, tasting only to titrate their white lightning. Shine already burned so ferociously on the inside; her spirit needed no exacerbation. He wished he could take credit for it, that fire. But he knew it was not his. Yet he protected it, nourished it, tried his best to temper it. She would be the strongest Strong, the best of the batch. This Shine honored him most of all, carrying his name along with his know-how.

God bless her. Life would not be easy for this one.

The birds were the first to sound the alarm: an anxious burst of calls and whistles, the flutter of wings and rustle of leaves as perches were vacated. There was the unmistakable crack of a tree limb being snapped that could only be made by a large animal.

Or a human being.

Then: a rapid-fire *bang, bang, bang* and immediate metallic reply of bullets hitting the copper sides of the boiler and condenser: *plink, plink, plink.* Shine flattened herself on the ground near the creek but Hiram was on his feet, the log seat turning over and spilling the lunch pail. An apple bounced down the bank like a red rubber ball.

Bang, bang, bang. Plink, plink, plink.

The hissing scream of the kettle as one bullet pierced the side at last, releasing a cloud of steam. There was a pause in shooting and Hiram—recognizing the distinct click of a Colt—knew it would be brief: a pistol's chamber held six bullets. The time for reloading would give him his one chance. He stumbled toward the entrance of the cave, where his Winchester leaned uselessly against the limestone wall. *Foolish old man. You let your guard down.*

A few more yards.

"Daddy! Get down!"

Hiram's fingers closed around the barrel of the rifle and in a split second, he had it to his shoulder, eye resting behind the sight. Finger on the trigger. His heart pounded in his ears. He stepped behind the closest tree, a hickory, its trunk not wide enough to hide his full frame but offering a partial shield. The firestorm of shots had come from across the creek on the right.

Bang. There was an explosion of glass, jagged shards splintering from the devastated jug as the bullet found its purchase. Pieces of glass landed with a tinkling sound on the dirt and gravel of the creekbank; a puddle of moonshine soaked into the ground.

Bang, bang, bang. Hiram heard a whiz near his right ear, then the *thunk* of a bullet embedding in the tree trunk in front of him. A stinging burn deep in his right thigh. Searing pain. *Goddamn it to shit.* He looked down to see the blood, a brilliant rose blooming out of the round hole in his brown pants.

"No!" A man's voice yelled out, panicky, from the left side of the woods, opposite the source of the bullets.

Hiram swung his Winchester toward the sound and fired once, the rifle kicking into his upper chest near his right shoulder where he steadied the butt. There was a scrambling in the trees, footsteps scuffling up leaves. He had gotten someone on the run, at least.

Then Hiram swung the barrel back toward where the bullet had come from. Waited for movement.

Bang. He could feel a breeze near his head as the bullets cut through the late-morning air. There. The Colt flashed and then disappeared once more behind a sturdy post oak. Time to reload again. Now was his chance. Hiram leaned out to the side of his own hickory, putting his right eye to the sight of the rifle and closing his left. *Gentle,* he reminded himself. *Soft squeeze.*

Boom. His index finger brought the trigger back to meet the metal of the trigger guard. The bullet only severed and dropped a limb near where he had seen the gun.

But Hiram had not quite kept count. Before he could pull back behind his tree to put in a couple more loads, he felt the bullet—the sixth round—enter his skull, right between his eyes. He blinked exactly once and dropped his rifle like it was red hot. He fell back, he and his gun hitting the unyielding Ozarks ground at the same time.

"Daddy! No!" He stared up at a piece of the sky, a fragment of blazing blue pottery edged by the high leafy canopy of blackjacks and red oaks. Then Shine's face was covering his view, her green eyes all fear and questions.

He wanted to answer them all. Tell her he loved her, this daughter of the spirit. *Spirits.* And Rebecca and Elsie, too. All his precious girls. But he couldn't make his mouth move, words come out. Shine's face was edged in a fuzzy red, as if she were being rubbed away with a bloody rag that was obscuring his vision. He felt her squeeze his hand, a desperate, iron grip.

"Hang on now, Daddy," she cried. "Don't you give up. I got you."

Where was she? He could hear her, as though through a long, dark tunnel. But all he could see was red. Darker. A crimson screen, like looking through a thickly leafed maple in fall.

"I will kill you bastards!" Shine was crying, hysterical. Why couldn't he use his arms? To comfort her. It would be okay. He was sure of it. If he could just . . .

Red black. The color of congealed blood. He wanted to blink, clear his vision. But it was getting darker. Where was Shine? His light? So very dark now.

Alta? Alta.

And finally: *black.*

Rebecca

Bob-white! Bob-white!

The quail was in the thicket by the fencerow. She couldn't see him yet, but the call was clear and sharp, unmistakable as the bird announced himself by name. Rebecca stood still, her long straight frame draped in her favorite loose brown canvas pants and tan cotton shirt with the sleeves rolled up. With her wide-brimmed hat forming a canopy of shade, she could have almost passed for a sapling herself.

She held her breath and released it slowly. She didn't want to frighten the bird. Yet. Rebecca felt the limp warm weight of three of the bobwhite's dead fellows in the bottom of the hunting bag against her hip. She had gotten a covey up a half hour ago, a frightening flutter of wings bursting out of a blackberry patch, and promptly dropped three with only two blasts from her shotgun. But the plump-breasted birds were petite; even if she kept both miniature legs and breast she would need a few more to make a meal.

Rebecca felt a nagging worry while she waited for her quarry to reveal himself. It was early afternoon and she had been hunting for hours, crisscrossing the wooded mountain up from the farm and back down again to the fencerows along the cornfield. Just after daybreak, she had looped by the place where her dad and youngest sister were likely making shine right now—although it had been quiet then. Hiram was probably hungover and late to get to work. Like most mornings.

She had been careful to stay on the opposite side of the creek from where the Strongs set up their still—she didn't want to leave tracks that might draw suspicion. But strangely, as she made her way through the stand of large red hickories and post oaks, she saw a human footprint. A single one, at the base of a tree that could offer both a hiding place and a clear view of the moonshine operation at full tilt on the other bank.

It was not her own. Nor anyone else's from the Strong family. First off, none of them would leave a footprint—they took extreme care to tread lightly and cover their tracks; their livelihood depended on remaining clandestine. But even if one of them had slipped up, their boot soles were worn slick and would leave a smooth, boot-shaped imprint in any dust or mud. This print wasn't pointed like a dress shoe or cowboy boot or shaped exactly like a Sears & Roebuck rounded-toed boot, either. It was a heavy work boot with a brand-new sole, sporting a pattern that Rebecca was unfamiliar with.

Judging by its depth in the dry dirt, the print had been made after a rain—and they hadn't had one for several weeks. Someone had been snooping around, and after the Strongs' close call with the prohis, Rebecca was worried. Maybe this footprint was left by the person who had ratted them out, gotten the feds up here on the mountainside in the first place. She needed to tell her daddy. It probably wasn't urgent since the footprint wasn't fresh. But she didn't like the idea of Hiram and Shine being spied on or their hideout discovered. They could both end up in jail. Or their operation might be destroyed, smashed, spilled and hacked to pieces—like that show she'd witnessed on Main Street put on by those prohis. Maybe both. Or worse.

She didn't want to ponder on what "worse" might be.

Bob-white!

If the bird didn't show himself soon, she would take a step and flush him out, shotgun steadied at her shoulder. Rebecca was a patient soul in general and felt safer in the woods than she did anywhere else. But the footprint put her on edge, ready to shoot. She had the urge to head home; to make sure everyone and everything were safe.

She slowly raised her gun in anticipation of the bird's sudden flight. Even when she knew birds were about to fly—and that she was the cause of a covey taking wing—there was still something startling about how they exited the safety of the brush piles. The brown-and-buff-bodied creatures rose in a furious cloud of thrumming wings, their calls shrill and alarming. She braced herself.

But instead, she was caught off guard by the brittle *crack, crack, crack* of a gun on the other side of the mountain, where the creek ran. Where she had been earlier. More shooting, then the fainter echo repeated over the forested hillside.

This was no rifle or shotgun. It was the distinctive pop of a pistol. No hunter. At least, no hunter of animals. Pistols were pretty much exclusively for killing people.

Ignoring the voice inside that told her to be safe, unload her shotgun, *walk, don't run,* Rebecca tore across the mountainside. Her heart raced, too, a rhythm mimicked in the *thump, thump* of her game bag hitting her hip while the shotgun banged against her back with each step.

She heard someone yelling, more shots. She ran through the cover of the woods, but she knew she needed to be careful. A spray from her shotgun would be a useless irritant in the face of a single, targeted bullet.

Please let them be okay.

When she broke through the last trees before the clearing on the creek, she stopped short: there, face up on the creek bank, was her father. And her youngest sister, holding his bleeding head in her lap and his rifle in her arms, Shine's face pale beneath its generous crop of freckles.

Rebecca did not need to ask. Shine only had to drop her eyes and she knew. Hiram was gone. She took in the neat hole in her father's forehead, the drip of blood leaking from that perfect circle as gravity pulled it down one side of his face. Slack mouth, blank eyes. The way her mama's had looked in those months before she finally passed.

"No, Shine. *No.*"

Her sweat went cold on her skin, even in the heat of the July sun. Her daddy, who had taught her to tend the tame animals on their farm; to track and trap, hunt and kill the wild creatures of the woods, fields and creeks. All with a reverence and care to take only what was necessary. But who had taken her father? With no regard for the life and lives he was connected to. Who depended on him. Loved him.

"We'll grieve him later, Becks," Shine said. "He's gone. And we need to track the fuckers who did this."

Rebecca stood rooted to the ground. She felt a rock-hard lump in her throat. She couldn't remember how to move.

"Go on, now. They got a head start but Daddy may have hit one of the pieces of shit before they ran. At least two of them, one from over there"—she indicated the right side of the creek—"and one from there on the left. Took off the way they came, I bet."

Rebecca removed the shotgun from her back, slinging the strap around and over her head. She ejected the two shells, set the gun and ammunition on the ground. Then she grabbed Hiram's gun from her sister, put her shoulder through the strap and reached into the nearby knapsack for a handful of rifle cartridges.

"Reckon this'll do me a sight better than a shotgun." Her mouth was a grim line. "You go get Gran."

"No. Daddy would want us to go together," Shine said, easing her daddy from her lap onto the ground. "Nothing to do for him now. We can't let them get away."

Rebecca shook her head. "We only got one gun between us that can do any damage if we run into trouble. And I'm the best shot."

"The bullets came from the right," her sister said, unmoved. Rebecca knew by the steely tone in her voice that Shine would be a part of this, right or wrong, safe or not. "So sure—you go that way. I'll go left.

"Besides, if I catch one, I'll be more than happy to kill him with my bare hands. Actually prefer it."

Rebecca hopped a few rocks through the creek and took off in the direction Shine had indicated, her rifle loaded with its muzzle pointed skyward. Out of the corner of her eye, she saw her sister heading in the same direction, farther to her left. She hoped to hell that Shine wouldn't mess up any trail that could be followed up on later. Rebecca was not only the best shot, but the best tracker. Shine didn't have the patience to go slow, always looking ahead at what was coming, not paying enough attention to where she was at. Or where she'd been. Shine might miss a bent stem, a loosed button or piece of thread on a tree limb.

Fifty feet from the creek bank, Rebecca found it: a tree with a dozen or more empty bullet casings at its roots. A strange crop, like cylindrical metal acorns. She picked up one, pocketed it. Left the rest. She needed to keep moving.

It wasn't difficult to follow the shooter. He had stayed on the game trail, leaving partial footprints—she recognized the pointed smooth sole of a cheap dress shoe—and trampled grass and plants on the sides where he had veered off in his haste or required a broader path than a dainty-legged deer. He was headed downhill, toward the east side of their property, wooded all the way down to the road. The acres of trees and scrub formed a natural barrier between the Strongs' patch of farmland and civilization. Hiram chose to leave it that way to discourage the unwanted visitor—and make sure even those who were invited truly wanted to be there.

The road. Rebecca's heart sank.

She heard the crank and whine of a motor starting up, the spray of gravel from a wheel thrust hastily into motion. She couldn't catch anyone now, on foot or with a bullet. The road was still a half mile away.

"Rebecca!" Shine had probably come to the same conclusion. "Over here!"

Shine hunched near a stand of pawpaw trees, their glorious limbs ribbed with oval green leaves that gave them the look of half-open umbrellas beneath the canopy of red oak giants.

"They're gone," Rebecca said, panting, as she reached her sister, who was bent over, hands resting on her splayed knees. She was out of breath, too.

"I know. Bastards," she spat. "But look here."

Shine pointed to a red splatter near her feet. It was the size of a silver dollar, splashed across the green striped hood of a jack-in-the-pulpit. The blood could almost be a bloom, or a berry, nestled as it was among the foliage. *Good job, sis.*

"Gotta be more where that came from," Rebecca said.

The sisters followed flattened plants and game trails that hosted footprints stretched apart: someone running fast. And increasingly large spatters of that cardinal-red blood. Rebecca would not be surprised to find that someone between here and the road, bleeding out or passed out. Or even dead. Hiram had found his mark.

But the blood went only as far as the road.

Gone. Along with whoever shot and killed their father.

The young women pulled up at the fence that edged their property along the rough red road. Empty—save for one last bloody drop near tire ruts spun a half-inch deep in the orange clay dust.

After a long moment, Rebecca unloaded her gun. Placing the two unspent cartridges in her palm, she let them roll around before tucking them in her pocket. How satisfying to have fired them into the worthless carcasses of the men who had done this. Not someone who typically sought revenge, Rebecca regretted not having the chance.

Her body began draining of adrenaline, leaving her flat. Despondent. But a glance at her sister told her that this dead end, this hopelessness, was only serving to get Shine revved up.

"It isn't right, Becks," Shine fumed, her hair loose and wild from running, the color matching her fury. "It isn't right."

She pushed down the top strand of barbed wire and lifted first one, then the other of her legs deftly over the fence. And then

Shine was running down the red dirt road, hair streaming behind her, boots pounding in the awful silence of that strange summer afternoon.

Rebecca watched her go, in awe of the way she gave herself over to running, arms pumping, legs stretched and striding, her body holding absolutely nothing back. She knew Shine would run out of wind, whether it took two miles or ten. And that she would follow along behind and be ready to pick up her sister where she collapsed. To calm her. It was what Rebecca did.

And by the time she and Shine returned home, exhausted and spent? After telling Gran and Elsie that Hiram was dead and gone and that it was up to the women to carry on somehow?

She knew her baby sister would have a plan.

That was Shine all over.

Heads

July 1929–April 1930

SHINE

C'mon, Cowboy.

Shine dug in her heels, even though the poor horse was already at a full gallop. *There.* The last turn in the road before the woods alongside opened into the few cleared acres that comprised Kinney, Missouri. The horse was lathered up, sweating something awful from the paces she had put him through. Her skirt tucked up beneath her thighs was wet where it touched his sides.

She gave the horse one last slap on the rump to urge him on, past the clapboard church where Elsie worshipped and prayed—probably for a husband. Then a few crooked frame houses, the farrier and, finally, Hanson's.

The general store was hopping today, a Saturday afternoon in midsummer. A clutch of women huddled on the front porch, exchanging gossip; some men leaned against the building chewing tobacco or smoking while others tended to horses tied on the front rail. But they parted like a hot knife through butter when Shine approached, pulling Cowboy up sharply and dismounting, with scant regard for the legs she exposed before her cotton dress fell back into place, stained with horse sweat and about a bucket of her father's blood.

The thud of her boots on the road acted like a judge's gavel in an unruly courtroom. Everything and everyone went silent.

The only sound was Cowboy, panting and snorting, sides heaving, as Shine lashed him to the tie-up. She hadn't considered what a sight she must be, blood-covered and face flushed with anger and exertion. And tears. Her dress a mess, her hair without benefit of a hat, sticking out from her head like thick orange flames.

"Shine? What in in the world—?"

She recognized the voice: Boyce Taylor, his farm two hollers over. He'd brought his youngest to Lidy with seizures. The typically jolly man had been scared to death the devil had the child in his throes. But Lidy patiently talked Boyce down, advised him to cook up a colt's tongue for the girl in a cast-iron pan.

No more epilepsy.

"Where's the goddamn sheriff?"

"Reckon he's in back of the store, swapping some stories," Boyce said. "You're bleeding, child."

There was a *thump* as one of the young women on the porch passed out flat just looking at Shine.

"Some assholes shot my daddy dead and they're gonna pay for it," Shine declared. "Now, get me the sheriff before I practice on some of you." She took her gun out of the holster, spinning it for good measure.

"What in holy hell—?" Sheriff Burkett pushed his way through the crowd of wide-eyed bystanders, having been apprised that there was a crazy firecracker of a girl packing on the porch.

"Shine's daddy's been shot," Boyce summed it up for the lawman. "Dead," he added. "And she's looking for some justice."

The sheriff hitched his pants, sagging beneath the shelf of his belly, and took a step toward Shine.

She cocked the pistol.

"Shine Strong, you put that down," said the sheriff. "We'll get to the bottom of this. But not with you waving that gun around.

"Bill, why don't you take Miss Strong's horse for a drink while she and I have ourselves a meeting." He gestured toward the taller of two men at the hitching post, who made a move to untie Cowboy, keeping a wary eye on Shine. She reluctantly holstered her gun.

The sheriff took her arm, steering her across Main Street where a maple tree provided shelter from the wicked July sun. And curious ears.

"I know it's those goddamn prohis," Shine blurted, shaking his hand off her arm. "I just need to figure out where they are."

"Well, it ain't here," Sheriff Burkett said. "Those boys packed up and hit the road. Bigger fish to fry in Arkansas, the lardy one said."

"Bigger fish, my ass. I'll fry him all right," Shine spat. "With some hot lead."

"I'm gonna pretend I didn't hear that. You better watch yourself, girl. Because the thing about it is, Shine . . ." Here he paused. "If you and your daddy were up to some shenanigans . . ."

"*Shenanigans?* Minding our business? Working on our land?"

"All's I'm saying is if you were doing something that wasn't a hundred percent on the up-and-up . . . there's nothing I can do."

Shine's heart clenched.

"How dare you," she spat. "You're supposed to protect the citizens of our county."

"That's right," he said. "My job is to protect the citizens. Not the criminals."

The sheriff touched the brim of his hat. "Best of luck to you. And my condolences to your gran and sisters."

John

They had barely made it over the Arkansas line when the adrenaline wore off. Flanagan's entire left side was on fire. Like he was in the bowels of hell being poked by the pitchfork of the devil himself. He'd taken off his shirt miles ago, insisting that McConnell tear it into strips and fashion a tourniquet at the shoulder. It didn't stop the blood from the front entry wound, though, so he had stuffed the pulsing hole with the leftover shirt scraps.

"I need a doctor," Flanagan finally admitted. The edges of his vision were fuzzing and he felt lightheaded. He could not die. Not because of the stupid idiot sitting unfazed in the driver's seat, popping handfuls of striped sunflower seeds into his mouth, chewing them like a bored bovine and then spitting the wet split husks out the window.

McConnell paused in mid-chaw.

"I never took you for a sissy," he said. "Even though I did put you in that dress one time. You made a beautiful bride." He slapped his knee at the memory. "Gawd, I miss New York!"

Flanagan tried to formulate a response but his tongue had thickened in his mouth.

Then everything went dark.

* * *

Sharp astringent ammonia.

Smelling salts. He came to in a dim parlor lit by a flickering kerosene lamp, shivering beneath a heavy blanket. A bespectacled face with a white walrus mustache hovered above him.

"There you are. You got yourself two pretty good punctures, son.

"Dr. Gaines," the man said, pulling back from Flanagan's face. He removed his wire-frame glasses and gave them a good cleaning with a handkerchief. "I was afraid you all were on the wrong side of the law when your partner came knocking on my door at eight o'clock at night. I don't cotton to criminals."

"But then I told him, 'Sir, we *are* the law,'" chuckled McConnell from a chair in the corner of the cozy room, closed off by a pair of dark cherrywood pocket doors.

"I've cleaned out both sides of your wound," Dr. Gaines went on, ignoring McConnell's inanity like Flanagan only dreamed of doing. "And given you morphine. You're a mighty lucky young man. An inch either way or a slightly different angle and you'd have been shot in the heart or an artery."

Flanagan didn't feel lucky at the moment. He tried raising himself off the exam couch. The doctor reached to steady him, placing a pillow behind his back to prop him up.

"Better sit before you try standing. I've shown your partner here how to pack the wound. Rinse it with rubbing alcohol and stick in clean gauze once a day. It should fill in after a month.

"I'd also suggest some time off the job," he said, quirking a bushy white eyebrow.

"Ha!" McConnell stood. "I told him that was impossible. I sure as hell can't fight the hillbilly brigade by my lonesome." He adjusted his belt buckle under the bulge of his belly. "But while I've got you, Doc, I've been wondering about my eyeballs. It's gotten where I can't see all that good."

Fantastic. From the man who has been driving me on backroads crooked as black snakes.

Dr. Gaines looked annoyed, but Flanagan could almost see the Hippocratic oath kick in as the physician sighed and sat down on a stool. Putting his glasses back on, he indicated for McConnell to take a seat in his exam chair, which was simply a parlor chair with a throw blanket on top to prevent staining.

"How long has this been going on?"

"Couple a years, I guess. Lot worse lately."

There were more questions, like rifle volleys; more answers in return. Flanagan's eyes grew heavy with the warm spread of the morphine through his body, an inner blanket matching the one on top of him. He was so tired. Of his job, where the rare success felt like a drop in the proverbial bucket. There was so much moonshine; a torrent, really. And bootleggers by the dozens, hundreds. He and McConnell were barely making a dent against all the criminality that had sprung up around illegal alcohol. He thought back to the idealism of his childhood, even his youth, when it seemed like he could fight it. He'd saved his dad, hadn't he?

"And, pardon the intrusion, but have you had . . . relations with more than one woman?"

Flanagan's ears perked up.

"Why, I most assuredly have!" McConnell's tone was disdainful. "I'd like to meet a red-blooded American man who hasn't!

"To tell you the truth," his voice turned sly, "I used to keep track. Notched them on the old belt, you know?"

Flanagan opened one eye. *Ugh.* He longed to stuff some of that gauze in his earholes.

"I was up near a hundred before I outgrew that belt." McConnell patted his belly, a fleshy round drum drooping over his waist.

But how many of those were *paid*? Flanagan couldn't imagine any woman who would choose to be intimate with that unappealing windbag.

"Hmmm." Dr. Gaines seemed to be processing the unsavory information. "Do you have, or have you ever had, a rash on your hands and feet?"

"Well, now, I own that I have," McConnell answered. "A few years back. Never could figure that out. But what does that have to do with my eyeballs?"

Dr. Gaines grimaced, as though the words he was about to say would cause actual pain to himself. Or McConnell. Although Flanagan didn't think the good doctor was a fan of his off-putting partner.

"And prior to the rash, did you note any sores or lesions on your . . ."

There was an awkward silence. Clearly Dr. Gaines had hoped McConnell would fill in the blanks.

"*Ahem.*" The doctor cleared his throat.

"On my what?"

"Your private parts, Mister . . . ?"

"McConnell." His partner was flummoxed.

"Or your rectum or anus, if I may add."

"Wait a minute," McConnell blustered. "Are you asking if I had sores on my *pecker*?!"

Whoo, boy. Flanagan—modest, decent man that he was—wanted to disappear into the floorboards. But a minuscule part of him was enjoying the show.

"That is precisely what I am asking," Dr. Gaines said. "Despite my supreme discomfort at doing so."

Flanagan held his breath in the beat of quiet that followed.

McConnell burst into laughter, deep belly laughs that shook his generous girth like a Christmas aspic trembling on a platter.

"Listen, Doc," he said, wiping his eyes with the back of his hand. "Now that you mention it, I may have had something like that years ago. But my pecker is usually sore from overuse, if you get my meaning."

"It would be hard not to," Dr. Gaines said.

"Did you just say 'hard'?" McConnell was off again, guffawing to beat the band. "Good one!"

"Mr. McConnell!" Dr. Gaines had had enough. "I am not sure

you are comprehending what I am trying to communicate, but I assure you, it is extremely serious."

McConnell stopped abruptly, eyes fixed on the doctor. Flanagan held his breath.

"I'm fairly certain you are suffering from late-stage syphilis," Dr. Gaines said. "And I'm worried the effects may be irreversible at this point."

Flanagan waited for McConnell to beg his pardon, interrogate him further about treatment, outlook . . . anything. But his partner was having none of it.

"Some doctor you are!" he scoffed. "If you can't tell the difference between a pair of eyes and a one-eyed snake, you're a pretty sorry specimen."

McConnell turned to go. "Get yourself together, Flannie. We're out of here."

Flanagan reluctantly got up from the sofa, steadying himself briefly with his one good arm.

"And watch out the next time you give a fellow an eye exam," McConnell said darkly. "Or you'll end up with a socket full of piss."

The door slammed.

Flanagan and Dr. Gaines looked at each other and shrugged. Or, at least, Gaines shrugged, while Flanagan winced with the effort.

"Son, a word to the wise: the symptoms of tertiary syphilis are not pretty," Dr. Gaines said, offering Flanagan the bag of gauze and alcohol. "Blindness, paralysis, pain. Not to mention paranoia, mood swings, even violence. I've heard mineral springs can mitigate the effects. But not reverse them. He shouldn't be in any job that uses a firearm. I daresay he shouldn't have a job at all. He could be a danger to himself and others."

Too late.

"But . . . Godspeed and God help you both."

Flanagan stepped into the warm July night and toward the driver's side of the truck, where McConnell had the engine running.

"Scoot over," Flanagan commanded. "I'm driving."

"You sure as hell aren't. Drugged up with only one good arm?" McConnell snorted. "Ha!"

"But I've got two good eyes," Flanagan shot back. There was a pause—but McConnell moved over.

And what I see is I need to get shed of you and this job.

Flanagan threw the truck into gear.

Lidy

She wore black. But then, Lidy had been dressing in "widow's weeds" for decades; they suited her. She wasn't in mourning for the husband she'd lost so many years ago. It had been all she could do not to dance a jig when the asshole died. An alcoholic who had regularly beaten her and Hiram—the last time within an inch of their lives. Who was so blackout drunk one night that he must have got into a rank batch of shine or drank the foreshots.

That's what people figured, anyhow. No one was surprised when he turned up dead, having bled from the inside out from whatever rotgut he'd ingested. Least of all her.

A woman had to do what she had to do.

Today, though, she also had on the black bonnet she wore to town—or to church if she was forced to go. Because today was her own son's wake.

Hiram.

If she squinted her eyes, she could imagine that the body laid out on the plank in the front room of their cabin was taking a nap. It wouldn't be the first time she caught her son at an afternoon snooze. Soon she'd have to give him a good shake, rattle those bones and dislodge the cobwebs of his dreams—or the leftover fumes from another good bender—from his skull. "Time to get the chores done," she'd say. "The day isn't getting any younger, and neither are you."

Parents shouldn't have to bury their children. But she'd seen it often enough in her decades of caring for the people across these hard Ozark mountainsides and the hollers in between. It hadn't been a dozen years since the Spanish flu tore through their sliver of the country like it had the wider world, not discriminating between old and young, mamas and daddies, soldiers, farmers or schoolteachers.

Lidy had helped all of them. Tried, anyway. Best she could tell, survival was purely a matter of luck or some inner strength or immunity that couldn't be predicted by looking at a person's outsides. She offered what she could in the way of fever and pain relief: herbal teas, poultices, her homemade tinctures. But when the body began to turn blue and the black-red blood started pouring from the lungs, there was nothing to be done. Move on to the next one with chills and fever and hope. Pray if you believed in God. Then burn and bury the dead. Holy Jesus, there had been so many dead.

She'd thought herself immune. And she had been, she and Hiram and the girls managing to keep healthy and whole.

Until now. But while Lidy knew most every granny cure available from her fifty-seven years in these hills, she had yet to come up with anything that could reverse the consequences of a well-aimed bullet to the brain. Or the hubris of those who willingly put themselves in harm's way for the making of a couple gallons of moonshine.

She wished she could do something about the stupidity of those doing the shooting. It was futile, trying to take out a moonshiner or his still. There were fifty more for every one uncovered or incapacitated in these hills. And a prohi ensuring there was one less hillbilly making shine did about as much good toward stemming the tide of illegal alcohol as a one-legged man in an ass-kicking contest.

No, Hiram was dead—and there wasn't a goddamn thing she could do about it.

It had been two days since Shine and Rebecca had loaded

Hiram's body across Marge's broad back and brought him home. She'd been standing between the rows of shelling peas and string beans, falling to her ancient knees when she saw them. Saw him. Pea pods scattered on the dark earth, petite green shrouds. Elsie had come running, hysterical, tried to pull Lidy up and embrace her—for a hug is what Elsie herself needed. But Lidy had remained stiff as a sun-dried sheet on a line.

Shine had torn into town, dead set on making someone pay for what had been wrought on her daddy. Lidy wished Rebecca had gone with her, to keep her hotheaded sister from doing or saying anything rash. But Rebecca wanted to get back up to the still, salvage and hide the equipment. Cover their tracks. Just in case the sheriff or anyone else came looking.

Lidy bathed Hiram. Laid him out the best she could, the clothes clean and crisply pressed—if not without mended places. The wake would need to be soon, before he started to stink. In this heat, even the living didn't smell that good.

She sent Elsie off to gather wildflowers and her granddaughter had outdone herself. Vases and mason jars—even watering cans and buckets—filled all four corners of the cabin and topped every surface, too. Black-eyed Susans, purple coneflowers, wild pink roses, a delicate bouquet of Queen Anne's lace—despite the flower's acrid smell and penchant for bringing in ants. Elsie had pulled together bunches of light purple phlox and hardy hibiscus with crimson blooms as full as Sunday dinner plates. She filled in around the blossoms with large branches of lavender, rosemary and even ferny asparagus leaves. Lidy knew her granddaughter was snipping away at her sadness with every upright sprig, every sunny floret or tight-lipped bud that met her blade. The result was as if the glory of outdoors had taken up residence within the four walls of the cabin, truly heaven on earth.

Lidy covered the one round mirror that hung on the wall, nailed a black ribbon wreath to the front door. She and Elsie had cleaned the cabin until it shone, the brown dirt floor swept smooth as a penny, lined two walls with a bench, chairs and several stools for those who wanted to join Lidy in her vigil.

Soon a stream of people would shuffle in to pay respects before she put him in the ground for good. He would finally be with Alta. She felt a pang when she thought on her now. The way she left this world.

Maybe a merciful God would forgive Lidy. Would pardon them both. And if not? Lidy didn't really believe in hell. She'd seen too much suffering on this earth to think there could be a worse place to go after you're dead.

It was November 1912. Mornings came silvery frosted down the mountainside, dressing the dried brown fescue, cornfield stubble and remaining dull oak leaves in lacy finery. The breath from the cattle, hogs and horses formed brief clouds from their mouths and nostrils. The chickens puffed up nearly twice their size in an effort to keep warm, while gray squirrels chattered and chipped away at walnuts, making piles of green-black hulls after eating the meat from the tarry innards.

Winter was fast approaching. And like the squirrels, the human beings on the hillside were also making preparations. Attention had turned from harvesting and preserving to laying up stacks of firewood in neat rows at the back of the cabin and butchering the fattened hog, rendering him into lard and fatback, salting away bacon and chops, jowls and brain, pickling hooves and tail. Care was taken to fill the chinks in the mud mortar between the logs that formed their two-room cabin and tarring the roof where it needed patching. The family's world was turning inward, after a spring, summer and fall of battling and harnessing the earth to produce what would sustain them during this dark, fallow season.

Lidy's thoughts turned inward, too. She had spent a month worrying whether Shine had the fortitude to survive being born so early, but the clenching fear finally released its grip. That left room for other concerns, the main one of which was Alta.

It had been more than three months since the "fall," the flight from hayloft to oblivion. Alta lay as still as she had from the beginning, covered in blankets on the cot by the wood stove. She was no more than a piece of furniture. There were times that Elsie would pull up a stool near her mother's head and let down her hair, brushing out every strand and then French braiding it into careful coils around her mother's ears. Or Rebecca might read her a page or two from *Farmers' Almanac*, the girl's favorite tome. Some mornings she would find Hiram in a chair at Alta's side, draped over his wife's body where he had fallen asleep after drinking the night before. But those times and interactions were fewer all the time. Was it becoming the norm to have Alta as a benign, nonparticipatory presence in their lives, going barely acknowledged? Or was it the arrival of Shine, with the demands that a new baby brings—along with all of the chances for snuggling, warmth, and goo-gooing? A life that gave back, mirroring smiles and emotions, versus a life that siphoned away love and energy without response.

That morning, Lidy had searched high and low for her dish towel only to find it draped and drying over one of Alta's stiff, stockinged feet. Definitely the work of an easily distracted Elsie.

A piece of furniture.

Lidy picked up the towel, a simple flour sack whip-stitched in blue at the edges, and knew in that instant what must be done. And done now, while she was blessedly and gloriously alone.

Hiram was squirrel hunting, hoping to bring home something for the stewpot to go with their surplus of carrots and potatoes. Rebecca was in the barn, mucking the stalls and likely daydreaming; of what, Lidy wasn't sure. And Elsie was outside with Shine on her hip in a makeshift sling so that the baby could accompany her on her round of chores—feeding the chickens and collecting their eggs, milking the cow and carrying the frothy pail to the cabin. Later, her little sister would be treated to a bottle made with the warm, slightly yellow liquid with its thick layer of unctuous fat. Elsie loved giving Shine her bottle, entranced by her thoughtful expression as she sucked in the milk, eyes searching

Elsie's face. The girl's tender countenance would be the closest thing this baby ever knew to motherly love. Not that she herself didn't love the little creature, despite everything, but Lidy's love was not nurturing or extravagant. She cared with cool efficiency, with an anticipation of needs met early—before the beneficiary may have even known what was wanted. But hugs and kisses were not her currency; practicality was her god.

Which is why, as she folded the stained towel into halves, then fourths, she lay it gently across Alta's staring face, covering those empty eyes. Then, reaching for a cushion from the room's only comfortable chair, she placed it square on top of the towel.

"I've kept your secret. Now I suppose you'll keep mine."

She did not ask her Maker for forgiveness; it wouldn't have occurred to her that she needed it. Instead, her only thought, as she pressed the cushion down hard around Alta's nose and mouth, was that she needed to get the vegetables chopped up for the stew and get the cornbread made and did she have enough cornmeal for a double batch?

But then Alta's arm shot up, fingers grasping and clawing the air and finding no purchase. Lidy, panicked, pressed the cushion down harder with her full weight. The arm jerked just once and fell to the cot again.

She felt no response beneath her hands, save the beat of her own racing heart in the center of her palms. She began counting, in the absent-minded way one might measure the time between thunder and lightning to see how far away a storm was. And when she reached five hundred, her own pulse slowed, she lifted the pillow and returned it to the chair. Then she peeled away the dish towel, which held slight imprints from Alta's eye sockets and a pair of wet stains along with one larger, made by her nostrils and mouth with her last breaths. Lidy draped it on the edge of the laundry basket.

Finally, she looked at her daughter-in-law, laid out with her grim, accusing stare. Maybe she had rushed her to the hereafter. That last twitch had spooked Lidy, even as she told herself it was nerves. Like the body of a beheaded chicken, detached from its brain but still with movement, if not life.

"You're a far sight better off than you've been in months," she said, using an index finger to close Alta's eyelids. "But I don't expect any thanks."

Lidy felt a sudden urge to wash her hands and did so with a dipper of water from the pail by the stove. She gave herself a thorough rubbing with a bar of lye soap, which never made suds, but left a brutal lingering smell she equated with clean. She dried her hands with fistfuls of her apron, smoothing it over her dress when she was finished. Then she went outside to the root cellar for carrots and potatoes.

Lidy positioned her chair right beside Hiram's body, within arm's reach. Never one for touch or shows of affection, she had the urge now to put her hand on her son's folded ones, her lips to his ruined forehead. As long as she could do those things, he wasn't gone. *Not yet.*

Outside, the Strong girls had pulled up a few chairs on the porch so they could greet mourners on their way into the cabin. She heard murmurs. Footsteps.

"I'm sorry for your loss."

Myrna Howard, a drab woman in a dark gray dress and practical boots, was shaking Lidy's hand. How had she gotten here? Lidy remembered when Myrna had knocked on her door, decades ago, desperate for something to make her husband desire her. She wanted children so badly. Lidy had recommended raw honey for fertility—along with a batch of her peach-infused hooch, instructing the poor thing to get her husband drunk and simply climb on top. Lidy had an inkling Hugh Howard didn't care for women in that way; it would be an uphill battle, so to speak. But she had to hand it to Myrna: she got a boy and a girl.

Then there was Molly, a younger woman whose fourth child had required Lidy to hurry on horseback to help pry the stuck baby out. When Lidy saw the deformed head, she used her quick hands to break the infant's neck before bundling and handing it to the exhausted mother with her regrets. A child like that—who knew how long it could have lived? And all the while sucking away the mother's energy, claiming a disproportionate amount of her time and attention. It was for the best. Molly had two more after that, perfectly healthy.

Sheriff Burkett showed up, hat in hand. "Wish there was more I could do, Miz Strong."

The cabin was filling up. Here was Boyce Taylor and his wife, Julia, and five girls, including the one who used to have seizures. A few people came in quickly to pay respects and left, uncomfortable with a dead body that so blatantly bore the cause of its passing. Others either didn't mind or their naked curiosity allowed them to sit a spell with Lidy and her grief.

But all of them were there to get fed.

"Gran, come see." Elsie insisted Lidy take a break from Hiram's side. "You won't believe it. Everyone sure loved Daddy. Seems they love you, too."

The spread outdoors was something to behold. Rebecca had set up a big plank on top of a two sawhorses under the oak; Elsie had covered it with one of her embroidered tablecloths, all curlicues and flowers. Earlier, Lidy had set out loaves of her fresh wheat bread, dusted with seeds and salt, along with two peach pies with their crisscross crusts of golden brown. But the rest was brought by neighbors. Pans of fresh-picked green beans boiled with bacon and black pepper or mountains of mashed potatoes. Plus plates of biscuits, jars of jam from blackberry to huckleberry and everything in between; heaping bowls of canned peaches, hot peppers, pickles and peas. Someone had brought a thick beef stew in a cast-iron pot, still steaming with chunks of carrot, red potato and onion. Skillets of cornbread in every iteration but—Missouri being a border state—falling into one of two camps: white Southern style, with a fine crumb and not a bit of sweet, and its more crumbly Yankee cousin, made with coarser yellow cornmeal, sugar and fewer eggs.

And the desserts! Molasses crinkles and cinnamon-dusted snickerdoodles, oatmeal raisin cookies and lemon bars, derby pie, and every type of fruit pie. Not to mention the dark golden pecan pies with their sweet syrupy glaze, sugar pie, and both sweet potato and pumpkin pie, too. Crumb cake and pound cake. Whole watermelons cooled and carved into red slices like giant smiles, easily held in hands large and small.

Lidy was not hungry, but the sight of the table and all the neighbors from near and far filled her. She did not help or heal with a balance sheet in her heart, or any expectation of reciprocation. Sometimes she left with a dozen eggs or a pound of fresh ground sausage. Or maybe a load of firewood would appear, stacked neat as you please when she opened her door on a fine crisp November morning. But she never asked for payment and if one wasn't proffered—sometimes there wasn't anything with which to pay—she didn't give it a second thought. These were her neighbors. Did she like them all? Not especially. But she cared for them, every last one.

Except *that* one. Her eyes fell on Jedediah Hanson, slinking along behind his parents. Trying and failing to blend into the crowd. She would have a few choice words for him, were it not her son's funeral. It irked her something fierce that he could sashay up here like he hadn't a care in the world, while her granddaughter might have been saddled with their mistake for the rest of her life.

It isn't right.

The lot of women wasn't right, in Lidy's opinion, top to bottom. Why, she'd give her eyeteeth to see a man birth a baby. She could good and goddamn guarantee there'd be crying and gnashing of teeth ten times that of womenfolk. *All bluster, no muster.* The good Lord knew what He was doing when he handed out assignments. There'd be no babies if it were up to men to carry and birth them. The end of the human race.

"Gran?" Elsie followed her gaze and, when she saw Jed, lowered her eyes. "Let's have a blessing and let these good people eat."

Lidy didn't like it, the shame she saw in her granddaughter's movement, that acquiescence to a man who committed the same sin she had—but would bear no punishment. Or, it would seem, do the right thing by Elsie. Thankfully, Lidy had already started putting things right—one glass of buttermilk at a time.

Suddenly, in the middle of the glaring July afternoon, there was thunder. Everyone paused their chatter and chewing long enough to look up, amazed at the single dark cloud zooming in to cover the sun, crowning itself with a halo of gold. Rain began to fall; they saw it approaching from woods below the house. Then it was on top of them: hard, pelting drops that darkened their hats and bonnets, wet their shoulders and spattered the bountiful table. The next instant, the nimbus cloud released the sun to reveal everyone in their damp but gladsome glory. There was laughter and clapping; some simply shook their heads.

Lidy's wrinkled face cracked into a rare smile. She had closed her eyes and turned her face upward to receive the last drops on her cheeks and forehead. A benediction. It was good luck to have rain at a funeral.

And that thunderclap? Why, it meant her boy's soul had made it through heaven's gate, everyone knew that. She might not be a big believer. But she took a measure of comfort in it all, nonetheless.

ELSIE

"Should anyone present know of any reason that this couple should not be joined in holy matrimony, speak now or forever hold your peace."

Brother Aiken took an anxious step back from the couple standing stiff as scarecrows at the front of his church. He slid an index finger inside the tight clerical collar and tugged, trying to loosen it. To breathe easier. Never mind the sweat staining his shirt. He needed air.

Elsie pitied him. She herself wished that Shine and Rebecca would sit down in the pews like normal people—was it too much to ask?—or at the very least, put away their guns. But there her sisters stood at her left side, Shine with her arms crossed and Hiram's pistol clutched in one hand, and Rebecca, taking a wide stance and holding her Winchester across her body like a soldier at the ready. She looked like she wanted to say something—her extremely untalkative sister!—but had decided against it.

The pastor's words echoed off the high ceiling of the nearly empty church. But afterward: stone silence.

"What God has joined, let no man put asunder," the perspiring pastor said, closing his Bible with a definitive thump. "I now declare you man and wife."

Elsie guessed this was all there was to getting married. She had higher hopes. Dreams of a lacy white dress and a headpiece of flowers with a half veil. High-buttoned white boots, new from the box. A bouquet of fragrant magenta roses from Gran's garden bound in a bow with white satin ribbon. Her mama's gold cross around her neck.

At least she had the necklace.

There hadn't been time for anything else. Gran had caught a whiff of something putrid and sour near her lavender bush—strangely brown and dying—and found large globs of turned, rotting cream dotted with shrunken cedar berries on the soil surrounding the plant. But what was Elsie supposed to do with those daily doses of buttermilk and tea? She had intuited they were *not* for her health.

Not long afterward, Gran spilled the beans about the baby to her sisters—and Shine had been adamant. And in an all-fired hurry.

"Time for a wedding," Shine said. And Hiram but a few weeks in the ground! He was probably rolling over in his freshly dug grave. Elsie squirmed. At least her daddy wouldn't have to know about her indiscretion. But he would have forgiven her anything, especially once he met his first grandchild. She knew it.

Her sisters had saddled up the horses, Shine riding with Lidy snug up behind her, Elsie perched in the saddle behind Rebecca. She was grateful for that, at least. Shine would've given her an earful the entire trip to town had she been on the other horse. And while she didn't feel anything close to Rebecca's approval, at least her oldest sister had kept quiet.

It was humiliating, really. The four of them, showing up at the Hansons' two-story colonial on the edge of downtown Kinney. Shine dismounting and knocking at the door around suppertime on a Tuesday night.

"I'd like a word with your son," Shine had said, all business, when Mrs. Hanson opened the door, then quickly shut it upon seeing that half her company had guns.

"Charles, come quick!"

Mr. Hanson had stepped out the door, removing a linen napkin where it had been tucked in the collar of his shirt.

"Sorry, ladies," he said, sizing up the crowd. "I'm afraid you caught us in the middle of dinner. What can we do for you?"

Mrs. Hanson, a plump, neatly dressed woman with her hair stretched against her skull in a severe bun, ventured out to peer from behind her husband's back at this strange assortment of Strong women.

"We're looking for Jedediah," Shine said, hands on her hips. "He's getting married tonight."

Mrs. Hanson gasped, putting a hand to her chest as if she'd been shot. Which she hadn't. *Yet.* "But surely we would know of it, were this the truth!"

Elsie watched in a dream state as Jed was summoned—her love!—and stumbled out the door to meet the angry mob of women with an air of bemusement. Like charming, attractive people do when they get caught out, able to erase a multitude of sins with a smile. And there *were* a multitude, she knew.

God help her, but she did love this beautiful man.

Elsie was probably the one person on or around that front porch who didn't want to skin him alive. She and the baby. She put a hand on her protruding belly as if to garner some support. An ally.

There had been the awkward explanation for the impromptu visit. Then the denials—first from the shell-shocked parents and then finally from Jed. But Elsie knew his track record, and his parents, in their heart of hearts, knew it, too. And Elsie was not the worst option for a wife for their wayward son. Not by a long-shot.

"Young man, if there is truth to this, then you must do the right thing," Charles Hanson said. Mrs. Hanson's chin jutted out in firm agreement. But her eyes were wet.

"Oh, it's the truth," Shine said. "We'll be seeing the results before wintertime. So if you want to see your only son get married, you best grab your hat and bonnet."

They had rousted the poor pastor from the rectory, his eyes behind the half-glasses growing large and round at the weaponry displayed by the Strong sisters. Far be it from him to stand in the way of love! Even if it meant setting aside his solitary supper for a few extra moments.

"You may kiss the bride?" Brother Aiken hesitated, as though this last piece might not be appropriate under the circumstances—kissing and more having clearly already taken place.

"Can't hurt anything," Shine said drily, as though reading his mind.

Elsie turned toward Jed. Up until this point, she had been afraid to look him in the eyes. Not because she didn't want this—she did, more than anything!—but because she was worried what she might find there. Would she see a man scanning for a door, a window, a hole in the floor? Wanting a way, *any* way, out? Or the slump-shouldered, hangdog expression of a man awaiting execution, the end of his life? Resigned to his fate.

She needn't have worried. Jed was a master of putting a good face on a situation. His eyes, though bloodshot, met hers straight on, as he reached for her hand and raised it to his lips. It felt like she'd been branded, and she fully expected to see the marks from his kiss on the back of her hand. But before she could look, he leaned in and met her mouth with his. Gently but firmly.

And smelling of drink.

Shine had more pressing concerns than Jed's show of decorum. As Mr. Hanson pulled up in their new Ford coupe to collect the newlyweds, she turned to Jed: "We'll be needing you and that car tomorrow. Show up around noon. We've got business to attend to.

"Enjoy your wedding night."

Elsie flushed pink. Despite everything, she *was* looking forward to it. Jed opened the back door of the Hansons' shiny Model A and motioned for her to get inside.

It wasn't the start to marriage that she had wanted. But her sisters and Gran would see. The Hansons, too. Jedediah had it in him to do the right thing, to be a good and godly man and live an upright life. Especially with her as his wife.

Elsie closed the space between her and her new husband in the back seat; hesitated before leaning her head on his shoulder, exhausted by all the hoopla and high emotions.

But happy.

Rebecca

"Becks, snap to! We got things to do before Jed gets here with that car," Shine said, giving her sister a shake.

The two had already been up the mountain to fetch the salvageable equipment Rebecca had hidden after the still got shot up. The good news: they would only have to replace one kettle, the big glass jug and some hoses. They would need a favor from a tight-lipped smithy to repair the other bullet-riddled copper kettle. The worm box was pocked with dents, but usable. They loaded everything they could on Cowboy's reluctant back, tied up the large wooden mash barrel in a tarp and attached it to the back of the saddle so he could drag it downhill.

Now they were calculating the amount of corn they had left in the crib, counting the bagged barley in the barn and—hidden beneath those—the enormous sacks of sugar. And the yeast, stored in airtight jars in a dark corner.

But Rebecca found herself going through every step at half speed, dragging her feet. She knew it was worry, a relentless sharp-toothed varmint gnawing away at her insides since the wedding yesterday.

Shine didn't like delays, whether caused by physical obstacles or attributable to laziness or lack of cooperation. But Rebecca was about the furthest thing from lazy there was.

"What's got your knickers in a twist, sis?" Shine finally said as they headed to the root cellar. "You've been moving as slow as molasses all morning. It's like you don't want to do this."

"Of course I want to do this," Rebecca said, hurt. "You think I don't want to keep our family warm and fed?"

"Then what is it?"

Rebecca sighed. "It's just . . . I don't see why you need to let the fox in the henhouse."

She propped open the cellar door and followed Shine into the cool damp. It took her eyes a minute to adjust to the dim light. They wanted to take stock of what they had in the way of hooch that was ready to be distilled into dollar bills. The Strongs were fast running out of cash after buying the sturdy pine coffin for Hiram and still in want of a replacement for the giant kettle that sported more holes than a slice of Swiss cheese. Not to mention their regular living expenses.

"Jed shouldn't be a part of the Strong family business."

"Too late. And honestly, Jed's too dumb to be a fox. More of a sheep." Shine shook her head. "Anyways, we need a car and a driver; Elsie needs a husband. It's pretty simple."

"You don't need a husband to have a baby," Rebecca said. "And I wouldn't trust Jed as far as I could throw him."

"Agreed," Shine said. "But don't forget that our sister is over the moon for that man. Might as well take advantage of a sad situation. Now we've got wheels for tracking down those prohis—and running our shine. Plus a connection to the Hanson coffers. No piddling deal."

Over the moon for that *man?*

Rebecca felt her throat constrict.

Tell her.

She'd had her chance. Her sweet Elsie in front of the church with Jed, drunk and barely managing to stand up. Brother Aiken asked if there was any reason they shouldn't get hitched.

The problem was, she hadn't really *had* a good reason before the wedding got rolling. No, she didn't want her sister marrying that worthless pile of horse manure. Elsie deserved better, even if her middle sister couldn't see that, blinded as she was by love, lust and the chance to get off the farm. Elsie had always loved playing house, torturing Rebecca with her imaginary babies, fine china and fancy furniture—no matter if they were really rag dolls made from clothespins, tea sets fashioned from acorn caps and heart-shaped redbud leaves with a stump slice serving as the dining room table. Rebecca was both husband and father by choice as much as assignment. Until Shine came along—what a relief!—and Elsie had a real baby to play with.

But the reason appeared to her as plain as day during the ceremony, as she stood hugging her Winchester to her chest. Shine had insisted on the guns and—while Rebecca thought the display overdone—she had to admit: they made an impression.

She had been admiring the couple up front. No one had prepared for this wedding and yet, Elsie glowed in a peach empire-waist dress that mostly concealed the swell of her belly and brought out the color in her cheeks. And Jed, while not sober, had cleaned up for dinner, a pressed shirt tucked into his work pants atop a pair of yellow leather work boots. The thick chunky soles gave Jed—who wasn't a tall man—an extra inch or so. *Vanity.*

But wait: those boots. Not from Sears & Roebuck or Red Wing—like most of the farmers and laborers around here wore. Special order. Probably expensive.

And those soles. Rebecca's heart dropped right to the floor.

But no. She couldn't prove anything. At least not without seeing the bottoms.

When she had gone back up to what remained of the still after the shooting, Rebecca had taken another look around, unrushed this time. She counted the spent casings—twelve, including the one she had pocketed earlier—by the red oak. There were the partial footprints that she found by that same tree and, downhill, similar tracks left by the person Hiram had shot. Different sizes, those prints. But all pointy with worn soles.

But that one lone footprint she had found early that morning near the still, the older one set deep in the dirt? What if Jed had been the one to lead the killers there? Or scouted it out ahead of time? He as good as killed her daddy, by her reckoning. And now he was standing there, saying "I do"?

That was some ice-cold water running through those veins.

But thoughtful, thorough Rebecca—slow to judge, slower to act. She couldn't pull the trigger. She saw her sister's face, looking up at her soon-to-be husband with a serene, shy smile.

And Rebecca held her peace.

She hadn't said anything then, and she sure as hell shouldn't say anything now—not without a hundred percent certainty. Not to Shine, who might take the idea of holding one's "piece" in a different direction—pointing a pistol at the maligned party. And God help the person on the business end of that barrel!

Shine had always been short on wait-and-see. Like now.

"Well?" Shine's irritation was evident.

"Why are you in such an all-fired hurry to get on the road? We lost that last batch of shine in the shooting and we don't have anything in production. The mash barrel is empty. Daddy's barely cold. Elsie just jumped the broom and her husband hasn't been educated on his job around this joint yet. *If* he's even up to the task."

"But . . . we can't let those prohi bastards get away." Shine's cheeks flamed.

"A couple of clowns like that?" Rebecca scoffed. "They're gonna leave a trail a mile wide. For one thing, Daddy slowed one of them down with a bullet. And believe me, the fat one is as good as throwing out breadcrumbs right now. He couldn't keep quiet to save his worthless life. You think folks aren't going to want to tell us what and who they've seen, busting up stills and causing people like us a world of hurt and trouble?

"We need to get organized," Rebecca went on. "Get some mash in the barrels, another batch or two of shine in the bottles. It's already August—that leaves us about two months to make hay while the sun shines. Or make shine while the sun . . . Oh, anyway.

"Who knows if we will get two solid weeks of good weather in November for fermenting? If we leave ourselves with nothing, we'll come back to nothing. And what if it takes a while to find those feds?"

She could tell Shine didn't want to admit that she'd made a good argument.

"You know patience isn't my strong suit." Shine thought for a moment. "But all right. We'll give the newlyweds a honeymoon while we make a batch—or three—of moonshine."

"Good. Now, if you'll excuse me, I talked more than I have in a month," Rebecca sighed. "I'll be using my mouth for chewing for the foreseeable future."

"If you're talking, I'm listening, Becks," Shine said, opening the cabin door to the rich, gamy smell of Gran's possum stew. "Those occasions are scarce as hen's teeth."

Jed and Elsie showed up after lunch. Late. They left the Model A parked on the side of the road and made their way up the rocky trail to the cabin. Rebecca and Shine waited on the porch, Shine tapping her foot impatiently—she didn't like a hitch in her giddyup—while Rebecca sharpened her hunting knife.

Elsie's face was pink with exertion—or maybe simple happiness, returning to her home a married woman at last. Jed held her by the elbow solicitously. He was playing the part of devoted husband pretty damn convincingly, even without a gun trained on him.

But they were less than twenty-four hours in.

"Gran, the happy couple's finally here," Shine called. She stood to give Elsie her seat on an overturned oaken bucket. Lidy emerged from doing the last dishes, wiping her hands on her apron. Rebecca dipped her middle sister a cup of cool water from the pail she had fetched from the creek.

"Thank you kindly, sisters," Elsie said, smiling. "This will always be the best water in the world."

"How's married life treating you?" Lidy cackled as Elsie

blushed. Jed, for his part, looked like the cat who had just eaten the canary.

But Shine was done with pleasantries. "I'm the one who called this meeting and I say we get down to business."

She outlined the plan: make more mash, distill more shine, load up the car in mid-October. Track down the no-good prohis who killed Hiram and make some much-needed cash along the way. Lidy, Rebecca and Elsie—as much as she was able—would hold down the fort till they got back. Hopefully a few weeks at the outside.

"But if it takes longer, you'll need to make the last batch or two of shine for the year, Gran," Shine said. "Think you can handle it?"

Lidy snorted. "I taught your daddy everything he knew about making hooch. But I'll need help hefting the mash barrels."

"I'll do it, Gran," Rebecca said.

"And I've been tending fires for laundry for years," added Elsie. "I'll enjoy stirring a big pot of mash instead of a cauldron of dirty clothes."

Jed needed no convincing to do the driving. His aversion to manual labor and the monotony of regular workdays made the prospect of moving moonshine and tracking down feds sound like a dream come true. What he'd been angling for, as a matter of fact.

"You'll have to keep your nose clean," Shine said, arms crossed. Lidy and Rebecca flanked her on either side, staring down at this new member of the Strong family with skepticism. "And your flappin' trap shut."

"I'm your man," he declared, puffing out his chest before grabbing Elsie up off her bucket and swinging her down from the porch to stand beside him. He kissed her hard on the mouth until Elsie pulled away, self-conscious at the display—even if she was a proper married woman. She likely didn't want to put her husband on the wrong side of the law after working so hard to get him on the straight and narrow.

"I already made this girl an honest woman. Even if it took some help. And I'm grateful to be part of the family," Jed said, dripping sincerity. "I won't let you down."

Rebecca had to hand it to Shine: she didn't roll her eyes. At least, not on the outside. But Lord, how she and everyone on that porch—especially the pregnant woman at Jed's side—hoped what he said was true.

Shine

Pine.

The sharp, rich smell of it permeated the dark hills, cutting the humid night air with its bite. A slender curve of moon, thin as a slice of one of Lidy's sweet onions, hung high above these Arkansas mountains as if giving a knowing wink to the car of bootleggers with a triple batch of their special brand of white lightning.

Shine rolled the window of the Ford coupe all the way down to flush out the cigarette smoke, and breathed in the scent of these trees so different from the hardwood-covered hills of her own beloved part of the Ozarks. She tried to calm herself, to ignore as best she could Jed's herky-jerky, distracted driving style which was helped not one speck by the rough road, barely wide enough for one car. The headlight beams bounced unevenly on the terrain in front of them, sometimes shorting out for a few seconds with a particularly hard jounce from a rut or hole in the road. *Ouch.* Like that one. Shine felt the reverberations up every single bone in her spine.

"Damn it!" Jed said, gripping the steering wheel tighter with one hand and taking such a long drag on his cigarette with the other that Shine could see the orange glow in the semidarkness of the cab for what seemed like forever.

Thank God I don't puke easy.

It was after midnight, and they had been on the road for hours, trying to make it to Mountain Home and a place to sleep. They had put Kinney and the farm in the rearview mirror, leaving the others to manage as best they could. Shine was arrogant enough to believe they would miss her, being the brains of the operation as well as the one to light the requisite fire under people's backsides. But she doubted anyone save Elsie would miss Jed.

The rumble of the Ford's motor was the only sound. Except for the gentle—or not so gentle, depending on how Jed took a particularly tight turn—sloshing of the moonshine against Shine's ribs beneath her hot, itchy clothing.

Indian summer in October. An unexpected burst of hot southern air from the jet stream on the heels of the first killing frost. Shine found it hard to believe that a week ago, what remained of the garden—bent vines heavy with a few leftover green tomatoes, browned and shrunken basil and sage leaves, a single head of bitter leaf lettuce—was crisp and laced in white. Walnut trees unceremoniously dropped what was left of their yellowed leaflets and the corn stubble in the field was browned and glazed.

Yet here she was, sweating like a pig in a thick wool coat held closed by Lidy's old brooch. She gave in and unclasped the piece of gold-plated jewelry for relief. It was hotter than hell, wearing the scratchy coat in this summer-like heat. But necessary. Because underneath, she was all tricked out in a vest created from rough muslin, with a large pocket on the back and two slender ones on the front flaps. The vest was held closed with two pairs of ties on the front, pulled tight to counter the weight of the moonshine bottles—a large flat one in the back and two wine-sized bottles in the front—that Shine wore over her dress.

But as uncomfortable as Shine was, she didn't have a choice. They were transporting hooch across state lines with flagrant disregard for the Eighteenth Amendment and the Volstead Act. Not that there were any boundaries for either; the "manufacture, sale, or transportation of intoxicating liquors" was prohibited nationwide, not just in Missouri and Arkansas.

Shine had done her homework, though, gathering that the enforcement part of Prohibition depended on the efforts of a few officers stretched as thin as sloughed-off snakeskin. And these feds—mostly men, like the pair that had shown up in Kinney—were loath to search a woman. In fact, it was illegal to do so in many states. Most prohis wouldn't bother to stop a car with women passengers. And even if a woman was arrested for bootlegging, juries were notoriously easy on females. They didn't have the stomach to put their grandmas, mothers, wives, sisters and daughters behind bars. It simply wasn't worth the feds' efforts to curtail them—even if they were accessories to major crime.

That's what Shine was banking on anyway.

"I may look like an accessory, but don't ever forget I'm the one in charge," Shine had told Jed as they loaded the Ford late in the afternoon, planning to do most of their traveling after dark.

"Fine," Jed had said. "As long as you don't forget I'm the one driving."

And talk about accessories. Taking Shine's research to heart, Lidy and Rebecca had designed the special vest and vessels for hiding contraband on the female form while Elsie did the sewing. Shine figured she had about a gallon and a half hidden on her person. And Jed had surprised them all by retrofitting the space beneath the car's back seat to hold a good ten gallons of moonshine and creating a false floorboard to hide another five.

They were a hundred or so miles into the journey—the farthest she had ever been from Kinney Creek and her family. But so far, so good.

Except that Jed was driving her crazy.

"Could you stop smoking for half a tick?" Shine's tolerance for Jed was already at zero. But the erratic driving of their precious cargo—both worn and stored in the secret spaces of this jalopy—coupled with the constant stream of smoke and profanity had her on the verge of homicide. If her sister didn't love him, she would have given him the heave-ho already.

Elsie must see something redeeming in him. But for the life of her, Shine could not discern what it might be. She supposed he would be considered good-looking. But Shine was of the opinion that what was on the inside greatly colored how one viewed the outer packaging. Another way she and her middle sister differed: Elsie loved a pretty package more than anyone she knew.

"Gotta stay awake," Jed huffed, blowing an especially large cloud in Shine's direction. "Watching for potholes in the headlights and John Law in the rearview," he said. "Think you could do better?"

"I do, actually." Shine shifted in her seat, trying to get comfortable. The flasks at her side and back made a sloshing sound, but were unyielding.

Outside her window, the trees went by, shadowy pine boughs barely outlined in silver by that sliver of moon. They made her feel insignificant. Alone. Sometimes it was hard, pretending to know the right thing to do. All she had to go on was her gut. And her daddy's voice in her ear: *"Shine Strong, there's nothing you can't do if you put your mind and your back to it."*

She wished he was beside her. Instead, she was riding shotgun with a man she didn't like or respect—and had to depend on for her life, as they took these steep, switch-backing Ozark roads in pursuit of some backwoods justice. And a few hundred bucks. She hoped it was worth it.

Damn it, Daddy.

She sure could use a little of his magic right about now.

They ended up spending the night in the car. If you could call it "night," those hours between two and six in the morning. It was dark, that much she knew. Not Shine's first choice, but they were low on gas and well past business hours—and she didn't want to chance running out on a lonely stretch of highway in the hills of Arkansas. They pulled off on a side road, not much more than a gravel path wide enough for the Ford to pass through unscathed by the brush and trees on either side. When they saw the hulking shadow of a falling-down barn, Jed pulled off onto a driveway of sorts leading up to it and killed the engine.

"Time for beddy-bye," he said. He opened the door and Shine could hear the creak of the trunk opening. Then he slid back into the front seat and slammed the door closed.

"Here. Take this." Jed offered her a blanket, but she already had on enough layers with the dress, vest, coat and underthings. She balled it up and used it as a pillow against the doorframe.

"Thanks."

"Sure thing, sis," he said.

"Let's not get chummy. I don't relish being related to you," she said. "We'll leave it at Shine."

Jed laughed his slow, deep chuckle which always sounded as though he felt he was the smartest one in the room and simply humoring everyone else by laughing at their inferior jokes or commentary.

"Don't worry," he said. "I'll keep on my side."

"If you've got a brain—and so far, I'm not a hundred percent convinced on that—you'll stay on my good side."

Jed grunted in reply.

Shine closed her eyes, but she didn't sleep. Not that she could, as Jed's rhythmic breathing eventually became a snore.

She couldn't stop her mind from scrabbling around, unsettled, latching onto one worry and turning it this way and that. When she finally forced herself to set it aside, another one was waiting in the wings: Would they find an open gas station soon? Should they lie low during the daylight hours or take their chances? How was she going to sell this hooch? How in the hell was she going to track down the two prohis she suspected in Hiram's killing? The farther she had gotten away from Kinney, the bigger the world seemed. And the likelihood of finding Flanagan and McConnell seemed slim and growing slimmer with each passing day.

The fingernail moon crept toward the horizon, disappearing around dawn.

* * *

Click, click.

Shine's eyes flew open. She had managed to fall asleep, after all. And now she was waking up to a scantly bearded young man with a shotgun aimed at the front windshield of the Model A.

"Don't shoot, for Christ's sake!" Shine held her hands up, as Jed came awake with a start beside her. "We aren't meaning any harm."

"You're trespassing on our land," the young ruffian said. "That's harm enough for shooting."

"Please, sir," Shine said, although it hurt her to kowtow to a hill-billy upstart whose patchy facial hair meant he was likely younger than she was. "I think we can help each other out."

Scruffy sneered. "Why would I want to help you all out?"

"Well, I heard the best shine in the country comes out of these hills," she continued, still holding her hands up. *Lord, it hurt to say those words!* Shine believed in her heart that there was nothing better than the Strong shine. But she could scarce afford to get shot here in the middle of nowhere in a pissing contest.

"Look," Shine said. "Can we get out and visit? We're trying to find the goddamn prohis who shot my daddy. That's the long and short of it. We've got no beef with anyone but them."

"No, stay where you are." Scruffy kept the shotgun trained on them, but his grip relaxed. "So you must be bootleggers, if you got a problem with a prohi."

"We might be," Shine said. "You seen any feds passing through? The two we're after said they were heading to Arkansas after they busted up a bunch of stills in our neck of the woods."

The young man ducked his head at Jed. "Get out of the car with your hands up and open that trunk. I'm betting you've got something might loosen my tongue."

Jed did as he was bidden, even though he knew as well as Shine that they would not be so stupid as to have any bottles of anything in plain sight.

"We're purt near dry as a bone," Jed told the youngster. "Dropped our precious cargo yesterday. But I reckon I've got my own personal flask of our giggle juice I could part with."

"I don't believe it," Scruffy said, his face screwed up in a frown. "Show me."

The young man hesitated, decided Shine was no threat, and followed Jed around to the back of the car.

She could hear the trunk being opened and rummaged through. She took the opportunity while the trunk blocked the back window to feel beneath her seat for her daddy's pistol. What felt like an ocean wave hit her square in the chest—and she was afraid it sounded like one, too. *Damn, I'm sloshing!* She righted herself in a panic while her displaced moonshine burbled back to the bottom of the bottles. *Glug, glug.*

Shine held her breath.

The trunk slammed shut. "Let's see the back seat."

Shine turned to see Jed accompanying Scruffy to the open driver's-side door, where he poked the shotgun barrel around in the back seat, moving Jed's hastily discarded blanket and hat. How foolish not to carry the pistol on her person; the same carelessness had cost her father his life! Not that she would shoot this annoying upstart. That wasn't going to help either of them get what they wanted.

"See?" Jed shrugged, holding his empty hands outstretched in the manner of someone who was sorry he couldn't help you. Pretty damn beguiling. He started to reach for his pocket.

"Whoa now," said Scruffy. "Keep them hands where I can see 'em."

"All right now, son, don't go off the deep end," Jed said, smiling. "Why don't you reach in my pocket and take my last smidge of hooch for yourself. Quality like that, a little goes a long way."

"Don't mind if I do," the youngster said, taking the flask from Jed's front pocket. He shook it and, satisfied it was full, leaned his rifle against his patched pantleg and unscrewed the cap. Tilting his head back, he took a slug so large it went down his gullet in a lump, like a black snake swallowing a hen's egg.

Wiping his mouth on the back of his hand, the young man whooped. "Holy *shit!* You ain't kidding! 'Preciate it."

"Thank you for your hospitality," Jed said, sweeping his arm at the overgrown drive, the ramshackle barn. "And if you could point us in the right direction, we'd be much obliged."

"If I was you, I'd head toward Hot Springs by way of Possum Kingdom," the young man said. "There ain't no laws there to speak of in that city. But the hills outside of it are filled to bustin' with stills and shine. You cain't walk to the outhouse without kicking one over. If I was a fed—and praise Jesus I ain't that kinda scum—I'd want to go where the pickings were easy."

"Amen," said Jed.

"*Possum Kingdom?* Sounds like a good place to play dead. Or plain old *be* dead," Shine said.

"God's truth? Someone else might fill their bellies full of lead before you do. It's stupid trying to part a mountain man from his moonshine," Scruffy said. "You can bet your bottom dollar he'll always be loaded, in more ways than one."

"I'd want to shake that man's hand," Jed said.

"Or *woman's*," Shine said. She was losing her patience.

The youngster laughed and shouldered his rifle again. "I wish you luck," he said. "And safe travels."

After Jed had pulled the coupe back on the gravel road and out of shooting range, he finally looked over at his seatmate. "You're welcome," he said, with a self-satisfied grin.

"For what? Nearly getting us killed? Or having our load lightened by a hillbilly barely sprouting chin hairs?"

"I had my Colt in the back of my waistband if we'd really needed it," Jed said. "Seemed better to let him think he was in charge. Got us a lead on the feds. And, near as I can tell, nobody got hurt. Except I'm down a couple ounces of shine."

Shine felt caught out. She didn't like making mistakes. *Even Jed was smart enough to have his gun ready.*

"Drive," Shine said in a huff. "We need gas. And I'll need the ladies' room or a nice wide tree. It's a hell of a long way from here to Hot Springs."

John

John took the doctor's advice to heart. Not for himself; there was no way he was going to step away from work. But for McConnell. The man obviously needed help.

So many things about the last few months—and years!—had fallen into place with the doctor's diagnosis. Not just the eyesight. But the paranoia. The increasingly erratic behavior. The rage. What Flanagan had accepted as McConnell becoming a bigger asshole with age actually had a cause.

The first thing he did when they got to Hot Springs was find McConnell a place to stay. The Happy Hollow Lodge offered a room for weekly rental and it was in walking distance of the hospital and the thermal springs.

The second thing was tougher: he quit the job. For both of them.

John put in a call to one of the higher-ups in Little Rock.

"You need to see for yourself what I've been working with here," Flanagan said.

The man had been willing to come to Hot Springs, and the meeting in the lounge in the bottom of the Marquette Hotel hadn't taken long. The partners shook hands with their superior, and then McConnell completely missed the chair he tried to take a seat in. The older woman at the check-in desk looked alarmed.

"Holy Christ! What kind of joke is that, moving a man's chair?" McConnell blustered, scrambling to his feet. His shirt untucked in the process, revealing the top crack of his wide, flat ass above his pants. Flanagan, embarrassed for him and by him, offered a hand up, which McConnell ignored out of pride. John was glad the hotel lobby was empty at this hour, save the front desk clerk. He noticed she had turned her back—on purpose, no doubt. No one should have to see this.

"What's the purpose of all of this anyhow?"

The senior agent looked long and hard at McConnell. "I know you've been a good soldier for Prohibition enforcement. But . . . we saw the trouble in New York. Kinda hoped it was something you could get out of your system with a change of scenery. And now with your eyes going . . .

"It's time you stepped down," he said holding out his hands as if there were nothing to be done. "We'll call it retirement. You'll get the pay coming to you. And your pension. But you need to take care of yourself now. And you're in the right place for that."

McConnell begged. Wheedled. Yelled and worked himself up into a lather. Eventually, he cried. But his supervisor was unmoved.

"Get this man settled somewhere and I'll take the keys to the jalopy," the agent said to John. Flanagan looked at the soggy, sad man seated at the table, holding his hands over his eyes to hide his tears. He remembered how he had been elated to get the experienced, outgoing prohi as a partner when he first came to New York. Before he knew what a buffoon McConnell was; what a punchline he would become. But they had put in a lot of thankless hours together—and a bunch of criminals behind bars. He owed him something.

"I'll see to him. But I need a new assignment," Flanagan said. He wanted out of Prohibition enforcement and into the FBI. "Prohi work is like sticking your finger into a hole in a leaky dam. New problems springing up everywhere and you have but ten fingers. I think I can do more good with the Bureau."

"I'll recommend a transfer through our Oklahoma City headquarters," said the agent, putting on his hat. "I'll be in touch."

The first few weeks had gone well. Flanagan set McConnell up with a doctor at the Army and Navy Hospital in Hot Springs, who concurred with the diagnosis he'd received. The prescribed treatment was a course of daily thermal baths and injections of salvarsan, made from an arsenic compound.

"Arsenic?" Flanagan was no doctor, but as a lawman, he knew his poisons.

"It's actually more dangerous for me to handle it than for him to get a shot of it. A minor dose won't hurt him, but it can kill the syphilis. Of course, he may be too far gone for that," the doctor said. "But let's try it and see."

Flanagan came to Hot Springs every few weeks to check on his former partner. McConnell had been dejected at first, consigned to retirement and a life that centered around bathing and shots. There was too much downtime, and McConnell was down. But after a month or so, John noted that McConnell had returned to his animated, over-the-top persona. He was the de facto mayor of Happy Hollow, introducing John to all the residents as his "sidekick." The regular turnover of guests at the motel gave McConnell a brand-new audience on the daily for those tall tales of his time as a prohi, and nothing warmed his heart more than the chance to hold forth about his accomplishments, real and imagined.

"You shoulda seen us take down the priests," McConnell would say, putting his arm around John, who would fidget uncomfortably as the stories unfolded for the captive crowd in the common area. "I mean, for the love of fuckin' Jesus H. Christ! Selling hooch in the name of the Father, Son and Holy *Spirits*!"

But then he would recount an exploit that John had never been a part of. That McConnell could not possibly have been a part of. Flanagan shrugged it off; part of the progression of the disease, maybe. There were other troubling signs as the weeks went by: slurred speech, forgetfulness. And he was having a harder time coordinating the simple act of putting one foot in front of another, like a toddler trying to master walking.

"Damn shoes." McConnell would foist the blame on whatever was convenient. "Damn sidewalk. Damn rug."

John saw to it that McConnell got a cane. Which he first groused about and then grudgingly employed. It wasn't easy, traveling from his new assigned territory of Fort Smith to Hot Springs every ten days to two weeks, but what was he supposed to do? He wasn't married to anything but the job; he had no close friends at work. Flanagan stayed for a day or two—careful to hide his FBI identity in that lawless city—and made sure McConnell was getting his treatments and shots, that his pension money was arriving on time and paid to Happy Hollow. And then he drove back in the beater of a used car he had purchased with his first paycheck.

Then came the day that he pulled up to Happy Hollow Lodge and found McConnell's room let out to someone else.

"He's been gone a week, maybe longer," the wizened old man at the front desk reported. "Said he was healed up and ready to get back on the job."

"But he was no such thing and he doesn't have a job to go back to," Flanagan said, exasperated and frightened, all at once.

"Healthy or not, truth be told, we was all gettin' sick of him," the old man said. "Yammerin' all day long. Knew everything about everything. Not sorry to see him go, no sir."

"Any idea where he went?" McConnell didn't have a car. How far away could he get? And he wouldn't have medicine. Or a doctor keeping tabs on him. His pension checks wouldn't find him, either.

"Nope. And I hope I never lay eyes on that bigmouth again. No offense if he was your friend or relative."

John shook his head. "Not related. By blood anyway."

Except for Hiram Strong's.

He walked to his car. What should he do? It was already close to dark. He guessed he would head to his lodging place for dinner and a good night's sleep. He'd look for McConnell in the morning.

Shine

Hot Springs, Arkansas, was nestled snugly in a valley of the Ouachita Mountains. For thousands of years, the area containing this "Valley of the Vapors" was home to many Native American tribes: Quapaw, Choctaw and the peaceful Caddo, who believed their people had originated from the steam of the springs themselves. While various tribes fought over valuable mineral deposits located a few miles north of the springs—to make their tools and weapons—the hot springs themselves were considered "neutral territory," a place where all could go to partake of the healing, spiritual experience of the thermal waters that bubbled up in such astonishing quantities.

A Spanish conquistador of Hernando de Soto's found these people and their sacred pools back in the 1500s. Thomas Jefferson was so intrigued by what he heard of the area that he commissioned two explorers, William Dunbar and Dr. George Hunter, to find out more. The land became part of Jefferson's "Louisiana Purchase," and as the explorers' reports of this enchanting place and its thermal waters spread, others came to settle there in what came to be called in turn "Thermopolis," "Warm Springs" and, finally, "Hot Springs."

The waters became so popular by the mid-1800s that entrepreneurs set up private bathhouse ventures along Hot Springs Creek and what would become Central Avenue. But the Supreme Court stepped in, declaring all their claims invalid, based on an 1835 bill signed by Andrew Jackson which set aside the land for recreational use—which essentially made Hot Springs the country's first national park.

Rows of majestic bathhouses lined Central Avenue, each in a different style or an eclectic mix of several—from the neoclassical Hale to the Spanish Colonial Revival Quapaw and everything in between. Thousands of bathers took baths in these grand buildings, which also housed beauty shops, card parlors with pianos, and exercise rooms. All featured inviting front porches where a person awaiting an appointment might sit on a rocking chair, lemonade in hand, and watch the world go by.

Now Shine Strong stood smack dab in the middle of it all. Jed had dropped her at the corner of Central Avenue and Fountain Street, in front of the enormous Arlington Hotel, for no other reason than it seemed like the hub of Hot Springs. She had never seen such a grand building before, more than ten stories, towering up into a sky the color of a robin's egg, so high it made her stomach feel as wobbly as one of Gran's egg custards.

There were people bustling everywhere; the streets were busy, too. Uniformed porters unloading and loading luggage out of a long line of late-model Fords as hotel guests came and went in this town that was host to healing waters. A newspaper and cigar stand was surrounded by businessmen taking a break to get the daily headlines, some gossip and a smoke. Farther down the sidewalk, the hotel hosted its own auto repair and gas station, featuring full service at the pump provided by well-scrubbed young men.

Shine gathered herself, straightening her shoulders and tossing back her orange-red locks, which were topped with a wide-brimmed, beribboned hat (Elsie had insisted she look like a lady, despite her unladylike mission) and marched right into the busy street. And if there had been any doubt, she immediately discovered that she was not in Kinney anymore—berated by honking and the skid of tires on gravel as cars swerved to avoid her. Shine ignored the yelling and the raised fists of irate drivers, keeping her eyes on her destination: the Southern Club.

A Romanesque building of white stone with a scallop of a half dozen arched windows on the second floor and a jaunty striped awning along the lower story, the Southern Club was *the* place for illicit drinking—and gambling and whoring, for that matter—in Hot Springs. And since it was the place to be, Shine knew it was where she wanted to market the Strong shine. She was just ignorant and brazen enough to decide that she would be doing the establishment a favor by introducing them to the Strongs' fine spirits.

After surviving the street crossing, she smoothed her dress, fixed her hat at the right angle and pulled open the door of the club. Even though it wasn't quite noon, the interior had a dusky feel, with low lighting and dark velvet drapes and chairs. The most light came from the reflection of a gilt-edged mirror on the wall stretching above the length of the immense black marble bar, polished to dazzling brilliance. Shine's nose was immediately hit with a combination of whiskey, heavy perfume and the greasy paper smell of cash money.

"May I help you?"

The voice belonged to a lanky, well-dressed man at the bar, enjoying what looked like a straight-up scotch or whiskey before lunchtime. Beside him, reading a newspaper, was a smaller, daintier man with a thin mustache and blond hair swept up in a slick pompadour. The points of a triple-folded lavender pocket square peeked from the jacket of his immaculate three-piece suit. A third darker, thickset man was behind the lacquered bar; he wasn't wearing a suit. But his white button-down shirt was neatly pressed, sleeves folded several turns onto his forearms, and he leaned on the bar as if the men had been deep in conversation.

"I'd like to speak to whoever is in charge of this joint," Shine said, putting on her most professional tone. She intended to be taken seriously. "Sir," she added. Serious didn't mean rude.

At this, the long-limbed man tipped back the last of his drink and set it down squarely on the bar.

"Do you mean *this*?" He motioned toward the bar. "Or do you mean . . . all of *this*?" Here he swept his arms around the room and toward the door from which Shine had entered. The men—except the one perusing the paper—laughed, seeming to find this hilarious. Or were they making sport of her, the country bumpkin in the big city, unsure of what was what and who was who? Shine didn't like that idea at all. It made her want to double down.

"I mean, who's the *boss*? I don't have time for guessing games, Mr. . . . ?"

"This here's the mayor," said the man behind the bar. "Mayor Mackey. He's pretty well in charge of everything that goes on in Hot Springs. And that's . . . Randy."

"*Randall.*" The blond man looked up briefly, arching a bored eyebrow in Shine's direction.

The bartender ignored him. "But if you need something from the Southern Club, I guess I'm your man. Merle."

Merle gave Shine the once-over, slowly, in a way that she did not like. As though he could see through her clothes, and not only to the moonshine, but down to her very skin. *You are* not *my man.* But business was business; she ignored the leering.

"Jace Strong," Shine said, sticking out her hand to shake the men's before they were offered. None knew quite what to make of her, this confident, fiery-haired young woman wearing a simple country dress down to her ankles and a heavy woolen coat in the middle of a sunny October day. But shake her hand they did—although it was not lost on Shine that Randall reached for his perfect pocket square to wipe his own hand off afterward.

"Most people call me Shine."

"Well, Shine, it's a pleasure to meet you. What can I do you for?" The mayor fished a tin of tobacco from his suit pocket and began rolling a cigarette on the bar with slow, precise movements. As if she didn't merit his full attention. Randall had already returned to his newspaper, pressing the center crease down with a slow swipe of his index finger.

"I don't know if I can talk freely." Shine hesitated. Would the mayor of Hot Springs have her arrested on the spot for bootlegging? She had planned on taking her product direct to the people who would sell it—bar owners, bartenders, maybe even pharmacists—but figured it would be on the sly. Shine hadn't expected to meet or deal with the town's highest official. Maybe an underling or some cops on the take. What does one offer the mayor for extending some grace and goodwill her way?

"You may," the mayor said, lighting his cigarette and taking a drag. He exhaled a cloud of blue-gray smoke in Shine's direction.

Shine frowned. This man was an ass—but she didn't come all this way to get shut down by some muckety-muck. "I come a couple hundred miles, in and around a bunch of creeks and hollers, and managed to avoid the long arm of the law to bring you the hands-down, damn-finest, bet-your-bottom-dollar, make-you-holler liquid refreshment known to mankind.

"It's our Strong family shine, and as we like to say, the 'Strong-er' the better. The *best.* If I do say so myself. And I believe I just did." Shine finally ran out of air.

The bartender broke out into applause. Randall abruptly stopped reading and looked at Shine with a mix of skepticism and genuine awe. Meanwhile, Mayor Mackey stared, open-mouthed, until his cigarette began to burn his fingers.

"Ouch!" he said, throwing the offending butt on the granite floor and grinding it out for good measure. "'Damn finest,' eh? Well, I have to hand it to you, Red, you've got the spiel down pat. But talk is cheap. And I've got about all the moonshine pouring into this city that we can handle."

"Not like this, you don't," Shine said. "And the name's Shine."

He shrugged. "What the hell? Go ahead, make me holler!" Here he waved at the bartender, who reached under the bar for four shot glasses.

This was her big chance. But getting a bottle of Strong shine ready to pour was going to be a production. She wished she could whip it out of thin air, unscrew the cap and pour each glass with a dramatic flourish.

Instead, she had to take off her clothes. At least her winter coat. And then she was going to need some help.

Shine unfastened Lidy's brooch at the top of the thick coat and then undid the rest of the buttons. She turned a half circle until her back was facing the mayor, who sat pop-eyed in stunned silence. "Would you be so kind as to reach that big bottle from between my shoulder blades?"

"Good God, I thought you'd never ask!" The mayor practically chortled. "You're full of surprises, aren't you, Red?"

Shine whirled around, the glass bottles of her vest clanking, a fierce look on her face.

"*Shine*," the mayor amended. "Sorry. Now, let's have a look-see into what you're packing. You know, you don't have to hide the stuff with a getup like that here." He winked at Shine. "Once you get inside our city limits, you're golden. Some people call Hot Springs the 'loose buckle on the Bible Belt,' " he laughed. "We are a soaking-wet oasis in the middle of a desert of dry counties.

"But I do admire the resourcefulness. And craftsmanship." He reached into the back pouch and pulled out the large flat bottle and set it on the bar. Shine removed the two slimmer vessels from the front pouches and lined them up alongside the big one.

"Now, what you all have to understand is that Strong shine isn't a one-trick pony," she said. "You got your straight shine, which is made with our own Kinney Creek spring water."

Shine poured three of the glasses perfectly even.

"Who's not drinking?" asked the mayor. "Randall?"

"I don't typically partake before lunchtime," he said with a studied Southern drawl. "But after that sales job and striptease, I find myself strangely curious. And thirsty."

The mayor eyed the bartender. "Merle?"

"Have you ever known me to turn down a drink? Especially

one I don't have to pour myself?" Merle smirked. "I think the little lady is trying to sit this one out."

"Little ladies don't know shit about shine," she said, trying not to lose her temper. This was too important to go flying off the handle, as Gran called it when Shine got her dander up and opened her mouth before her brain had a chance to catch up. "And I know this here's the best stuff that'll ever cross your lips. I don't need a snort at eleven thirty in the morning to prove it."

The mayor was obviously enjoying this chance to tease a country girl. "But how do I know this is moonshine and not some grand scheme to unseat the town leadership by means of poisoning or some such?"

Shine pushed a shot glass along the bar toward each of the men. "Drink up," she said. "If poison ever tasted this good, why, people'd be lining up to drink their way to their heavenly rewards."

The men finished at the same time, slamming their shot glasses on the counter in unison.

"*Damn*," said the mayor.

"That is some fine panther piss you got there," said Merle. Shine thought she detected a note of admiration in his voice. And a bit more respect.

Randall sat with his watery blue eyes bulged out, mute.

"I'm intrigued," said the mayor. "What else you got?"

"Well, that should be more than enough," Shine retorted. "But you're in luck. The Strongs like variety in their moonshine. We add a dollop of this and that, whatever's in season or suits our fancy. Smooths out that hard stuff with a little something extra. Subtle. You'll see."

Here, Shine reached for one of the slender bottles and began refilling the glasses. Randall covered his with his hand, shaking his head no.

"I've had enough," he squeaked.

But the other two men threw back the shots, no hesitation this time.

"Sweet Jesus." The mayor wiped his mouth on the shirt cuff

peeking out from the sleeve of his blue linen suit. "I feel like I ate a slice of my grandmother's peach pie—then got kicked in the gut by my grandad's mule."

"You're welcome," said Shine, pleased.

"All right," the mayor said. "Now, Miss Strong—Shine—have a seat and let's figure out how we can welcome the Strong stuff into the Hot Springs family. Merle here will make arrangements for the club's share—"

"We'll take everything you've got," Merle interrupted. "In an exclusive—so the club is the only place you sell to. *If* you've got the production," he said. "I'm not interested in one or two bottles, no matter how good it is."

Shine did some quick calculations. If Gran and Becks distilled everything they had in the mash barrels right now and the good weather held—*and* they could avoid the feds on the return trip to Hot Springs . . .

Rebecca would say that was a sight more "ifs" than was comfortable. But she wasn't her sister. She would take her chances, by God.

"Kinney Creek isn't in danger of drying up anytime soon," said Shine. "The Strongs, neither. We put lightning in a bottle like nobody's business. I can deliver fifteen gallons today and another fifteen in two weeks. Twenty-five bucks a gallon."

That might be a stretch. A big stretch, if she was being honest. Everything would have to go right. But if they could pull it off? They would be solvent, secure, for the first time in their lives. And she liked her odds.

"I'm not big on hyperbole, except for my own, Miss Strong, but I know you aren't exaggerating. That's a mite high but . . . I like your stuff. And I like your style," the mayor laughed, pumping Shine's hand. "It's a deal."

"Deal." She shook Merle's for good measure, nodding at Randall, whose hand was gingerly rubbing the length of his throat. "I'll have my driver bring round the shine this afternoon."

But there were a few other pressing matters. She needed some cash. And a place to stay while she looked for a couple of murdering feds.

"I'll need a down payment," she said. "Twenty-five dollars should do. And I'll take the rest this afternoon when I deliver the fifteen gallons. For this run and the next."

She was glad they couldn't see her sweating beneath her homespun hooch vest. She had asked for more money than she had seen in one place her whole entire life.

But the mayor didn't bat an eyelash. "Merle, get this girl some green and seal the deal."

Maybe she should have asked for more.

"And if you could point me toward a place to stay, I'd be much obliged," Shine said. "Nothing fancy," she amended. "I've no need for all the extras at the Arlington."

Merle scratched his head of black, greasy hair. "A few Southern Clubbers have stayed at Bernyce Ward's place on the edge of town. It's a mile or so walk. Or you can take the streetcar. Not pricey. But decent. And safe for a young woman on her own."

Shine didn't like the way he smiled. Wolfish. Predatory. She put on her coat and turned on her heel.

"Pleasure doing business."

Shine wasted no time sending Jed back for the second load of moonshine.

"See you in a couple of weeks," she said, after they unloaded the first batch at the back door of the Southern Club. "Soon as you and Becks can get that shine bottled up and on board the Model A. Then we'll be golden."

"Easy as rolling off a log backwards." Jed slid into the driver's seat and cranked down the window.

"I wish Daddy was here to see it," Shine said. "He shoulda taken the middleman out of the equation years ago."

Shine reached through the window and placed a crisp twenty

in Jed's palm. "Here's gas, food and lodging." Then she pulled the thick envelope from her dress pocket. "Get the rest of this home safe and sound to Gran."

"Will do," he said, tucking the stash beneath his seat. "Back in a flash."

Shine patted the Ford on the hood as Jed fired up the engine. Everything had gone so smoothly; better than she had dared to hope. She would settle in at the boardinghouse—and turn her full attention to tracking down those prohis.

Elsie

She held the sleeping infant in her arms, inspecting each of his hands for the hundredth time, taking in the slender fingers topped with pink moon-shaped nails. A head of pale downy hair, upturned nose and that sweet mouth with a thin droplet of milk trailing from one corner; a mouth that still moved as if nursing, the baby dreaming of his mother's breast, so recently removed.

Elsie had felt a trickle of water between her legs yesterday morning, the day after putting in a full shift at the mash kettle, where she had stoked the fire and stirred the contents for what seemed like forever. Made more difficult with Gran looking over her shoulder the entire time, passing judgment as she threw in handfuls of yeast and overripe fruit. Pawpaws this time, Elsie had noted, wrinkling her nose. The smell made her want to throw up, it was so cloying. But she knew that sweetness was a good sign for the moonshine they were making. So she ignored her nose and kept at it.

All that hard work seemed to kick off a different kind of labor.

Clara Hanson had helped her change and made her comfortable in the high four-poster bed of the guest room—now hers and Jed's—and sent for Lidy. She knew her limitations. Clara was much more comfortable behind a cash register than between the legs of her recently acquired daughter-in-law, trying to catch a baby. But you could bet she would be at Elsie's side, anxious to meet the grandchild she had given up on ever having.

Hi.

Elsie named him Hiram; Hi for short. Jed hadn't been here to weigh in, off on a bootleg run to deliver that last big batch of hooch to Hot Springs with her big sister. But the Hansons seemed to approve her choice.

Well, Daddy, you finally got your boy.

She couldn't wait for Jed to meet the baby. Their son was absolutely perfect. And Hi would complete their circle of love, which Elsie was loath to admit had not felt whole. She hadn't wanted her sisters to coerce Jed into marriage. He would have come around without the threats and guns, the spectacle the Strongs had put on. If only Gran would have let her talk to him!

But she wanted the marriage so much, she wanted *Jed* so much, she had acquiesced. Just in case his good intentions weren't enough to get him to the altar in a timely fashion. And she would have been hard-pressed to stop the firestorm that was Shine on a mission.

Her wedding night had been disappointing, though. Disturbing, even. After the hubbub at the house and stint with Brother Aiken at the church, the Hansons had driven the newlyweds home in stunned silence. Clara had hastily made up the bed in the guest room and left the bride and groom alone, mentioning a headache.

Jed removed his shirt and belt and then sat in the rocking chair by the fireplace. An empty bottle and a half-finished glass of spirits sat on the mantel from a few hours earlier. Before he had known he was getting married. Jed swallowed the remainder in a single gulp.

"Well," he drawled, after ruminating a long moment and rubbing the back of his neck. "I feel like I got a serious case of whiplash. First your daddy tells me to stay away. Then your sisters show up like two trigger-happy Annie Oakleys to hustle me off to church. It makes no damn sense."

Elsie didn't know how to answer. *Daddy* had kept Jed away? Was there a single person in her family who thought she could take care of herself? Her face burned.

Jed belched. "Hope you got what you wanted."

"I just want to be with you," she faltered. "To be your wife. And raise your child with you."

"How do I even know it's mine?" He shook his head. "Far as I recall, we were together just the once."

Elsie hung her head. "Twice," she whispered. She remembered everything about those evenings after church, the drive home, pulling over at a pretty spot. The moonlight on the back seat. The slow, careful way he had undressed and caressed her, the whole time declaring his love for her, and exclaiming on her beauty as he uncovered her inch by creamy inch.

How could he forget?

"I . . ." She paused, embarrassed. "You are the only one I've ever . . ."

Jed laughed, but not with warmth. "I've heard that one before," he said ruefully. "Well, might as well have what's legally mine. Take off that dress."

Elsie cringed. *What?* She had envisioned embraces, kissing. Laughter and talk of their future, which all began tonight.

Slowly, mechanically, she undressed. The peach dress with the multitude of pearly buttons took some time. Her boots, her stockings. She pulled her white slip over her pooching stomach, her breasts, and finally her head, feeling the scratch of the lace-scalloped bodice as it touched her face. She wanted to die of shame as she stood revealed, the swollen bump undeniable in her thickened middle.

Jed watched the show without expression. "You're pretty far gone, aren't you?

"Well, lay down and spread your legs," he said, callously. "I suppose I can close my eyes and manage somehow. It's my wedding night, after all."

It took two minutes at most. Elsie lying on top of the bedcovers, shivering with shame and cold, even in the oppressive heat of a late-summer evening. Jed didn't even take off his pants, just unzipped them and climbed on top of her, closing his eyes and squeezing her swollen breasts until she cried out. Everything hurt as he jammed into her without so much as a kiss or caress to help her body along. Then a single groan before his body went limp: he had passed out on top of her.

Tears leaked from the corners of Elsie's eyes onto the freshly ironed eyelet pillowcase. *This wasn't how it was supposed to be.* Putting her palms on his shoulders, she pushed against his dead weight with all her strength. He rolled onto his back and immediately began snoring, a wet rumble vibrating his slack mouth. Then she swung her legs over the side of the bed and located a chamber pot in the corner of the lamplit room to relieve herself. The urine burned her tender parts as it came out in a rush, the slow drip of semen after. Then she scrubbed at herself with the washrag and pitcher of water set out by Clara until she felt clean, dug out the new nightgown from her valise and put it on. She crawled beneath the covers on her side of the double bed, careful not to touch her sleeping husband, and reached to turn out the lamp.

Tomorrow would be a better day. It had to be.

And it was.

Jed, for his part, woke up sober and didn't seem to remember much from the night before. He looked surprised to open his eyes and find her there beside him.

"I thought I dreamed you."

He reached for her again and she quivered, thinking of the shock and pain of the night before.

But he was gentle. He traced her face with one of his fingers and placed it on her lips, as if quieting her worries, her fears. A slow, deliberate pull at the ribbon that held her nightgown closed at the neck had her aching for him to go further, to touch her like she remembered.

Afterward, he held her nestled in between his arm and chest, her face resting on his shoulder.

"Good morning, Mrs. Hanson," he said. She turned her face up to his. Elsie couldn't help herself: she smiled.

"Good morning."

That was the moment she understood she had married two different men. There was the dashing, devoted—if somewhat aimless—Jed that she fell in love with. And the snide, cynical one who was having a self-destructive affair with a booze bottle. That Jed frightened her. She knew she would have to do everything in her power, God help her, to keep Jedediah Hanson on the righteous path.

Later, standing with Jed in front of that rigid line of judgmental Strong women as Shine outlined the plan to exact justice and save the family from financial ruin, Elsie had felt a twinge of something akin to pride. Her *husband* was going to help them.

They needed him.

And he needed them, too. Shine was giving him a purpose; she believed he could come through for them—him and his Model A. That belief was something he hadn't ever had, working out back at the store. His dad had decided long ago that he was good for nothing. But Elsie knew: he was good for *something.*

"I won't let you down," Jed had said.

Elsie didn't see the skepticism in her sisters' eyes or the scorn in the twist of her gran's lip. In the cool shade of that front porch, she saw a man with real promise. As real as the promise they had made to each other in the front of that church.

She placed the infant in his cradle and stretched. Lord, she was sore. Birthing a baby, building a fire, stirring a mash pot. She needed to rest, regain her strength. She was a mama now. And that meant Lidy was all by her lonesome on the mountain. She would be needing help, even if she was too stubborn to ask for it.

Thank God Jed, Rebecca and Shine would be back soon.

LIDY

The stillness woke her.

It was not yet daylight, but Lidy was done sleeping. She wasn't used to the quiet; it unsettled her. To be the single human being in the cabin. It felt strange, unnatural. Hiram gone. And now Rebecca was on the moonshine run with Jed, meeting up with Shine in Hot Springs. Elsie in town with the new baby.

Little Hi. She couldn't lie. When Elsie named the child, it had touched her heart deep down where she hadn't felt anything for a long while. Since Hiram died. As if her feelings had been buried along with her son. But the birth a few days ago had reawakened her, banished the numbness she wore like a second skin.

"Gran, isn't he a perfect peach?" Elsie had been wrung out yesterday from the long hours of labor, but blissful holding the bundle that was the prize for her efforts.

Lidy agreed: he was. Plump and pink, a halo of golden fuzz on his head. Slate-gray-blue eyes that would lighten to match his mother's or father's shade of blue. And a dimple! An angel had kissed Hi on his way out of heaven—and on the right cheek. The child would be lucky.

Was already lucky.

A wave of shame washed over her, remembering how she had

done her damnedest to rid Elsie of that baby. But he had the good fortune to have an unexpectedly fierce mama beneath that delicate beauty and despite her diminutive size. Elsie had always intuited more than her sisters, understood human feelings and behavior in a way that Shine did chemistry and numbers or Rebecca did nature and living creatures.

It gave Lidy pause sometimes, wondering what Elsie thought she knew. About her. About Alta. She had never said anything beyond a few questions as a child. Asked flat out why her mother had jumped—insisted she had *seen* her jump—even though Lidy told the girls she fell. Was Lidy to lessen the grief of two granddaughters by irreparably harming the third?

Your mama never meant to die. She just didn't want you, Shine.

No. Best keep the truth hidden, buried along with Alta near the woods.

Elsie hadn't called Lidy out for her herbal offerings that were purportedly for strengthening Elsie's womb, either. Instead, she dumped them where she knew her gran would eventually look. Letting Lidy know in the language of a limp lavender bush that she knew the treachery in her heart. Lidy felt watched when Elsie was around. More than watched. *Seen.* In all the worst ways.

The first rays of sunlight found their way through the front window, turning the wooden logs of the cabin a golden brown. Lidy's mind turned to all the chores that needed doing. Starting the fire. Hauling water from the creek. Feeding and watering the horses, mules and cow. Milking. Scattering some grain for the hens and gathering the eggs.

Then there was the batch of moonshine that she and Elsie had been smack in the middle of. The barrel of mash was still sitting out in the barnyard and needed to be rolled into the barn for storage. But Jed, Rebecca and Shine would be back for the distilling any day now. She was counting on it. There was no way in hell she could do all that lifting by herself.

At least she was spared from cooking. She didn't need more than a piece of day-old cornbread and some jerky. Maybe an apple, if she felt like a trip to the root cellar.

The rooster crowed.

Lidy rose and met the day.

Shine

It hadn't been that easy getting her foot in the door at Bernyce Ward's.

"I only board respectable ladies and gentlemen," the stoop-shouldered old woman had said, taking in Shine's homemade dress and pilling woolen coat that had seen better days on several sets of shoulders. Her eyes were sharp, dissecting the young woman in front of her as if assessing a junked car that might be sold for parts. Shine stood straighter.

"I've got a good job and I don't want trouble," Shine said. "I'm trying to make some money to send home to my gran and sisters since my daddy passed."

"And what might that job be, may I ask?" Bernyce Ward had not just fallen off the turnip truck. She knew a young girl like the one in her front parlor had limited options for making money, and ninety-five percent of those were unsavory. Not befitting her tidy, reputable boardinghouse.

"The Southern Club—"

"Absolutely not," said Miss Ward. "Why, I shouldn't even let you stand in my living room with a 'job' like that! The women under this roof have sterling reputations and employment. As do the gentlemen."

"I will try not to take offense," Shine said. *Old biddy.* A glance around the parlor told Shine that "sterling" was more about money than propriety. Everything was clean and neat, but the sofa had a sprung coil that gave it a slight bulge on one end and the floral rug frayed at the edges. Bernyce Ward needed a good-paying customer. "I am helping keep the books. I have a good head for figures and I've been doing the ledgers for my family since I was a schoolgirl."

"Hmm." The older woman sniffed. "You still look like a schoolgirl if you ask me. How old are you, anyway?"

"Eighteen, ma'am," Shine lied with ease. *Close enough.*

"All the same, I can't have a Southern Club girl here," she said. "I have four boarders right now: a schoolteacher, a seamstress, a nice young man who is starting out with First National Bank. Plus a clean-cut salesman who stays on weekends when he's passing through on business."

"So an accountant would fit right in."

"*Accountant* sounds pretty highfalutin for that sordid place," scoffed Miss Ward. "Like putting lipstick on a pig."

"I don't wear lipstick." Shine gave a saccharine smile. "But I guess I can put a better face on this. How about Andrew Jackson's?"

Shine took out her change purse, and with a quick snap of the twisted metal prongs, she opened it to display the folded twenty she had procured at the Southern Club. She smoothed the bill before holding it out. "Will this do for a month's room and board?"

It was satisfying, watching Bernyce Ward try to pick her chin up off the floor. Everything had a price. Even propriety.

Dollars always make sense. That's what her daddy would say—and if he were here, he would be greasing that wrinkly palm, too.

"I provide breakfast and supper," she said. "If you'll be late, you must let me know so I can make a plate and keep it warm. My three rooms for women are upstairs. Yours is the one at the end of the hall. You'll need to be in your room by ten p.m. Lights out at eleven.

"Bedding should be brought down on Saturday mornings, along with your towel and washcloth." She paused, looking hard at Shine. "And this should go without saying, but absolutely *no* male callers upstairs."

"Of course," Shine said.

"Supper is at six," Miss Ward said. "I'm expecting a full table tonight."

Shine unpacked the few clothes she had in her satchel and hung her one extra dress in the closet. She only found two hangers, which confirmed this place was not as choice as Bernyce Ward would have one think. People who stayed here didn't have much.

"Hi, I'm Birdie."

A pointed face peeked around her half-open door. Before Shine could say anything, the rest of the young woman slid into the room and flounced onto the one wooden chair. She crossed her legs primly, clasping her hands around the sharp corner her knee made beneath her mid-length navy skirt. "What kind of trouble are you?"

Her thin face was angular but her large blue eyes, like violets, softened her look somehow. The mouth was turned up in a grin.

"Trouble?" Shine startled. Was it so obvious she was on the wrong side of the law?

"I mean, no one would park themselves here if they had other options," Birdie said slyly. "Where ya working?"

"The Southern Club," Shine said, proud she had managed to get in cahoots with the city's best casino and watering hole.

Birdie's large eyes widened, which Shine thought impossible, given how they already dominated her face. But she had surprised Birdie.

"The Southern Club?" Birdie let out a low whistle. "And Miz Ward let you stay here?"

"She did."

"Well, wow and holy cow," Birdie said. "Most of us who work there have to lie about it. Hard to find a good place to live with two squares for two-fifty a week. And old Bernyce likes to pretend she's got standards."

Shine realized with dismay that she had paid double. No wonder the old gal had started salivating when she paid her up front.

"So . . . are you the schoolteacher or the seamstress?"

"I'm the seamstress," Birdie giggled. "That's what I told old Bernie. But I couldn't stitch a straight line if my life depended on it. I work in the laundry room at the club. Pretty close, right? Slaving over tubs of hot soapy water and bleach, getting the whites white. It doesn't pay much, but beats working in the bathhouses. And my boss said I can move up. There's lots of jobs there. What about you?"

Shine faltered. How much should she divulge to her obviously chatty guest? "I'll be stocking the bar," she said, pleased at her own cleverness. "And helping to keep the books."

True on both counts.

Her new friend was impressed. "You must know how to cipher. Can you read?"

"Sure," Shine said. "I had plenty of book learning. I've always been good with numbers and I happen to know a bunch about booze, though I don't drink it myself."

"You got family?"

"My mama and daddy are both dead," Shine said. Her throat tightened. She hadn't gotten used to that last part yet. "But I got my gran and my sisters back home in Missouri. One just got married and is having a baby any minute."

"You're lucky." There was wistfulness in Birdie's voice. Shine hadn't thought herself fortunate, with her mama dead before she knew her and Daddy shot dead smack in front of her. But there was all kind of suffering in the world. And she did have the love of her family, however reduced in size.

"My parents both died of the Spanish flu and I lost three of my eight brothers and sisters. The five of us got parceled out to different families around, mostly farmers. I ain't seen any of 'em since." She smoothed her skirt as if she were trying to smooth out her memories. "Soon as I could, I came to the big city to find work.

Wanted to make my own way instead of killing myself for a couple who saw me as a hired hand more than a daughter or a ward.

"I quit schooling when Mama and Daddy passed," she went on. "I wasn't much good at it anyhow. No matter how hard I tried, the numbers and letters didn't go together like they were supposed to. Like how everyone else saw them.

"But laundry, I can do." She scooted closer to where Shine was seated on the bed, tightly made up in white sheets and topped with a handmade quilt. "And," she added in a whisper, "the food is a whole lot better at the club. So I eat a big lunch. That way I can pick at what's most tolerable on Bernie's table. She stretches her meat so far you can see through it."

"Well, no one can stack up to my gran when it comes to cooking anyway. I imagine I'll get by." Shine rose with an audible sigh. She was starting to wonder if she was going to have a roommate rather than a hallmate.

But Birdie got the hint. "I'll let you finish settling in," she said. "Then I'll see you at dinner—or what passes for dinner around here.

"If you're lucky, you'll get to sit by the salesman," she said slyly. "*If* he's in town this weekend. He's all kinds of good-looking, but sorta quiet. I'm not sure what he even sells. But the banker is boring, a real snooze. Pasty as a biscuit and talks nonstop about his mother."

"Thanks for the warning." Shine started closing the door, even though Birdie wasn't quite through it yet. "I'm not really looking for a man, though."

"Aw, that's no fun!" Birdie's disappointment was plain. "Well, we'll see about that. I'm in need of a good husband, myself. A rich one. So I don't have to work anymore! A girl can dream!"

Shine closed the door with a not-so-soft click.

Actually, she *was* looking for a man. Two of them. And they better hope to hell she didn't find them.

Rebecca

A little farther to go.

Rebecca tapped her foot impatiently against the floorboard. Once they got to Hot Springs, it was a simple matter of unloading. Shine would meet them at the back door of the Southern Club at midnight and—if everything went according to plan—they would get a good night's sleep and head back to Kinney tomorrow morning. They would have a full tank of gas and full pockets after emptying their Model A of its clandestine cargo.

Rebecca was looking forward to traveling lighter, that was for sure. Beneath a nubby woolen shawl, she wore two galvanized steel half-cylinders she had crafted to curve around her midsection and hold a gallon and a half of hooch each. Far worse, though, than the merciless metal cutting into her sides was the dress she was wearing beneath. That was even more painful.

Rebecca didn't wear dresses.

At least, she hadn't since she was a child. She preferred the all-around cover and comfort of a pair of sturdy work pants. And since she spent the majority of her time outdoors, helping in the cornfield or climbing fences and trees or wading in the chilly creek water, Lidy had let it slide. Pants were practical, like the girl who wore them.

But right now, the most practical item that Rebecca wore was a floral cotton dress of Lidy's, let out at the seams to accommodate

Rebecca's broad back and straight waist. Dressing the part of a lady was key to their safety: hers, Jed's and their precious moonshine's. Shine had assured her that no self-respecting prohi would search a woman. A *lady.* The makeover hadn't been easy, though. Her gran had had to add another four inches of lace at the hem for decency. Rebecca was nearly six feet tall, and Lidy's dress would have shown decidedly too much ankle without alterations.

The last seventeen miles to Hot Springs were the curviest, and for some reason, that spurred Jed to drive faster rather than slower. Like her horse, Cowboy, when he sensed they were close to home: he stepped up the pace. But this was a whole lot faster—and Rebecca wasn't holding the reins.

"What's the hurry? Whether we get there at ten or ten fifteen, it doesn't make any difference. We'll have to kill some time till midnight anyway."

"Quicker I get there, the sooner I can relax," said Jed, eyes focused on the road revealed in the beam of the Ford's headlights. "I'll be getting me a drink or three while we wait."

Rebecca knew that was part of it. Jed never missed an opportunity to wet his whistle. But she also knew that this was the leg of the journey—despite the harrowing dirt roads and the alarming twists and turns—where they were most likely to run into the law. And while having a woman in the car should be enough to keep the local police and feds from stopping them, it wasn't a sure thing. Despite his posturing, Jed was nervous. Maybe he really did need that drink.

"Well, you're driving like a twitchy rabbit."

"Aww, shut it, sister," Jed said. "I got this under control."

Rebecca gripped the armrest. It didn't *feel* under control. But Jed wouldn't want to harm his precious coupe. She suspected Jed cared for this car more than he did Elsie, the way he fawned over it, constantly tinkering with the engine and washing it to a dazzling shine. He had taken on his role with gusto, researching ways to mold his Model A into a moonshine-running machine. Since he got back from Hot Springs, he had added more carburetors and new intake manifolds—even over-boring the cylinders—to increase the car's horsepower.

And that was only the engine! Rebecca had pulled Cowboy up to the barn last week and found Jed in the back of his beloved car with the upholstered seat bench torn out and sitting in the road. A spotted hen was taking advantage of the comfortable perch that had appeared seemingly out of nowhere.

"What in tarnation?" Rebecca was taken aback by the wholesale dismantling of Jed's love object.

"Trying to see if I can put in a few compartments behind the seats to hide more shine," Jed said as he emerged from the back of the car, wrench in hand. " 'Course, I'll have to work on the suspension if I do. Otherwise, the car will ride too low when she's fully loaded. And the cops would be on us like flies on shit. Whattya think?"

"I think you're nuts," Rebecca said, deadpan. "And I didn't know you had an honest day's work in you. So color me surprised."

"Why, thank you very much?" Jed laughed, giving her a low bow. "I wouldn't call it honest, so maybe that's the key. Here, let me show you something."

Jed reached for the dashboard to turn on the lights, which glowed weakly in the noonday sun. Then, to her amazement, he flipped a switch beneath the steering wheel and the glow of the taillights immediately disappeared, leaving only the headlights on.

"I think I'm supposed to be impressed?"

"I thought you were the one with the common sense," he said. "If we get in a chase with the cops, I cut the taillights. We can still see the road, but they can't see us nearly so well.

"Go on and say it: I'm a genius."

Rebecca grunted. "You're something, that's for sure."

She had kept a wary eye on him since noting those fancy work boots on his wedding day. He was still on probation in her book. But it made her hopeful to see her lazy brother-in-law engaged with something besides drinking and idling away any time he wasn't at the store. At the same time, she knew everything Jed did to and for the car cost money. Big money. And they had to cover the additional equipment, more ingredients, gas money and Shine's expenses at the Hot Springs boardinghouse. Not to mention the cash money required to grease the requisite palms; the product giveaways that warmed official bellies while clearing both the sinuses and a pathway to selling the Strong shine in that town. They were a long way off from turning a profit from their bootlegging—one more oversized load, in fact.

Jed wouldn't have given a thought to any of that. He was raised with a safety net. No matter how far off the path he veered, his parents would pick him up—albeit reluctantly—and dust him off. Not *cut* him off.

The Strongs? Not so much. They had always been a hand-to-mouth operation. Their safety net was knowing they had strong backs and smarts. Rebecca hoped that was enough to balance out Jed's proclivity for extravagance.

"Holy shit!" Jed's swearing swooped Rebecca right out of her rambling thoughts and back into the front seat. They'd hit a pothole, bouncing the Model A so hard that her head hit the ceiling.

"Watch where you're going, why don't you!" Rebecca had barely settled back into her seat, rubbing her head, before the car's undercarriage scraped the ground, a front tire crawling out of a large pothole.

"No time for that." Jed checked the rearview mirror. "Passed a turnoff about a quarter mile back. Soon as I started down this hill, I saw a pair of headlights turn on. Hang on tight, because I aim to outrun these motherfuckers."

"But you've got me, decked out in my Sunday best," Rebecca yelled over the jouncing and grinding of the gears as Jed threw it into low. "They won't arrest us. Isn't that the whole point of having a woman along?"

Her right side slammed into the passenger door. "Jesus! You're not much of a driver."

"Well, you ain't much of a woman," Jed said. "And we're a couple miles out of Hot Springs. I'm not about to get slowed down by a pair of prohis with a hard-on to empty our tanks or throw my wily ass in jail. Better to beat a path to the city limits, where we're safe."

The headlights were getting closer. Rebecca felt her heart skip a beat. She didn't particularly want to take a chance on being inspected. She'd heard that some of the more barbaric officers loved groping suspected bootleggers, particularly those in dresses—even if it wasn't likely she would be put behind bars.

"Watch this," Jed said. He floored it and the car jolted ahead, sounding as if the engine might explode. *Up, up, up* and then a lurch around a curve that had Rebecca feeling as though she had left her stomach behind. At the top of the hill, the headlights behind them cut into the back window, illuminating a slice of Jed's face, resolute. Whoever it was had closed the gap and Jed was not about to be caught.

"I think I remember a fork in the road past the next turn."

In less than a minute, the Model A was there. Jed cranked the steering wheel hard toward the right and had no sooner gotten onto the tiny road when he reached under the steering wheel to cut the taillights. Then he quickly backed up about twenty feet and cut across some low brush, taking the left fork of the road instead.

"Take that, you S.O.B.s! That should throw them off," Jed said, laughing. Rebecca didn't like the sound of that laughter, dark and devil-may-care. He was enjoying this—the thrill of the chase—while she felt that her life could be over any second.

Once again, he mashed the gas pedal down and took each of the hairpin turns on the way down the mountain sharply, tossing Rebecca from side to side, bumping the window and then the gearshift and back again.

"Jed, slow down! *Now!*"

"I can't."

She looked over at him while holding on to the dashboard in front of her with one hand, her other white-knuckled on the door.

"Goddamn it, Jed, I said slow down! Or I will absolutely kick your ass when this thing finally stops."

Jed said nothing. So when Rebecca turned toward the driver's seat to make a further plea, she froze at the look on his face. He was terrified.

"I can't!" He was screaming, yet she could barely hear him over the noise of the car as it continued to pick up speed. Pine boughs and low scrub scraped the sides of the car with whining and cracking sounds as Jed wrestled the steering wheel to keep it in the ruts of the rough road.

"*Can't?* Or *won't?*" Rebecca's blood boiled, anger taking over for fear. She would rip his arm off and beat him to death with it. And not have an ounce of remorse.

"No brakes!" Jed yelled, pumping the pedal like a madman. *Is he* crying? *Jesus. This fraidy-cat piece of shit is going to kill us both.*

"Hang on!"

Rebecca did her best. She put her arms straight out against the dashboard, feeling a worsening nausea as the headlight beams lit up a giant Scotch pine coming up at the next sharp turn. *Sweet Jesus.* She braced herself for impact as the trunk of the tree loomed larger and larger, the thick red-orange crackle pattern of the bark layered like a cabin roof. And then: a last-second swerve. She felt the car go up on two side wheels as Jed cut the sharp curve and land with a resounding *whump* back onto all four. Rebecca was just turning to congratulate him when she saw another tree, even larger than the last.

She didn't even have time to scream.

The Model A hit the loblolly pine square in the front bumper, the force of it crushing into the hood and shattering the windshield. The car bounced back from the tree and off the constricted road, tumbling long-ways down the steep hillside, loosing a shower of shale and limestone and taking out some shallow-rooted saplings clinging precariously to the side of the rocky mountain.

The car came to rest on its battered roof at the bottom of the ravine, a single front wheel spinning. For a moment, there was no sound but the creak of that solitary wheel, as the useless headlights cut into surrounding brush. Then the slightest *drip, drip* of liquid as it fell in fat droplets from the floor of the car onto Rebecca's bleeding face.

Peaches.

It was the smell of the Strong moonshine that brought Rebecca around, leaking from the compartment hidden in the floorboard. She opened her eyes. Why was she looking up at the floorboard instead of down?

Dear Jesus.

She had never felt pain like this. Rebecca squeezed her eyes closed, then opened them again—had it been a few seconds? A few minutes?—when she heard Jed moaning, moving around. Everything snapped back to her then: the headlights, the curves, the brakes failing, the tree.

She released a deep primal groan.

The pain. Sharper than her daddy's bucksaw. She felt as if her leg had been cut clean through like a piece of cured firewood.

"Holy shit." Jed squeezed himself out of the driver's-side window and hurried to the other side of the car. Rebecca dangled there unnaturally, held aloft by one long leg pinched below the knee, held fast between the crushed floorboard and the dash of the upside-down car.

The metal moonshine containers strapped to her body were still heavy with hooch, and sliding from their previously secure position around her waist and ribs toward her breasts and armpits. One tin was badly dented and leaking a steady stream of moonshine. He untied the contraption; Rebecca's side had a deep jagged cut from the metal. He set about trying to pry her leg free, to loose her from beneath the crushed dashboard, but it was awkward, reaching in through the window.

"Fuck!" Desperate, he left her hanging, went to the rear of the car and managed to kick the latch of the trunk open and grab a crowbar. By this time, Rebecca's intermittent moaning had become more of a panting scream.

Sticking the tip of the iron bar into the spot where dashboard met floorboard, but careful to avoid Rebecca's knee and upper leg, Jed pried with everything he had. "Shit, shit, shit!" Nothing moved. He leaned on the bar with as much of his weight as the difficult angle would allow. He had about given up when the metal rod broke through the wooden part of the dash enough to release the leg. Rebecca fell to the car's ceiling in a heap of skirt, petticoats and pure agony.

Then Jed was grabbing her under the arms and pulling her through the window, trying unsuccessfully to hush her.

"Steady now." He almost had her torso out of the car window. Her clothes and wrap were bunched up under her arms and in the way. "You never have known how to wear a dress."

When he got both legs out, he dragged her the few extra feet to the front of the car, setting her down so that he could see her in the headlights.

There, right beneath the knee, her lower leg hung at a ninety-degree angle from the kneecap—but not in a way a leg is made to bend. And sticking out of her skin like a large, chipped piece of porcelain was a leg bone, broken off uncleanly, a rotten branch splintered from a tree trunk.

Jed turned away from her broken body, put his hands on his knees and vomited. He wiped his mouth and scraped-up head with the tail of his shirt, plopped down beside his ruined Model A and waited for the headlights to die. Or someone to show up and help them out of this mess. Off of this godforsaken mountain. Anyone would be welcome right about now.

Even a couple of motherfucking prohis.

At least she wasn't screaming anymore. But not because the pain had stopped. Jed had seen her leg, so he knew: Rebecca had simply passed out.

Shine

Dinners at the boardinghouse were everything Birdie had promised: gray, tasteless and scant. The last part was probably a blessing.

It was Friday night, and Shine poked her fork tentatively into a gray chunk of potato. Gran would be horrified that this was what was considered a passable meal. And that she was paying for it! She hadn't eaten a single decent dinner the past two weeks. But . . . beggars could not be choosers and she needed this place for the time being.

"Would you pass the beans, please?" A stick figure of a young man reached for the bowl, his ears seeming to redden from Shine's request. This was the banker-in-training, Mr. Harold James. She had also met Miss Sarah Phillips, the schoolteacher, with her dark hair pulled back in a French braid and a complexion as chalky as one of her classroom erasers. She seemed talked out, probably from holding forth with a classroom full of hip-high hellions. She held her mouth in a thin line except to take the occasional mouse-like nibble of food, as though she had to work up to it each time. Shine could relate.

Bernyce Ward sat stiffly at the head of the table, with Birdie chattering away on her right side. Shine was on her left, but there wasn't room to get a word in edgewise with Birdie carrying on like she did.

"Can you believe the Babe lost a thousand dollars at blackjack today?" Birdie was giddy with her hot piece of news, gleaned from the steamy laundry room of the Southern Club. "The man can hit a ball five hundred and thirty-five feet out of the park and into the alligator farm clean across the street, but he can't add a few cards to make twenty-one?"

Babe Ruth was one of hundreds of baseball players who had fallen in love with Hot Springs over the years. Most enjoyed it during the months of spring training held there—teams like the Brooklyn Dodgers, Chicago Cubs, New York Yankees and the Boston Red Sox. But the Babe was so smitten he started visiting in the off-season. Golfing, hiking, betting on the ponies, taking more than a few mineral baths and enjoying the nightlife, too.

"One is skill and the other is mostly luck," Shine said. "It's not that surprising."

Birdie's face fell as flat as the custard awaiting them for dessert.

"Still," she said. "A successful man like the Babe shouldn't get taken in."

"I'm more disturbed by the lack of a moral compass," Miss Ward said, pursing her lips as though she had eaten something distasteful. Which Shine knew she absolutely had. The gravy served with the stringy pot roast was more gray than brown. But at least it matched the meat and potatoes. "Our baseball heroes should not be gambling or anywhere near a place that allows it. That behavior is typically accompanied by drinking and other devilry. It's not seemly."

The boarders chewed that thought over with the same enthusiasm with which they met the roast, prepared to a state of doneness Lidy would have pronounced "whangleathery." It was quiet but for the sound of forks and knives on porcelain and the rhythmic grinding of the tough meat by all.

There was one empty place: the salesman was late. But rather than make a late plate for him like she had professed to do for those who gave her fair warning, Bernyce apparently wanted this man to join the table, tardy or not. *If he knew what was good for him, he would stay away.*

"Will Mr. Smith be here tonight?" Birdie's tone was hopeful.

"He had business he thought might keep him late," Miss Ward replied, looking wistfully at the empty plate.

There was the sound of the front door opening and closing. "Speak of the devil, I'm sure!" Birdie practically jumped out of her seat, clapping.

The wrinkled edges of Bernyce Ward's mouth turned up slightly. "I'll put together a nice warm plate," she said, scooting her chair back to rise.

At precisely that moment, Mr. Smith appeared in the entrance to the cramped dining room, holding his fedora. He was so tall, he had to stoop on his way through the doorframe.

Shine took in the boarder all at once: the neat dark suit covering a crisp white shirt that peeked out of his jacket at cuffs and collar; black hair, pomaded slightly and parted cleanly to one side; steely blue eyes set in a fine face with a scatter of freckles.

She pushed back her chair, too, and stood. Then Shine reached into her pocket for the pistol in her dress pocket, having sworn—after what happened with the thirsty young man with the shotgun somewhere in rural Arkansas—that she would never again be caught unprepared.

He was even more handsome than she remembered.

"Say your goodbyes, Flanagan," she said coolly. "I'm about to dispatch you to the hereafter. Which in your case is an eternity in burning hellfire."

There was a sharp gasp as everyone around the table took a breath, goggle-eyed and fearful.

"Shine!" Birdie was frantic, clearly wanting to stop whatever was happening—but too frightened to move from her chair. Like the rest of the boarders and their hostess. "There must be a mistake," she said. "This is Mr. Smith, not Flanagan or whatever you called him. We can vouch for him!"

"This is not 'Mr. Smith,'" retorted Shine, keeping her pistol trained on Flanagan, who held his hands up in a gesture of surrender. "Are you?"

Bernyce Ward trembled on the edge of her dining chair. "I do *not* allow firearms, not to mention shooting, in my establishment! I must ask you to put down your weapon and take leave of this house. *Now.*"

"Not quite yet, Bernie." Shine enjoyed the way Birdie's eyebrows shot up. She might as well have fun while she could. Because it was about to get pretty serious around here. Too bad there had to be so many witnesses to Flanagan's imminent demise.

"This man shot and killed my daddy," she said. "And now he's gonna pay for it."

"Miss Strong—" Flanagan began.

"Don't 'Miss Strong' me," Shine said. In her revenge fantasies, she had always come upon the guilty prohis unaware, announced herself and unloaded her pistol before the surprised feds could get a word out. But here they were, she and Flanagan both caught off guard—and in a room full of onlookers, no less. "And please stop yapping."

She felt her finger, thick and heavy against the trigger. Going numb. *Just a gentle squeeze. Like Daddy taught me.*

"I didn't kill your father, I swear," Flanagan said. He met Shine's gaze, ignoring the single staring eye of the pistol between them. The rest of the diners were silent—either terrified or fascinated by what would happen next. Or both.

"And I can prove it."

Shine shook her head. This wasn't how it was supposed to unfold. Shine wanted to mete out a healthy portion of justice to this man who had destroyed her family and move on. She would deal with the fallout later.

"*Please.*" His voice was steady, insistent.

She didn't say yes. But she didn't say no, either.

Slowly, without moving his eyes from hers, Flanagan removed his suit jacket, draping it over the empty chair that had been saved for him. He undid the top button of his shirt . . . and kept going until the entire thing flapped open on both sides. This he took off as well, placing it neatly on top of his jacket.

Flanagan was down to a thin short-sleeved undershirt which clung to his well-built chest.

But he wasn't finished yet.

Flanagan reached to his waist, where the T-shirt was tucked into his trousers, and tugged it free. Crossing his arms in front of him, he grabbed the hem of the T-shirt and began to pull it up over his chest, his head and hair disappearing briefly until he had the entire thing off and balled up in one large hand, exposing his arms and chest.

Whump!

Bernyce Ward passed out cold and tumbled gracelessly to the floor. Her legs were sprawled, her shirt dress pulled up to reveal the tangle of garter clips and bands that were holding up the tops of her stockings, stretched to the breaking point by her thick leaden legs.

Birdie screamed. The schoolteacher and the young banker went rigid beside each other, white as the dining-room tablecloth.

But Shine was oblivious to everything except the half-naked man in front of her. She lowered her arm at last, the pistol loose in her grip.

John Flanagan's chiseled chest was marred by an angry red wound below his left clavicle where his shoulder attached. Shine watched, mesmerized, as he made a quarter-turn to reveal the exit wound from a bullet on the back of his upper left arm.

He turned back to face her. "Satisfied?"

Shine nodded mutely. Her eyes brimmed with tears. "But . . . you were there."

"I'm so very sorry," Flanagan said. "I was."

"Are you all gonna leave Bernie on the floor like that?" Birdie blurted. "I mean, she's not my favorite egg by a long shot but you've put her in a kind of compromising position."

The schoolteacher went to cover the old woman's legs, tugging down the bunched dress with both hands. "I've got smelling salts in my room," she said. "And may I ask, Mr. . . . *Smith*, if you wouldn't mind putting your clothes back on while I'm gone," Miss Phillips sniffed. "*Some* of us are ladies."

"Awww, you're no fun!" said Birdie. "This is the most exciting dinner we've ever had here. *Wow!* I mean, since no one actually got shot or died," she added.

Flanagan made short work of putting on both shirts, dispensing with the jacket for the moment.

"Can we talk?" He was at Shine's side now. She felt empty. Bereft. Robbed, if she were being honest. He took the pistol from her hand and guided her out of the dining room by her elbow, leaving the chaos of Bernyce Ward and the boarders behind. He led Shine to the front porch, where a dilapidated swing and rocking chair sat empty. Flanagan helped her onto the porch swing and hesitated before sitting down beside her.

Shine stared straight ahead, beyond the fenced front yard, where a single streetlight cut the blue-gray darkness. She felt Flanagan next to her, heard his steady breathing in the evening stillness.

"You know, I ought to shoot you anyway," she said at last.

"I wouldn't blame you," Flanagan replied.

Shine turned to look at him, surprised. She couldn't see his features there in the half darkness, but his tone was genuine.

"Hmmm."

"But would you like to hear my side of the story first?"

Shine considered this. "Then I can shoot you?"

"If you feel you must," Flanagan said. He paused, waiting.

"Well, by all means," Shine said, settling against the slatted back of the porch swing and setting it in motion. "Start talking."

John

McConnell had been pissed. He didn't like the fact that a redhead girl and her redneck family had made him look like a fool. Getting stuck in that smokehouse like Winnie-the-Pooh was bad enough—but when they left the Strong place empty-handed, McConnell had sworn he would get them back.

"No one does that to R. J. McConnell," he said, puffing out his chest and regrettably distending his potbelly. "Those hillbillies just made their last batch of hooch."

A year, maybe even six months ago, Flanagan would've laughed it off. He had heard McConnell's bluster and bullshit before; it would blow over. It always did. But that last stunt in New York where he had them dressed in wedding finery to infiltrate the ring of bootlegging priests? And the way he busted those bottles in the streets of Kinney, insisting everything be not just rendered useless, but reduced to smithereens? He was getting more extreme. What passed for success in days or weeks prior didn't hold enough drama or charm for McConnell anymore. He wanted big plans, bigger busts, fantastic fireworks of his own making. He was like a junkie—and Flanagan felt he was taking more risks and breaking more rules to get those highs.

They had gone west for a week or ten days, making a few busts deep in Ozark County around Gainesville. Even found a still hidden in a privy on some land near the North Fork of the White River in Tecumseh.

"I knew we were into something when there wasn't any downwind stink," McConnell said. "Proves them people's got shit for brains, I swear to Almighty God."

But when Flanagan suggested heading farther west toward Springfield, McConnell dug in his heels. He couldn't let bygones be bygones, by God. He wanted to head back toward Kinney for "one more crack at the Strongs."

He and Flanagan stopped at the general store for some supplies, garnering more than a few dark looks. Flanagan paid while McConnell made his way out back, remembering the young rake who had tipped them off in the first place. When John emerged from the store, he found McConnell deep in conversation with Jedediah Hanson.

"I came upon their still last week on a Sunday stroll. It was a ways off the beaten path," Jed said, winking. "I might remember the exact location for some long green. Or a nice jug of that Strong shine."

McConnell made one more purchase: a Colt revolver.

"What's that for?" Flanagan asked. "You know we can't be armed."

"Insurance," McConnell said, wiping down the gun with an oil rag. "I don't want to find myself toes up in a shallow grave for finding the wrong man's still. I've still got the dimples in my ass from the whack job that peppered me with shot last month.

"Besides, I'd like to put the fear of God in that family of wiseacres on the side of that mountain."

"I won't allow it," John said.

McConnell stopped cleaning the revolver and sized up Flanagan. "I'd like to see you stop me."

"Anything we find, anyone we arrest, it all goes to hell if either of us is carrying," John said. "You know that. What's the point of doing our job if you're going to piss it all away?"

The squat man grunted and made a show of putting the gun away in the neat lidded box it came in.

"I'll keep it in the truck," he said. "But you'll thank me someday when that piece saves your skinny ass."

Flanagan didn't like it. But he could live with it. Sometimes he thought this was what parenting must be like: giving in to lesser, unimportant things so you could refuse to negotiate on the big ones.

Yet he could have kicked himself for being so naïve, for believing McConnell would be a man of his word.

That July day in the woods, they had followed Jed's directions and were rewarded by the smell of a burning fire. They had split up, McConnell going farther north so that they could come up on the still from two sides. Moving slowly and deliberately so as not to make a sound, John spied the still, about fifty feet away across the creek and up the bank. There was the flame-haired young woman, getting a drink from the creek, laughing at something her daddy said. The old farmer, perched on a log, eating his lunch from a silver pail.

Flanagan had found a thick white oak to hide behind. He would let McConnell make the bust, like he always did. Let him satisfy his thirst for the dramatic. John handled the cleanup, the decidedly unfun part of the job: issuing citations for infractions, cuffing the felonious, loading up the moonshining equipment amidst howls of protest and the potential for a fistfight.

He was used to it.

But he was not used to shooting. Or being shot at.

Crack!

John felt a stab of pure panic as he registered what must have been McConnell stepping on a fallen limb, sending several birds into a flurry of wingbeats and worried calls.

Bang, bang, bang.

Plink, plink, plink.

He would never forget those sounds, the twanging of bullets

and the reply as they found their mark on metal. McConnell had surprised him by opening fire on the copper still and kettle and exploding the glass jug at the end of the drip coil in a million pieces.

John had frozen in his tracks, stopped breathing. He couldn't believe it—and didn't know what to do to stop it.

Everything happened so fast. He saw the open laughing face of the redhead, turned like a moon toward her father, how her expression changed in an instant to shock and fear. And the man, the moonshiner, Hiram Strong, his placid look of contentment twisted into dogged determination as he scuttled toward the gun leaning against the karst wall above the creek.

Then McConnell had done the unthinkable.

Bang, bang, bang. John saw the red bloom of blood in Hiram's thigh before he stepped back behind a slender tree.

"No!" He couldn't help himself; he wanted it to stop.

Pyoowwww.

He was rewarded for his efforts toward peace with a searing pain in his left shoulder. John had looked down to see that his body had not been solid enough to stop the projectile, but perhaps had slowed it down. There were two holes: one in his shoulder and another on the back side of his upper bicep. And then there was blood, leaking out both sides of him as if he were a faulty dam.

More shots from both directions. And the anguish of the girl's cry: "*Daddy! No!*"

Even in his frantic state, running back toward the road and the waiting truck, his shoulder on fire, the hurt in her voice cut him nearly in two.

He had held his wounds tightly, trying to staunch the flow, and scrambled down the hill to the dirt road. McConnell arrived a few minutes later, puffing and sweating, tossing the gun in the seat between them.

"What the hell did you do?" John was furious. At McConnell. At himself. And he was *shot*, goddamn it! He wasn't even sure he was going to be okay.

"Gave the motherfucker what he had coming," McConnell said. "That's one less hillbilly in the moonshine biz. Permanently."

Now John knew he wasn't going to be okay. Ever.

"Why are you looking at me like that?" McConnell said, flooring the gas pedal and spraying gravel in their wake. "I just saved your fucking life."

Shine

"You can bunk here."

There hadn't been anywhere else to put her. All the male waitstaff, bartenders, cooks and dishwashers were boys and men. They lived in apartments, boardinghouses or in tent encampments outside the city along the river. So Merle put her with the female part of the operation: the prostitutes.

It was a simple setup: two sets of bunk beds, one on each side of the room. A single window opposite the door with no curtains, since the view was the wall of the dark brick building a few feet away from the Southern Club. Nothing to see. And no one to see in. One dresser with four drawers. A tiny closet. One chair. The beds weren't made, but a stack containing a pair of thin sheets, a pillowcase and a pilling gray blanket sat folded at the foot of each stained mattress; a single lumpy pillow lying forlorn at the top.

The bunk room was at the end of the hall on the top floor of the club, where the "girls" slept or hung out when they weren't working. The other rooms along the corridor—with its rich carpet and gold-flocked wallpaper—were for "business," although Shine knew the business was pleasure. It made her skin crawl. But now wasn't the time to be squeamish.

Merle wasn't pleased to be showing Shine around. The bar manager obviously felt it was beneath him. He was probably pissed that Mackey had given her a job in his bar without asking first.

But she hadn't known what else to do.

She had been sitting on the porch swing with Flanagan, making plans to search for McConnell.

"If what you say is true, I won't need to put a bullet in him," Shine said. She was reluctant to give up the satisfaction of a well-aimed piece of lead, but it sounded like McConnell was dying a slow, painful death. Why should she put him out of his misery?

"Please tell me his dick is going to fall off," Shine said. "If it hasn't already. That would make it perfect."

Flanagan colored. "Um . . . I don't know," he confessed. "But I'd say it's pretty much out of commission."

"Nonetheless, I'd like to see for myself," Shine said.

Was it possible for Flanagan to blush any harder? It was sort of endearing.

"Well, I'm sure he would be . . . *ahem,* not averse to showing you," John managed. "If you must."

"Oh, Lord," Shine laughed. "I don't need to see his pecker. I just want to know he's as bad off as you say."

John looked relieved. "But promise me you won't kill him. It would be unfair, like shooting fish in a barrel."

"Like how he shot my daddy so fair and square?"

John grimaced. "It's a lot to ask."

Shine sighed. "I don't want to shoot a sick old man. Even if the bastard deserves it."

They decided to go first thing in the morning. She figured she had one more night at the boardinghouse. Bernie would likely give her the heave-ho when she was up and around again after the kerfuffle around the dinner table. Might as well get packing.

But right as she stood to go inside, a black car pulled up to the house, and a man in a brown suit jumped out, door slamming.

"I'm looking for Jace Strong," he said, coming up the sidewalk at a fast clip.

"That's me." The dread she felt as he approached the porch and removed his hat nearly flattened her with its weight.

"I'm sorry, ma'am. There's been an accident. Your brother-in-law sent me to fetch you. He's all right. Scrapes and bruises. But your sister's hurt real bad. Might need her leg cut off."

Shine couldn't speak. Flanagan had thanked the man and sent him on his way.

"I'll take you," he said.

The rest of the night had been a blur: seeing Rebecca in the hospital bed like a mummy, bandages on her head and torso. And the leg. The doctors had managed to get the bone set, but there was no guarantee it would take. If the leg did heal, she could have a bad limp. It was too early to tell. She would need to be in the hospital for several months. Not to mention the hard work of rehabilitating the leg and her weakened body afterward.

Jed stood sulking in the corner of the hospital room, the bandage on his head the lone indicator that he had suffered any trauma at all. Shine fought the urge to inflict more damage.

The dumbass! Trying to outrun some prohis when they probably wouldn't have blinked an eye when they saw Becks in the front seat! And worse: knowing now that he was the one who led Flanagan and McConnell to the still; that none of this would've happened except for the actions of her pathetic bastard of a brother-in-law.

She barely restrained herself.

All of this was going to cost money. A ton of money. And Jed had emptied their load in the thirsty Arkansas ground. A load she had already been paid for by Merle; money she had sent home with Jed for Gran to take care of their bills.

She had Flanagan take her to the mayor's house.

"Jesus, Red, it's nearly eleven o'fucking clock." He had answered the door in his robe, his highly annoyed face taking in his late-night visitor. Shine registered a jolt of surprise to catch a glimpse of Randall scurrying behind the mayor in his robe, too. The mayor didn't show any signs that he had noticed, his eyes focused squarely on Shine, but he did shift his body slightly to more fully cover the opening. "This better be good."

It wasn't good. But it was enough to collect the sympathy and favor she sought. She could work at the Southern Club as a bartender. He would talk to Merle.

"But not till morning, for the love of God and all that is holy," he said, shaking his head. "Good night, *nurse*."

Now here she was at the Southern Club, getting the nickel tour from Merle.

"Shower and toilet are down the hall," he said. "Grub is on your own, but the cooks might make you something on the cheap if they're not busy.

"Drinks are on the house when you're off the clock," he continued. "You aren't old enough to drink though, if I'm guessing right. But hell, if you can hold your own glass that's good enough for me. It's up to you whether you can hold your whiskey."

Shine pondered this. Missouri didn't have an age restriction on alcohol consumption now and never had. But for some reason, Arkansas didn't have a drinking age until a few years ago—*after* Prohibition began. She wasn't sure what the point was.

"Show up at three thirty p.m. every day except Sundays." Merle paused. "And if you turn out to be a slow learner . . . well, I'm pretty quick to fire dead weight. Making shine doesn't really qualify you to sling drinks, no matter what the mayor thinks."

"Are the mayor and Randall related?" Shine flashed on the image of the two men in their robes at midnight. Something didn't make sense.

Merle rolled his eyes. "The mayor's a little funny. But he runs this town like a well-lubricated machine, no joke."

Shine frowned. She didn't think the mayor's sense of humor had been particularly notable.

Merle, as if sensing her confusion, grimaced. "Listen. All I'm gonna say is you got a lot to learn. Like keep your eyes open and your yap shut."

"Got it," Shine said. "Anything else?"

Merle's face soured further. "I'd watch my step when you're up here. You might get taken for a whore."

"Thanks," Shine said. "Smart advice. You might get taken for a genius."

Merle lifted a dark, woolly worm of an eyebrow. Her tone could mean she was either in awe of him or being a smart aleck. He didn't know her that well yet, but she could tell he was leaning toward smart aleck.

Careful. You need this gig.

After he closed the door—harder than they both knew was necessary—Shine sat down in the room's lone chair. She needed to think.

But first she needed to cry.

She didn't generally indulge in tears, saw them as weakness and a nuisance. Shine had never known what to say to make tenderhearted Elsie stop crying. Or her daddy, either, for that matter, when he was deep in his cups and the loss of Alta would return to him as fresh as that first day and turn his grief liquid, too.

Daddy, where are you when I need you?

She let her eyes brim over, swiping at the overflow hastily, as if someone might catch her. And when she felt emptied out at last, her eye sockets rubbed red and raw, she took stock of the room: the cracked plaster walls empty of artwork, one bare bulb illuminating every barren corner, the window showing the next-door building so close she could have thrown open the sash and touched it.

Fitting. She had run into a brick wall.

Shine did the math in her head. Again. And the numbers never came out any better. Merle had paid her the twenty-five-dollar down payment, then another seven hundred and twenty-five dollars in cash for both batches of moonshine. More money than she had ever seen, let alone held in her hands. And now one of those loads was soaked into a steep foothill of the Ouachita Mountains.

She had kept the deposit and an additional twenty bucks but sent the rest back with Jed. Now his car was going to need extensive repairs and she had no idea what Rebecca's hospital bills would be. Based on what the doctor said, it could be months. How would they pay for that?

And it was November. Getting too cold to make another big batch of shine; that would have to wait until spring.

Then there was Gran, alone on the farm. Elsie, big as a house—or with a baby by now—was living in town now, helping the Hansons at the store. Rebecca was supposed to return to handle the bulk of the chores; Shine, too, after dealing with the prohis. That was impossible now.

That left Jed, an apparent traitor and certified numbskull. He would be about as useful as tits on a boar hog when it came to farming. And Gran would as soon shoot him as look at him. That was a match made in hell if ever there was one.

Well, they'd have to be grown-ups about it. Everyone was going to have to chip in, shoulder the load. She would write Gran before her first shift at the bar. She needed some of that money to pay what they owed Merle for the wrecked batch of shine. If she was lucky, there would be some left to fix the car. She would put Jed and that note on the first Missouri Pacific train going north, which would get him as far as Hollister or Branson. He would have to make his way to Kinney from there.

And as for her? She would simply be the best bartender in Hot Springs, even if she didn't know an old-fashioned from a sloe gin fizz. Yet. The way she figured it, she might be stuck here for a few months, but the harder she worked, the more money she would make. And the quicker she and Becks could get back to Gran and the farm—and the Strong shine operation.

Shine stretched out on the bottom bunk without even putting on the sheets. She needed rest, something she hadn't had since the night before she pulled a gun on Flanagan.

Flanagan. That was a silver lining of sorts. Since she was stuck here, she'd have more time to track down that asshole McConnell. See if he was truly suffering and, if not, make damn sure he was when she left him. And she realized she was not averse to spending more time with Flanagan, who honestly seemed sorry for his part in what happened to Hiram. He wanted to help her, and right now, she was short on allies.

He had seen her at both her highest and lowest points. When she was carefree and making moonshine—then holding her daddy in anguish as his life drained away. And pointing a pistol at him across a dining room table, which felt like a bit of both.

She had seen him without a shirt. And that was a sight she wouldn't forget anytime soon.

Eyes closed, alone in the bleak room on the thin bare mattress, Shine's cheeks grew hot, there in the dark. Eventually, she slept.

Rebecca

She wished she were dead.

If she had come across a fawn in the woods with a shattered back leg, crushed ribs and a dislocated front leg, she would have shot it in the head without a second thought. And if Jed had been half a man, he would have helped her out of her suffering the night of the accident. She remembered him vomiting, like the chickenshit he was, when he looked upon her broken body.

Near as she could tell, no one was going to perform that merciful act for her today or anytime soon.

The first time she opened her eyes, she thought she actually *had* died and arrived in heaven. So much white. So many angels—also in white. She was surprised, given her religious leanings: she believed in a Creator and in nature; that was as far as she could go. But somehow, she had slipped through the pearly gates on that slim ticket.

But no. These were nuns. And she was in the hospital. St. Joseph's Hospital in Hot Springs, Arkansas. Rebecca wasn't familiar with Catholicism, so it took her a while to figure out that these were sisters, nurses. Not the heavenly host. She should have known by the sheer amount of pain in her body, which was not consistent with the lack of earthly suffering advertised by those with a belief in the hereafter.

She was lying down, her ruined leg hanging from scaffolding at the foot of her bed on a series of ropes and pulleys. There were beds on either side of her, other patients with various ailments and pains. Barely enough room for a nurse to squeeze in between. Or a visitor.

Shine was her first. Rebecca didn't know how she found out about the accident or knew where to find her. But she was there, the bright flame of her a welcome sight in this colorless, pain-filled existence.

"Hey, lazy bones," Shine said. "Lazy *broken* bones. What are you doing in bed? I believe I had scheduled a delivery and you're about two days late."

"And a dollar short," said Rebecca. She groaned from the effort of speech. Three broken ribs and a deep wound in her side where the metal moonshine container had cut into her. That part of the batch survived, Shine reported.

"But the rest of it . . ." Shine shook her head.

"That idiot Jed," Rebecca said. "He's alive and well, I suppose."

"He is," Shine said dispiritedly. "For now, anyway. He swerved to avoid hitting the tree. So *he* didn't. But you sure as hell did. Lost the shine in the back-seat compartments and the floorboards, too, which makes me madder than a hornet. And his daddy isn't going to be happy about the damage to the car, either.

"But not a scratch on him," Shine continued. "And that's not from living right. He asked if he could come see you."

Rebecca closed her eyes. If she ever saw that idiot brother-in-law of hers again it would be too soon. She wouldn't be here if it weren't for him and his misplaced sense of derring-do. None of them would be here if he hadn't done what he'd done.

"He can go to hell."

"Mmm-hmm. Told him as much myself," Shine said. "He's been staying at a place around the corner till I can get him on a train. The old Model A is going to take more money than we have to get up and running. But it's no skin off his ass. Three squares a day and nothing to do but drink and get up to all sorts of no damn good. If Elsie was picturing a pretty scene where baby makes three, she's gonna be disappointed."

"She should count herself lucky not to have to look at him twenty-four hours a day," Rebecca said.

"But that's all he's good for, looking at," snorted Shine.

"Not if I could get out of this bed and rearrange his smug mug with my two fists."

Shine laughed, in spite of her sister's complete seriousness.

"I mean it, Shine." Rebecca's face contorted. Getting worked up made the stitches in her side hurt. "He's no damn good. I'm pretty sure he ratted us out to the prohis."

"I *know* he did," Shine said. "Flanagan told me."

"Flanagan? But—"

"Long story. I almost shot him across the dinner table. He told me everything. How McConnell shot Daddy. And Daddy shot him. Anyways, I wish you'd told me sooner, Becks."

Rebecca grimaced. "I wasn't a hundred percent."

"Classic Becks." Shine sighed. "Well, the sad part is we're all married to him now, like it or not," Shine said.

"*Ugh*. Get me out of here," Rebecca said. "What's Gran going to do without me?"

"Becks, there isn't a whole lot she could do *with* you, given the shape you're in. The doctor says it will be months before you get your leg healed up and working again."

"We can't afford that," Rebecca said. "And we can't afford all this, either." Here, she waved her left arm, the lone limb she could move without causing herself pain.

"Don't worry, big sis," Shine said. "I got us covered. I'm a working girl now."

"What?"

"Meet the newest bona fide bartender at the Southern Club."

"But . . . a bartender doesn't make much. Moonshine is what's been keeping us liquid. So to speak." Rebecca smiled weakly.

"True enough," Shine said. "That's why, as much as I want to strangle Jed right now, we've got to get him back to help Gran with the farm and maybe another batch of hooch before winter. We got paid up front for the shine that ended up watering the Ouachita Mountains."

Rebecca heard a wobble in her baby sister's bravado.

"*Shit,* Shine. Are we going to be okay?"

"Don't worry." Shine gave Rebecca a confident pat on her good leg. "Bartenders may not make a good wage. But I've heard the tips are terrific."

Shine

The first time he came into the bar, Shine nearly dropped the bottle of whiskey she was holding. She had heard of him, how he liked to come down from Chicago to drink, gamble and carouse. But she never expected to lay eyes on him herself, let alone serve him a cocktail.

Al Capone. Gangster. Bootlegger. Murderer. And regular vacationer in Hot Springs. Scarface loved to golf, visit Happy Hollow Amusement Park, bet on the horses at the racetrack and—like everyone else—take a nice soak in the healing waters.

It was about four o'clock in the afternoon on a Tuesday and things were slow at the Southern Club. So slow that Merle had gone out to take care of some business and left Shine in charge.

He hadn't liked the idea of a woman behind the bar; it wasn't done. He believed females belonged beside the male customers, encouraging them to drink too much and linger too long at the craps table or roulette wheel. Or on the third floor, flat on their backs, with whoever had paid for their time or services on top.

"Or however they like it," he said with a smirk.

Shine didn't like that smirk. She didn't like Merle, who let her know there might be *other* ways to help repay her debt. But she loved being behind that gorgeous lacquered black bar. Shine was a fast study, learning how to make anything and everything the thirsty crowd at the Southern Club might desire—an old-fashioned, sidecar, gin rickey or Tom Collins. Drinks neat, straight up or on the rocks. Martinis that were dirty, extra-dirty or downright filthy.

But she was at her best when she went off script. If someone answered her "What'll you have?" with "What's good?," Shine was off and running. She loved showcasing the Strong moonshine, with its smooth burn or fruity flair. And Shine often cut the standard spirits with sparkling sodas or fruit juices. The women who frequented the Southern Club loved her concoctions, so much more delicious to sit and sip than a cheap unadorned glass of hooch that hit your innards like a hot burning coal—and was almost as tasty. Why just drink to get drunk when you could enjoy every swallow along the way? Shine calibrated the right balance of sweet, sour and salt in her creations, plus she knew how to finish, garnish and heighten a drink's appeal with a salute to Lidy: snippets of rosemary, thyme and basil; crushed mint; colorful slices of strawberries, melon and peaches; hot peppers and cool cucumbers along with the standard olives, lemons and limes.

Plus, Shine had a certain charm. Who could resist being told by an attractive, flame-headed young woman to "stop swilling the cheap stuff" and "hang on to your hat" as she set down a cocktail she came up with especially for you?

Everyone loved her. She was good for business. *Very* good.

The squat, dark man in the rumpled linen suit and black-banded fedora was intrigued. He had his boys keep an eye on the Southern Club from their fourth-floor room at the Arlington and let him know when the redhead was serving up drinks. He had gotten bored with his standards—Manhattans and Southern fizzes—because everyone was afraid to make his drink wrong. So they made it exactly to order, every single time. He should have been flattered to inspire such fear in the hearts of the bartenders of Hot Springs that they kept their cocktails uncomplicated. But Al Capone was a man of insatiable appetites—and restless, too. He was on vacation, and he was tired of drinking the same stuff he got in Chicago, served up with the same deference.

Two of his men had left him in the car to scope out the club, and returned with the "all clear." Capone stepped out of the 1928 armored Cadillac with the inch-thick glass and solid rubber tires that he kept in Hot Springs. Even though the town was off-limits for hits and Mafia-related revenge, Capone had been targeted once on his way back to the Arlington from another club. Afterward, he had the nearly ten-thousand-pound Caddy shipped to Arkansas on the Rock Island Railroad.

When he slid onto a barstool in front of Shine Strong, she was immediately drawn in by this sallow-skinned, jowly man with the dark circles under his eyes. They were the same on some level, willing to do whatever it took to survive and to keep their families safe and cared for. Maybe their means and definitions of "family" were miles apart, but the end goals were aligned. He was smart. And he understood people very, very well.

Just like Shine.

Her hands trembled around the slender neck of the bottle of rye and she gripped it tighter. Her gran would say he's just a man. *Puts his trousers on one leg at a time like everyone else.*

Shine placed a napkin printed with the Southern Club name in front of her first customer of the evening.

"And what would you like, Mr. Capone," Shine said, her matter-of-fact voice belying her anxiety at serving the biggest of the big-time gangsters.

"I'd like very much for you to call me Alphonse," said the man, removing his hat.

Shine didn't believe in getting overly chummy with her customers, preferring professional distance—even as she captivated them with her blunt, folksy charm. But this was Al Capone. It couldn't hurt to have a man like that in your corner—especially if your main gig was making and moving moonshine.

It sure wouldn't be good to have him as an enemy.

"All right, then, Mr. Alphonse. What would you like to *drink*?"

Capone's dark eyes sparkled.

"I'm on vacation," he said. "I want someone else to decide what I'd like for a change. You got a problem with that?"

"Nope. I love being in charge, Mr. Alphonse. Ask anyone in my family. Or around this joint. I've been here one month and they're accusing me of bossing them like I own the place."

"I am not surprised, Miss . . . ?"

"Call me Shine," she said. "Shine Strong."

"Are you kidding me?" The lines in the gangster's brow deepened. "A bartender named after hooch?"

"Not exactly how I got my nickname. But yeah. As I like to say, everyone loves the 'Strong stuff.' "

"Then I'll have a glass of the 'Strong stuff.' However you see fit to dress it up."

This would be fun. *If* she didn't have a heart attack doing it. She could substitute a garnish or a mixer for either of his usuals and call it her own. But that would be the same drink with different window dressing. Or she could start with his favorite rye whiskey—Templeton Rye, from way up in Iowa—and riff on that. Predictable. Almost cheating.

Shine wanted to knock old Alphonse's well-made socks off. And showcase her family's own brand of shine. If it went well, who knew what that could mean for the Strongs? Now was not the time to play it safe.

As if Shine would ever play it safe.

She reached below the bar to her stash of "extras" and removed a gorgeous, ripe peach, from a last-of-the-season batch brought all the way from Texas. Grabbing a sharp knife and a cutting board, she quickly cut the fruit in half, expertly slicing between its fuzzy round shoulders along the suture. Once cleanly halved, the peach easily popped out its pit when she touched the tip of her knife beneath it. She set half aside and quickly diced the other into pieces. She chose a rocks glass from the shelf behind her and filled it with fresh ice. Then she threw a handful of dripping peach chunks, a sprig of mint and a spoonful of her brown sugar simple syrup into a silver cocktail shaker, muddling the contents briefly but thoroughly—too much muddling would make the mint taste bitter.

Capone was mesmerized by all the activity on his behalf. Then she added ice, two shots of the Strong's peachy shine and rattled that shaker like her life depended on it. Maybe it did.

She strained the chilled liquid into the glass, splashed ginger beer on top and then garnished the sunset-colored drink with fresh mint and a peach slice.

Shine placed the glass in front of Capone; it was perfection.

Capone raised an eyebrow. His two bodyguards at either end of the bar watched with interest in the ensuing silence. By Shine's count, it was a full fifteen seconds. Enough time for sweat to trickle down her armpits.

The gangster raised the glass to his mouth and took a large swallow. It was so quiet she could hear his throat open and close. Capone placed the glass back on the bar. But his face, lined with three visible knife scars on the left cheek and neck, showed nothing.

"What do you call it?"

"I haven't named it yet," Shine admitted. "It's an original. What would you call it?"

"Damn good," Capone said, his mouth quirking up on one end. "This is what vacation *should* taste like."

Shine and the two men on either side of the bar relaxed at the same time.

"The 'Damn Good' it is then," Shine laughed. "And you know where to find it."

She left him to his drink. The late-afternoon regulars were beginning to trickle in, filling in the stools at the bar and needing her attention. She noticed, however, that Capone was given wide berth.

A few of her customers—Jimmy, from the cigar shop at the Ohio Club, and Bert, from the mayor's office—surreptitiously asked her to serve them up "what *he* was having." Before long, the

Damn Good was sitting pretty in front of a whole slew of men and women at the Southern Club bar. When Shine was able to take a breath, Capone was gone.

But beneath his empty glass, there was a twenty-dollar bill.

The first of many. Because for the rest of his three weeks there, Capone made the Southern Club his first stop on Tuesdays and Saturdays, before heading to the racetrack. He requested the Damn Good until the peaches ran out. Then he gave Shine her orders.

"Surprise me," was all he said.

And she did—sometimes more successfully than others. But Capone enjoyed the unpredictability, something he wouldn't—and couldn't—tolerate in life outside of Hot Springs, Arkansas. The one thing he insisted stay the same was the bartender: he wanted to be served by Shine herself.

The last time had been the best.

She had made Capone the Shine Strong version of a "Southside," one of his go-to drinks, named for the district of Chicago where his men were king. It was typically made with gin, lime juice and fresh mint, but Shine mixed some of the last of the Strong shine in the lime juice, in lieu of gin, then garnished the drink with a jalapeño instead of mint.

"Whattya call it, Shine?"

"I call it the 'Hot Side,'" she said slyly. "It'll put the 'hot' in your springs."

Capone had laughed, waving for a second drink for his associate on the stool beside him. They were obviously talking business, something Capone was generally loath to do while he drank. It must be important.

"When I sell liquor, it's bootlegging," Capone groused. "When my patrons serve it on a silver tray, it's *hospitality*."

She hadn't meant to eavesdrop. But it was second nature as a bartender, surrounded as she was by the chatter of the bar customers, the waitstaff, the cooks in the kitchen behind the swinging doors calling out orders and barking at each other or anyone who got in their way. Her ear filtered out what she wanted or needed to hear, whether it was a fresh drink or someone asking for the check.

"I've had two runs busted in the last two weeks," he said to the man in the pinstripe suit beside him. "Two trucks full. Prohis dumped our shine into the street and it was like someone busted open a hydrant. Jesus. I can't afford that kind of hit on the regular."

"Gotta be a way to disguise the stuff better'n that," the man agreed. Shine got the feeling the man would agree with anything Capone said. Not that she blamed him.

"Excuse me, Mr. Capone—"

"Alphonse."

"Yes, Mr. Alphonse. I couldn't help but overhear . . . and well, I once heard a prohi say that sometimes the best hiding place is in plain sight."

The heavyset gangster scooted back on his stool, amused. "You don't say? And you know where I might find some plain sight to hide my hooch?"

"Well, you mentioned the shine running in the streets like water," Shine began, nervous now that all eyes were on her. *Me and my big mouth.*

"What if you use Mountain Valley Spring water trucks to move your shine? Those trucks deliver big glass bottles of water all over. Your stuff's as clear as water. Who would know the difference?"

There was a long pause. Shine stifled the urge to prattle on, watching Capone's brow wrinkle. Was he angry? Or simply thinking? Then he slapped the bar with his open palm.

"I'll be *goddamned.*"

The gangster threw back his head and laughed; his yes-man followed suit.

"Shine, you're pretty bright." Capone chuckled at his own joke. "And you might be onto something."

He left her a hundred-dollar bill. Nearly a third of her debt, erased! Shine, elated, picked up the cash and found a business card, too, scrawled with a name and address in St. Louis.

"In case you want to do your own thing," Capone said, as he got up from his stool. "A friend who can help you get started."

Shine managed an unsure smile.

"Don't worry," Scarface said, as if she had said something out loud. Had she? "Totally on the up-and-up. Friend of my sister's who knows the mayor there. I know you're an honest gal. Mostly honest, anyway."

He gave her a crooked grin.

She heard later that Mountain Valley had been bought by an outside businessman. Rumor had it the giant glass bottles could only be distinguished as water or moonshine by someone who knew Capone affixed the shine labels upside down. Anyone else seeing the truck laden with "water" bottles wouldn't give it a second glance.

Genius.

Lidy

The old Guernsey cow rolled her cud around, chewing absentmindedly as she kept one bored brown eye on Lidy, standing near her hindquarters with the milk pail. Lidy struggled to bend her creaky spine enough that her bony backside could meet up with the wooden stool. Getting up was even harder. But she managed it once more, taking satisfaction in the feat every time. She was old, but she could still milk a cow.

Lidy started with a few long strokes high up on the udder with her thumb and forefinger, then curled her remaining fingers around one of the teats as she pulled down, expelling the milk. The squirts hit the pail in a metallic rhythm and soon she had covered the bottom with frothy white. Lidy thought about what she might do with what the cow provided. Maybe let it sit so that the rich yellowish cream would rise to the top and allow her to make a batch of butter, keeping the rest for a hot milk cake for Elsie.

Rich cream and skimmed milk. They spoke to Lidy of haves and have-nots. While she had never felt destitute out here on the mountain, they had never had extra. But more than many. The Strongs owned their land and had always saved their own corn seed, put up their own hay. They never missed a meal, even if they were scraping the bottom of the flour bin or eating last season's mealy potatoes.

But times were harder now, and not only for farmers. She had heard stories of the runs on the banks. City folks lined up around the block to retrieve the hard-earned dollars they had deposited inside the walls of those buildings purported to help them save and grow their investments. Money that—somehow—could no longer be touched, stacked, folded or separated from its reluctant fellows with a freshly licked thumb. Imaginary money, it would seem, since there was nothing but paper ledgers to vouch for its existence. Disappeared. There was desperation; men in three-piece suits flinging themselves from the tops of skyscrapers as an alternative to facing total financial ruination for themselves and their clients. And families.

Lidy found it hard to wrap her mind around the idea that money could evaporate into the ether. Made her proud of the way she had squirreled away cash in a tin can when she could and paid her debts. Avoided credit at Hanson's. What people were calling a "panic" seemed far away, a gray-black cloud on a distant horizon, destined to pass them by.

Until a few weeks ago.

Eugene Sacks had been the first to show up at her cabin door, hands shoved awkwardly in his front pockets. He hemmed and hawed, mentioning the dry weather and potential for a hard winter. Lidy asked about his wife and their grown son who had a family of his own now.

"Gene, let's get down to brass tacks," she said, thinking of the logs burning low in her woodstove and the water she needed to heat for her hard-boiled eggs. "What brings you here? You and yours enjoying good health?"

"Yes, Miz Strong, thank you for asking."

The man's clothes were worn thin but clean and neatly patched. He kept his eyes on his boots, their scarred leather tops tied to the soles with rawhide to extend their lifespan.

"I hate to ask, with all the troubles you've had," he said. "But your son give me an I.O.U. for some fence posts and shingles. I was hoping to let it go after he passed but . . ."

The man produced a grubby piece of paper with torn stitching holes at the corners: a label off some type of feed sack, the back with a dollar amount written in pencil and Hiram's scratchy signature.

She paid him. She had the money Jed brought back from Hot Springs from that first run of shine. There had been bills for Hiram's coffin, repairs to the still equipment. Another large barrel for mash. But she had about half the money left.

But soon there were more empty hands and hangdog looks at the door. Hiram had borrowed the neighbor's bull to service his cow with the promise of compensation. The mule that replaced the one gone lame last year hadn't been bought outright, but with a signed note given in lieu of payment. And that didn't even cover the debts she found on her most recent trip to Kinney. Seemed everyone had a note from Hiram or a tab she hadn't known about: the farrier, the saddle shop and, most discouraging, the barber shop—which apparently had a hush-hush saloon hidden in back for those who needed fortifying before, after or instead of a shave or haircut.

"Sorry to dun you, Miz Strong, but times being what they are . . . I can't let it go. I know you understand."

Lidy's face turned crimson. She didn't question any debt, knowing Hiram as she did. She berated herself for wanting to believe that they were getting by better and more easily than seemed possible. She had been blind to his borrowing, like she had ignored his weakness for drink. It was all of a piece. The hiding of sins, the burial of grief and pain beneath the thin veneer provided by alcohol.

She should have known better. Dug deeper. Paid closer attention. Hiram was battling for his life and livelihood long before the shootout at the still.

So she squared all the debts, using nearly every dollar she had. But once Jed, Rebecca and Shine came home with the cash from the second batch of shine, they would be more than all right.

Lidy rose from her stool with a groan and patted the cow's rump. The milk pail was full to the brim, thick and foamy with bubbles.

She frowned, noting the creamy surface marred by a large black fly, frantic and drowning in the white sea.

She reached with one gnarled finger and flicked it out. The creature, dazed and wet, sputtered in the dirt at her feet.

She stepped on it.

Lidy pushed open the barn door, careful not to slosh the milk. There, across the barnyard, sitting on the front porch as if she had conjured him: Jed. He held his head against his hands, which were clasped as if in prayer, his elbows resting on his knees. One of the Hansons' horses was tied to the corner post, switching its tail to worry away the horseflies.

"I never thought I'd say it, but you're a welcome sight, son."

Lidy expected one of his full-of-himself grins. But he didn't raise his head.

"Jed?"

The young man in front of her didn't dress like her grandson-in-law. He was ragged and filthy, a knobby knee sticking through a hole torn in his brown pants, shirt untucked and shoes with broken laces tied in knots rather than bows. And when he finally looked up at Lidy, she gasped. Jed's usually lean handsome face sported a scabby raised cut on the forehead, his greasy hair hanging on either side like soiled wet straw.

"What in the world . . . ?" Lidy had so many questions crowding her mind, the whys and the whats and the hows. But one made her go instantly cold; she couldn't keep it back.

"Where's Rebecca?"

It didn't take long to sort. Jed held out the crumpled envelope from Shine, the note inside written with her granddaughter's typical combination of bravado and understatement.

Lidy looked up at Jed. "She needs three hundred dollars. And she's asking as though I should have it."

Jed didn't blink, his blue eyes cold as cat-eye marbles. But his jaw clenched.

"Something tells me we've been taken," she said. "But only one person knows for sure."

Nothing.

"Are you going to tell me where the rest of that money went? Or am I going to have to beat it out of you?"

Jed lowered his eyes. "It's in the car."

"The car? Well, why didn't you collect it before you came home? I swear, you don't have the good sense God gave a goose!"

"I mean, I put it *into* the car. The new taillight rig, the storage compartments behind the back seats, in the floorboards. Souping up the engine. Rebuilding the suspension to handle the extra weight . . ."

Lidy's heart sank. "There should still be some left, even so."

Jed still wouldn't meet her eyes.

"You been cattin' around, son? Wasting funds on women and whiskey?"

"No women," he said. He had the nerve to sound indignant. "But a few whiskeys. And I might've put some on the horses down there in Arkansas. I was going to make it up to you all, I swear—"

Lidy slapped him hard across the left cheek. Shock flashed across his features and he reached up to touch his face, striped with the imprint of her fingers. But before he could say anything, she delivered another crack to his right with her open palm, rough and reddened.

"You *might've*?" Lidy spat. "Well, you *might've* thought of someone other than yourself for once in your goddamn pitiful life. That wasn't your money. That was *our* money. And I'll be taking it out of your hide," she said. "You best get yourself to town and let your wife know you'll be staying here sunup to sundown, except for Sundays.

"And knowing Elsie, she'll have your worthless ass on a hard church bench when you aren't here.

"You'll get to decide which version of hell is worse."

Elsie

Elsie loved every minute at Hanson's General Store, spending most of her waking hours behind the counter she had once stood in front of with longing and awe. Her father-in-law had seen the potential right away in her beauty and bubbly nature. And her work ethic.

"She is a welcome addition up front," said Charles Hanson, thinking of the way the register rang with sales to his female customers seeking the right fabric for a dress or ingredient for their cabinet. Not to mention the men, who might order more than they needed of almost anything to spend more time in conversation with Elsie.

Meanwhile, Clara Hanson was delighted to watch Hi while Elsie helped Charles at the store. She had never enjoyed the necessary small talk that sales required. And it made her deeply uncomfortable when a customer had to ask—again!—for credit when she knew getting repayment would be like squeezing blood from a stone. She left Charles and Elsie to it, preferring to bathe and powder her grandson, and send each of his perfect piggies *to market, to market to buy a fat hen* and then revel in his giggles.

"The light blue of this gingham shows off your eyes," Elsie said to Nan Giddings, she of the notorious never-buying, always-time-wasting ways.

"Do you really think so?" The woman held her purse handles

tightly, but she leaned in toward the counter to look more closely at the cloth that Elsie unfolded with flair on the oaken countertop. "Hmmm."

She took home two and a half yards, smiling all the way.

"Nice work, daughter-in-law." Charles Hanson gave her a curt nod.

Elsie let out a satisfied sigh. It felt good to show her own value to the general store and the Hanson family. Especially with Jed helping her gran with the farm while her poor older sister recovered enough to return. She and Hi were two more mouths to feed, bodies to clothe and house. Neither of the Hansons made her feel beholden. But Elsie had seen the tense line of Charles Hanson's jaw and the vermillion vein that throbbed at his temple when he looked over his ledger books. Extending credit to someone who didn't have the cash for their cornmeal and flour. Or needed a new wheel for a hay cart. A tonic for an ailing child. And those ledger pages contained something else: a tally of money owed and paid for the goods themselves. Costs had risen with wholesalers, too, leaving the Hansons in the uncomfortable middle, losing money on both sides. They had needed a few credit extensions themselves.

Elsie had always thought that people who had money and a grand home didn't have real worries. That their hardest decisions might be about, say, the precise color of lace for finishing a fine new dress or the best make and model of a shiny coupe or roadster.

Her Bible said that God "maketh His sun to rise on the evil and on the good, and sendeth rain on the just and on the unjust." Rich and poor alike. She had told herself rain wasn't nearly as bad when you had an umbrella, a fancy parasol provided by money and privilege.

But she had learned this wasn't true. Charles Hanson anguished over customers not having enough to eat, unable to scrape a living out of the dusty earth. He knew he could stave off suffering for a while if he wished to do so—and he did. But the books were getting bleak and his demeanor along with them. Elsie swore his dark hair had turned white overnight.

And what of her own troubles?

Dog tired from long days on her feet behind the oaken counter and evenings devoted to Hi after she relieved Clara from her grandmotherly duties, Elsie was weighed down by the knowledge that her husband had hurt both their families with his recklessness. She knew Lidy had given Jed the what-for. And while she didn't know exactly what Charles had said to his son when he confessed the Model A as a total loss, that dressing-down had Jed silent and morose for days.

Jed had left for Hot Springs as a man with a puffed-out chest and straight spine, full of confidence in what he would do as part of this new family. What he could do. But a month later, he was a changed man.

"Jed!"

Her heart fell when she saw him. Filthy. His clothes stained with sweat and the cumulative detritus from his journey in train cars, hay wagons, and farm trucks and on his own two feet. Mile after mile on red clay roads had ground his good leather boots down to nothing. His dark blond hair fell in greasy strips to his collar. And he smelled of strong liquor.

Clara was there, too, wide-eyed with worry and Hi on her hip.

"Meet your son," Elsie had said, taking the baby from her mother-in-law and holding him out to Jed. An offering. A gift. A prayer. "This is Hiram. Hi. He's been anxious to meet his papa."

Jed didn't say a word. His red-rimmed eyes focused briefly on the infant before he hung his head.

"I need a drink."

"What you need is a hot bath and a good night's sleep."

Elsie handed Hi back to his grandma. Then she hustled Jed into the house, running the deep clawfoot tub full of steaming water. She helped him remove his ruined clothes and loosened his broken, knotted boot laces. Then Elsie sat down on the toilet beside the tub and begin to pour water over her husband's back and head. She scrubbed him with a washcloth and a bar of rosemary soap, rubbing with the ferocity with which she had formerly attacked a stubborn stain on a washboard. His skin reddened as it finally gave up the grime she swiped at, relentless in her task. But even when there was nothing left to scrub, she kept at it, lathering and scrubbing, hoping to find her husband somewhere beneath it all.

And he hadn't touched her once. She had covered his face in kisses, stroked the stiff back that was turned toward her in their bed. But it was as if he was afraid to see his failure reflected in her face, her eyes. In the person who had worshipped him, bowed down to his beauty and charm, overlooked his shortcomings and taken pride in the man that she had shaped and fashioned into a worthy partner.

"Dear Lord, please bring my husband back to me."

She had whispered the same prayer on her knees for weeks, wishing him home and safe. And now that he had returned, she found herself continuing the same plea, night after night, week after lonely week. She prayed that his work on the farm would heal him, return him to wholeness. So when she saw him on those precious Sundays, they could restore their tenuous connection. Go to church together. Share a meal with his parents. And find sanctuary in each other's bodies in that four-poster bed. She asked that they could be a family, her and Hi and Jed.

A family with a mama *and* a daddy. It was all she had ever wanted.

Rebecca

The hospital stay was excruciating. The way the doctor and nurses manipulated all the ropes and pulleys on her devastated leg. She refused the pain medicine as soon as she was conscious and able to push away the spoonfuls of morphine she was being proffered by those bulky white angels hovering at her bedside. Rebecca didn't like the way the medicine made her mind hot and foggy, the bad dreams—of being chased, hunted and trapped with no means of escape—that came with it. Her mouth dry, as if full of feathers, in the mornings.

But worse than the pain was the boredom. She passed the time in between Shine's visits by writing brief, unadorned letters to Lidy and Elsie, missives with a mention of a lunch menu or a thunderstorm. Or she stared out the high window of the ward, where she could see a branch of a walnut tree and the birds who perched there: mostly dull sparrows, but occasionally the burst of cardinal red that made Rebecca feel as if life might be worth living.

If she could get out of this place.

"Doc, I can't take it anymore," Rebecca said. "I'm going to make a break for it."

Dr. Peebles, a harried but kind older man, looked over his black glasses with alarm. "You realize, Miss Strong, that you can't walk, let alone run, at this point."

"I know. But I can't survive in here much longer. I'm about to rip these cables off and take my chances."

"Well, you've been here for six weeks now—"

"Six weeks and two days."

"As I was about to say, it's early, but I could send you to the baths for healing. And massage, to bring the blood to your muscles and promote strengthening."

"I'll sit in a tub of boiling hot water if it means busting out of here," Rebecca said. "But I've been drinking the stuff since I got here. I don't think it's helped one whit."

"You'd be surprised what the minerals in that water are doing. Healing you can't see," the doctor said. "I'll write you an order for the baths and massage, once a day for two weeks. Then we'll go from there."

Rebecca's eyes started to sting—and she was not a crier. "I can't afford that, Doc."

The doctor looked surprised. "Your sister has had no trouble covering your bills," he said. "She told me to do whatever it takes to get you up and around again.

"And I must say, it's very difficult to say no to your sister," the doctor added, his tone that of someone who had tried and failed. "She seems to believe nothing is impossible."

"Nothing is," Rebecca said, "for Shine."

The next weeks were grueling. Rebecca was released from her cast and the contraption on her bed that had been supporting her leg, but walking was still impossible. It took two of the strongest sisters to get her out of bed and onto a gurney so that she could be driven to Bathhouse Row—and everything Rebecca had not to scream out as she was transferred to the back of an ambulance. The pain in her leg was a violent stab; she feared passing out or throwing up. But she swallowed her suffering; the more normal she acted, the quicker she would be released.

And the ride to Buckstaff Bathhouse! She felt every bump, rock, pothole and rut on Central Avenue like a personal assault, staring up at the roof of the ambulance and wishing she *would* pass out. Sometimes she counted backward from a hundred to divert her attention; in darker moods, she enumerated the ways she would like to make Jed suffer for doing this to her.

Unloading was painful, too. Rebecca was hoisted from the gurney into a sitting position in a wooden wheelchair by the ambulance driver and one of the young Black bathhouse employees. But sitting up felt more dignified, even with her troublesome leg sticking out ramrod straight in front of her. *Progress.*

Central Avenue was lined with enormous southern magnolias with glossy green leaves, which softened the look of the gorgeous tan brick colonial bathhouse. Eight stately white columns stood like sentries across the front, with tall arching windows on the first floor between each pair of columns. The second story had square windows beneath the building's entablature with "Buckstaff Bathhouse" in all-capital roman letters; a shorter third story above the facade hosted decorative concrete vases between each of the seven windows.

Rebecca surveyed the staircase, which was also quite grand—both in width and number of steps—and wondered how she would ever make it inside. Worse, a number of bathhouse patrons were sitting in rocking chairs and wheelchairs or standing at the base of the building's many columns. She didn't want an audience.

But she needn't have worried. The same muscular man who had unloaded her into the wheelchair pushed her to the bottom of the stairs. He spun her chair around and proceeded to bring her up backward, one surprisingly gentle bump at a time. *Bless you.*

Once inside the foyer, he turned Rebecca's chair forward and pushed her toward a large marble reception desk. She gawked at the minute tiles that made up the expanse of floor around her: the central part in front of the desk consisted of white hexagonal tiles, dotted with black-centered gray flowers made with hexagons, too; the sides were banded by gray square tiles lined in dark orange and broken up by black and orange geometric patterns. It made her head spin.

The young man took a left, past the staircase at the side of the reception desk, and deposited Rebecca in front of two metal doors that closed together in front of some hidden room or passage. "Miss Blanche will take you from here."

A large light-skinned Black woman in a short-sleeved white dress acknowledged Rebecca and punched a button before grabbing both handles of the wheelchair from behind. A bell sounded and the doors in front of her slid open, disappearing into the frame of the door. Miss Blanche pushed Rebecca into the metal cage that barely had room for her wheelchair, plus her attendant's sizable body.

To Rebecca's amazement, the doors closed and there was a metallic groaning before their cage began to rise up off of the floor!

"What in the—" Rebecca's stomach felt as if it had dropped out of her body and stayed on the first floor of the building. "Let me off of this thing!"

"Pardon, ma'am, this here's the elevator. It's the best way to get you upstairs," Miss Blanche said. "Women go on the second floor, men on the first. Don't you worry. You're safe as can be."

Miracles never ceased. Maybe this was the first of several she would experience here in this place that promised healing. Rebecca had just begun to relax when the crazy ride was over. The doors opened onto a large open room where a half dozen Black women of various ages, all wearing the same type of white dress as Miss Blanche, sat around a rectangular table. Their dying chatter echoed off the tile walls and floor as Rebecca was wheeled into the room.

A short, muscular young Black woman with her hair slicked back beneath a white headband rose from the table.

"Eulalie, this here's Miz Rebecca Strong," said Miss Blanche. "She's supposed to have a bath and massage."

"Pleased to meet you," Rebecca said.

Eulalie eyed her curiously. "Good Lord in heaven. Ain't you a sight!"

"Now, mind your mouth, Eulalie," Miss Blanche said. "Sorry,

Miz Strong. She's one of the best here and the doctor says you're supposed to have the best. But you won't ever have to guess what's on her mind."

Eulalie wheeled her to the dressing room, a long line of stalls with curtains that slid back to reveal wooden benches where one could sit to remove clothing and a metal locker in which to store belongings.

Rebecca felt a surge of panic, an urge to flee. But how? And on what? She looked down at her left leg, shrunken from disuse even above the knee. And the calf where both leg bones had splintered and barely avoided amputation? Desiccated, like the smoked skin of a chicken wing dried and stretched over its frame, no meat to speak of. Rebecca wasn't going anywhere.

"You used to being the strong one, huh?" The young woman parked Rebecca in the back of the room and came around to face her. "Well, best get used to some help. I imagine we'll both know when you don't need it anymore."

Eulalie pulled several towels and a crisply folded white sheet from the cubicle shelves on the back wall, placed them on Rebecca's lap and resumed their journey into the adjoining room.

More miniature white hexagonal tiles, broken up by the occasional blue and gray hex design, shaped like snowflakes. But the room was anything but cool, with steam vapors rising toward the ceiling in wispy clouds. A long row of soaking tubs stood against one wall, each in its own private stall with a white sliding curtain. Large pipes ran along the wall with spouts directing the hot spring water into each tub, which was mounted with an agitator to make the water bubble while the patient soaked.

Eulalie pushed the wheelchair into one of the stalls and pulled the curtain closed. She took the stack of linens from Rebecca's lap and placed them on a metal chair.

"Ready?" Her dark, wide-set eyes were gentle, as if she did not want to hurt Rebecca—even with her gaze. Eulalie tilted her head slightly and Rebecca understood she was asking for permission.

She drew a deep breath. "Okay."

Carefully but efficiently, Eulalie began removing Rebecca's clothes—first the gown-like top from the hospital, then the graying undershirt that served as a both shirt and brassiere for Rebecca's boyish frame. Her lean chest barely suggested breasts, and Rebecca had never cared for the suggestion. She preferred a tight man's cut that kept her slight curves out of sight and out of her way.

But having someone else remove it made her self-conscious of her body. Not solely her breasts, but also the jagged scar down her side where the moonshine container had punctured her and broken her ribs. She was not merely unwomanly, unattractive; she was broken, damaged. Not fit for the human gaze. She closed her eyes.

Eulalie kept at her task. Rebecca felt her presence, kneeling beside her. Her sure hands coaxed her undergarments down the straight lines of her hips, beneath her bottom and then down each leg. She tried imagining that she was getting ready for a plunge in the deeper parts of Kinney Creek at the base of their mountain, skinny-dipping with her sisters when the July heat made any other activity unbearable. She wasn't self-conscious with them; they knew each other's bodies like they knew each other's minds, noting the differences without judgment. How delicious it had felt, drying on a flat rock beside Shine and Elsie, feeling the sun warm through every inch of her skin, the shadows of tree limbs crossing her closed lids, the sound of a dragonfly buzzing nearby and landing on one bare shoulder. It never lasted long. Fair Elsie had to retreat to the shade of the trees after twenty minutes. Shine got bored and quickly took to throwing pebbles at her older sister, Rebecca ignoring her until the pebbles became rocks. Forced to rise, she would chase her sister into the depths with threats of death or dismemberment, Shine laughing wickedly, egging her on.

Shine. They were miles away from Kinney Creek now, weren't they? Swapping their innocence and ice-cold creek water for this outlaw town with its thermal springs and promise of an easier life.

Easier money. But it had been a far sight from easy. She wanted to go home.

When she opened her eyes, Eulalie was peering into her face. "You all right?" She made her way to the faucet, where with a quick turn of her wrist, she unleashed a steaming torrent of water into the deep, rectangular tub.

"Knock-knock." A musical voice outside the stall announced another attendant, who ducked inside the curtain. Another set of assessing eyes. But Rebecca felt no longer felt judgment; it was more like the taking of a pulse or listening to a heartbeat. She was exactly how and what she was, and that was okay with these women. "Mmm-hmmm. We got you, Miz . . . ?"

"Rebecca."

"That's a nice name. From the Good Book," the tall, wiry woman said. "I'm Maybelle. You ready, Eulalie?"

Moving in synchrony, Maybelle got behind her, reaching under the arms, while Eulalie took her legs, careful to keep them together and touching the wounded one as lightly as possible. And as if they had counted to three—although Rebecca heard nothing—they had her up and into the hot water.

"Ouch!" The water was boiling hot. Rebecca looked down at her naked body, certain she would see her skin come off in this roiling, steaming water.

"I'm just so much stew meat," she said, dejected at the sight of the wasted muscles, the raw red scars—and not realizing she had spoken her thoughts aloud. But Eulalie let out a hearty chuckle.

"You feeling sorry for yourself now, Miz Rebecca Strong?" Eulalie reached for a scrub mitt. "I can throw in some onions so you can have yourself a good cry." She paused for a beat. "Or you can decide to get better."

Rebecca was grateful now for the scalding water that reddened her skin beyond its ability to show shame. She *had* been feeling sorry for herself. But this woman bent beside her tub, so intent on scrubbing her skin to bring the blood to the surface and reinvigorate her shrunken flesh: she would not abide it.

It hurt—the sloughing of skin, the unknotting of desiccated muscle—but Rebecca understood that she didn't have to be in her pain alone. She had never asked for help in her life. And now she wondered . . . *why?*

She began looking forward to her time at the Buckstaff. The gradual lessening of the pain until—over the days and weeks—there became room inside her to feel something else.

Shine

Shine had never had a friend before. She hadn't needed one; she had her sisters. Her memories always involved tagging along with Elsie and Rebecca. Trying to keep up on the walks to the one-room schoolhouse near Kinney. And once she got there, learning as fast as she could, longing to join them in the upper group. She had no use for her peers, zero interest in gossip or fashion or tittering about love and who was sweet on whom. It was bad enough to listen to Elsie carry on about those subjects on the walks to and from school while she and Becks pelted each other—and occasionally a dismayed Elsie—with hard green walnuts or lumpy Osage oranges.

But Birdie had somehow become her friend.

Shine figured she had seen the last of her after she pulled her pistol on Flanagan that night at the boardinghouse. She knew she wouldn't be seeing Bernyce Ward and the rest of them anytime soon. Or ever.

She had no regrets.

So it had surprised her when, in an almost identical reenactment of their first meeting, Birdie stuck her head in the door of her bunk room at the Southern Club.

"Fancy meeting you here," Birdie laughed. "If you don't mind me saying, you look like you could use a little company."

Before Shine could reply, Birdie had breezed in, carrying a hand valise and a hatbox, managing to close the door in her wake.

"And I could use a place to flop."

"But—"

"But nothing! Old Bernyce threw me out on my ear."

"I hope it wasn't guilt by association."

"Naw. Plain old regular guilt." Birdie looked around the room and decided on the bottom bunk, beneath where Shine slept. She tossed her bag on the bed and headed to the closet door, where she found a shelf for her hatbox.

"Perfect." She flounced down on her new bed across from Shine, who was seated on the room's single chair, polishing her boots.

"Well. What was the last straw?" Knowing Birdie, it would be interesting.

"Nothing special. I blabbed my mouth about goings-on at the Southern Club one too many times," Birdie said. "I guess it was hard for Bernyce to keep pretending I was a goody-goody seamstress when I knew the big roller on the craps table the night before. And who was three sheets to the wind!

"She came to my room with a favor, some mending she needed done. And I mean to tell you she had an evil twinkle in her eye," Birdie went on. "Asked me to patch a glove and hem a bathroom curtain.

"I said I'd do it, thinking I'd sweet-talk someone into doing it for me later. But *no.* Bernyce said she'd be happy to keep me company while I did it. Since an expert such as myself should have both things done lickety-split.

"I guess I don't need to tell you how that went." Birdie rolled her eyes. "I couldn't thread a needle to save my life and when I finally did, my stitches looked like something a two-year-old might make.

"She got this pleased look on her face and thanked me. Then she told me I could pack my bags and find a place more suitable for girls like me.

"So, here I am," Birdie said, her tone jubilant. "Can't say I'm sorry to be out of there. Now I can get that promotion I been promised. Working out at the tables. More money. Nicer outfits. Getting my drinks for free."

"Oh, Birdie," Shine said, frowning. "No. You don't want to do that."

"You can't have all the fun up front, Miss Bartender. My boss talked to Merle. It'll be so much better than being a washer-woman. And I'm not getting any younger," she said, batting her eyelashes at Shine. "Nineteen and not yet married? I gotta get out of the laundry while I've still got my looks."

"I'd much rather wash the Southern Club sheets than get them dirty," Shine said firmly. "You can do better, Birdie. I know it."

Birdie's eyes flashed. "I *am* doing better, Shine Strong. I may not have a head for figures like you, but I got a figure that turns heads. Might as well use what the good Lord gave me.

"I'm supposed to sit there, make pleasant conversation and look pretty," she went on, sticking out one shapely leg, turning it this way and that, as if checking her stockings for runs. "You know, make sure everyone's ordering plenty of drinks and putting money on the tables. It's perfect."

Shine shook her head. "There's more to it, I'm afraid."

Birdie laughed. "It's good money, Shine. And I don't mind co-zying up for it. The way I see it, a few good months or maybe a year? I'll meet someone interested in more than one night. Some-one who wants Birdie to make a nest with him. And if I don't?" Here she shrugged. "I'll have plenty of money in my purse, a few nice frocks and shiny new shoes for a change.

"Try to be happy for me, Shine."

In that moment, Shine saw Elsie. Stunning, younger and more innocent than her years, with dreams and ideals that were never going to be realized. But who was she to say a person couldn't dream? Or hope?

Or maybe—just maybe—get lucky.

"I guess I won't mind having you around."

"Thatta girl," Birdie said, clapping her hands with glee. "What shall we do first?"

Shine couldn't deny it: Birdie made life a lot more fun. Gave her something more to do than ruminate on how she was stuck in this town and this job. When Shine was behind the bar, and business was slow, Birdie would perch on a stool and pass the time with silly stories and her analysis of everyone and everything going on at the club. She shared Shine's distaste for Merle, and loved to imitate his short-man swagger anytime he was out of sight, wiggling her eyebrows for effect.

"Shine, you missed a spot," she would say, pointing to a nonexistent place on the immaculately polished bar. "For someone named Shine, you're a pretty dim bulb!"

The two of them would laugh together—deep belly laughs—until the swinging doors behind the bar would flap open and Merle's irritated mug would appear.

"I'm running a business here, not a hen party," he would grump. "Put a lid on it, ladies."

And even when business was hopping, Shine and Birdie would exchange knowing glances: which man needed another round, whose pockets were empty and could be—gently but firmly—ignored. Who was in the dough. Shine loved hearing her laughter, cutting through the smoke and the clicking of dice and ice cubes in near-empty glasses. Birdie made every moment a party.

But Sundays were the best: a full day off. No obligations at the Southern Club. Birdie would shake her awake and have a plan together before Shine could wipe the sleep from her eyes.

Sometimes she and Birdie would go off on an adventure. Like the time they went to the alligator farm. Birdie knew someone; the brother of one of the dishwashers at the club. Herm was his name, and he let them in without paying. It was good for business anyway, two good-looking young women like them, laughing and having fun amidst the emus, monkeys and alligators. He even took their picture sitting beside one of the docile gators—a large ancient specimen named Doc—and made it into a postcard.

"Aren't we something?" Birdie was elated. "I swear, Shine. This place is the craziest town on earth. Alligators and gangsters and tons of hot, bubbly water coming up out of the ground like magic. I wouldn't go back to the farm if you paid me a million dollars. Well . . ." Birdie considered this. "Maybe a quick trip back for a cool mil. But this is my town now. It makes me *feel* like a million bucks, you know?"

"I would love to go back to my farm. With Rebecca," Shine said. "And you wouldn't have to pay me. I miss my gran and Elsie. I'm an aunt now, Birdie. And I haven't even met my nephew."

"Well, the fact is, we're both flat broke. But we're in the right place to remedy the problem. We'll find some good-looking businessmen to marry," Birdie said, twirling a piece of her long blond hair. "It's a matter of time."

"I've told you I'm not interested in settling down."

"But what about that handsome fella who keeps showing up? Mr. *Smith*. He must have a good job. He's got a car. And he's obviously sweet on you."

"It's not like that, Birdie." Shine's throat got blotchy in an instant, her entire face not far behind.

Birdie sat back against the steps that led to the alligator farm gift shop, crossing her legs at the ankle and smiling skeptically. "Okay then, Shine. Why don't you tell me what it's like?"

Rebecca

When Dr. Peebles discharged Rebecca from St. Joseph's, it was difficult to know who had been more relieved, Rebecca or the good doctor. The entirety of her five-month stay, she had hounded him, pleading her case any time the poor man dared peek his head in the room.

He didn't, however, release her from his care. Even though she begged him and her sister to have mercy. To send her home to Missouri. But Shine stood firm with Dr. Peebles: Rebecca needed to get stronger, to get along on her own two feet. She had to be able to navigate the journey—including stairs, uneven streets, and sidewalks—without help.

"Believe me, Becks, I'd have you on the first train back to Missouri if I could," Shine said. "Lord knows Gran and Elsie want you home. But we both know you can't do it alone. Yet."

Shine had even investigated a round-trip train ticket for Eulalie to accompany Rebecca, after her sister had remarked on how the bathhouse attendant innately understood where her pain was—and how to move her to minimize it.

But Shine found out there were rules. No one who looked like Eulalie was welcome in a passenger car that carried white people. And Rebecca wasn't allowed in the colored car, either. The sisters didn't understand it. Because while they hadn't seen any Negroes before coming to Arkansas, they had quickly grown accustomed to the various shades of humanity that peopled the streets of Hot Springs. In fact, there was a thriving business community on Malvern Avenue, right off Bathhouse Row, with Black-owned hotels—like the National Baptist Hotel—plus the Pythian Bathhouse, physician offices, barbershops, restaurants and music venues all along what had become known as "Black Broadway" standing alongside white ones.

But as successful as they were, they were separate. Just like the train cars.

So instead, she hired Eulalie to help Rebecca with her rehabilitation. It wasn't much money, but with the dwindling hours and clientele at the Buckstaff these days, Eulalie had welcomed the supplement.

"She can even stay with me if you like," Eulalie said. "Since I'm tending to her anyway. My roommate and I wouldn't mind some help with the rent. *If* you all are comfortable with that," she amended.

Rebecca couldn't imagine a place or a person—outside the farm and her own family—that she would feel more comfortable with. Eulalie had become a friend.

"She's like you, sis," Rebecca said, talking it over with Shine. "Says her mind. No BS. And she doesn't let me get away with anything."

"Sounds perfect." Shine had been relieved. Her plan had been to beg Merle for one of the extra bunks in the room she shared with Birdie and—occasionally—other "girls" who crashed there after a hard night's whoring. But the Southern Club had two flights of stairs and no elevator. It wasn't feasible.

So Eulalie took her home, a ground-floor apartment she shared with another woman, June, from the Buckstaff. It was cramped but convenient, right by the streetcar stop at Malvern Avenue.

That first night, after a simple supper of collard greens that rivaled her gran's, June excused herself and began making up her bed on the living room couch. Eulalie guided Rebecca to the bedroom and showed her the single bed where she would sleep.

"But . . . what about you?" Rebecca asked. There was a kerosene lamp on a rickety bedside table and a worn oval rag rug on the floor between the one twin bed and the door.

Eulalie pointed to the rug. "I'll be right here. In case you need me."

"I can't let you sleep on the floor!"

"Well, *you* sure as hell can't sleep there," Eulalie said. "I'll be fine. It's only a few weeks. Till you're ready to fly the coop."

She opened the cramped closet and pulled out two extra blankets, making a pallet and pillow beside Rebecca's bed. She gestured for Rebecca to sit down on the bed. Just like at the bathhouse, she removed Rebecca's shoes and stockings, worked the pants down the long legs, navigating gently the right thigh atrophied above the scarred knee and lower leg. Rebecca removed her own shirt down to her thin undershirt. She didn't feel ashamed anymore; she had grown used to Eulalie's deft and gentle touch.

She eased down and Eulalie helped her lift her legs into the bed, turning her on her side to face the wall how she liked it. She tucked a sheet and then a blanket around Rebecca's body, which nearly touched both the headboard and footboard with its length. When Eulalie was satisfied, she rested a hand briefly on Rebecca's forehead before removing it.

"Good night."

"Good night," said Rebecca. She heard Eulalie undressing; soon, the kerosene lamp was turned down. There was the rustle of blankets as Eulalie nested, made herself comfortable. A sigh.

Just a resting stop on my way home. She closed her eyes and tried not to think about all the hard work that lay between her and Kinney. One step at a time.

It was a miracle.

That's what Dr. Peebles said when Rebecca was finally able to walk on her own. She bore some terrible scars on her side; her right leg was misshapen and the way the bones had knit themselves together made it a good inch shorter than her left, giving her a distinct limp. And although she would never admit it, she still hurt and knew she probably always would.

Rebecca would say her healing was *not* a miracle—not in the sense of some inexplicable transformation from broken to whole. Healing had been hard work. Daily soaks in Hot Springs mineral water and massages that loosened her muscles and eased her pain had helped. But mostly it was the countless hours of rehabbing, using the equipment in the gym at the Fordyce Bathhouse. Samuel Fordyce had spared no expense, outfitting the place with peculiar machines designed by the Swedish physician Gustav Zander that had become all the rage, with "Zander Institutes" popping up all over Europe in the mid- to late-eighteen hundreds and New York City, too.

Stretching, leg lifts, spine alignment, torso twisting: Zander mechanotherapy machines were designed to address a person's every weakness, defect or ailment using weights and levers to vary resistance—and Rebecca did them all three times a week, with Eulalie helping her in and out of each contraption. There was a chair rigged for a seated user to strengthen their biceps with a series of pulleys and levers mounted at the sides, a vibrating bench to help with digestion and even an undulating, saddle-like metal seat, meant to mimic the healthful effects of horseback riding for those who were unable to mount a real animal.

"It's no Marge," Rebecca commented sourly.

Eulalie had also accompanied Rebecca on her physician-prescribed walks in the hilly park behind Bathhouse Row. The government land was laced with walking trails designed by German physician Dr. Max Oertel and completed fifteen years prior to improve visitors' heart health. The graduated trail system was color coded, and Rebecca had worked her way up from yellow to green and blue and now, finally, red.

At first, Eulalie had taken her on the easiest route, pushing her to the trailhead in a wheelchair and then handing her a pair of crutches. Then a walker. Eventually, Eulalie offered her arm. After a month or so, Rebecca graduated to a cane. Now she carried it mostly for confidence—and to keep Eulalie from hovering as Rebecca made her way painstakingly up the trail and back down, quicker every time. Although she did miss holding on to Eulalie.

"Becks, you're about ready to take me in a footrace," Shine said. She and Flanagan often joined the pair for a Sunday afternoon walk after searching for McConnell, though Rebecca didn't care for onlookers. But Flanagan knew when to keep his mouth shut, unlike her sister. "What do you think, Eulalie?"

"I think I don't want to witness that." The compact woman at Rebecca's side shook her head, amused by the sisters' banter. Mostly one-sided, as Shine talked a blue streak and Rebecca barely spoke. "I can tell neither of you likes to lose."

"That's the Strong in them," Flanagan said sagely. "They can't help it."

Maybe the Strong women couldn't help who they were deep down, that core of pure obstinance and determination. But grit and guts had stood them in good stead so far, the same qualities that kept Rebecca pushing herself day in and day out. In the gym. On this hillside.

No, her healing was not a miracle by any stretch. But she did believe that something mystical had happened to her here in Hot Springs.

Some*one.*

John

He still stayed at Bernyce Ward's when he came down to Hot Springs from Fort Smith every couple of weeks, although he knew if the old woman suspected he was anywhere close to Shine Strong, she'd give him the boot.

"Fat chance," Shine said. "That woman has a thing for you, even if she is twice your age. Maybe *three* times! It's pathetic."

"Well, a fellow's got to take all the good will that's offered," Flanagan said mischievously. "Pathetic or not."

"*Hmmph.*"

The two usually met for breakfast—Flanagan footing the bill. Shine protested at first, but eventually relented; she wasn't used to being treated. He could almost feel the tally marks clicking in her head, who owed what to whom. Flanagan kept track of the number of times he got her to smile. Let down her guard. She was a double-walled castle surrounded by a moat—and the water was full of starving alligators. But Flanagan wasn't one to shy away from a challenge.

They spent the day driving around Hot Springs and environs, pulling over at gas stations, dry goods stores and a few ramshackle houses right on the road. Flashing around a photo in hopes of finding leads on Flanagan's old partner. But so far, no luck. It was as if the old prohi had set out from Happy Hollow and walked—somehow, some way—off the edge of the earth.

"There was a time when every speakeasy in New York City had this guy's picture behind the bar," Flanagan told Shine. "Everyone knew R. J. McConnell. For better or worse."

"Worse, I'm sure."

John understood why Shine had no love for the man who had so brutally taken her father from her, even if he was old and sick as stink. She likely found it curious that he felt such an obligation to the problematic prohi. John wasn't sure he understood it himself. Beyond the brotherhood of the badge and bureau, his loyalty stemmed from believing McConnell's intentions were good—even if his behavior was at times unpardonable. Like when alcohol had his own father in its throes.

At any rate, Shine had promised not to kill McConnell on sight, and it was an agreement he dearly hoped she would honor if they ever laid eyes on him.

This Sunday, they decided to try Bathhouse Row again. McConnell had loved his soaks in the thermal springs, even if he hadn't liked the arsenic shots and mercury rubs. Maybe he was still managing to get treatment somewhere. John and Shine made their way up Central Avenue, inquiring at the Lamar and the Buckstaff, the Ozark and Quapaw and—finally—the grand Fordyce.

The bathhouse's beauty was dizzying, with high marble-covered walls and a terra-cotta fountain on either side; stained-glass clerestory windows tinted the light that hit the sparkling ceramic tile flooring. This was Hot Springs's finest bathhouse, financed nearly fifteen years earlier by Samuel Fordyce, a wealthy railroad tycoon who credited the healing waters with saving his life. He spared no expense, intending to build a spa that would rival the best in Europe.

Shine stood beside John in the lobby, mesmerized. So much grandeur down to the last detail. There were signs to the bowling alley, the billiards room, a reading lounge, rooftop garden and the spas—one side for men, the other for women.

"Oh, I wish Elsie could see this! And Gran," she said, turning in a slow circle and gaping at the painted ceiling. "Gran would be complaining it's too much. Wasteful! But Elsie would want to try everything, the more wasteful the better!"

A few customers waited in comfortable, high-backed chairs. One well-dressed woman in an elegant feathered hat with an open book on her lap stared at Shine. Registering the gaze, Shine stuck her tongue out at the woman, who quickly went back to her book.

The visit to the front desk didn't take John long.

"No luck."

Shine frowned. "Wait. If the man is broke, he wouldn't be in a place like *this*, would he?" She threw a glance toward the woman in the hat.

"True," said Flanagan. "The pamphlet at the desk advertised nineteen dollars for a course of baths. That's nearly a dollar a day, and his pension—if he is even getting his check—wouldn't come close to covering that."

"Excuse me, sir?" The young desk clerk in a neat gray dress beckoned to Flanagan and Shine. "I couldn't help but overhear," she said. "If your friend is indigent . . ."

"He's as white as we are," Shine interrupted.

"She means *poor*," Flanagan said, apology in his voice. Shine looked mortified.

The young woman cleared her throat. "We offer free bathing to those with no means. All the bathhouses do. But it requires a physician's order. If you think he's not under a doctor's care, I'd suggest the Government Free Bathhouse. They can't refuse anyone under law. But you won't find it on Bathhouse Row." Now it was her turn to blush. "It used to be called the 'Mud Hole.'"

"Thank you kindly," said John. "Could you point us in the right direction?"

They backtracked their way down Central Avenue until they reached Reserve Street, which took them along the edge of the park. But John and Shine didn't stroll or linger along the way like the other couples there. They walked briskly in lockstep, looking for the free bathhouse supposedly four blocks in.

Unlike the impressive architectural masterpieces along Bathhouse Row, the unassuming white brick building they found was a single story. But it was a far sight from "Mud Hole," newly constructed and clean. That was a relief; John did not wish to see McConnell wallowing in actual mud, fitting as it might be.

Inside, a frazzled desk attendant barely registered the photo that Flanagan held out.

"I'm sorry," she said, peering over her glasses. "We get so many people here. Sometimes several thousand a month."

"Please. He was my partner. We were Prohibition agents together."

"A *prohi*?" The woman's spectacles slid a quarter inch down her nose as she studied John intently.

"Yes, ma'am," Flanagan said. "*Former* prohi. Both of us."

The woman reached for the photograph and studied it. "Well," she said, doubt in her voice. "We did have a regular always bragging about his time as a prohi. Said he loved throwing bootleggers in the slammer."

"Sounds like McConnell!"

"But he was older, skinny as a rail. Covered with blisters. We sent him to Army and Navy up the hill, assuming a government man like him probably served. Couldn't ask him. He wasn't making any sense at that point. Pure gibberish. I don't remember a name."

Flanagan's shoulders fell. He sensed Shine beside him, her spirit sagging along with his. The whole thing was hopeless.

"When was this?"

"A few days ago? Maybe a week." The woman pushed her glasses back up on her nose. "Now, if you don't mind, I need to get back to work."

Shine

The Army and Navy Hospital stood above Bathhouse Row, high up on Hot Springs Mountain, abutting the large green expanse of the park, with its walking trails, scenic views over downtown and the Rix observation tower, poking up above the trees. When creating this first general hospital for both Army and Navy personnel nearly fifty years prior, the government had chosen the location solely for its proximity to the healing waters. Now the building was in transition, the original wooden structure being systematically replaced by a brick, mortar and steel behemoth that would hold five hundred beds.

"I don't know about you, but I've about had my fill of hospitals," Shine said to John from the passenger seat of his dusty black Plymouth. "Rebecca got sprung from St. Joe's and not a second too soon. It's a marvel anyone gets well in a place like that. All those weak whiny people lying abed, getting served trays of overcooked food and being poked and prodded every minute of the day!

"And the smells! If you aren't sick already, that's enough to get you there," Shine said. "Give me one of Gran's cures and a kick in the pants any day."

She was chattering; she knew it. Like some silly, empty-headed girl. But she was nervous. She knew the chances of McConnell being here were slim to none, but . . . Flanagan seemed hopeful. Or maybe he was happy to have a lead, no matter how unlikely.

Shine stole a glance at him, his countenance serious as he guided the car up the curving road on the backside of Hot Springs Mountain to the front of the hospital. She liked his calm blue eyes, so fair in the way they assessed a situation; his unruffled demeanor, so unlike hers. She—unsurprisingly—had been in such an all-fired hurry to get there that she had suggested going on foot, using the stairs that started from Bathhouse Row, and included hundreds of steep steps to the top of the hill and the hospital's back entrance.

"Trust me, it's faster to drive," he had said. "And I know you love a good shortcut."

Shine could not argue with that, even while she wondered if he might mean she played fast and loose with the law. Was that a smile tugging up the corner of his mouth?

Inside the hospital, John and Shine headed to reception, only to have their hopes dashed: R.J. McConnell was not a current patient.

"I'm sorry," the clerk said. Her silvery-gray hair was braided and pinned in a coil atop her head. "I wish I could help."

"But my partner was quite ill, so he wouldn't have been discharged quickly. We were told he was speaking nonsense when he was brought here. Do you have a separate facility for people with addled brains?"

Shine was impressed. The mild-mannered ex-prohi was tenacious. Insistent but not obnoxious.

The clerk pursed her pale lips. "There is one other place he could be, I suppose."

John and Shine leaned in.

"The morgue."

"You mean . . . he's *dead*?" Shine hadn't come all this way to find her mission already accomplished.

"If he's there, then yes, he is most assuredly dead," the clerk sniffed.

"Sounds simple enough to check," John said. "Could someone show me to the morgue?"

"*Us*," Shine chimed in. "Let's go."

* * *

She shivered. The morgue was an antiseptic cold, delivering a sharp clean bite to the skin and the inside of her nose. She flashed back to her karst cave hideaway with water so cold it hurt to touch it. That cave had been so full of life: the exuberant greens of lichens and moss, the silken rainbow skin of a trout, delicate brown and pink crawdads, their shells made rosier by the water.

This room was full of death. White walls, silence. And in the center, two sheet-covered forms on a gurney. She inched closer to Flanagan.

Dr. Reynolds—a nervous middle-aged man swallowed up by his long white coat—approached the first body, his black dress shoes echoing off the empty cement-block walls. He began to turn down the sheet of the first form, gesturing for Shine and John to come nearer.

Shine gasped. The man's long sallow face was missing part of its cheek and jaw, revealing an ulcered tongue, white and patchy, and blackened molars. The lips had been eaten away, giving the corpse a disturbing grin.

John's hand found her elbow, steadying her. She allowed it.

"Mouth cancer," Dr. Reynolds said. "Left mostly untreated. Does he look familiar?"

Shine and John shook their heads. Even with half the face missing, they knew this wasn't their man.

Dr. Reynolds revealed the top half of the second body, bare and hairless. The man was short and emaciated, extra skin puddling around him like a second sheet. His body was pocked with ulcers and lumps, dulled by death into a mottled grayish purple. The skin on the fleshless face had pulled back, the skeletal grin showing two rows of rotten teeth.

Shine covered her mouth. Flanagan cringed.

"This isn't him, either," Shine said. She recalled the day at the farm when Flanagan and McConnell had shown up, nosing around. How the fat bastard got stuck in their smokehouse. There wasn't enough fat on this man to make a single strip of bacon.

The doctor had started to cover the man up when Flanagan let go of Shine and reached out to stop him.

"Wait," he said. "Would you mind turning him over?"

The doctor couldn't hide his surprise. "What would the point of that be?"

"Just being thorough," John said. "I'm sorry. It's my training. But I think I'd rest easier knowing I'd left no leaf—or body—unturned."

It took both men to flip the corpse over, even though it wasn't heavy. The cold stiffness made the body completely uncooperative, and for one awkward second, it looked as though it might roll off the gurney. Flanagan stopped it with his hip.

John drew in a sharp breath. The naked backside was wide, flat and ashen from its time on the cold, steel table. In addition to sores and ulcers, there was a scattering of dark, freckle-like spots on one chilled cheek.

"It's McConnell!" he shouted. "Why, I'd know that derriere anywhere! I spent hours bent over it with a pair of tweezers, trying to get out the buckshot he took in the backside from an unhappy moonshiner. Couldn't get it all. He may have—or be—less of an ass now. But the pellets don't lie."

Shine couldn't believe it: the months of searching for the man who killed her father were over. And she couldn't exact a single sliver of justice. Or put the fear of God in him. Curse him, shame him, tell him off. He was already dead. The son of a bitch was beyond any earthly pain she could inflict.

Shine turned and fled the room, her footsteps echoing down the basement hallway like repeated open-hand slaps to a face. Up the closest stairs. Then out the dense wooden double doors that gave in reluctantly to a ferocious shove of her hands.

Alone at last, she collapsed against the back of the building, an expanse of brick broken up only by the occasional window and vent. Shine reared back her head and howled, a painful exiting of all the grief she had set aside on the bank of that creek, holding her father's bleeding head in her lap and setting her sights on vengeance. That hate and hope had fueled her, kept her going. With McConnell gone, she had nothing left but her own pain.

Sobbing, she slid her back down the brick wall, the rough bricks catching at each vertebra of her back through her cotton dress until she was on the ground, her forehead pressed against the tent of her skirted knees. She wanted to crawl inside the hurt and disappear. Drown in it. Die. *Now what?*

Then the groaning gasp of the heavy doors again and Flanagan was there, yanking her to her feet, pulling her against him. Her whole body shook as his arms locked around her, quieting her with their strength, like a tuning fork vibrating until touched by something solid and still.

And then he held her tighter.

When she pulled away at last, swiping at her face with her sleeve, she found herself looking up into a concerned pair of piercing blue eyes.

"I . . ." She didn't know what to say. *Thank you? Leave me alone? Please . . . just hold me. A little longer this time. Maybe forever?*

She was cried out, flat and empty as an old flour sack. But before she could figure out what to say, Flanagan put a gentle hand on either side of her face and kissed her.

Somehow, they made it back to the entrance of the Southern Club. It wasn't a long drive; neither of them spoke.

When he opened her door, she tried to rush past him, desperate to put the frigid finality of the morgue behind her. Shaky and vulnerable, she did not feel like Shine Strong at all. She didn't know who she was without someone at whom to funnel all her hurt and rage, her grief and disappointment.

And that kiss!

After the initial shock of his lips on hers, her body had answered his soft questioning kiss for her, a warm tingling spread through her faster than a mountain wildfire, and before she could think, she was closing her eyes, pressing her mouth back against his. *I'm melting.*

What *was* that?

Wrong, that's what it was. They weren't on the same side. She had been fooling herself to think they ever could be. How could she forget that John was part of it, the hole in her heart that was Hiram? Despite his efforts to make up for his partner's crime, his own inaction.

Flanagan caught her by the wrist.

"Shine. I'm sorry. I shouldn't have—"

"Stop." She couldn't look at him. She had fallen completely apart in front of him, shown weakness when she needed to be tough and resilient. And she was a traitor.

Because she felt a genuine sadness that this was over. Whatever *this* was. More than a hunt; a shared mission. She had enjoyed partnering up with Flanagan, counted the days to the weekends when he returned to Hot Springs determined to find McConnell. Walking the avenues and streets of the city with him, careening the curved roads in his car and exploring all the nooks and crannies, hills and hollers of this land of vapors.

Like the steam from the thermal springs, those times had vanished into thin air. What had brought them together was gone. Dead. Cold and stiff in a sterile hospital basement. And there couldn't be anything more.

She pulled away. Flanagan let go of her wrist. "I'm so sorry, Shine. Please, let me help you."

"I think you've helped enough," Shine laughed bitterly. "I need to get out of this hellhole. There were two things keeping me here, debt and payback—and it looks like McConnell's headed to hell without my assistance. So, once I pay what I owe to the club, I'm free and clear."

"I could—"

"No." Shine's pride couldn't take another hit. "I don't want your money. Get on back to the Bureau. Put away some real bad guys or something."

John's shoulders slumped. She was glad to share some of her hurt, pass it around.

"Well." He paused, at a loss. "I'll be at Bernyce Ward's the next few days. I'll get McConnell out of the morgue and into a plot somewhere. Try to locate any family. Let the guys at the Bureau know. Then I'll head back to Fort Smith."

When she didn't respond, he dug in his pocket, fumbled to open his wallet. "Here's my number. If you need anything. *Anything.* Just call."

"I won't." Shine turned on her heel toward the back door of the hotel, which she opened with a flourish—and slammed with a bang.

Flanagan was left standing by the open car door, his mouth similarly agape, unable to form words that might stop her.

But at least she had taken the card.

Rebecca

At first, the evenings after supper with Eulalie and June were mostly spent in conversation or companionable silence. June was a farm girl from around Crow's Station and she loved swapping tales with the new roommate. The crops of that rich land by the Saline River differed from those on the Strongs' hardscrabble mountainside—but the hard work and occasions for hilarity were much the same. But Rebecca could tell that Eulalie was antsy. That she wouldn't have stayed home if it weren't for her.

"Go on," Rebecca said on the third night, when she saw Eulalie glance at the clock for the fourth or fifth time in as many minutes. "Don't let me stop you from going out or doing what needs doing. I don't need a babysitter."

Turned out that Eulalie loved this new music—jazz—that had made its way from New Orleans, snaking up from the Mississippi River the same way the bluesy sax and syncopations crawled up her spine and made her want to dance and sway. Kick up her heels after a day spent bent and sweating at the Buckstaff. She loved it all, from the big names who could fill the auditorium at the Woodmen or unknowns at a hole-in-the-wall off Malvern.

"But—"

"I'll be fine."

Rebecca had never been afraid of being alone. And it thrilled her, each night, watching Eulalie's transformation—magnificent magenta-flowered dress and pair of purple heels replacing her Buckstaff whites; touches of warm color to her cheeks and lips; eyes rimmed with kohl, enlarging their dark beauty. She made Rebecca think of her gran's zinnias, bold and brilliant, every compact petal distinct, popping against the backdrop of brown garden soil.

And later, in bed, she smiled to hear Eulalie slip in the door, humming, the smell of cigarettes, sweet perfume and sweat permeating the darkness. She pretended to be asleep, relishing the ritual as her friend paused beside her bed, touching her head gently; a simple, silent good night.

But one night, as Eulalie put on her hat and Rebecca opened a book, she looked at her ward and waggled a finger.

"Uh-uh. Not tonight," Eulalie said. "It's my birthday and you're going with me."

Rebecca had protested. Used every excuse she could think of, from her limited wardrobe to her limp. But her friend insisted.

"Girl, you may be alive. But I can tell you: you ain't living. Let's go."

It was a blur. Stepping into that dark hazy room, reverberating with the jaunty rhythms—a combination of blues and ragtime, plunked and pummeled; brass and keyboard, voice and drum. Contagious. Dangerous. And the way the musicians played their pain, blew out their agony and chased their joy. Rebecca had not heard or seen anything like it.

Eulalie helped her into a seat at a back table and slid into the chair beside her. Rebecca must be a sight—a raggedy white country girl dressed in dungarees in a room full of dark faces. But after a few heads turned briefly she realized: no one was looking at her. She gave herself over to the music then, yearning along with it, keeping time by tapping her hand on the tabletop. Delighting in the laughter that spilled over from the low-lit, drink-filled tables and onto the dance floor.

She didn't drink; she didn't need to. Looking around, breathing in the smoky damp air in the hot room and watching the swirl of colors as men and women moved together, dancing closer than their own shadows: it was as intoxicating as it was loud. Attempts at conversation were futile—and that was fine. It was enough to be inside the music, with her friend. For a few hours, she forgot the hurting, the jazz soothing and massaging her from the inside out.

Rebecca didn't want it to end. But those few hours were taxing. She wasn't used to so much walking, so many people. So much sound, color, emotion. Eulalie sensed it and tugged at her sleeve, pulled her slowly to standing.

Time to go home.

She slept as soon as her head hit the pillow. But while her body was exhausted from a morning of pushing her limits at the gym and the walk to and from the club, Rebecca's mind was keyed up from the jazz; from all that teeming humanity in one room. Her dreams were tangled, a combination of the familiar edged with danger, strangeness. She was in the woods, hiding behind a red oak, watching Shine and her father tending the mash pot. It was idyllic, the vibrant rich greens of summer and the accompaniment of birdsong: cardinals and Carolina wrens, punctuated with the percussion of the pileated woodpecker. Rebecca could happily inhabit this space, this time, forever. Her sister's laughter, her father's smile. She didn't feel excluded, but as if she were sharing in the warmth of their bond, a bond that she helped to create and protect.

But then: gunshots. And in her dream, Rebecca could not lift either her Winchester or her feet, all leaden and rooted in the ground like the tree that sheltered her from view. But not from seeing.

"No!" she cried out, her lungs gasping, body sweating. Yet still she couldn't move, forced to watch her father and sister cut down like so much firewood littering the bank of the creek. Why couldn't she help? Why wouldn't she do something? Anything?

Rebecca awoke, blanket thrown off, sheet damp and twisted between her legs. Her heart beat like a bass drum, frighteningly loud in her ears. For a moment, she didn't remember where she was. Her face was wet; she had been crying.

But then there was that hand on her brow. The reassurance that she was okay, it was a dream. A terrible dream. Eulalie unwrapped the sheet from Rebecca's legs, taking care not to jostle the scarred one. Rebecca felt cool relief as the sheet was flapped and straightened before fluttering down around her body once more. The blanket replaced lightly on top.

She closed her eyes, facing the wall once more, and exhaled, grateful for her friend in this place.

"What would I do without you?" she whispered.

To her surprise, the sheet and blanket at her back rose slightly, letting in the cooler air of the room.

And a warm body.

Eulalie slid in beside her and curled her compact form around Rebecca's longer one. Even through the nightdress, she felt Eulalie's thighs and knees against the back of her own, the woman's stomach firmly against Rebecca's bony rear, Eulalie's breasts pressed against her back. She stiffened, the entire length of her body on alert in the darkness. What would happen next?

What did she hope would happen? Every nerve and sinew of her body came alive in the safety of that bed, her eyes wide open. Eulalie brought her arm over Rebecca's side and rested a hand on Rebecca's stomach. She felt all five fingers and palm on her skin as if she had been branded. But no pain. Simply the pleasure of touch, which she hadn't realized she needed, so different from the cool efficient hands of a doctor or nurse. Or a bathhouse attendant.

Eyes still open, Rebecca took the hand from her stomach and slowly guided it to her chest until it rested there. A pause. The only sounds were their breathing, hers and Eulalie's, synchronized. Eulalie's hand cupped her small breast and she closed her eyes. Her nipple hardened beneath the sure palm.

Rebecca felt the imprint of Eulalie's mouth, soft on her shoulder. The body behind hers suddenly felt as natural and necessary as a second skin. As if the two of them shared the same breath, a heartbeat.

It was like coming home; to a place and a feeling that was both familiar and unknown. Traipsing across the hilly woods of her Ozark land, taking worn paths and exulting in the landmarks of trees and creek and clearing in search of an elusive critter or bird. Finding instead something new or breathtaking where she least expected it: a clutch of minuscule bluebird eggs in a cavity where she had only seen woodpeckers, a spotted fawn curled nose to tail in the brush of an untended fencerow, a hollow oak that homed a hive of bees, its walls of waxy cells thick with golden honey.

The comfort of sameness, the astonishment in the unanticipated.

Eulalie's warm hand on her heart felt like a blessing.

HEARTS

1933

Shine

Time both crawled and sprinted by. Night after long night the same, and yet the calendar turned at a fast clip. Like those flip books Shine had seen, where the drawing changes almost imperceptibly from page to page, but when you fan through them rapidly with your thumb, there is the appearance of movement, of motion.

Shine wanted desperately to move on, head home. But the severe slowdown and stagnation of the nation's economy had finally hit Hot Springs. It took exponentially longer for coins to add up to dollars, stunting her ability to pay her debt. Capone was in prison—and no one had tipped her better, before or since.

"You can go a long way on a smile," he'd told her once. "But you can go a lot further with a smile and a gun."

All she had was her smile—having hocked Hiram's pistol months ago—and it was worn thin.

But she kept going, even though she felt like a prisoner. Three years in, Shine still serving up drinks to the wide swath of humanity that frequented the club with her trademark sass and creativity. Any given Saturday night, she was equally happy to hand a frou-frou cocktail to the good Christian woman who would be holding her aching head in the church pew the next day as a straight-up bourbon to a banker, baseball player, bootlegger or a big-time criminal like Capone. She had even gotten used to waiting on the occasional unconventional couple—a pair of men or women who gave off an almost imperceptible aura of "more than just friends," even if they rarely touched. So unlike the men and women who couldn't keep their hands off each other, cozied up at the craps tables or deep in the corner cushions of a high-backed wooden booth. Shine understood it was different for those couples. Like the mayor and Randall. They were typically discreet. But she felt their connection, as intense and real as any other. Maybe even more so because of that public physical restraint.

But no matter who you were—or who you came with—once you made it through the door at the Southern Club, you were *in*.

Sure, there were a pair of well-dressed men at the doors—crisp black suits and shoes polished to a shine that rivaled that of the sleek black bar—checking to make sure you had the right word or the right friends. But once inside, the world was your oyster. Whether you fancied a game of blackjack, a turn at the poker table, a cigar at the bar with a stiff shot of whiskey and a pretty arm hang, it was yours for the asking.

As long as your wallet was full.

But still: there were customers who rubbed her the wrong way. The kind who spoke down to her or looked through her as if she was as transparent as an empty highball glass. Men, typically, who acted entitled to anything they desired. Or anyone.

One of those was Frank "Jelly" Nash. Some said he got his moniker as a kid known for his love of jelly beans and maintaining a sharp appearance. Others said it was a nod to the explosives he used to crack safes during his considerable bank-robbing career—some two hundred jobs, all told—and for which he had been serving time in the penitentiary in Leavenworth, Kansas, up until a couple of years ago. Having won favor with the deputy warden as a handyman and sometime chef, he was given an errand outside the prison one day and never came back. He was still on the lam.

He got to Hot Springs whenever he had a chance. It was pleasurable to take a vacation, to enjoy the horses and the healing springs. But mostly to take a break from life as a wanted man. The code in Hot Springs held that this was a neutral place, and people like Nash made the most of a few days of untroubled freedom.

One cool Saturday night in March, a boisterous crew came through the doors, and Shine looked up, dismayed to see Jelly and his pals roll in. They were a bunch of arrogant bastards—they didn't tip well, either.

They split up, Jelly and his girlfriend Frances cozying up at a high-top table, while two men headed toward a poker game. One burly, frowning man stood near the door, keeping an eye out, while the remaining three plopped down at Shine's bar. One had dark curly hair cropped close with a touch of gray at the sideburns; another had shaved his large head so cleanly that it reflected what light was in the bar, giving him the appearance of a lightbulb. But the one in the middle seemed out of place: not much older than Shine, with a painful-looking crop of acne on his cheeks and forehead, no facial hair save the peach fuzz on his chin.

"What'll you have, fellows?" Shine was polite but not warm.

The two older men wanted whiskey neat, but the younger one was unsure.

"Make it three," the curly-headed one said. "We gotta grow this boy up to a man tonight. It's his birthday."

"Well, happy birthday," Shine said. The young man blushed, his acne disappearing briefly into the red background. "Sure you don't want ice in yours?"

"No," he replied. "Reckon I can handle it."

His compatriots slapped him on the back in approval. She set three tumblers in front of them and poured out the amber liquor in three equal measures.

"All at once now," said the bald one. The youngster looked nervous, but at his buddy's count of three, all the men downed their drinks and set the glasses on the bar with a thump.

"Another round."

It was a crazy night. Whether it was the hint of spring in the air or the full moon, Shine wasn't sure. But by nine, the place was crammed tighter than a new pack of cigarettes. She was a whirling dervish behind the bar, serving up the basics of bourbon, rye, whiskey, scotch and gin along with her unusual takes on classics—and her own special concoctions, though the Strong shine was long gone. That size crowd meant Merle was working, too. But the good-looking, drink-slinging redhead at the Southern Club had her own cult following, and that made what would be a good night of business even better.

Shine kept a wary eye on Nash and his friends. He was canoodling with his girl, the two of them oblivious of everything but each other and their next round of gin and tonics. The three at the bar took several more slugs of whiskey before trying their luck at the craps table, the younger man trailing crookedly behind his friends. The next time she stole a glance in that direction, she saw Birdie had perched on the chair closest to the young man, her head tilted toward him, her contagious laughter audible.

She tried to make eye contact with Birdie. She knew that man—barely more than a boy—probably didn't have the pocket money to keep her happy all night, so she shouldn't waste her time. And she wanted Birdie to stay far away from anyone close to Jelly Nash.

But Birdie ignored her, fluttering her eyelashes at the awkward boy and managing to get a drink out of the curly-haired man behind him. She whispered something in the youngster's ear, red seeping into his round face like a wine spill on a fresh bar towel.

Later—she wasn't sure how much—the bald one sidled up to Nash's table. They conferred conspiratorially, sly grins and a thumb jerked in the direction of the young man. Birdie had hold of his arm, practically propping him up, while he had the grin of someone who could not believe his good fortune: a stunner of a girl sitting beside him, a half bottle of bourbon warming his insides and a party all around. He could get used to this.

Nash opened his wallet and tossed a crumple of bills on the tabletop. The bald man unfolded them, smoothing them longways in his hand before heading toward his young colleague.

"Happy birthday, Gordy," he said, his voice booming above the hubbub of the bar and gambling tables. The crowd at the club settled into a low chatter as everyone turned an interested face toward the pronouncement.

"Everyone . . . on my count!

For he's a jolly good fellow
For he's a jolly good fellow
For he's a jolly good fellow
Which nobody can deny!"

The bar broke out into applause, while the man of honor shook his head with disbelief and delight.

"And hell, son, that's just for starters," Baldy continued. "In honor of your big day, the fellas went in on a present for you."

Gordy's mouth turned up in a loose, liquid smile. "Well . . . thanks, I reckon. You boys are swell."

"Hang on to your hat now. You don't even know what we're giving you." The bald man slapped his thigh, enjoying the spotlight. "Actually, we're taking something instead."

Gordy frowned. He didn't understand what was being cooked up in his honor.

"Your *cherry*!"

The whole establishment burst into laughter, as both of Gordy's drinking buddies got under either arm and helped him off his chair. Then Birdie got up and began to lead them and a few others from Nash's gang past the bar and up the stairs to the second floor.

"Birdie!" Shine hissed as her friend bumped up against the bar, squeezing her way through the crowd. "That one's drunk as a skunk. He doesn't know which way is up."

"*Shhh*, Shine, I swear! I'm not stupid," Birdie said. "I haven't sat by him all night getting him drunk off his ass not to make some green. I won't have to lift a finger. Or my dress, either one."

Birdie gave her a wink.

Shine hated this part of the club, the ugly underbelly that emerged when men drank and gambled in this dark corner of the world where no one could see their deeds. Why did men see fit to order up a woman like they might a sloe gin fizz or a steak-and-potato dinner? And consume them with no consideration of their humanity?

Shine watched the drunken entourage stumble up the staircase.

It was after two a.m. when Shine had wiped the last glass dry and swept the floor behind the bar. She was tired to her marrow, but it had been a good night. Her tip jar was full for the first time in ages, even after tipping out the boys in the back. And Merle's percentage.

"Decent job tonight," he said, as she handed him his due. "Wish we could have a month of Saturday nights like that."

Shine wished that, too. The sooner her debt was settled, the sooner she would be home. She thought May, maybe. In time to be of real help to Rebecca in the fields and Gran in the garden. Shine could almost feel the damp dirt between her bare toes.

Home.

When she got to the top of the staircase, someone was sitting outside her door at the far end of the hall. She hurried over the burgundy rose-patterned runner that cut through the center of the wood hallway, her quick footsteps muffled in the pile of the wool rug.

Gordy? The young man was slumped against the wall beside the door. His head rested on his chest, covered with wet chunky vomit, and he stank of booze. Gordy's pants were pulled down to the pink hairless knobs of his knees. Shine was grateful his shirttails covered everything above that.

She knew by the gurgling snore that the boy was alive. She would need help moving him, since he was in no shape to cooperate. But he would be fine there the rest of the short night. Maybe even learn a lesson.

Shine opened the door slowly, expecting to find Birdie or another one of her ever-changing roommates asleep, and she didn't want to wake anyone.

But the overhead light was on. No one was in bed.

Instead, Birdie lay on her side on the floor, as still as if she were sleeping.

"Birdie?" Shine never knew her friend to overindulge to the point of passing out. She liked to nurse a drink while she was on the clock, but nothing more. It was bad for business—and too dangerous.

"I have to keep my wits about me," Birdie would say. "Gotta stay a step ahead of these johns."

Shine rolled her friend onto her back, as tenderly as she would a sleeping child. And oh, Lord, she was sorry. If she hadn't recognized Birdie's mauve dress and blond hair, she would not have known her at all. Birdie's eyes were swollen shut, face blackened with deep plum-colored bruises, and she was missing a front tooth. A hank of her long blond hair had been torn out by the roots. The slinky dusty-pink sequined dress that she had been so proud of—"I'm *uptown*, now, Shine!"—was torn top to bottom, revealing one breast, its skin broken by a full set of bite marks. Blood and a clear slime oozed from between her legs, staining the back of the dress beneath her.

Birdie moaned.

It was several days later before she could talk. Apparently Gordy hadn't known what to do when his buddies dropped him face-down on the velvet bed piled high with pillows. And he wasn't in any shape to do it, either. The men had closed the door behind Birdie, leaving the two young people alone in the dim room with its rich velour curtains and plush pile rug.

Birdie could hear them laughing and carrying on outside the door. Poor Gordy passed out, and she made him as comfortable as she could before letting his comrades know that the young man was finished for the night. But the men hadn't been satisfied: they'd paid good money for him to get an education, hadn't they? The bald one thought maybe he should show Gordy how it was done. Birdie had protested, said she would get the manager to work something out. But that enraged the man. He had shoved her back in the room, Curly right on his heels, angling for a gander at the goings-on.

Birdie had ended up hosting the entire gang between her legs that night, against her will. She couldn't tell Shine who was after Baldy or who was last. Or how many were in the middle. All she knew was that she had begged for them—for it—to stop. Around the third or fourth man, she had wrestled an arm free and poked someone straight in the eye and was in turn beaten around the face and head so badly that she passed out.

Shine was apoplectic. But what could she do?

That night, she had cleaned her friend as gently as she would a newborn, removing her ruined dress and underthings, washing her pale body with a soft damp cloth and wringing it out in a pail of warm, sudsy water, over and over again. Patting the cuts and bruises of her face, she applied a salve that Gran always used, made with yarrow, and some arnica paste to lessen the pain and fade the contusions quicker. She washed the blood from Birdie's scalp where it had clotted around the new bald spot, the size of a half-dollar. Then she put her in one of her cotton nightdresses, hefted her into the bottom bunk and tucked her in.

Out in the hallway, Gordy snored softly. *Stupid bastard.* His so-called buddies had left him behind after they had gotten all the sport from him they could. Like Birdie. Shine saved her rage for them. But she couldn't let Gordy completely off the hook.

She knelt down and took off his shoes and socks. Then she pulled his pants, belt and boxer shorts the rest of the way off. She cringed at removing the vomit-covered shirt, but decided she must. He should have nothing and nowhere to hide when he woke up from his bourbon-induced slumber.

His belt was a poor grade of leather, but pliable enough. Shine grimaced as she bound Gordy's ankles together and gave the belt a good yank to tighten it. Then she tipped him over so that he was on his side, reaching for his wrists to tie up with his ankles. When she was finished, he looked like a hairless, pink-skinned pig that had been hogtied for branding, butchering or neutering. Gordy should count himself fortunate she was not equipped for any of that.

She left him in the hall. It was nearly four in the morning when she climbed up to her top bunk at last. Her friend's breathing below her was labored, air drawn in slowly and let out like a leak from the swollen nose that could easily be broken; it was hard to tell with the puffiness and bruising. Shine turned on her side, unable to sleep, even though she was enervated.

Nash and his friends were gone the next day. Gordy, too. Miraculously. She wished she could have witnessed his eventual escape. Even Harry Houdini would have needed assistance with her fine handiwork.

And it turned out, Birdie had suffered much worse than a broken nose.

In the weeks after the rape, Birdie began to look more like herself, as the bruises faded and Shine brushed her blond hair to hide the bald patch on the right side of her skull. The gaping hole in Birdie's mouth from the missing tooth was the main physical remnant and reminder of what had happened. But her spirit was broken.

She could do nothing but lie in bed, curled up on her side. Shine did her best to get food and water in her before her shifts, asking Birdie's favorite chefs in the kitchen to make her something special. But nothing appealed.

"C'mon, Birdie," she coaxed. "One bite. Good girl."

There was nothing Shine hated more than powerlessness. She was unable to return her friend to wholeness. And she couldn't make the bastards who broke her pay for their crimes. With everyone on the take, from beat cops and sheriff's department lackeys on up to the mayor, narking got you nowhere. Except in trouble. Trouble she could scarce afford, as she tried to scrounge, scrape and save her way to freedom from this corrupt place so many considered paradise.

If this was heaven, she would gladly choose hell. At least there, she figured people had to own who they were. What they did.

Merle told Shine that Birdie had to go. "She's been lying around for two weeks. I can't give every broken-down whore who needs it a room. I'm running a business here, not a charity."

"Have a heart, you son of a bitch," Shine said, heated.

But he had shrugged, given her a regretful smile. "I told you there's creative ways to pay your debts. Or hers. Let me know if you change your mind."

God, he sickens me. She didn't know what to do, but she sure as hell wasn't going to take any favors from Merle—or offer any, either.

She did the only thing she could think of: she got Birdie cleaned up, dressed and packed and, swallowing her pride, hopped on the streetcar to the boardinghouse with her friend in tow. Merle may not have a heart, but she thought maybe, just *maybe,* old Bernie might.

Turned out, she was right. The old woman had been reluctant to open the door when she saw Shine on her stoop. But then she caught a glimpse of Birdie, hunched and looking at her shoe tops. Bernyce Ward shook her head, and guided her into the kitchen for a cup of tea. Whether old Bernie was acting out of compassion or filling the vacancy she happened to still have now that "Mr. Smith" no longer came to town, Shine didn't know. Or care.

"Poor child," Bernyce Ward said. "Not the brightest but always so cheerful. It's like the sunshine's been sucked out of her. Didn't approve her choices, but she never hurt a fly."

Shine gave her the money Birdie had saved—which wasn't much.

"I'll cover her after that's gone," Shine said, cringing inside. This would set her back a month or more. But Birdie's safekeeping was worth it.

"Who knows?" Bernyce Ward said with a sniff. "Maybe I can actually teach the girl to sew instead of just lying about it."

Shine had to smile at that, patting Birdie on the shoulder. "That would be a welcome miracle."

Birdie didn't respond. Shine cleared her throat. "Well, I thank you, Miz Ward. I know you don't owe me any favors."

"Indeed I don't," Bernyce Ward said superciliously. "But I'm not doing it for you. And I no longer offer boarding to so-called 'bookkeepers' after your pistol-pointing incident. If you are or were ever a bookkeeper. Which I doubt."

"Oh, I definitely keep the ledgers," retorted Shine. "I would venture to say my entire young life has been spent figuring out who is owed what by whom. And how to make sure those who deserve it get their due. If that isn't bookkeeping, I don't know what is."

Someone needed to be held accountable for what had been done to Birdie. Shine wanted to cut the nuts off every single man who had come into the bar with Frank Nash that night, make steers out of that bunch of bulls. Put an end to their bullshit.

But Jelly Nash took the brunt of her blame. He should have been in prison! Instead he was free as a bird, causing irreparable harm to innocents like Birdie—and Gordy, if she was being fair. Bankrolling the "fun" for his friends, then blowing out of town and back into hiding.

Shine bided her time, chiseling a hard edge to her hatred the way a man might put a knife blade to a whetting stone, sparks flying against that white-hot edge that would—when it cooled—cut you so quickly and cleanly you wouldn't even know what happened.

Rebecca

The crops were stunted. Crippled by lack of rain.

It was June. Corn stalks were reluctantly emerging, squat and deformed, from the first acre they'd planted a month back. She and Jed had finished walking the rows—if you could categorize such crooked lines as constituting "rows"—and he had gone to the barn to put away the mule before lunch. He rarely made an appearance at the farm these days unless specifically asked by her or Gran. Or to bring Elsie and Hi out for a visit. But though Rebecca handled most all the chores these days, standing on the plow while driving the mule was still difficult. And she needed to get this second field seeded.

Rebecca marveled at the way the sky could remain so cloudless and blue. Unmoved by the plight beneath it. Refusing to shed the tears that could heal this dusty dry land. Even on the rare occasion when a burgeoning black cloud would form on the horizon, the sky withheld its gifts, the thunderhead skirting along the edges of earth as far as she could see, skipping their piece of mountainside once more. She hoped someone somewhere got that relief, that moisture that meant the difference between a viable corn crop and hunger and want. She had heard of horrible dust storms on the plains that made farming impossible. Missouri wasn't that bad off yet, thank God. And they were blessed with spring-fed Kinney Creek for the garden and watering the few remaining farm animals.

Still: she felt stunted and crippled, too.

Being home these past three years had been a balm to her soul in some ways. To walk their woods—albeit more slowly and with pain—and hear birdsong again. Take a currycomb to her horse's hide and feel the rippling, warm flesh respond to her ministrations. And coax green life from the fallow fields and garden.

But there was a lack, a hole that refused to be filled, even with these things and places that had never left her wanting. As long as she was free to walk under the sun in its heavens, to share space with other living creatures, whether in leafy woods or wildflower clearings—or even the plodding back and forth of field work—she had never felt alone. Or needed anything more.

She missed being touched. Not only the press of warm skin against hers, although she hungered for that. But the touching of her heart by another human being, a connection that transcended body and language. Someone who understood her without her saying a word.

That last morning in Hot Springs, when it was just the two of them, Rebecca held Eulalie in the streak of sunshine that made its way through the coarse kitchen curtains. Shine was coming soon to get her to the train station.

But when Rebecca pulled back, her lover would not look up into her eyes.

"I have to go."

"I know that. That's been the goal the whole time. Congratulations."

That smarted. "You got me back on my feet. I'm grateful to you, Eulalie," Rebecca said.

"Grateful, huh?" What she saw in Eulalie's face nearly broke her: the large dark eyes, luminous and watery; the generous mouth that nearly always held humor, turned down on both ends. Defeated.

"Well, I healed your leg all right. But I can't do nothing about your head."

"I don't know what you mean."

"What do you *want*, Rebecca Strong?"

She hadn't had words then for what she wanted; the irrational urge to close and lock the doors of that apartment, to keep them suspended in the warmth of that streaming sunlight together. But the farm was where she was needed.

She said nothing.

Eulalie took one of Rebecca's hands, put her lips to the palm and then closed the fingers around it, as if keeping that tender kiss safe, protected from the hardships ahead.

"Let me know if you figure it out."

Then Shine was at the door.

On the platform, Shine stood waving exaggeratedly as the train began to pull away, making a spectacle of herself as she sent her big sister home at last. Rebecca smiled, placing her hand on the window. For Shine, yes; but also for one who wasn't allowed on that platform.

Goodbye.

What she had discovered in Hot Springs would need to stay there. She had no reference for the myriad feelings she had: moments of hot roiling emotions, bubbling up from her depths, countered by the calm contentment of a placid farm pond at dawn. She had enjoyed camaraderie and friendship with her sisters. But Rebecca had known instinctively that she was not the marrying kind. That if Noah had tried to find a match for her amidst the torrents of rain and rising floodwaters, he would have failed. And she had made peace with that.

But that was before Eulalie.

She had mailed letters the first year, short missives that Shine hand-delivered to her friend. But because Eulalie couldn't read or write, anything Rebecca sent would have to be read by Shine or someone else. So the reports on the corn crop, the farm animals and the weather were as dry as the drought-ravaged fields they showcased, an unsatisfying one-way correspondence that resembled nothing so much as entries from her beloved *Farmers' Almanac.* Frustrated by what she couldn't say, Rebecca quit writing altogether. But she never stopped thinking about Eulalie.

"Rebecca!"

She snapped her head around toward the sound of Jed's voice, panicked and breathless. He appeared at the bottom of the field, waving his arms over his head.

"Hurry! It's Lidy."

Lidy

She was in the garden when it happened.

It was late spring, when plump rusty-breasted robins hopped on the rich earth of the neat garden rows in search of worms and dun-colored sparrows tugged at pieces of Lidy's loose straw mulch to build their nests.

She had picked a pint of red strawberries, turning back the rounded, rick-racked leaves to uncover them, hidden beneath. Lidy allowed herself a berry or two, letting the sweet warmth of the sun-soaked fruit dissolve on her tongue.

She stood, eyes closed, enjoying the trickle of sugary goodness down her throat. But then her throat constricted. A sharp, sudden pain at the top of her skull, like a bolt of lightning out of the cloudless azure sky. She dropped the basket of berries, which scattered like droplets of blood on the ground.

Lidy's eyes flew open, but she couldn't see from the right one. Everything was red. She needed to get to the cabin, rest for a spell. But she was dizzy, the ground strangely buckling beneath her feet as she struggled to put them one behind another. Why did her right side feel so heavy, leaden?

Was she dying? *Lord, no.* There was so much still to do! So much to put right.

She didn't want to die. Not yet.

* * *

Sun on her eyelids, turning everything an orange red. Morning. Maybe it had been a dream: the garden, berries and beating sun. And the weakness. The falling.

A bad dream.

Lidy opened her eyes. The walls of the cabin, as they should be, wood a warm umber where it was touched by sunbeams. Her cast-iron skillet hung on its nail. A pair of brown boots by the door: hers. The wooden pie safe with its punched tin windows that served as her medicine cupboard.

But here was Elsie, in a chair beside her cot, chin on chest, asleep. She should be at the store. Or with Hi.

She must have fallen after all. But she was fine. Lidy would wait, let the poor thing get a few winks. Lord knew Elsie was run ragged between the child and Hanson's.

Lidy resumed her inventory of the cabin. The front door with the doormat she fashioned from a culled feed sack, repairing the holes and filling it with sand to keep it from sliding around before sewing it closed. The daintier flour sacks she had stitched into curtains for the window, using a cheerful red thread. It gave her satisfaction to see her handiwork, pretty and practical. She never embraced the concept of beauty for its own sake, but utility combined with beauty was undeniably pleasurable. She strove for it, even if she couldn't always achieve it—usually due to a lack of resources rather than imagination.

Her nose was cold, one of the few parts of her exposed. She was covered from toes to neck with a light blanket. The fire had probably gone out.

Lidy turned her head toward the woodstove—but her head didn't turn. She could still see only the view in front of her and at the periphery of her vision.

That was odd.

She would get up and stoke the embers she knew were nestled rosy and warm in the gray wood ash.

But her legs would not swing over the side of the cot. Lidy was used to the reluctance of her aging limbs to obey her wishes but had never been refused before. She reached for her right leg, to help it along.

Her hand could not move, her fingers could not grab. Panicking, Lidy began to thrash—but the thrashing was inside her brain, her body as still as a stone. Her eyes alone could move, opening and closing. Blinking.

Lidy was trapped in her own body.

She began to sweat profusely, her heart pounding. Lidy scanned the room again, looking for . . . what? A way out? Some sign that this was not really happening, that this paralysis was simply in her mind?

As if Lidy's panic had rippled out into the room and touched her, Elsie awoke with a start. Her eyes immediately went to Lidy's face. And whatever she saw there, whoever she saw there, made her smile.

"Gran! You're here!"

Where else would I be?

The indignity of it was the worst.

Elsie had been thrilled to know she was alive. *Truly* alive. Not merely a husk of a human being like Alta had been. Lidy's mind was quick as ever.

But her body was hopeless. Lidy closed her eyes while Elsie jostled her legs and hips to wipe her filth and change her underthings. She couldn't feel anything, but being unable to control her shit and piss filled her with shame.

And the way Elsie would come at her! Sometimes with a spoon, but usually a straw with some type of nourishment or water. Lidy could not sip; she could not swallow. She flashed back to the strawberry patch, where she had begged for her life. For more days and nights on this spinning globe, in her glorious parcel of it.

But if this was life, she wanted to die.

And it wasn't going to be easy.

Elsie

It was a springtime Saturday and there was a line out the door of the general store. Soon the earth would be warm enough to host all matter of seeds and kernels in its dark womb, pushing up stalks and stems through the topsoil. Then the unfurling would begin: tender bent shoots uncurling toward the sun, while leaves unfolded in their brilliant green glory.

The human beings felt it, too, this awakening. Despite the drought and difficulties, hope rose in them pure and sweet as sap. Farmers checking and oiling their implements, repairing broken or imperfect tools in anticipation of that soon-to-be time when they would score the earth like a loaf of hearty wheat bread and sprinkle it with seeds. The women longing to banish the drab grays and browns of winter with a new frock made with a light cotton weave in gentle pinks, buttery yellows and light lavenders and embellished with pearlescent buttons, a bit of lace.

Elsie was greeting her next customer when Jed burst through the front doors. His breathing came in hard puffs, his eyes frantic.

Lidy had been struck down.

Elsie left the store in such haste that she was still wearing the apron that held her receipt paper and sharp scissors for separating yards of fabric from a larger bolt; she forgot her bonnet. Jed had ridden into town on Cowboy, pummeling the recalcitrant horse in the withers with his heels. The horse seemed to understand the urgency of the situation and allowed it, even though the man on his back was not a person he particularly liked. When Jed oversaw the feed, hay and water, they never appeared at the same time of day—and sometimes didn't come at all.

Jed had found Lidy in the garden, stretched out stiff as a fence pole near the berry patch. He had come in from the cornfield when the sun was straight up overhead, hoping the old woman had put together dinner for him and Rebecca. They needed a break from the work—and from each other. Jed had been struggling mightily with the plow, cursing as he tried to keep the sharp angle of the blades cutting the earth in straight rows behind the mules; his sister-in-law watching the proceedings, mouth in a hard line, silently cursing him.

"Gran wouldn't have approved your husband's profanity, but I know she preferred it over mirth," Rebecca told Elsie later, as she ministered to Lidy, still and silent on her cot in the cabin. "She warned him this morning not to laugh while planting the corn or it would be irregular."

Elsie knew her sister was trying to cheer her, to keep her from worrying herself into a useless tangle. But it was of no help.

The next week was horrific. Seeing Gran—her invincible grandmother—brought so low. She who constantly buzzed, busy as a hummer in summertime, with vinegar in her veins that gave her a sass and strength few could equal.

Now Lidy lay helpless. Even young Hi, at three, could do more than his great-gran. The stroke had left her paralyzed, unable to control her bowels or bladder. She could not chew or swallow, and Elsie was at her wits' end, trying to get water and nourishment into her.

But those eyes.

The dark look that they gave her when she attempted to get water or sustenance into that unmoving body! Those eyes, still so black and sharp, able to cut Elsie to the quick. They were portals inside her gran's suffering. Lidy couldn't formulate speech, not even a guttural growl or grunt to indicate her needs or preferences. Her once talkative gran, who always had a word—usually the last word—and now could not utter a single one.

But Lidy was alive inside. Unlike her mother, whose essence evaporated while her physical body labored on, even giving birth. Elsie's heart twinged to think of it, two decades later.

Elsie had come back from the henhouse one morning with Shine on her hip and a basket of eggs on her arm. Putting the eggs on the table, she lowered Shine into the woven basket lined with a blanket on the floor where she slept. From there, the baby could be moved around or watch the family's goings-on with her curious slate-blue eyes not yet turned to emeralds.

Elsie kissed her mother on the brow. If she didn't have other chores, she would unplait her mother's dark brown hair, brush it a hundred strokes and braid it once more. But that morning, when she put her lips to Alta's forehead, it was cool. Much too cool.

Where was Gran?

She picked up her mother's wrist and pressed it with her two fingers, feeling for a pulse, like she had watched her gran do a hundred times. She waited patiently at first, then with increasing alarm. Elsie dug her fingers farther into the chilly flesh, which left dimples when she released it.

Her mother's eyes were closed. Was she dead?

That's when she saw the dirty tea towel, folded neatly and hanging over the side of the laundry basket. She could almost make out a face: damp dents where eyes might be, then two wet spots for nostrils. A larger stain for the mouth. It was as if her mother had become a spirit.

When Lidy had reappeared from the root cellar, she nearly dropped her carrots and potatoes when she saw Elsie studying the tea towel so intently.

"What on earth are you doing, child?" Gran set the vegetables down.

"I thought I saw Mama in here. Her ghost." As Elsie held up the flour sack, Lidy nearly fell over with fright.

"Give me that."

Elsie handed her the towel and watched her gran collect herself, putting her face together as if assembling a quilt square from the scrap basket, disparate shapes and colors made neatly into a whole.

"Your mama's gone to heaven," said Gran. "She's an angel, not a ghost."

Elsie threw herself into her gran's arms then, arms that closed stiffly around the girl like a metal gate creaky with disuse.

"She's in a better place."

But Elsie didn't buy it. *This* was the best place. Here, with her and Rebecca and Shine. And her daddy. She buried her face in her gran's apron front and cried until she couldn't. Lidy, using the spectral dish towel, swiped roughly at her granddaughter's tears before sending her out to tell Hiram and Rebecca the news: Alta was gone.

It wasn't until later that night, lying on her pallet with her sister, unable to sleep, that a thought froze her heart.

How did Gran know Mama was gone without even checking?

The towel. Not her mama's ghost, but her very spirit. *Her breath.*

She stopped herself from shaking her big sister awake. *If* she was asleep. Rebecca hadn't said a word since she and Hiram had rushed into the cabin. He had been hysterical; she taciturn, taking it all in with her serious dark eyes. She turned and headed to the barn to take solace in her animals. To touch their living hides and coats, rub their noses and ears. Desperate to feel warmth and the steady beat of a heart where she could not find them in that cabin, on that cot. Elsie envied Rebecca that comfort.

Instead, Elsie snuggled against her sister's slender back, breathing in her tangle of stick-straight hair that smelled of hay and sunlight, sweat and dust. She tried to match her breathing to that of her strong, silent sister. Maybe that would make her strong, too.

She tried to tuck away her fear, swallow it whole. Why did Gran say Alta had fallen when Elsie had seen her jump? Why did her gran stop her mama from breathing? Her gran loved her, loved all of them. She wouldn't hurt anyone. Or lie to them. Would she?

Elsie kept her observations and questions to herself. She grew up and—while she didn't exactly banish the worries from her mind—she covered them up, layers upon layers of tissue and time. Like a burl on a fine, straight oak, the knobby growth enclosing a scar or wound caused by some type of stress, disfiguring the tree. Except Elsie's was on the inside, a tight bumpy knot way down deep. So deep she could almost forget it was there.

Until her gran gave her that first glass of buttermilk. Then another and another. Trying to take Elsie's baby like she'd taken her mama. Deciding for everyone who lives and who doesn't and when.

Elsie had been confused and angry ever since.

SHINE

The violet bruises on Birdie's face and arms faded to the sick yellow-green of a southern tornadic sky and then disappeared altogether. She was talking again—not constant chatter like before, but glad of company and conversation. But she didn't laugh the same way, head thrown back and mouth open in a full-throated gargle of delight. Her smile was rarely discernible in the straight line of her mouth. Maybe it was the missing front tooth. But she was diminished, defeated.

The June sun was pure white light in the blue Arkansas sky, full up with galloping white clouds, a herd of woolly, unruly sheep. Shine was sweating, despite taking the streetcar to the boardinghouse. She went to the back, where Bernyce Ward made clear she was to be received. Shine was not "backdoor company" in the way of close family or friends. Bernyce simply didn't want that reckless, eyebrow-raising redhead on her front stoop for all the neighbors to see.

Even so, Bernyce had softened on her. Shine had kept showing up for her friend—and footing the bill. That went a long way in Bernyce Ward's book.

Shine had no sooner knocked when Bernyce opened the door and pulled her inside.

"I need to tell you something," she whispered.

"Please tell me it's good news," Shine said. "I've already had enough bad for two lifetimes at least."

"I wish I could." Bernyce's whisper was now a hiss. "But . . . Birdie is with child."

With *child*?

Shine let the idea sink in—then promptly rejected it. "Well, I'm not Lidy Strong's granddaughter for nothing. There's ways to take care of that."

Bernyce's mouth puckered. "That would be well and good if she were interested."

Shine shook her head. A young woman like Birdie—with no education, no skills, no family support, no money and no husband—wasn't destined for much of a life as it was. Add a child to the mix? The odds were not in her favor. So dismal, in fact, that Shine figured there wasn't a drunk at the Hot Springs racetrack who would take them.

"She needs some sense talked into her is all."

"Who needs some sense?" Birdie stepped into the cramped quarters of the kitchen.

"Miz Ward was filling me in on the . . . *situation*."

"*Hmmm*." Birdie sniffed. "A situation sounds like a problem that needs fixing."

"Birdie, have you thought this through? How will you look at your child and not be reminded of how he came to be? That half of his being is from a man who . . ."

Shine couldn't finish. Her hands clenched into fists at her side. What she wouldn't give to punch and pummel the men who attacked Birdie. Punish them. Especially Frank Nash, who so cavalierly plunked down his money, encouraging his pals to help themselves, to use Birdie up, treat her as if she was disposable. Like trash.

"That's not this baby's fault," Birdie said, a glimmer of her old spark in her eyes. "And remember, this wee one is half me, too. That's more than enough."

"And how will you care for it. I mean, *him*. Or her."

Birdie's face took on a dreamy expression as she reached into the pocket of her cotton dress, its shiny black buttons barely holding the fabric closed over her chest and stomach. She opened her palm to reveal a half-finished bootie, crocheted from fuzzy white yarn.

"Miz Ward is teaching me how to sew, knit and crochet," Birdie said. "I'm much obliged to her, Shine."

Birdie leaned over and gave the old boardinghouse owner a peck on the cheek. Bernyce Ward blushed. She was not accustomed to receiving affection or kindness. Or portioning out any of her own. Until Birdie showed up, needing her to nurse and mother her. Like the child she never had.

Shine felt her fists relax.

Wonders never cease.

It was nothing short of wondrous that Shine caught sight of Jelly Nash that very afternoon. Actually, the miracle of it was that she *recognized* the bastard when she saw him.

She was heading back to the Southern Club to change clothes before her shift. Walking down Central Avenue, she performed the same mental calculations she always did, never coming up with an answer that pleased her. How much money did she have in the drawstring pouch around her neck? How much did she still owe? She was so close to paying off Merle; twenty-seven dollars more. Shine would be on her way home in a few weeks; a month at the outside. Back on the farm with Gran and Becks. She could almost feel the earth beneath her bare feet, smell the rich hopeful scents of early summer in the flush of wildflowers filling the fencerows. And she would finally meet Hi! She knew Elsie was itching to show him off, her letters chock-full of charming anecdotes about the child.

But then, that's what Shine had been saying to herself for nigh on three years now. Then someone or something unexpected always raised a needy hand so the number never seemed to go down. Like her old boots, heels so worn-out that one finally broke off. Birdie's woes. Everything cost money. And these days, it was harder to make it. So many slow Saturday nights at the club, when the few coins in the tip jar clanked an unhappy tune. She had spent other unpleasant moments at that bar, too, spurning Merle's advances. But downtrodden as she was, Shine felt lucky to have a job.

She breezed by the White Front Cigar Store, the folding doors flung wide in the warm spring weather. Cigars were the literal smoke where there was figurative fire—like high-stakes poker games taking place in the back room to the side of the front counter. Shine had gone two storefronts farther when she stopped in her tracks. Had that been Frank Nash leaning on that counter? She did an about-face, walking by briskly a second time. It hadn't been her imagination: there he was, puffing a fat cigar. Twenty pounds heavier, mustached and wearing a flimsy toupee. And glasses! But it was Jelly, no doubt. She would know those dead sharklike eyes and sharp nose anywhere.

Shine darted down the alley, taking the back way to the club. No need to sashay by for a third look. She was already worried he might have noticed her noticing *him*.

Once inside the club, she slammed the door and collapsed against it, pulse racing. She had imagined having her chance to take out Frank Nash, it had fueled her in those dismal days after Birdie's assault, like her need for payback kept her going after Hiram's murder. But what could she *do*? Slip him a mickey? Shine had to smile; it would be obvious who was responsible. Shooting him would be the most satisfying, but completely out of the question. Even if she still had her pistol, the mayor and his minions wouldn't like their "neutral territory" breached by bullets. It wasn't good for the gangster business.

If she couldn't put him in the ground, she would at least like him behind bars. He should be in prison in Leavenworth right now, not gallivanting around the country, vacationing without a care between crime sprees. Hurting innocent people along the way. But no local lawmen would be interested in returning the fugitive to Kansas.

Her heart rate gradually slowed. Then it came to her.

She stepped from the back-door alcove into the kitchen and looked around. Sam, the big-bellied fry cook, was hunched over his grill and deep fryer and didn't look up. Duck, the dishwasher, busied himself with a broom, sweeping up the worst of the dirt and dropped food from the greasy tile floor.

"Hey, boys," Shine said. "Merle around?"

"He headed to the bank before it closes," said Duck, talking around the cigarette that hung from one corner of his mouth.

That gave her ten minutes, fifteen tops. Shine pushed through the swinging doors separating the kitchen from the bar. The place was empty, high-top tables and barstools vacant, and beyond, the green felt tables where gamblers would try their luck were like lonely fields of perfect farmland, fenced in by their wooden frames. Before long, the room would be humming with brawny bouncers, white-shirted-and-bow-tied blackjack and poker dealers and craps box men, readying their cards or dice. Maybe the sly shaved deck here or a weighted die there. The way the workers titrated their gaming pieces mirrored the way Shine put together her cocktails—and with similar results: they kept the customers coming back for more.

She strode to the corner of the bar by the register and pulled out the heavy black telephone from underneath. The candlestick-shaped device had a bracket protruding from one side, which held the conical earpiece, attached to the whole contraption by a black-and-white cord. At the top was a mouthpiece, while the base displayed a rotary dial with numbers. Shine panicked; she had seen Merle operate the thing, but had never made a phone call herself. But she sure as hell wasn't going to let that stop her.

Glancing once more around the room, she took a deep breath and began dialing the only number she had memorized by heart.

John

He'd been surprised how easy it was. The biggest arrest of his FBI career. Hell, the biggest of his *entire* career, including his years as a prohi. He had captured the "most successful bank robber of all time." And all he had to do was take him by the arm and say, "Come on, Nash."

His partner, Agent Blackwood, had taken Frank "Jelly" Nash's other arm. And a third officer—Billy Deeds, the police chief of McAlester, Oklahoma—had stepped behind, pressing his revolver into the criminal's back to make sure he didn't try anything funny. But Flanagan had slipped those silver handcuffs on the slimeball all by himself.

Clink, clink. The sound those cuffs made closing was music to Flanagan's ears.

And this guy was a slimeball. Several hundred bank robberies across the Midwest. A few murders. Several prison escapes. Busted marriages where he didn't even bother with divorce papers.

But what Nash's boys had perpetrated on Birdie? That was unforgivable.

John couldn't believe it was Shine's voice on the end of the line. He assumed she had thrown away his phone number after all this time. After that kiss. Shine Strong had made it clear she wouldn't be in communication with him until the streets of hell had frozen over.

Ice-skating, anyone?

But John couldn't lie: he had hoped her call was more of a personal one, that she might have changed her mind and wanted to see him. But she *needed* him—and that was something. Shine's story got him riled up; he thanked her for the tip and immediately hightailed it to downtown Hot Springs. And crossed his fingers for a glimpse of the enigmatic, maddening redhead, too.

The plan was for Flanagan, Blackwood and Deeds to drive Nash back to Leavenworth. But the criminal had a lot of friends.

By the time their Buick reached Benton, Arkansas, a line of eight men blocked the highway and Blackwood barely squealed the heavy-duty tires to a stop before hitting one of them. He rolled down the window, and a thick-jowled sheriff put his face next to his.

"What are you boys doing with this man?"

"Taking him back to prison, where he belongs."

"I'm gonna need some ID," the sheriff said. "You understand."

What the three lawmen in the car understood, after producing their badges and paperwork, was that it could take forever to get through Arkansas if they got stopped at every wide spot in the road with a sheriff trying to do someone a favor.

After they were pulled over by a few hard-to-convince policemen in Little Rock, it was clear they needed plan B. Flanagan called regional headquarters in Oklahoma City.

"Better put him on a train, boys."

The crew made it to Fort Smith, Arkansas, to catch the 8:30 p.m. Missouri Pacific train to Kansas City. From there, Nash would be escorted by car back to the penitentiary in Leavenworth. He'd been free for years after busting himself out—but the party was over.

Now Flanagan, Blackwood and Deeds were on the train, scheduled to arrive bright and early at Union Station. Deeds had been on Nash's trail for a while now, after a bank robbery that left a teller dead and another customer wounded. The FBI agents had brought him along to ID Nash. And the fact was, the Bureau still didn't allow their agents to carry guns, and they needed protection. Nash was connected—and not exclusively to bank-robbing, murderous riffraff, but also to the mob.

Blackwood sat next to Nash, still handcuffed, while John sat across from them on the high-backed seats in the passenger car, a fold-down table between them. The angular Deeds, all pointy chin and sharp elbows, stood at one end of the train car, gun in hand. The FBI agents had arranged to have the car to themselves; no one save the conductor and some higher-ups at the railroad and FBI headquarters needed to know a prison escapee was on board. It would be unnerving for passengers to see Deeds with his revolver on full display.

The prisoner slumped against the seat in a bored fashion. Flanagan took inventory: a sweep of blond hair above a pair of oversized ears and large nose. Wide mouth topped with a mustache and twisted in a perpetual sneer.

Nash looked John square in the eyes. They were cold, those eyes. Flat black buttons. Reptilian. John didn't know how women found Nash attractive, yet he had seen the third and latest wife in the cigar shop, crying buckets as her new husband was cuffed and hustled off to prison. Did she know he wasn't even divorced from the previous wives? Maybe she didn't care. He was a powerful man, even on the run. And he had been free so long he may have seemed invincible. Some women found power and the underlying potential of violence a kind of aphrodisiac. That, and money.

"What are you lookin' at?" Nash curled his lip contemptuously. When Flanagan finally looked away, Nash grinned. He had confirmed his theory: the FBI was weak. A joke.

"Probably that dead animal on top of your head," Deeds chimed in from the corner of the car. "Flip that cheap rug up, why don't you, and let's see what's underneath." He motioned to Flanagan, who tugged on Nash's hair. Sure enough, it gave way with Flanagan holding what looked like a lifeless rodent in his hand.

"Ha!" He couldn't help it. Nash was bald as an egg, save for the stripes of adhesive from the toupee.

"Take it easy with the hairpiece," Nash whined. "It set me back a couple hundred bucks."

"You won't need to look pretty where you're going," Deeds said. "In fact, it's probably better for you if you don't, if you catch my drift."

Nash seemed nonplussed by the entire drama that was playing out. As if he knew how it would end, how they all knew it would end: Nash getting out of it, somehow, some way. Like this was a nuisance—and they were wasting his time.

John balled his right fist in his lap. He was not a violent man—but what this man had wrought on others made him want to be. First the nose. Then that smug mug.

"You sorry lot are gonna regret this," Nash said.

"Shut it," Blackwood said, turning a stony gaze on Nash. He was short and fair, built like one of those new British tanks Flanagan had seen in the papers. No one with a brain would cross Blackwood. He had zero patience for anything except the rules and punishing those who went outside them. Criminals were like roaches to him: filthy and always showing up where there was a mess—or making one of their own. He would enjoy exterminating them with the heel of his boot. But he would settle for putting them in the slammer.

Nash couldn't. "My boys are gonna hear about this. They'll be none too happy, I can tell you that." His voice was steady, a man delivering facts. No trace of fear or worry.

And that sneer again.

"Yeah, your girl seemed pretty torn up about it," Blackwood said. "All that screaming didn't seem to rally the troops, though."

"Leave her out of this," Nash snapped.

"My bet is that your friends are pretty sick of you," Blackwood went on. "I can see how that would happen."

"Don't be so sure."

Nash closed his eyes and turned his head. Soon the only sounds were the wheels rolling, a rhythmic metallic hum, and the *thump*,

thump of the car as it passed over the rail joints. And Nash, mouth slack, snoring.

The train pulled into the west side of Kansas City's Union Station right on time. The enormous Beaux Arts–style building was a marvel: gray stone arches and columns with ninety-five-foot-tall, ornately decorated ceilings hung with three magnificent chandeliers, each weighing in at 3,500 pounds. And it was practically new, a decade or so old, designed by Chicago architect Jarvis Hunt to replace a more modest station that was prone to flooding. Every day thousands of people traveled through the station, a crossroads for those heading west and east.

The Missouri Pacific train was one of many loading and unloading that early June morning. Streams of passengers disembarked to make their way toward home, stretching and yawning from overnight trips, while others dashed fresh-scrubbed and harried to their early trains. In the crush, no one paid much attention to Chief Deeds, who stepped off the Fort Smith arrival, motioning for the others to stay back until he had scoped out the platform and inside of the giant station. They would have to navigate the entire width of it to get Nash out the doors and into the car that awaited them in front.

Nash stood and stretched. In the nearly twelve hours since they had left Fort Smith, a shadow of black stubble had appeared, making him look even more sinister. Blackwood took his arm, guiding him to the exit, while Flanagan covered the rear.

At the all-clear signal from Deeds, the remaining party of three disembarked onto the platform, where they were met by four more lawmen.

"Special Agent Vetterli," said one of the two in plainclothes. "This is Agent Caffrey. And we've got two of the KCPD's best, Hermanson and Grooms. Gentlemen?"

"Agent Flanagan and my partner, Agent Blackwood. And our security detail here is Police Chief Billy Deeds, from Oklahoma. He's okay." One of the men chuckled; there were handshakes, back claps. Each man taking the measure of the others. The local officers took stock of Nash, who held his chin up defiantly. He needed no introduction.

The Kansas City policemen took either side, since they, unlike their FBI counterparts, were armed; Deeds brought up the rear. The group made their way across the shiny marble floor of the Grand Hall, where a giant dual-sided clock—each face more than six feet in diameter—showed 7:15 a.m. Flanagan couldn't help but gawk, turning his own face skyward. He'd heard about this "Big Ben of the Plains," but seeing it was something else entirely. Time as it ticked by on this massive clock seemed even more precious somehow, something to be noted with a touch more solemnity than what was indicated by a typical watch or timepiece. But neither the grandeur nor scale nor weight of the giant clock—more than one thousand pounds!—could make time go any faster or slower. Or provide more of it to one person over another.

Time's up. Flanagan's relief was tinged with a sense of satisfaction. That Nash would soon be back behind bars where he belonged; that justice would be, belatedly, served. He hoped that every second, every hour, dragged by. Nash was close to forty, in the prime of his life. To be locked away again would surely be excruciating.

When they reached the doors to the outside, there was a perfectly timed pause, the group in sync like a caterpillar: one brain moving all those legs. Hermanson drew his gun, pushed open the door and surveyed the parking lot. He motioned for the rest to come out.

"My Chevy sedan is over there." Agent Caffrey pointed toward a white late-model car on the front row.

Flanagan shaded his eyes. The light from the sun shone pure and dazzling on the smooth stone of the station. A kelly-green lawn surrounded the parking lot, edged with beds of red roses in full bloom, softening the hard edges of the enormous station. He was a long way from Ohio.

Something about the light—the way it pierced his vision,

warmed through his suit down to his bones—made him feel alive. Almost giddy, although that wasn't appropriate for the occasion. For an instant, he was transported back to an Ozarks mountainside on another summer day, chasing a different, elusive creature that didn't want to be caught.

Shine. He wished he could go back to that day. To that afternoon when it was she who had captivated him with her spirit and wit. Not to mention that fiery beauty; she looked every bit the Irishwoman herself, in the middle of that godforsaken rock farm. But they had been on opposite sides from the start. And doomed to stay that way. Maybe someday she'd forgive him, even if she never wanted to see hide nor hair of him again.

Caffrey went to the driver's side of the sedan and opened the door. Nash made to get in the back, but Blackwood steered him toward the driver's seat.

"You sit behind the wheel until the others get in, then move over," Blackwood said. "We'll give you the best view."

Blackwood got in the back seat, behind the driver. Flanagan scooted toward the middle, with Deeds following to take the back seat directly behind the prisoner. The other three Kansas City lawmen waited near the front of the car until it was fully loaded. They would ride in a second sedan and accompany Nash and his entourage to Leavenworth.

"All set?" Caffrey made to get in the driver's seat—but never got the chance. Flanagan saw movement to the right of a deep green car parked close by. Two men. With tommy guns.

"Let 'em have it, boys!" It happened so quickly: shouting and a hail of bullets, like the sudden ferocity of a pop-up rain shower in the middle of an otherwise sunny day.

But this one wouldn't end in rainbows.

John had barely turned his head to face the front windshield when it exploded with a horrific crack and shower of broken glass. A large spray of blood covered the passenger window and he saw Nash slump in his seat, the top of his bald head blown clean off. Caffrey was down, outside the open driver's-side door.

"What the—"

He and Blackwood fell forward in the back seat as the next blast of bullets riddled the front of the car. Deeds made a gasping gurgle and collapsed onto Flanagan.

"I'm . . . hit." Blackwood was bleeding from somewhere. "Bad."

More bullets. It seemed to go on forever, an unrelenting hell. Flanagan's mind filled with flashing shards, pieces of his life as sharp as the window glass in his face and neck. His mother, humming happily in the kitchen. Laughter. He and his brothers and sisters, jumping in a pile of crimson maple leaves. His dad standing clean and sober in a church pew. A hot-tempered redhead running down a Missouri hillside in a pair of cow shoes.

I'll never catch her now.

A pause in the shooting. The acrid smell of sulfur mixed with blood. Footsteps. Movement somewhere outside the car. Shadow. A sudden darkness overtaking the light.

"They're all dead. Let's get out of here."

Elsie

At first, Lidy mostly slept. But after a few days, she began waking regularly, as if she were on her usual schedule, up with the dawn and slumbering when the shadows in the cabin grew long.

That was when Elsie first noticed the difference in her eyes. There were sullen and murderous looks when she approached the cot with anything she intended to put into Lidy's body somehow. But Elsie saw something altogether different when she put a compress to her gran's forehead or took one of her limp, knobby hands in hers: a fleeting gratefulness. Relief.

She began chatting with Lidy then. Elsie, always more comfortable with talking than silence, was relieved. The one-sided conversations made the hours pass more quickly, seem more hopeful, as though she was chatting with a friend—even if she was talking to herself.

"How do we feel today, Gran?" Elsie would ask as she cleaned her gran like she had her infant son, wiping and changing her, avoiding the eyes as Lidy beamed out her discomfort and shame. She moved to more pleasant tasks as quickly as she could. "Would you like some beeswax on your hands?"

Instinctively, she looked at her gran as if waiting for an answer. In the few seconds it took her to remember there would not *be* an answer, her grandmother's eyes slowly blinked. Once.

"Gran?"

She opened the tin of beeswax and dipped a fingerful. Holding it to Lidy's face, she asked again: "Would you like some on your hands?"

One blink.

Elsie tried something else. "Would you like a bit of broth through the straw?"

The eyes sparked. Fear? Irritation? And then they blinked again, slowly. Twice this time.

Elsie was delighted. After the beeswax, she went about the room, touching various things and asking her gran yes-or-no questions. Did she care for an extra blanket? Two blinks: no. Would she like the window open? One blink. Did she want Elsie to read from her Bible? Two blinks, faster this time, as if emphasizing her dislike.

Gran was in there, after all! Maybe she could come back to them.

It didn't take long to understand that Lidy wasn't as happy about her situation as Elsie was. After a day or so of communicating the basics—yes to a blanket, no to having her hair brushed; yes to building up the fire, no to being read to—Lidy became more petulant.

No, no, no.

Elsie had Jed and Clara bring Hi to the cabin since it seemed she would be there for a while, her mother-in-law reluctantly parting with the boy who had started running—walking no longer satisfactory to get him quickly to the next curiosity. And that smile! Breaking open the round, rosy face like the sun bursting from behind a puffy pink cloud. He loosed himself from Clara's embrace and raced toward Elsie.

"Mama!"

"Let Jed know if you need me," Clara said, trying to keep her eyes away from the body on the cot, but then finding myriad other things that distressed her: the dirt floor, the cramped living space, a woodstove that served as a cooktop, the rough-hewn furniture, a single smudged window. She preferred not to know in such stark terms how the other half—or ninety-five percent—of people lived. What she surmised from her customers was enough, as they watched hawklike while she measured and snipped and weighed their household staples, fists clutching their meager cash or coins. The thought of Hi playing on this floor made her feel faint.

"You'll have your hands full with Hi and your grandmother," she said.

"You're right, Mother Hanson," Elsie said, reaching for her boy and breathing in the lavender goodness from the top of his freshly shampooed head. She had loved kissing him there, before the skull closed over the soft spot he was born with, feeling his heartbeat against her lips. "But I miss him so."

"And we miss *you*." It was true: the store hummed along much better with Elsie and Charles teaming up in the front. Her husband would never say it, but he preferred his daughter-in-law's company to hers there. Clara had never been as quick or nimble; she hadn't known what to say to these people with their covetous eyes and mouths. Elsie was something special, having been of that crowd, knowing their wants and needs without making them feel less than. The women wanted to be like her; the men just wanted her—or, at least, wanted to be given her attention, even if it was for a pound of nails or for choosing a comb or a bit of lace for their women.

Elsie wished her own husband felt that way. It hurt when Jed didn't agree with his mother. He stood silent, ready to bolt, eyes looking at everything in the cabin except her.

She closed the door behind her husband and mother-in-law with relief. She loved Clara and felt lucky to have been taken in by her—despite the less-than-ideal start to her and Jed's marriage. But oh, it felt good to be with Hi and Gran in this place where she had grown up! This room where she had shared a pallet with Shine and Rebecca, at the table where they had done their sums and spelling words, the same dinner table where they had eaten and laughed with Hiram hundreds of times.

So many good memories. So many tough ones, too.

Because she couldn't look at her gran like that and not see her mother in that same spot so many years ago. Or Hiram. Both of those bodies stilled; one stone-cold dead and the other might as well have been.

But Gran was still breathing and feisty as ever inside her skull, behind those watchful eyes.

Elsie took Hi on a tour of the cabin, picking him up and waltzing him from the door to the window, wiping a clean hole in the glass for them to peer outside at the barnyard and beyond. She touched the one photo of her mama and daddy on their wedding day. There sat Alta with those dark eyes, unsmiling as was the custom; Hiram behind her, one hand resting on her shoulder, unable to keep the grin from his face, custom be damned. He must have had to hold still forever to get it so perfectly clear.

The same single wooden shelf that held the framed photo also held the handful of books the Strongs owned. The fat, ancient-looking family Bible that Lidy opened only to add to the family tree in front, meticulous squares full of names and dates, outlined in boxes and connected with lines and dashes. A birth. A marriage. Or a death. Lidy didn't use the Good Book for meditating on Scripture, but no one else dared touch it, either.

Most of the books were Alta's. Elsie had long ago adopted her mother's diminutive white Bible. But there was a book of poetry, a slim *King Lear* bound in dull green leather and Alta's prized copy of *Little Women*, the black fabric of the cover worn down to the fibers with so much reading and rereading. How she and Rebecca had loved when Alta read to them around the woodstove! She was Amy, through and through; Rebecca was the smart tomboy, Jo. That was before Shine showed up, uncategorizable as any single March girl.

Elsie's tour of the room took her to the pie safe, where she had vague memories of cooling, crisp-edged fruit pies before Lidy had made it her own. Hi reached out one dimpled hand to the tin window which caught his eye, the way it gleamed in the light.

The punch-hole pattern was a trio of tulips, and Elsie delighted in naming the flowers for him and counting them, too, using his index finger to trace each bloom and stem.

"One, two, *three*."

Elsie turned to find Gran awake, gaze fixed on her and the boy.

She drew hers and Hi's hands from the cabinet. It was still Lidy's, even if she couldn't open it or stock it with her herbs or tinctures.

But Lidy seemed to want her to touch it. Her gran blinked twice when she removed her hand and then, when Elsie tentatively pressed it against the door again, there it was: one quick closing and opening of the eyes.

"Do you need something, Gran?" Elsie waited. One blink.

Of course! Her gran would know what she needed better than anyone, even Elsie, her sometime helper and apprentice. She swung open the door and her gran complied with one blink.

What did she need? A tea that might go down better than water? She touched the jar of sassafras leaves.

No.

Definitely not tansy. But maybe what Gran called "senny" or sienna? Mostly a laxative, but . . .

No.

Red pepper for cramps. White oak bark for stomach trouble. Slippery elm tea for stirred-up bowels.

No, no, no.

Elsie reached farther back into the cabinet. These were bottles that rarely saw the light of day and she didn't know what was in them. But she held them up, one by one, trying to find the remedy her gran seemed set on.

She emptied the entire cupboard, the kitchen table a jumble with dried leaves and berries in glass jars and tins, a mortar and pestle, bags of dried herbs, bottles of tinctures and salves.

No.

On her tiptoes, Elsie reached into the darkest corner of the safe's top shelf and pulled out a compact bottle with a ridged exterior crafted from cobalt-blue glass. Her trained hands and eyes knew that both of those qualities meant one thing: poison.

For those who were blind or could not read, this special bottle was the equivalent of a skull. There could be no mistaking the color or the feel of its ribbed surface in the palm of your hand. And this was most likely arsenic. Elsie set Hi on the floor and opened the bottle slowly, not wanting to stir the potentially hazardous contents into the air.

Whitish-looking powder.

A single blink.

What? Her gran must be mistaken. This was not a healing herb or medicine.

She recorked the bottle and began to put it back on the shelf. But something cold and ominous crossed her heart like a shadow. She looked at her gran once more.

Blink, blink.

Shine

Shine wowed a pair of lovebirds in Hot Springs for their honeymoon with two flutes of champagne and strawberry liqueur garnished with half of the same heart-shaped red fruit.

"Every marriage should start off sweet and bubbly," Shine said, setting the slender glasses on the bar. "But trust me, you're going to need something stronger, whether it's next week or next year. Or next round. I've got you covered."

Normally, Shine would have gotten a kick out of the way the two made moon eyes at each other, as if to say, "Who, *us?* It's always going to be champagne and strawberries."

But while Shine continued to go through the motions—filling and refilling drinks, cleaning the barware, restocking towels and napkins and garnishes—her heart wasn't in it. Her insides were a molten mass of worry since one of the mayor's men had burst in with the news a few hours ago: Frank "Jelly" Nash had been grabbed up that afternoon in Hot Springs by the FBI.

It was all her regulars could talk about.

"Snatched the son of a bitch up in broad daylight in the middle of Central Avenue," said one man. "Smoking a Cuban at the White Horse!"

"Goddamn G-men didn't even show a weapon," said another, shaking his head. "Jelly shoulda let 'em have it."

The mood at the Southern Club was somber, dampened by

pervasive feelings of shock and disbelief. And fear. If one of the biggest, baddest bank robbers of all time wasn't safe from arrest here, what did it mean for the small-time gangsters, petty criminals, hoodlums and con men? Who was next?

Someone had broken the code, the "neutral territory" notion that had been honored since the first people had discovered the Land of Vapors. And the town would be reduced to nothing but those titular thermal waters if that were to change. Commerce—both the illegal and legal—depended on that and each other to make Hot Springs the prosperous paradise it was. Even while the country suffered, the town still managed to scrape by.

Shine hovered at the edges of conversations. So far it didn't appear anyone knew how the FBI found out Nash was in town. Maybe it would be okay; Nash back in prison and no one the wiser. But right as she started to relax, the talk took a darker turn.

"Well, I'll bet you dollars to donuts that Nash's buddies will show up to make sure he doesn't go back to Leavenworth," said a sour red-faced man at a barstool.

"Make that a 'Jelly' donut," snorted his shorter, bearded friend. "I pity the G-men on that doomed mission. They'll be lucky to make it to breakfast."

Then both men laughed, an ugly chuckle that made the hair on the back of Shine's neck stand on end. She hadn't considered what could be in store for Flanagan. She figured it was over once he arrested Nash. Had she unwittingly sent Flanagan into harm's way? If the possibility had arisen in the immediate aftermath of Hiram's shooting, she would have shrugged.

"No skin off my nose," she might have said. "If something happens, I expect he's getting his just desserts."

But she didn't feel that way anymore. What she did feel was complicated. She had gotten to know John Flanagan. And no matter how she sliced it, he wasn't a bad man. In fact . . .

Shine stopped there. No need thinking on things that couldn't be. Or of that one incredible kiss. But she definitely didn't wish ill on the man. If she were the praying type, she would have sent a few words heavenward on his behalf.

Instead, she focused on wiping the bar of any evidence of spilled drink or food. And she kept her face similarly blank.

Back to business.

It was nearly noon, and Shine had come in early for her shift. She hadn't slept all night, eyes wide in the dark, worrying about Flanagan getting Nash safely to Leavenworth. She folded bar towels like an automaton, barely able to focus. The radio in the back of the Southern Club bar blared big band music, the preferred background for Sam and Duck and the rest of the kitchen crew to do their cleaning and prep work. There was an abrupt scratching sound, needle across vinyl, as Duke Ellington's latest was interrupted on KTHS to deliver a shocking news bulletin.

Frank Nash was dead.

They were calling it the Kansas City Massacre—and for good reason.

The notorious bank robber and prison escapee had been shot down in cold blood while in the custody of the lawmen who were transferring him to Leavenworth. Two men with tommy guns had opened fire on the car being used to transport him in what appeared to be a botched rescue attempt. Nash never made it out of the Union Station parking lot. Worse: multiple officers were dead. Kansas City was in an uproar.

Behind Shine the kitchen fell silent for a few seconds before erupting into mayhem, the clatter of silverware and pots and pans abandoned to sink or stove, brooms and mops dropped to the tile floor. Gasps and shouts.

"What the *hell*?"

"No way our man Nash got got!"

Merle burst out of his "office" in the back of the kitchen, a bathroom that served as his changing room and—Shine suspected—a place to catch a few z's when things were slow or his hangover demanded it. He also kept the books there, on a desk across from the toilet. Shine found the whole operation disgusting, but appropriate. It was a dirty business.

"Jesus H. Christ!" he shouted. "The mayor called. Nash dead is a fucking disaster. For all of us. I'm heading to his office for a meeting."

The news spread like a house afire. Everyone in Hot Springs was heated. And more than a little worried. The bubble that had protected their burbling thermal springs and the rash of illicit activities surrounding them had burst wide open. Who had ratted Nash out to the feds?

Shine stood motionless. The shouts, the kitchen chatter, the banging pans and slamming doors—it was as if they were all far away. She was trying hard not to collapse. The tower of neatly folded towels fell to the floor as she reached toward the bar to steady herself. The noise in her head was at high volume, threatening to split her skull open. And it had one refrain on repeat:

Flanagan is dead. I killed him after all.

When Merle reappeared an hour later, his face was a thunderous dark cloud ready to let loose with some lightning. And it was no secret where those bolts were headed. He strode straight to the bar where Shine had finally taken a seat, wiping silverware with an oiled cloth to remove watermarks and return them to a high polish. Trying to tamp down her panic.

"*You.*"

Merle was fuming but he also looked . . . *fearful*? She felt a sudden chill. But there was no way he could know what she had done. And she wouldn't let him bluff her into confessing.

"You told on Nash," Merle said. "The mayor has friends in the Bureau. There was a call from here to the FBI in Fort Smith yesterday afternoon. And it sure as hell wasn't me."

Shine shrugged, shooting for a nonchalance she didn't feel. She had no idea that calls could be traced! *Holy shit.* "Hmmm. I could say the same. Maybe you had your eye on a reward. I bet Nash's head would bring in more bucks than a whole year of Saturday nights in this joint."

Merle lunged, grabbing for her throat.

Shine slipped around the bar, shoved her way through the swinging doors and ran to the bathroom "office." She slammed and locked the door behind her—just in time.

"Let me in, you bitch!" Merle pounded on the door.

Shine eyed the silver lock she had managed to slide across the door after closing it in Merle's furious face. She hoped it would hold. Shine didn't know how she was going to get out of this—*any* of this. This bathroom. This town. This disaster.

She was a dead woman.

"You're guilty as sin and you know it," Merle blustered. "I know it. Do you think Duck and Sam don't know where I was yesterday at 4:07 p.m. and won't vouch for me? You ignorant red-haired hillbilly!"

Those were fighting words. Anger overcame fear. Ignorant? She'd show him. No one would pin anything on Shine Strong.

She surveyed the cramped bathroom that was both her current prison and safe space. There was a mirror over a porcelain sink stained brown by a perpetual rusty drip; black whisker bits dusted the bowl. The toilet sat underneath a narrow window, cracked open for much-needed ventilation.

There were two hooks on the wall. One held a grubby hand towel and Merle's beat-up fedora; the other a belted pair of Merle's pants along with a wilted shirt stained yellow around the collar. Yesterday's clothes. Merle's black leather bag of toiletries rested on the back of the toilet. She rummaged through them, unsure what might help her out of this mess. Or at least postpone the inevitable.

Merle pounded the door again.

"Fine," he growled, rattling the doorknob for good measure. "Stay in there for all I care. The mayor and some of his boys from the force will be here any minute. You can choose the civilized way to come out—or they can bust the door down and drag you by the hair, you double-crossing ginger. I don't give a good goddamn."

She heard his footsteps recede. The kitchen staff, which had been stunned speechless by the chase and accusations, resumed a tentative hum.

By the hair.

Shine didn't respond. She busied herself with a pair of scissors she had found in Merle's bag, along with a dented tin of black shoe polish and a shaving brush. She surveyed herself in the mirror.

"Goodbye, Shine," she whispered. "Or . . . so long for now."

She gathered her wild orange-red hair as if she was making a ponytail, holding tight near her scalp. Then with a few quick snips, the long curls fell into the sink. She looked in the mirror, fascinated: her wide green eyes and pale, freckled face were now framed by an uneven mane of spiky, carrot-colored locks.

No time for regrets. Shine popped open the tin of shoe polish and, taking a generous gouge, smeared the greasy goop between her palms. She rubbed it on top of and then through her hair, until it was a flat, ugly black. Then she dipped the shaving brush into the tin and touched the bristles above her top lip.

Nice mustache.

A knock at the door, more polite than the earlier pounding.

Merle was back.

"Open up, Shine. Party's over."

Not yet, you S.O.B.

Shine unbuttoned her dress, fingers fumbling, until the whole thing fell in a brown heap around her ankles. Quickly, she pulled on Merle's pants, threw on his smelly shirt and tucked it in before belting the whole ensemble, cranking it to the tightest setting—and praying the pants would stay up.

Merle was done with polite. The door shook in its frame with the next assault, rattling the sliding lock, too.

"Open up right now or we're busting this thing down," Merle yelled. "And no one gives a shit if you get hurt in the process."

Grabbing the fedora, she climbed up on the toilet tank and pushed at the window, a foot high and only slightly wider. It was open a crack. With her free hand, she shoved it out as far as she could, the rusty hinges resisting with a groan.

Could she fit? It didn't matter. She had to try.

She tossed the fedora out the window.

"Ready, guys?" Merle rallied his cronies for the takedown. "Count of three."

Shine put both hands on the edge of the window frame and tried to boost herself up. But the metal cut into her hands and she slid back down the wall. *Jesus.*

"One . . ."

She took a deep breath and jumped again, this time ready for the pain, as she gripped the edges of the window tightly and hefted herself into the open frame.

"Two . . ."

She hung, suspended, half in and half out of the window. She could see the ground of the back alley, the hat which had rolled on its rim and landed by a stinking overfull trash can. Her legs kicked behind her, touching nothing but the stale air of the bathroom. The belt buckle was stuck on the window frame and her body took up every inch of space; she couldn't get her hands inside the bottom of the frame to loosen herself.

Shine wiggled slightly from side to side. *Shit!*

"Three!"

The wooden door withstood the first two rams with a thick pole. On the third try, Merle and the three Hot Springs policemen—two men on either side of the ramming rod—splintered the whole thing into pieces, their bodies falling heavily to the tile floor with the impact.

When the dust settled, Merle stood up, pulled aside the broken door by its knob and stepped inside.

"Shine?"

He was talking to an empty room. The only evidence the young woman left behind was a crumpled dress on the floor. And a sink full of curly orange-red hair.

Above him, a warm summer breeze blew through the open window, carrying the ripe smell of stale piss and rotting garbage.

"God*damn* that girl!"

Lidy

"Are you asking me to murder you, Gran?"

Lidy had put her granddaughter in a terrible position. Not what she wanted. But she hadn't asked to be reduced to an unmoving slab of flagging flesh, either. Hadn't she lived her entire life preparing for the worst? Whether canning extra green beans and ripe tomatoes in advance of a hard winter or carrying a potato in her pocket to prevent rheumatism, Lidy constantly readied for whatever life might mete out.

Except this. This *life*, which she would not acknowledge as living. She, who had imagined and lived through the very direst of moments, had not in her mind's eye seen an ending like this. What a fantastic failure of imagination. She had pictured a gradual or even a sudden decline in her health as she aged—eaten up by cancer or crippled by arthritis that would slow her by inches and then by miles. Or the heavy crushing pain of a heart attack. Frightening, but mercifully brief.

What Lidy was experiencing day in and day out on that cot was anything but merciful.

So she asked Elsie, in the only way left to her, to do what she could not: dispatch her to the hereafter. Her middle granddaughter had balked.

How to respond to Elsie's question with her limited vocabulary of blinks? No, she was not asking to be murdered, simply released from captivity. *No* to murder. *Yes* to death. But that wasn't the question now, was it?

Her eyes welled up. Something Lidy couldn't control anymore, either. A fat, salty drop collected in one corner of her right eye and spilled over, hurrying down the slope of her gaunt cheek.

Elsie dabbed it away with a handkerchief.

"You know I can't do that," she said. But her tone was uncertain.

Lidy had no way to reply. *Yes, you can? No, you won't?* It didn't matter. Lidy remained in the horrible in-between. Nothing would happen.

Not yet.

But Elsie had more mettle than the young woman herself knew. Lidy only prayed she would realize it sooner rather than later.

The next morning, Elsie bustled around the kitchen with a sense of purpose. As if a plan had been crafted, a decision made. Did Lidy dare hope her wish might be granted?

She had raised her granddaughters the best she could. Kept them warm and fed and safe. Taught them right from wrong. How to be strong. How to *be* a Strong: hardworking, curious, kind, loyal. And yes, she had protected them. Not with the ephemeral warmth of hugs and kisses, but with the thick, hard shell of curated truths that covered the tender flesh of their young selves. Their pure hearts. Lidy controlled what she could so that they didn't know absolutely *everything*. Not the hurtful things.

They didn't need to know all the pain their gran had seen people through. Lidy had served as midwife, priest, mother and mediator as she eased her corner of humanity from birth to death, through sicknesses of mind and body. She had dealt with the results of sins and arguments, accidents, ailments and agues. Had she helped a few sufferers meet their maker early to mitigate their pain? Spared some babies a life with parents who couldn't feed or love them? Lidy had played God, wielding her quiet power with cold-blooded calculating or warmhearted acts of kindness, depending on your point of view. Nothing was black or white, though. And she had been comfortable in the gray. Even with her own family.

She had saved herself and Hiram from her brutish husband because no one else would. And she would tell three young girls that their mother had fallen from a hayloft in a terrible accident—not that she had jumped in an attempt to end the life of the third! Or the reason why. So now, who would gently place the tea towel and pillow over her own wizened face? Who would show her mercy?

"Gran," Elsie began, her voice soft. Apologetic. "I've thought about what you asked me yesterday. And I think we should pray on it."

Blink, blink.

Elsie gave a wry laugh. "I knew you'd say that."

She had a Bible in her lap. It was Lidy's own, the large, black leather-bound family Bible passed down from her own mother and kept dusted but unused on the single shelf of books in the cabin. The inside cover had been painstakingly lettered in elegant script, both hers and that of the matriarchs before her, a record of births and deaths and marriages captured in curving loops and straighter strokes of brown-black ink.

But Lidy didn't let anyone touch that Bible—not that there had been much clamoring for it over the years. Elsie was the one girl who had taken to church, and she had inherited Alta's Bible. But now, here she was, holding the Good Book like a right, not a privilege. And Lidy, powerless to stop her.

"Brother Aiken says when he has a troubling question on his heart, he lets his Bible fall open to whatever page it wants to. The answer is usually right there, ready to help him through."

Blink, blink. Faster this time. *No.*

Elsie was not deterred. She thought her gran simply didn't want anything to do with prayer or Scripture. But Lidy had a more pressing reason not to want her granddaughter cracking open that Bible: there was something she had not dealt with, decided about.

Like the Lord, separating wheat from chaff, tossing the latter into the fire. The typically decisive Lidy had wavered for twenty years about what to do.

He who hesitates is lost.

The truth would not—could not—be folded, flattened out or hidden away forever.

The musty tome parted near the middle, revealing an ivory envelope browned with age at the corners and bearing a single scripted name on the front. *Alta.*

"What is this?" Elsie frowned, turning the letter over and opening the delicate flap.

Blink, blink.

But Elsie wasn't looking at Lidy. She was scanning the page that was filled front and back, written in an ink that had aged to a light red brown. Her face changed expressions as quickly as an Ozarks sky—from sunny empty cerulean to threatening nimbus clouds.

"Gran, what does this mean?" Elsie, who never cared for math but had sharpened her skills at Hanson's, swiftly did the calculations. An early spring visit; a late fall baby. "Why did you keep this from us?

"From *Shine*?"

ALTA

1 July 1912

Dear Alta,

I hope this letter finds you well in both body and spirit. I have been worrying and praying about both since I saw you in the spring, a goodly while ago now. I hope it is not upsetting to you that I have thought of you every day, no, every minute of every day, since then.

There is so much I wish I could say to you, to your beautiful face that has become like a homing beacon to me as I travel these roads in hard country, bringing the Word of the Lord to those who have sore need of it. I have been through the dry desert that is Oklahoma; a thirsty land and a thirsty people, many who do not know the Lord and are eager to have the comfort of His saving grace shared with them. My preaching will take me to New Mexico and Arizona, Texas and then up through Arkansas and possibly Missouri again on my way home to Lexington, Kentucky. I'll continue my journey on foot, though I will not turn down a kindly offer of a ride along the way should one be proffered!

Forgive me for writing. I know you forbade me and I swear I will honor that wish after I dispatch this letter. But I feel a burning need to tell you that I have tortured myself over our meeting that day in your garden, as you rose from planting seeds in the barren beds like a saving angel, with apron rather than wings. But a lovelier countenance I do not believe exists, even held up against the host of heaven.

You asked how you could help me. It was biblical, I believe. And simple: "For I was an hungred, and ye gave me meat: I was thirsty, and ye gave me drink: I was a stranger, and ye took me in." I remember how you gasped when I removed my hat as I stepped inside your cabin. I told you that I burned so intensely for the Lord that I couldn't quite contain His fire within me. I thought then that I might have caught the glimmer of a smile.

As I sat at table with you, slaking my thirst with your cold creek water and filling my empty belly with fatback and cornbread sopped in fresh milk, I could feel that you hungered, too. But your starvation was one of spirit. I do not know if it was the act of breaking bread together or the promise of spring around us, but I felt a camaraderie and kinship of spirit immediately. You must also have felt it? For soon, we were talking and laughing like long-time friends.

Until you began to cry.

I will keep close those things that you unburdened from your soul. Your life is much too hard, your heart too frail and fragile. When I asked if I could pray with you and took your hand across the table, I meant only to aid and strengthen you. Please know this.

I still think with shame of all that happened after. I would say that we were both moved by something greater than ourselves, the Holy Spirit, perhaps. But I know our Lord's commandments, and I cannot make excuses. I pray for forgiveness. Yet I still find myself unable to be wholly sorry.

I will want to see you on my return trip if you and the Good Lord will allow it. I swear I shall be happy to be granted the hospitality of your smile, nothing more.

I remain faithfully yours in Christ,

Robert Smythe

Elsie

"And be ye kind one to another, tenderhearted, forgiving one another, even as God for Christ's sake hath forgiven you."

Elsie sat near the front, listening to Brother Aiken's sermon, being delivered with such fervor that the man's thick neck was close to popping his collar open, buttons be damned. She had come to church this morning for solace, to be reminded of the rewards of suffering. For the strength to make difficult decisions. Or to do nothing—which might require that she be even stronger.

She didn't love the message.

It was easier to be angry and hurt by the sinners in her life than to forgive them. Hiram with his drinking and the moonshine making that had cost his life. Her mother, pregnant by another man, ending her life trying to take Shine's. And Gran, daring to play God, deciding who lived and who died; withholding truths, keeping secrets. How could she live with herself?

Now Lidy didn't want to live at all. And wanting Elsie to hasten her death! But whether she did or didn't, Gran was not long for this world. Elsie had sent word to Shine right away, but Lidy might not last to see her granddaughters gathered around her one final time.

Elsie was grappling with another sinner, too.

She had forgiven Jed before. For all of it. For his recklessness with Rebecca. Losing all that money—and causing Shine to have to stay behind to repay it. But he couldn't seem to forgive himself. He had been demoralized by what had happened in Hot Springs. And afterward, working uncompensated at the Strong place for Gran, lower than a hired hand. Elsie had seen him at his lowest, "lower than whale shit," he called it. He could never be the man he had once been in her eyes. And for him, there was no coming back from that.

Then: the whispers.

He was drinking. A lot. His assignment on the Strong farm meant he hadn't regularly shared a bed with Elsie for a while. But even after Rebecca came home and the corn was planted, he still spent the odd night in Hiram's old lean-to room when she needed an extra hand. Or so he said. In town, he chose to sleep in the undersized bedroom downstairs; the maid's room back in the days when they could keep a maid. Jed didn't want to share a room with a "bawling baby," he said. But even when Hi stopped nursing and Elsie put him in his own room, Jed didn't return to hers. Theirs. She knew the arrangement allowed him to come and go as he pleased. With whomever he pleased.

Jed had brought her and Hi back to town yesterday for the night. Rebecca had insisted Elsie take a break from watching Gran and she hadn't argued. She desperately needed a good night of sleep in a comfortable bed. To go to church. Get her head and her heart straight. Then leave Hi with Clara and return to the farm for as long as it took Gran to die.

Clara was delighted to have the boy back again, had been at loose ends without his sunny presence, the endless energy and questions. Hi insisted on seeing his "Paps" at the store, and Clara jumped at the chance to run to Hanson's to show him off.

That had left Elsie and Jed in the foyer at the bottom of the staircase, where they would part ways: she would head upstairs and he would continue toward the room off the kitchen. But she was tired of being by herself. Of being left alone.

"Jed, please. What have I ever done but love you?"

He looked surprised by her words. But then he set his jaw. "I don't believe you ever loved me. Your family only loved what I could do for them. Used me up and then spit me out when things went bad," he said, every word as biting as if it had teeth. "Treated me like I was nothing. Worse than nothing."

"That's not me, Jed," Elsie's voice wavered. "I've tried to make it nice for us. For our family."

Jed shook his head. "You've made a good life for yourself. But I've never really been a part of it. Part of the Strongs. I wanted to be, way back. But now I don't remember why."

He started toward his room but she put her hand on his arm and raised her chin. "Well, if you insist on breaking our marriage vows, I will ask that you find somewhere else to live. I can't abide it under my nose anymore."

His laugh was raw, as if years of swallowing his bile had roughened his throat. "You can't kick me out of my own family home."

"Your parents would be quite discouraged to find out the kind of husband and father you are—if they haven't heard it elsewhere already. Let alone want it happening under their roof."

"You're wrong." Jed was furious. He pinned her against the wall, his sour breath in her face, while she absorbed the heat from the full length of his body pressed against hers. "I'm their golden boy. You're just one of my mistakes they've seen to do right by."

"You're not the golden boy anymore," she said. "Hiram is."

Jed closed his hands around Elsie's throat. How strange that anger could distort his fine features, turn him into someone unrecognizable. Ugly. Elsie reached for his hands with hers, trying to pull them from her neck. She couldn't scream. Or breathe. Why did it look like his bulging eyes were about to burst from his head, when it was her throat that was cut off, the blood vessels in her eyes aching at their breaking point? She tried to wrestle away, kick at him.

But Jed tightened his grip, like wood clamps turned to the tightest notch. "Don't you talk to me like that."

Her vision went black at the edges. She no longer felt pain.

There was a noise from the yard. Hi's laughter; Clara's teasing tone.

Jed dropped Elsie like a pile of laundry, his furious footsteps receding, punctuating what he had done. What he had left unsaid. Somehow, she was able to breathe again; deep, desperate lungfuls of air that weren't enough. Coughing and crying without sound, snot dripping from her nose, she got herself on all fours. By the time she heard footsteps on the front porch, she had managed to drag herself upstairs, where she fell onto the bed, panting.

She didn't go down for dinner.

Church, once a balm for her soul, was now a torment. And not because she sat alone—although that was painful. Jed hadn't shown up here for months. Maybe years.

It was more the looks that she got. Or *felt,* drilling into the back of her head as she sat in her pew. Pitying glances had replaced envious ones. Smugness that came of knowing someone's business—and they surely knew her husband wasn't coming home every night. The worst was wondering who in that holy building was betraying her. Or knew the person doing it.

Watching her fall, be reduced to a mere mortal; she who had dared to set her sights on more. Wanting to be a different kind of wife and mother than she had, a family that was whole.

They were enjoying how she was brought low. Even with them. Or worse. At least they didn't marry a drunk or a cheater. "Let that be a lesson," she could almost hear them say in tittering groups in the churchyard or over Sunday dinner. "Money can't buy you love—or happiness."

And then, "Pass that red-eye gravy, if you please." Forgetting all about her.

She was glad they couldn't see the pair of purple thumbprints on her neck.

Elsie sat in her pew a few moments longer, after the final prayer and the exhortation from Brother Aiken to "go forth to love and serve the Lord." She took a calming breath, pulled back her slouching shoulders.

Elsie couldn't wait any longer for the Almighty to answer her prayers, for her gran *or* her husband. Or to expect a handsome prince to deliver her "happily ever after." The most important stories are the ones we tell to—and about—ourselves. And her story could no longer be one of weakness and wishing, of deference and denial. If she desired a different ending, she would have to act.

In a moment, she would gather her purse and Bible and face the congregation, the pastor and everything that lay outside those hand-carved wooden doors. And walk right on through them all. She would do what she needed to do.

It was time to rescue her own damn self.

Shine

She stopped running after she made it out of the long alley behind the Southern Club. Shine straightened her stolen fedora and walked at a businesslike clip, eyes focused ahead on the sidewalk ahead of her. Trying for calm. Then she ducked into the pharmacy to wait. Shine resisted the urge to touch her sweating upper lip, afraid to smear her mustache.

There would be a trolley soon; it stopped here every ten or twelve minutes on its way through town to the railroad station. She prayed to a God she wasn't sure she believed in that she hadn't just missed one. A mile or so to safety. But the clock was ticking. Merle and his friends would be on the streets, in the alleys. Everywhere.

But they were looking for a red-haired girl.

She busied herself with an issue of *Life* magazine on the rack near the front of the store. The cover was an illustration of a bored blonde in a fancy black satin evening gown, standing in front of an array of current news headlines: "Reichstag Bows to Hitler," "Roosevelt Shuts Banks," and "120 Die in Quake." The title of the illustration was "Nothing Ever Happens."

Didn't she wish that was true! She could write a few headlines, too: "Mother Dies Falling from Barn Loft," "Moonshiner Shot to Death by Prohibition Officer," or "Bootlegger Wrecks Car and the Family Business."

"You gonna buy that, mister?" A man's voice sent a jolt of fear through her. Was he talking to her?

Mister.

"I can't sell it to no one else, the way you got it bent this way and that."

Shine didn't trust her voice. At the counter, she put the magazine down and impulsively added a chocolate bar on top. Fifteen cents for the magazine, another nickel for the candy. She tried to act like frivolously spending her hard-earned dimes was nothing new. Reaching for the pouch around her neck, she extracted two thin dimes.

"Have a good day," the clerk said, sliding the money off the counter, plunking the coins into the cash register drawer.

Shine didn't look up. She didn't want anyone to examine her closely. To see the scared, poorly coiffed young woman in the too-large men's clothes and hat that had seen better days.

At last: the squeal of brakes and hydraulic hiss as the trolley stopped in front of the pharmacy. Grabbing her loot, she stepped out on the sidewalk and swung herself up onto the streetcar.

Ten minutes later, she had a one-way train ticket to Missouri.

Shine took a seat by a window overlooking the platform, so she could see trouble coming—whether that was Merle, the mayor, or anyone else on a manhunt. *Womanhunt.*

But the only familiar faces were in the row beside her: the honeymooners from the bar the night before! The man was by the window, reading *The Hot Springs Sentinel-Record* with the headline "Five Slain at Union Station."

Shine turned her face away. Something hard blocked her throat, as if she had swallowed a brick. *No tears.* Even if it hurt to hold them in. She couldn't think about Flanagan right now. She had to make it back to Gran and Elsie and Becks.

A tap on her left knee made Shine jump. She was busted; the jig was up! But it was the woman honeymooner, leaning across the aisle.

"You look different in the daytime," she whispered with a conspiratorial smile. "But I think you need to check your mustache. It's a smidge . . . smeared?"

She pressed a compact mirror into Shine's hand as the train groaned, pulling away from the station.

"And thank you. That cocktail was the best drink I've ever had in my life."

Rebecca

"'Bout time you made it home," Jed had said when he picked her up at the train station three years ago in the Hansons' horse and buggy. "Your gran's nearly killed me off getting the plowing done and every other chore under the goddamn sun. She's taken her pound of flesh and then some."

"Reckon it was her due." Rebecca had reluctantly taken his hand to boost herself into the wagon. She wouldn't have required his help before the accident. Hated needing it then. "Oh, and good to see you, too."

Jed shook his head. "Thought you might be appreciative. All I done in your stead."

He tossed her canvas bag into the open buggy and swung himself up onto the bench that had room for two.

"Nice wheels."

Jed grunted. She'd gone and pissed him off. "Your daddy's, I s'pose." Might as well heap it on; his irritation made an inadequate but pleasurable balm for her soul.

It was a stonily silent ride to the Strong place.

Rebecca had returned with her hands itching to rearrange her brother-in-law's pretty face. But once she saw her beloved farm lit up in that tentative spring sunshine—the serene greens of the pasture grass, waving a warm hello; the regimented rows in the cornfield, patiently awaiting planting—she forgave all. Or at least decided to live and let live.

Jed had stepped up at the farm in her absence. Under pressure from Gran, no doubt. Yet he had done the work. Not with care or precision—or even an understanding of growing things or the animals that fed them, whether by providing eggs, milk, meat or labor. If they weren't exactly flourishing, they were alive. And for that, Rebecca had been grateful.

By summer, they'd come to an understanding about the work. Rebecca handled the care and feeding of the animals; Jed hauled the water to fill their troughs and buckets. She yoked up the mules; he guided the plow behind them under her watchful eye, correcting him if he veered off course or used an overly heavy touch with his whip. Or his words.

She helped Gran get the garden planted; Jed watered while she weeded everywhere that didn't require her to bend her bad leg. He used the hoe for the rest. The women harvested and shelled, stemmed, skinned, sliced and chopped—then pickled, cured, canned and preserved. Rebecca fell into bed most nights as soon as supper was over and the sun slid behind the hills, brilliant colors of cantaloupe melting together and then blending into darkness.

Since Gran still had the bedroom and Jed had claimed Hiram's old lean-to room off the back, Rebecca made do on a cot by the woodstove. She could've slept on the floor and not known the difference. She was bone-tired. But they had managed.

Then, after that first fall harvest, Jed laid in a few cords of wood and went back to living in town, coming to the farm only on request. He figured he'd done his time. She and Gran weren't sorry to see him go. Shine would be back by spring; they would get by.

Except she wasn't.

The depressed economy had eventually thrown a sopping wet blanket on the city of Hot Springs. Just as the Strongs' fortunes were dashed in that devastating October car wreck, many of the rich had lost everything in the more famous crash of '29, too. Numbers were down. So were tips. What Shine had predicted would be a six-month stint in the flush, fat times had turned into three years.

Soon.

It would be good to have Shine here at last, with her strong back and her grit. Rebecca would even welcome home the mercurial moods and Shine's ability to nurse a grudge, tending it with the care others might bestow on a baby. All of that served to make Shine interesting; kept *life* interesting for all of them. Her sister was aces in tough situations.

Like yesterday, when Rebecca had gone to town for provisions—a twenty-pound sack of flour, a jar of honey Elsie had insisted on for Gran's bedsores, and a new splitting wedge to replace the one Jed had pounded into an overlarge stump that neither of them could bust free.

Jed had been nowhere in sight when she walked Cowboy to the back of the store to load. Rebecca had dismounted and left the horse waiting while she went to the storeroom door. She was loath to venture inside; there were always men sitting around, whittling and swapping stories. She had raised her fist to knock when she heard a voice: "I don't know how you do it, juggling them girls, keeping 'em up in the air like you do."

"Not to mention that pretty filly you got at home," someone added.

"Definitely burning my candle at both ends." It was Jed, holding forth loudly. "And I thank God and Jesus for my extra-long candle."

The backroom burst into dirty laughter, edged with something like admiration. Rebecca had turned away, face burning.

She helped herself at the flour barrel and took off for home.

Now, this late June morning, Rebecca weeded rows of corn with her hoe to give the corn plants more room to grow. Hacking weeds from the hard cracked earth didn't do the crops much good without water. But it stilled her mind, which was turning over her worries about Jed and Elsie like a river rapid, raging over the rocks, shifting and shaping them over time.

But she didn't have a half-million years to smooth the edge off these troubles.

The dinner bell jolted her out of her thoughts. She glanced up at the sun, not quite overhead. Earlier than usual. But hell, she'd eat. Rebecca had been starving since she got back to the farm and Kinney Creek. She was working hard, harder than she ever had. But she had never been so hungry, ravenous; as if craving something to fill a bottomless emptiness, her body barely more than sun-browned skin stretched over bones.

As she rounded the corner of the barn, the cabin came into view. Elsie was on the edge of the porch, her hand still holding the rope of the dinner bell. But her face was turned toward the path leading up from the woods.

They had company. A young man, from the looks of it, likely someone come to pay a last visit to Gran. There had been a number of those lately, once word got around. Somebody grateful for a life she'd saved or birthed, a body she had healed, a worry she had listened to or a mind she had eased.

Or maybe he was a peddler or a preacher, passing through. Selling household tools or salvation.

Elsie screamed. The young man, surprised, looked up so that Rebecca could see the face beneath the brim of the dusty fedora. And what she saw made her break into a stumbling run, faster than she could easily manage, dragging her bad leg as she went. But she didn't care.

The young man ran, too, meeting her halfway between the house and the barn.

"Shine!"

"*Becks!*"

The sisters threw their arms around each other, laughing, making a slow circle in the dry dirt of the barnyard.

"Let me in, you two goofs." Elsie had jumped down the porch steps, wiggling her way into the embrace. That's when Shine's fedora fell off and rolled into a fresh cow plop, sending Shine into another fit of laughter—and her two sisters into shock.

"Holy moly, Shine!" Rebecca gawked. "You look like a match that's been all used up, skinny as a stick and black where I should be seeing orange flames."

Elsie's mouth hung open. "And is that . . . a *mustache?!*"

Shine's eyes grew wide and she began swiping hard at the shoe polish that remained on her upper lip. "I forgot all about that darn thing!"

They sat on the porch then, as she told them about the trouble with her friend Birdie and how she had turned in Frank Nash to the FBI. Her narrow escape from Merle, the mayor and his minions.

"Once they figured out I had squealed on Nash, I was in hot water and I don't mean the kind they pay to take a bath in down there," Shine said. "I'm not bragging, but I'm kinda famous around Hot Springs."

Both sisters looked at her with raised eyebrows.

"Okay, I *am* bragging," Shine laughed. "I got popular by slinging the Strong shine and lots of other libations at the Southern Club. So there was no way I was going to get out of town as my usual redheaded self. I had to improvise. Do you like me better as a brunette?"

"Shine, I couldn't love you more than I already do," said Elsie. "But you look like a tatty version of Charlie Chaplin's little tramp. You're going to need lye soap and plenty of elbow grease to get that polish out of your hair."

"Yeah, or you're going to give Gran a good scare," Rebecca said.

"Speaking of the old gal," Shine said. "Where *is* Gran? I thought she might've missed me. Even if she isn't the hugging kind."

Total silence. That's what it felt like, although surely the birds still sang and the cicadas buzzed their metallic melodies, hidden in the trees and high grass of the fencerow. Rebecca looked at Elsie; Elsie stared back.

"*What?* What is it?" Shine's smile was gone, wiped away like the smear of shoe polish above her lip.

"I thought you knew . . . that you must have gotten the letter I sent. Gran's had a stroke," Elsie went on, tearing up at the telling. "It's bad, Shine."

Shine shook her head as if to clear it. "But she's alive, right?"

"If you can call it that. She can understand us perfectly. But she can't speak a word. Or move a muscle," Elsie explained. "And she doesn't want to be alive, that's for sure. Let's go inside. I'm sure she's heard all the commotion and is waiting for you."

At that, the three young women fell in line from oldest to youngest, Rebecca opening the door for Elsie and Shine to step through before closing it behind her.

"Gran? Look what the cat dragged in!" Elsie's voice was falsely bright.

Shine recoiled as she took in the scene inside the cabin. Rebecca was shocked to realize she had become accustomed to Lidy lying there, shrunken and helpless, taking up maybe a third of the space on that slim cot. Pale skin draped loosely across bones, like laundry pinned to the thin lines of her body. When had that iron-gray hair turned a wispy white? The only signs of life were those eyes, black coals in the ashen ruin of her face. Shiny. Alert. Waiting.

But Shine barely skipped a beat. How Rebecca admired her that ability! Shine made her way to Lidy, giving her gran an awkward squeeze and a kiss on the cheek. Rebecca remembered coming upon Lidy laid out in the garden, thinking her gran dead. The soul-lightening relief when she had found the faint pulse, followed by the crushing understanding, later, that Lidy would never recover. That she would never hear Gran call her name again. Eat one of her famous peach pies. Or sit with her on the porch in companionable silence, shelling peas.

"Now, Gran, what's this I hear about you being lazy?" Shine pulled up a chair beside Lidy, took one of her gran's limp hands. "I reckon you've earned it and then some, all the years of hard labor you've put in."

Lidy's eyes filled and slowly leaked, unchecked, from their corners.

"Now, Gran, don't tell me you've gone soft." Shine playfully poked Lidy in the ribs. Nothing.

"Well, don't worry. I'm home now. You got all three granddaughters to keep you going."

Blink.

"That means yes," Elsie was quick to explain their special limited language. "Two blinks mean no."

"Well, you always said life is easier when you keep things simple, Gran," said Shine. "Wish I'd done a better job of that the last few years."

Elsie bustled around, giving Lidy some water through a straw, while Rebecca pulled up another chair and a footstool so the three of them could surround their gran. Close the family circle, its remaining members together at last.

Shine regaled them all with her adventures since she'd left Kinney Creek. From her and Jed being held at gunpoint by a thirsty young mountain man to selling the Strong shine to the Southern Club. Rooming with Birdie. Waiting on the likes of Babe Ruth. Getting tipped by Al Capone.

"I swear, Shine!" Elsie exclaimed. She had missed this, the stories, the way Shine spun her escapades into towering tales, with her as the outmanned underdog surviving on her wits and wiles—and sometimes the wave of a pistol. Rebecca, too, had relaxed back into her chair, caught up in the story. She marveled at her baby sister. For her venturesome spirit, yes, but mainly for the fact that she was here. Home at last.

"Weren't you scared old Scarface would shoot you dead if you messed up his drink order?" Elsie went on. "Or put you in a pair of cement shoes and drop you in the hot springs?"

"Nah," Shine said. "The man was a fan. Of me *and* our shine. Why, one day he gave me a hundred-dollar bill! I coulda been home in a few weeks instead of a few years if everyone was as good a customer as old Snorky!"

By now, the sun was well into its afternoon arc, but the women kept listening, laughing, mesmerized by their sister's stories—and the miracle of being together. At some point, Elsie made butter sandwiches; Rebecca fetched a pail of fresh Kinney Creek water for tea. It was as if Shine's words were weaving a web around them, suspending them safely in the present with no worry about the past or what tomorrow might bring.

It was glorious.

Later, after a break for chores and tending to Gran, the women reconvened for a light supper of cornbread and last summer's green beans from a jar. Elsie dipped into Lidy's precious crock of bacon drippings, plopping a spoonful on the warm beans. A special treat for the occasion.

Someone lit the kerosene lamp at Lidy's bedside, turning the light low. The burning eyes had finally closed, their gran exhausted from the afternoon excitement. Staying awake and keeping her mind engaged had taken a toll.

Shine pulled the blanket up to her gran's chin and tucked it around the thin body. Then she sat back at the table with her sisters, like when they used to gather after the dishes were cleared and cleaned to do their ciphering and perfect their cursive script. And poke, tease and make faces at each other when Gran wasn't looking.

"But what about those prohis? What happened to Flanagan?"

Unsurprisingly, Elsie still remembered the dashing prohi who made her drop an apronful of fresh eggs that summer day. What a mess! But nothing like the disaster that would come later, with Hiram shot at the still while Shine watched.

Flanagan. Rebecca looked hard at her baby sister. This was interesting. Would Shine admit how Flanagan had spent all his free time with her, searching high and low for that murderer McConnell? Trying, she knew, to make up for being party to Hiram's death? Or report the way he had looked at her like Shine was the be-all, end-all—and how everyone from Birdie and Bernyce to Eulalie and anyone else on Central Avenue with eyes in their heads assumed they were a couple? How she sent him back to Fort Smith once they had their man—or found him dead, anyway—oblivious of how much he seemed to want to stay? To be *her* man?

Shine was smart and perceptive when it came to making mash and moonshine, plans and schemes, calculations and contingencies. But when it came to listening to her heart, her youngest sister was deaf as a post.

Maybe it was not knowing her mama. And losing their daddy. Shine was hell-bent on preserving what she had left at all costs, pouring all her hope, effort, dreams and energy into their family, wanting to keep them safe. Keep them *Strong*. And to hell with the rest. She hadn't had the time to consider what she wanted or needed beyond this small sphere of love. Rebecca might not have, either, if she hadn't been laid up with her ruined leg and time to think. About how life was too magnificent and precious to be lived alone. That enlarging your circle didn't dilute love, but miraculously multiplied it. That the heart was a roomy organ, for sure—if you opened the doors.

But what Shine owned up to wasn't at all what Rebecca had expected.

"I killed Flanagan," she said. "Without even firing a shot."

Lidy

Elsie fidgeted by her side for most of the afternoon.

When she wasn't sitting, she dusted and tidied, even when a white-gloved finger would have wiped in vain to find a speck of dirt. Afterward, she helped herself to a dipperful of the fresh creek water from a bucket on the porch. Inspired, she had tried to force some down her gran's throat with a straw, as though she didn't want to drink alone. Lidy felt the cool wet hit her thick fat tongue—she imagined it like a cow's tongue, long and purply gray, covered with bumps like gooseflesh—which expelled the water out of the corners of her mouth.

"Maybe I got a drop or two down your gullet, Gran," she sighed, patting Lidy's face dry with her dish towel. Then she sat and began fidgeting again. Lidy, hawklike, noted the way her hands worried the dusty blue chair cushion she held in her lap. She stood again, pacing and staring out the window for a long while before making her way back to her gran's side, where the restless squirming would begin anew.

Maybe her middle granddaughter was reconsidering her request to be put out of her misery. Elsie had returned from church a few days ago resolute, as if she had thought things through, made a decision. Or left it in the Lord's hands.

Elsie's skittish behavior today could have more to do with Jed coming by, rather than reconciling Lidy's wishes for an early exit from this earth. Shine sent for him to clean out what remained of his belongings from Hiram's old lean-to, where he stayed while helping out. Jed had been a sorry substitute for Rebecca, but beggars couldn't be choosers—and Lidy hated to admit how close the Strongs had come to being beggars. After Rebecca returned, he mostly moved home, sleeping at the farm when she needed an extra hand. Lidy thought he liked having two places—made it that much easier to be thought somewhere he wasn't. But now that Shine was home, they had need of that room.

What could Lidy say of his time here? Chores generally got done. No animals died of thirst or lack of food, although she suspected they had been shorted a meal here and there. The corn seed was sown. Some plants made it to knee high. But nothing had done well in this drought. That could not be laid completely at her grandson-in-law's dragging feet. But fences went unmended, and the hayfield, with its stunted stalks, still needed threshing to even partially replenish the loft.

Mostly what Jed had done here was eat and sleep. Lidy made sure he had a hot supper, even if it was warmed over from the day before. She never sat at the table with him; she had nothing to say and it was clear he felt the same. Theirs was a partnership built on the mathematics of mistakes, not mutual like or respect. He owed them. And, by God, Lidy would have her due. After supper, he would grunt a goodbye and head to bed. The slant-roof addition to the cabin was more like a shed than a real room; it could only be accessed by the outside. Hiram joked it was an attempt to claim some peace and quiet away from all the womenfolk. But he built it onto the house in great sadness, when he wasn't sure he wanted to live at all, and it showed.

There, Jed drank whatever he could procure, nicked from the Strong family stores, Hanson's or elsewhere. Lidy could gauge the quantity by how quickly he got up the next day. She rose with the rooster at dawn, but Jed didn't appear sometimes until late morning, snagging the cold biscuit she left for him on his way to the barn or fields. Jed also slipped off, from time to time, after chores or dinner. Lidy didn't know exactly where he went, but she was certain it was not to climb into Elsie's bed in town. Lidy kept that knowledge close, like a festering wound under gauze. Who would she tell?

She chose to stay silent. Lidy was already run ragged between her chores and the garden, where she worked so hard for such a pitiful harvest. These past few years, she had to coddle every slight seedling into the most meager of fruiting or vining. Lidy needed what work she could wring out from the unsavory young man.

And now? She couldn't warn Elsie if she wanted to. Her granddaughter, holding the cushion from their one good chair in her lap. Lidy noted the high-necked dress she wore, even in summertime. She recognized what it meant, having had her own scars and sorrows to cover up in her day. Jed had finally crossed the line with the only person who truly loved him.

Elsie turned the round cushion as though she were searching for an edge, something to hang on to, but couldn't find purchase. A life preserver. The opposite of what Lidy craved.

Please. I'm ready to go.

When the sun started easing its way into shadow, Elsie lit the kerosene lantern hanging on a square nail near the door, even though there was plenty of daylight left. Lidy hated the dark. It wasn't fear, exactly. But being unable to move had sharpened her instincts, her desire to see what was coming for her, even if she could do nothing about it. Elsie always made sure Lidy was asleep before turning down the lantern and heading to bed in the room that had been Hiram and Alta's.

Elsie took in a deep breath beside her, releasing it slowly. "Gran, I've been thinking—"

Lidy's spirit perked imperceptibly in its prison of flesh.

"I prayed on it." Elsie's voice wobbled. But her eyes were steady as she met Lidy's. "I asked for strength. To discern the right path. And do what needs to be done. I've come to think it's not a sin, helping you do what you can't do for yourself."

Yes.

Lidy blinked—just once—but feared closing her eyes, even for the briefest of seconds. Worried this tenuous understanding could evaporate in that slip of time. That Elsie would change her mind.

"Maybe you don't deserve my help. But mercy isn't about deserving, I guess." She leaned down and pressed her lips to Lidy's forehead, creased and cracked like dry leather. "I'm ready if you are, Gran."

Lidy did not hesitate. She bestowed a single blink of blessing. Closed her eyes as the cushion came down to meet her, softness on her face. Then firm. Stifling stiffness over her nose and mouth. The slow burning of the remaining air in her lungs, devoid of precious oxygen, trapped; the uptick of her heartbeat, pattering and then beginning to pound with lack.

Bang!

The unmistakable sound of a rifle shot from the direction of the barn.

"What in the world—"

Elsie's arms sprung up, releasing the cushion, which fell to the floor and rolled harmlessly on its edge in a long lazy loop before falling flat at last, a milky-blue eye staring blindly at the cabin ceiling. By that time, she was out the door. She slammed it closed with such force that the kerosene lantern jolted from its nail, shattering the glass globe into sparkling shards on the hard dirt floor.

Rebecca

The hunting wasn't very good.

The drought had been rough on birds and critters, too. Berries, seeds, leaves and insects weren't as plentiful; water dried up in creeks and ponds. People all over these hills hunted what animals they could find to fill their bellies with no thought to how those creatures might be replenished. Deer were practically nonexistent. And Rebecca's beloved quail could scarcely be found in coveys; she was fortunate to find a pair or a singleton hiding in the hedgerows. Still, she had shouldered both rifle and shotgun on the off chance that today would be her day.

Her heart wasn't in it. She was worried sick about her family. Gran, for starters, barely hanging on—and not a thing to be done about it. But what was eating her alive was anxiety for her sisters: one hurt, and one hell-bent on hurting someone else.

Last night, after Gran had fallen asleep, the three sisters prepared for bed. Rebecca planned to sleep on a pallet by Lidy; the other two sisters would share the bedroom. Rebecca stripped off her shirt and pants, content to sleep in her undershirt and favorite pair of long johns, shiny and thin with wear. Shine unbuttoned her dress and threw it haphazardly over the chair, then sat down on it to remove her boots.

"My dogs are barking," she said to no one in particular, shaking out a pair of odoriferous stockings. "Standing behind a bar all night is tough, but it's nothing compared to a full day of farm-work."

Elsie didn't make a move to put on her nightgown.

"What are you waiting for?" Shine said, poking her head through her own, a simple straight cotton shift that hung to her knees. "Seems marriage and motherhood would make you less modest, not more."

Elsie shrugged. "I'll sleep in my dress tonight," she said. "My nightgown's in need of washing."

"You'll be hotter than Satan's house cat in that getup," Shine said. "I don't know why you're wearing that high-necked thing in the summertime anyways."

"I'm fine," Elsie replied. But she didn't look at either sister.

"Hold on a minute," said Shine. "What's going on?"

She turned to Rebecca, as if the two of them were in cahoots. But Rebecca shook her head.

There had been a pause, a beat of silence that held the three of them suspended, like a soap bubble floating free on the breeze for an instant, but duty-bound to burst. As if they all knew that what happened next would change everything.

Slowly, mechanically, Elsie reached for the topmost button on her dress and undid it. Her eyes remained straight ahead, staring at something, anything other than the flabbergasted face of a sister. One after another, the buttons disappeared until the bodice of her dress fell open at last.

Her slender throat bore a matching set of dark purple bruises, as if a criminal had been inked and thumbprints pressed on the tender vellum of her skin.

But then, of course, he had.

Elsie bowed her head in the deathly quiet. Those soundless, wordless fifteen seconds felt like a lifetime. Then Rebecca and Shine both breached the space between them, holding their sister while she cried.

Shine was incandescent, chewing Elsie up one side and down the other for not telling her sooner, raging against her brother-in-law and scaring the absolute bejesus out of Rebecca. Gran's eyes had flown open, taking in the chaotic scene. Maybe Shine wasn't that good with feelings after all.

"How could I be such a fool? You might've moped around for a month if we hadn't made you two get hitched," Shine railed. "But you'd have gotten over it. I let myself be blinded by that man's cheap charm—and my desperate need of his Model A coupe. Both of them, worthless junk."

"I wanted that marriage, Shine. With my whole heart," Elsie said, wiping her eyes. "You didn't *make* me do anything."

Rebecca wouldn't have been surprised to see steam coming off her youngest sister; she was that hot. What she could see were the gears in Shine's head, grinding away.

"I've got a mind to finish that one," Shine said. "The only thing that kept Jed safe this long is the fact that you loved him."

"I still do, Shine," Elsie said, her voice dull. "But he doesn't love me. Or Hi. No one can make him."

"But I *can* make him leave," Shine huffed. "I'll ride to town first thing tomorrow and tell him he needs to get his stuff. And then I'll persuade him that he needs to go. Leave town for good. Laying hands on my sister? That dog don't hunt."

But Rebecca did. She hadn't wanted to hang around the cabin all day, waiting for Jed to show up. She needed some fresh air. She'd grabbed her guns this morning and left Shine to stew and Elsie to fret. And Gran to lie there and watch the whole thing.

But walking in the woods and wading through knee-high fescue failed to soothe her. She felt the weight of her worry, a boulder in her lower belly. Rebecca couldn't shake the feeling that something was off. Like the eerie yellow stillness of a sky that hadn't yet lowered a funnel cloud—but soon would.

Rebecca turned her nose toward home. She took a trail that led her across the slick stones of Kinney Creek where Shine and Hiram had once made their moonshine: the Strong stuff. That meant their high-quality shine, naturally. But also what they boasted about being made of themselves. It had been a good while since Rebecca had felt up to her name.

Limping slightly, she quickened her pace. Something told her she didn't have the luxury of being weak anymore.

SHINE

She was in the barn loft, waiting for Jed. She had told him to meet her there after he gathered his belongings from the lean-to room.

"One of the loft doors is stuck closed on its track," she said. "I need you to help me give it the old heave-ho. Ladders are still tough for Becks, although she won't admit it."

"You Strongs. Always trying to squeeze the last juice out of a man, I swear to God," Jed grumbled. "If it doesn't take long, I guess. I need to get home before dark."

Home. Shine almost snorted. A grown-up, married man—a father!—living with his daddy and mama. While Jed may have hated his time on the farm, he had liked having somewhere else to stay. Or *say* he was staying. But now that Shine had come home, he didn't seem heartbroken to relinquish his room or role as sometime farmhand.

"Glad you all got enough hands around here," he said. "Finally."

"I reckon we do," Shine replied. "Rebecca and I got the farm chores covered. And Elsie is caring for Gran until . . ." Here, she had paused. "Until she doesn't need to anymore. Then she can get back to you and Hi, where she belongs."

As if I'd allow that to happen.

Jed hadn't replied. But the way he looked at her then stuck in her mind like a piece of rusted barbed wire. Was it "I don't care" or "You don't know shit"?

Either way, she didn't like it. That look had cemented her conviction that she was doing the right thing now.

She was glad that the lean-to only had an outside door, so Elsie wouldn't have to lay eyes on the bastard. And Rebecca had gone hunting, hoping to rustle up a squirrel or rabbit for tomorrow's stewpot—and stay out of the fray. When Shine had joked that she'd gotten out of the habit of eating critters, Rebecca had shot back that any meat was a treat these days. Gran had sold the boar hog and then the sow, to make ends meet. And when the old milk cow gave birth this spring, instead of fattening up the steer for their own larder, Lidy sold him as well. There wasn't anything to fatten him with—and the money he fetched helped them catch up on their bills after another hard winter.

Shine had about given up hope when she heard the creaking whine of the barn door. Footsteps followed, as Jed walked to the ladder that led up to a square-cut hole in the loft floor. There was the squeak of each wooden two-by-four nailed into the wall that served as a step on that ladder.

Jed's hatless head popped through the hole, shaking a few stray pieces of straw from his dark blond hair. With his hands on the edges of the opening for leverage, he boosted his body into the loft.

"Which one is the problem?" Jed stood and eyed the loft doors, dusting off his forearms and shirt impatiently. He was irritated to be held up from whatever he was looking forward to in town. A hot dinner at the Hansons'; a burning shot of whiskey. Or maybe he had a warm body waiting for him.

Shine stood up from her seat on a squat stepladder. "Actually, you're the problem, brother."

The pleasing peaks and planes of Jed's face twisted in confusion, then annoyance. "Quit jacking with me. I got places to be."

"Don't I know it," Shine said. "I could almost take it if you were just a spoiled idiot who can't drive worth a crap and damn near broke my sister's leg off. Who lost half our money. And pissed away even more. I've been wanting you gone since that prohi told me you tipped him off about Daddy's still," she went on. "And to think we welcomed you into our family after you got him killed."

"Now, hold on." Jed backed slowly toward the opening of the loft. "You all didn't 'welcome' me into this fucked-up family. Your daddy didn't want me anywhere near it. And as I recall, there was a gun to my head at the wedding. Or at least pointed at some vital organ—"

"That's been the real problem," Shine interrupted. "The wedding. You married my sister. Who loved you, for some reason. Thought a leopard could change his spots, I guess. Instead, you cheated on her. But even with all your sins, shortcomings and sheer stupidity, I could've let bygones be bygones."

She pulled the pistol from the pocket of her overalls.

"Whoa! Let's not get crazy," Jed stammered, smirk suddenly replaced with fear.

"But now you've gone and laid hands on her." Shine shook her head slowly, as though regretful of what she was going to say next. Even though she wasn't—not by a long shot. "She's better off without you. We all are."

Jed's face paled. He looked shiny, sweating in a sunlit strip of the loft strewn with several inches of hay and straw.

"You aren't gonna shoot me now, Shine." He made a nervous sound that approximated laughter. "That doesn't make any sense."

"You're right," she said. "I'm not going to shoot you. First off, you aren't worth a goddamn bullet. And second, why should I do the dirty work and take the blame when you can do it yourself?"

"The hell I will," Jed said. But his voice cracked. His eyes scanned the scene in the barn loft as he began to understand what Shine had in mind.

There was the stepladder that she'd been sitting on. And above her, barely hung over the highest beam in the barn loft, was a loop of rope—the end of which she had wrapped several times around a hook on the wall that was typically home to a pitchfork. Jed watched open-mouthed as Shine untied the rope and let out the length, so that the noose came down about six feet off the floor.

"You crazy bitch," Jed said, his tone a combination of fear and disbelief. "You wouldn't."

"I would and I am," she said. "But first things first."

Shine took out a sheet of folded ledger paper from her pocket and handed it to Jed, along with a sharpened lead pencil.

"You need to write a note."

Jed stared at the pencil and paper.

Shine stepped closer, nudging his shoulder with the slender barrel of the pistol. "Go on, now. Get cracking."

"What . . . am I supposed to say?" Jed whined. "I never been much for writing."

"Well, you can start with 'Dear Elsie' and continue with how sorry you are," Shine said stonily. "Sorry for not being the man and husband you needed to be. And for letting down Hi. Sorry for hurting her. For hurting the entire family. And for breaking her heart in pieces."

"Hold on, you're going too fast," Jed said, hands shaking as he tried to still the paper and write. "I can't keep up."

"Ha!" said Shine. "You never could. Wrap it up with the fact that she will be better off without you; the whole world will be. Sign it with love. Or just plain Jed. I don't really give a good goddamn."

She watched Jed trembling. It was much worse knowing you were about to die than to have it happen out of the blue. The heaviness of Jed's dread was palpable. And Shine felt that should be part of it, part of all of this. To increase his suffering like he had done to their family, every last one of them: Hiram, Gran, Elsie, Becks. Little Hi.

But Shine was nervous, too. For all her big talk and bluster, for all the hours she had daydreamed of making someone pay for killing her daddy or beating and raping Birdie, she'd never actually ended anyone's life. It was surreal, this moment in the loft. Her brother-in-law, using the top of the footstool for a desk as he struggled to make sense on the page. He was left-handed; how had she not known that before? His face was a study of concentration and desperation, the triangular tip of his tongue above his upper lip as he pressed the lead against the lined ledger paper.

Jed scribbled another few words, folded the paper and handed it to Shine. There were tears in his eyes.

"C'mon, Shine," he pleaded. "You made your point. Loud and clear. I can change. I *will* change, I swear."

Jed began crying in earnest. "*Please.*"

Shine steeled herself.

"Your own parents love Elsie better than you. Plus, she's a more valuable employee than you ever were. And young Hiram!" Shine shook her head. "You think they'd choose your sorry ass over his if it came down to it?"

Jed hung his head; he knew she was right. But that didn't mean he was ready to give up living. He lunged for the pistol.

But Shine was ready, sidestepping so that Jed ended up face-down on the hayloft floor. He raised his head, pieces of straw and dust clinging to his wet cheeks.

"I'm not gonna do it," he declared. "You're gonna have to shoot me."

This wasn't going how she had imagined it. She didn't have time for these antics. Rebecca would be back from hunting before long. And Elsie was in the cabin with Gran—but she might begin to wonder at Jed's horse still tied to the barnyard fence.

She tried to focus on the task at hand. "Get your sorry self up and on that stepstool," she said through her teeth. "Now. Because if you want shooting, it's going to be a whole lot of bullets in a bunch of painful places before you get dead. I'll make certain of it.

"Be a man, for once in your goddamn life."

Her words broke him.

Jed climbed on top of the stool. He gazed up at the ceiling of the barn loft, at the thick beam hung with the noose meant for his neck. Shine lowered the rope down so he could reach it. Jed closed his eyes, tear tracks on his dirty, unshaven face. Then he placed the rope around his neck with both hands.

"Any last words?" Shine faltered, keeping the gun pointed at him there on his perch. Now that it was here, now that it was time, she was suddenly unsure. Revenge had sounded so sweet, teasing and tantalizing her with its promise of peace, of satisfaction of justice being had at last, sustaining her over long months and years. But was this who she was?

Jed opened his eyes and stared at her, as if he could see the contents of her heart. He wasn't crying anymore. He clasped his hands together in front of his waist.

"Nah," he said. "I best be getting on."

She almost put the gun down, started to tell him that he could have that one last chance. But before she was able open her mouth, he kicked the stool away from his legs, his full weight coming down on the rope at his neck.

"No!" Shine screamed. In that same instant, there was the unmistakable whine of a bullet, its report echoing through the thick hot air of the loft.

Jed fell to the loft floor with a sickening thud. The end of the rope snaked up and over the beam with a hiss and ended up in a loose coil beside him.

Shine looked down at the pistol in her hand and dropped it as though it had scorched her.

What had she done?

Rebecca

She had one chance. She had to get it right.

Rebecca took a breath and aimed her rifle at the narrow target. Gave the trigger a gentle tug that belied the tension she felt throughout her body.

Bang!

The rope holding Jed by the neck was nipped neatly in two and fell into pieces around the still bulk of his crumpled body, which hit the loft floor first.

"What the—" Shine's voice was shaky, relieved.

Rebecca was visible from the shoulders up, poking through the loft floor. She double-checked her foothold on the ladder rung before laying her rifle down at the edge of the opening. Removing the shotgun that was slung loosely around one shoulder, she set it alongside the rifle, before raising the rest of herself into the loft.

"I might say the same," she said, standing. She surveyed the setup, hands on her hips. "Executing some cowboy justice around here?"

"I lost my damn mind for a minute," Shine said. "Not that this piece of shit doesn't deserve to meet his maker."

"Christ on a crutch, Shine. Who died and made you God?"

"I almost did." Jed rolled over slowly onto his back. "Died, that is. You Strong women need to make up your minds," he rasped, rubbing his throat. "I can't take this. Also, I think I pissed my pants."

"I . . . it's just that . . ." Shine, for once, was having difficulty formulating a reply. She exhaled heavily. And were those *tears*?

"The harder I try to hold this family together, the more it pushes apart. And this one here, lower than a snake's belly. Ratting us out. Cheating us. And hurting Elsie six ways to Sunday."

"You made me family, whether you like it or not, Shine Strong." Jed had pulled himself up to sitting now, his hands resting on his splayed knees.

"Well, you sure haven't been much of a husband or a father," said Rebecca. "Shine's got a point. But that's not a hanging offense."

"Shit, Becks! I would have done it straightaway after Daddy died if you'd have told me what you knew. He never would have gotten to marriage and fatherhood if you weren't so goddamn slow to cogitate. That would've saved a hell of a lot of suffering for all of us."

"But you're not that person anymore, Shine." Rebecca's tone was stern, but also held a sense of wonder. "None of us are. And that's a blessing."

A sudden creak of wood stressed by the pressure of weight and movement caught everyone's attention at once. Elsie's head and upper body appeared in the hole in the loft floor.

"Well, isn't this a fine how do you do?" The apples of her cheeks were pink. "You girls know I don't like to miss a party."

Rebecca and Shine were struck silent. Jed stared at his wife with slack-jawed amazement, as though he were seeing a vision. And as she climbed through the loft opening and stood to full height, all she lacked were wings to complete her look of vengeful angel.

"Nothing like the sound of gunshots in one's own barn to pique the curiosity," Elsie went on drily, dusting off her dress. "Either of you gals care to explain what is going on here? Or *you*?" Here, she pointed at Jed. "Lord knows I'd love to hear it."

"We were just—" Shine faltered, looking at Rebecca, who, as usual, said nothing.

Jed scrambled to his feet, hands extended as if to embrace her. "Elsie. Thank God you're here. These sisters of yours damn near had me taking my own life! At gunpoint," he added. "There seems to be a misunderstanding."

"Don't touch me," Elsie warned, stopping her husband in his tracks. He lowered his hands to his sides, waiting for whatever came next. "I think they understand you all too well, unfortunately. But what they seem to have forgotten is that I'm a grown woman, capable of making my own goddamn decisions."

"That's right!" Jed agreed. "Tell them how it is. How we—"

"Shut it," Elsie said. "There's no 'we' anymore. You've made sure of that."

She turned to her sisters. "Well?"

Reluctantly, Shine reached into her pocket and pulled out Jed's note, holding it out to her sister. Elsie scanned the contents.

There was an awful moment. Then Elsie surprised everyone by smiling. But it was a rueful smile. She looked at Jed. "Well, that's about the size of it. You haven't been good to me. Or Hi. And the world *would* be a better place without you. At least, our corner of it."

"Elsie, come on. We can figure this out." Jed recovered his swagger, despite the piss-stained pants. That confidence that he could charm his way out of the situation, even one as sad and dire as this one.

"Get out," she said. "And don't ever show your face around here again. Or in Kinney. Or anywhere there's a person who knows you. You're dead to me. And if you show up again, I can guarantee you'll be dead to everyone else, too. Graveyard dead.

"I won't save you from the Strong sisters a second time."

She looked at the note in her hand, folded it. "Your parents will be sad to read this. But they love Hi. Don't worry. We'll be more than all right without you."

Jed's face registered first shock, incredulity. And then: anger. He looked furiously from sister to sister, hoping for a chink in the mortar, a break in the wall of their solidarity.

None was forthcoming.

He shook his head. "You Strongs think you've got it all figured out, and better'n everyone else. Even God Almighty. I'm glad to be rid of the lot of you."

He started toward the loft door but then paused, glancing toward Shine's pistol, which still lay on the floor.

"Don't even think about it," Rebecca said. "And leave your nag where she is or I'll shoot her out from under you. Dead men don't have need of horses. You're lucky to walk out of here on your own two feet.

"And no necktie."

Lidy

With a soft *whoosh*, the kerosene leaking onto the floor from the broken lantern shot up in a burst of orange-white flame.

Lidy's eyes lit up, too. *What is this?*

She watched curiously as the forked tongues of fire licked upward in that brief instant, catching the bottom of her colorfully embroidered curtains. The whole window went up in flames as the old dry cloth caught fire.

As a younger or more mobile woman, Lidy would have grabbed a rug or dish towel and beaten the blaze into submission—like she always had. Squelching anything that threatened to cause them harm. She had been putting out fires, literal and otherwise, the entirety of her time on this earth.

But now it was her distinct pleasure to let this fire burn. To consume everything it touched. Lidy was spellbound, fascinated as the flames flicked at the dry, cured wood of the window frame, like a kitten tentatively sticking a rough tongue into a bowl of milk and then lapping with increased greed.

The fire spread across the floor, following the trickle of kerosene to the rug and Lidy's cot by the woodstove. The metallic tang of the spent fuel filled her nostrils, but she didn't panic. The flames slowed at the thickness of the braided rug, smoldering, content to blacken the fibers before flickering again, boldly advancing toward her once more.

That's it. Come closer.

Her lungs began to sting as smoke curled upward in hazy ribbons, encircling the fire like dancers, outfitted in gauzy white. She couldn't even cough, her body betraying her so brutally, so unapologetically.

The first hot orange tendril caught hold at the hem of her wool blanket, hesitant at first but then with increasing urgency. The flame beckoned her with its thin yellow-blue fingers.

Sorry, you'll have to come to me.

Tentative, almost shy, the blaze receded out of her sight at the foot of the bed, before bursting again in an exuberant greeting. It was like a strange game of peekaboo, but she knew that the flames would find her.

It was awful to watch: the relentless fire devouring first her blanket, then the thin dress beneath. To feel her own flesh heating, an unbearable burning, that gouged deep molten pits in her shriveled frame. The flames stretched toward her neck and face.

Excruciating. But she could not turn away.

She welcomed this death; she had been made for it, hadn't she? It hurt like hell—beyond human imagining. But she would burn, a satisfying ravaging of this ruined body, this necessary heating of herself for what could be wrought. The purifying power of flame to turn waste to ash and release the soul, the restless and ready spirit inside her boiling up at last to become vapor, to *rise* and *rise* and *rise.*

If anyone had been there to capture that misty essence, they might have been able to bottle her up once more, that clear burning spirit with an unexpected kick. But alone, untended, she rose: unshackled, unbottled, dissipating into the air of the cabin before reaching the window, the woods and fields beyond. Past the chattering creek and the crushed velvet dark of the mountain at dusk, the cottony clouds hovering on the horizon, shot through with the brilliant hot pink beams of setting sun.

It was dazzling, all this beauty. But she couldn't stay.

Blink . . . blink.

Shine

Shine fastened the top button of her wool-lined coat, the chilly December wind reminding her that—despite the denim sky hung with a brilliant sphere of sunshine—it was nearly winter. A glorious gift of a day this time of year, warm enough to work comfortably outside if you were dressed for it.

She had set up in the barnyard, building a large, crackling fire as if it were laundry day. But she wasn't cleaning clothes or sheets today. Shine had brought all the distilling equipment out of the dark corners of the barn, bent on washing and disinfecting the kettle, coils, jugs, jars and barrels of the family's clandestine business. All out front, for anyone to see. It didn't matter anymore.

Prohibition was over.

It wasn't that the country was suddenly pro-drinking or that the evils of alcohol had been eradicated once and for all.

Hardly.

But the cash-strapped country had realized it was missing out on the tax and job potential of illegal alcohol. FDR had made a campaign promise to legalize drinking and was swept into office with all the force of a fresh-tapped keg of whiskey. People were exhausted by joblessness, homelessness and the "Hooverville" shantytowns that had sprouted up as a result of the Great Depression and put their meager hopes in a new president and his "New Deal."

It felt like maybe America was off to a fresh start. With a long way to go, to be sure.

Sort of like the Strong family.

There was the horror of that night in June six months ago, when she and Rebecca and Elsie had smelled the acrid smoke and tumbled on top of each other, getting down the loft ladder and out to the barnyard. They found the cabin completely engulfed, flames forming an ominous aura above the cedar-shingled roof as it burned. The three women sprinted toward the porch as the single glass window in the front shattered, a shimmering wall of heat halting them before they reached the steps.

"No!" It was Shine they had to hold back. Elsie and Rebecca grabbed her arms as she strained to get to the cabin. And Gran. Shine, who had always burned with the belief that she could save her family, made helpless in the face of this conflagration.

"We can't let her die!"

But even as Shine cried out, all three sisters knew their gran was beyond help, already gone. When Shine eventually gave up resisting her sisters' grip, they fell into an awkward embrace, holding each other up. The ferocious flames ate away at the only home they had known, an insatiable monster that made the roof collapse into the belly of the cabin where their gran surely lay; the sturdy beams of the four walls blackening and leaning inward, enclosing Lidy like a burning coffin. There were no tears; those would come later, and in a great flood that could have extinguished a lesser blaze.

It was what happened afterward that reduced each of them to tears. How, before the remaining embers of the burned beams had cooled or the smoke dissipated, people emerged from the woods and from across the fields, from nearby mountains and the low-lying, echoing hollers. Some carrying stewpots and pans, woven baskets full of pies and pickles and preserves; arms laden with blankets and pillows, rugs and dish towels, clothing and coats that could scarcely be spared. Farmers showed up with adzes and axes, hammers and nails. Men with horses dragged lumber up the trail from the road while others marked and felled the straightest trees from the nearby woods.

Caring for the Strongs like Lidy had cared for them.

"So like your gran to go out in a blaze of glory," Sheriff Burkett said, thumbs hooked on his belt loops as he watched the men, young and old, push up first one and then another of the walls of the new cabin. This version was an undeniable upgrade, with a common living space and two proper bedrooms.

They buried Gran's bones next to Hiram. Just the three of them, the Strong sisters. Gran would not have wanted a big funeral. They held hands in the kaleidoscope of light from a raucous summer sunset and took turns naming the things Lidy had bequeathed them: to Shine, the primacy of family; to Elsie, strength; and to Rebecca, the ability to know her own mind.

"Right or wrong, but never indifferent," Elsie said. "She was a Strong, through and through."

"As are we all," Rebecca said, squeezing Shine's hand.

Afterward, Elsie returned to town. "I showed the Hansons the note Jed left," she reported. Her in-laws had read it with sadness, but not surprise.

"We lost him years ago," Clara had said, blotting her eyes.

"They wanted us to stay. Me and Hi. They need me at the store. I've never been that useful on the farm anyhow."

"Yeah," Rebecca agreed. "All those times you thought you were pulling the wool over our eyes, saying you were going to help Mama, fetching fresh water or going to the outhouse while we were in the fields? You'd stay gone as long as humanly possible while we did the grunt work."

"Was it that bad?" Elsie had the decency to look embarrassed. She laughed. "I did hate farming, though!"

"Not like I loved it," groused Shine. But she knew as well as Rebecca that Elsie didn't belong here.

Rebecca did, though. She loved the land and all its creatures. It felt like her cradle, she said, her comfort and safe place among the stoic oaks and hickories, alongside her chattering childhood friend, Kinney Creek.

"It'll be my grave, too," she said, without a trace of sadness.

But Shine . . . where did she belong?

As she scrubbed the scummy layer of dust from a large glass jug, she considered the question. She loved her sisters. But she wasn't a farmer or a hunter at heart. She had loved this place because of the bond she shared with her daddy, making their mash, distilling their spirits drop by satisfying drop in wordless synchrony.

And now to know Hiram might not have been her father after all? That her mama made her with someone else, some flame-headed man of God? Shine rubbed even harder at the jug beneath her hands. It was overwhelming.

"No more secrets," Elsie had said, sharing the letter she had pocketed from Lidy's Bible. "And no more lies. Even if it hurts. But this doesn't change anything, Shine."

Shine read the letter penned by the preacher to her mother so long ago, grappling with the idea that her sisters might be half sisters, her father and gran not blood relatives at all. And how her own mother, her true flesh and blood, had jumped—not fallen!—out of a barn loft to be rid of her.

"Elsie's right," Rebecca had said after reading the letter. "You're my sister as much as she is."

What did they mean? This changed *everything.*

Shine poured boiling water through the copper coil until it ran clear. She wiped the outside gently with a cloth before setting it on a feed sack in the sun so it could dry completely before she stored it away. Maybe for good.

Prohibition was over, but was she finished with shine? The big city breweries had begun fermenting beer months ago. And soon the distilleries would be supplying spirits to the masses. And no one here drank the stuff; they didn't need it for tippling *or* tinctures. She had considered opening a saloon in the back of Hanson's. It had been Elsie's suggestion, amazing Shine with its cleverness.

"You think you're the only Strong with good ideas?" Elsie laughed, pleased when Shine stared at her, dumbfounded. "Baby sister, you've got another think coming."

But Shine felt unsure. Untethered. Restless. Rebecca could get by with a greatly reduced farming operation now. Nothing was really holding Shine here. And yet, she stayed. As though she were waiting for something but didn't know precisely what. She only knew she was missing it.

She walked up past the barn toward the woods to grab some limbs and sticks to stoke her fire. Passing by the plot of cleared land where Alta and Hiram—and now Lidy—were buried, she paused. As a child, she had come here regularly; it was something her sisters did and she felt compelled as well—even though she had never been held by her mother, except in the womb.

Shine would visit the grave, with its rough wooden cross that bore her mother's name, although rain and sun conspired to erase it. She could tell who had been there before her by the offerings she found: an empty booze bottle left by Hiram; a handful of wilted wildflowers bound with twine from Elsie; a fluff of feathers or an abandoned robin's egg from Rebecca. Once, Shine had found a rabbit's hind foot chopped neatly at the joint and completely crawling with ants—also a gift from Rebecca. That one she had kicked off into the grass, knowing her sister would never be the wiser.

Shine had not known what tribute to leave for her mother. So she gathered rocks, chosen with care from the surrounding fields and forest by her childish hands—milky calcite, chalky limestone, a thin square of shale, pinky quartz or a chunk of iron pyrite with its false gold glint—and made awkward cairns on that sacred ground. Rocks. Shine marveled at the choice; she hadn't known then how appropriate it was to leave her mother something as hard and unyielding as her heart had been that day she jumped from the loft. As unforgiving as the half-buried stone that met her head.

And yet: Alta hadn't wanted to die, had she? Her mother had been frightened, maybe, at the price of her mistake. Another child to care for. Who wasn't her husband's. She was likely exhausted, desperate. Hoping for a fresh start, maybe. Who knew? Shine had lived long enough now to know she would not want to be judged—or punished—so harshly for her worst transgression or mistakes. She had felt that all too keenly.

Like bringing Jed into the family, only to have him nearly kill both her sisters by vastly different means. Or how she had tried to make amends for what happened to Birdie—and ended up losing Flanagan forever. Why hadn't she kept her mouth shut? And leave justice for Nash up to God. Or the vermin of the criminal underworld, by whom he would have likely met his end eventually, just or not.

Revenge had been all she wanted for so long. Satisfying. And if not easy, at least straightforward: an eye for an eye, a tooth for a tooth. But mercy? Forgiveness? That was tougher. More complicated. Meandering. Certainly not achieved in one hotheaded instant. Shine figured it might even take forever. But the hard work of it—the deep breaths, the cleaning out, the letting go—made a space begin to open inside her for something else. Something *good.*

Clang, clang, clang, clang, clang, clang—

The *dinner* bell?

The simple copper bell that graced their front porch, that their gran had used to summon them all to countless suppers, was the one thing that hadn't burned up in the fire. The singular sound snapped Shine back to the present: the graves, the woods beyond, the fire she had left dying and untended in the barnyard.

—clang, clang, clang, clang, clang, clang—

Rebecca kept at it, ringing the bell so relentlessly that Shine was sure the clapper would snap off. She rang it like Gran used to when there was danger. Like when those goddamn prohis showed up.

Shine lurched forward, pulling her feet from the ground as though they were mired in quicksand. And then she ran.

—clang, clang, clang, clang, clang, clang—

It couldn't be.

Shine rounded the corner of the barn, panting, her heartbeat hammering in her ears. Her shoulder-length auburn hair was wild; she had lost her hat somewhere along the way.

She didn't see Rebecca on the porch, easing up on the pull rope; she didn't even notice the bell had stopped ringing.

All she could see was the tall, dark-haired man in the suit, standing beside the cabin, his hat in his hand. His blue eyes fastened on her as if she held the answers to all of life's questions. Or at least one of them.

"Flanagan!"

Shine did not hesitate. She kept her gaze locked on him in case he was a mirage, a ghost come to haunt her. A dream that could disappear into the ether. She ran straight into his arms; the young man barely had time to open them. Shine jumped up, locking her legs around his waist, her arms thrown tightly around his shoulders, head buried in his neck. He smelled like fresh soap and starched linen. She wasn't about to let him go.

"Shine Strong." Flanagan's face was not quite enough real estate to contain his grin. "You're a sight for sore eyes."

"You're supposed to be dead!" Shine drew her head back to look at him, frowning. He set her back down.

"You're telling me." The young man shook his head. "I've been shot at so many times I think it might be open season on John Flanagans."

"But . . . Union Station? All the headlines said four lawmen had died."

"They did. And my partner was badly wounded." John's face was somber. "But somehow, some way, I dodged those bullets. And believe me, there were about a million of them. That was the longest thirty seconds of my life.

"I knew I was going to die," he said, then hesitated. "And all I could think about was you. How awful it was that I wouldn't see you again."

Shine turned a color that nearly matched her locks. She glanced at the porch, but Rebecca had done her the kindness of going inside. No one to see her blush but him.

"Afterwards, when I realized I *wasn't* dead, I had no choice," he went on. "If you're the one person who survives something like that unscathed, you get the message. I stayed in KC till my buddy got out of the hospital, but after that, I turned in my badge."

He paused. "Then I went back to Hot Springs to look for you."

"But I was gone," Shine said. "I had to hightail it out of there, hop the first train after hearing Nash had caught his lunch in Kansas City. Left Merle and the mayor in the dust. And poor Birdie"—she hung her head—"I didn't even get to say goodbye. And she won't answer my letters. She's probably mad at me."

Flanagan lowered his eyes, shifted uncomfortably.

"What?"

"Let's go inside," he said, finally. Awkward. "I've brought someone I want you to meet."

Flanagan had brought someone along? Like a girlfriend? Or a *wife*? That seemed pretty cruel, but then, men were dense sometimes. Scratch that: *people* were dense sometimes. She hadn't known how much she had felt for this man until she thought he was dead and gone. Why should she expect he would care about her? Beyond friendship, anyway.

She was bad at this. And Shine didn't like being terrible at anything.

"Okay," she said. She would play along, swallow her feelings. Be happy that he was alive and wish him all the best. Because she *was* glad. Her soul had felt immediately lighter when she'd seen him there by the porch, as though it had kicked off its Chicago overcoat a la Al Capone and sprouted wings.

Shine climbed the two steps up from the yard and turned the doorknob. She made her face neutral, bracing herself for whoever and whatever awaited inside.

She gasped. There, seated on their one good chair, was Eulalie, who looked up at Shine and Flanagan with an enormous smile. Rebecca knelt beside her with one hand resting on the chair arm, her usually stoic features softened with wonder, while her other rested protectively at Eulalie's elbow. And Elsie was there, beaming as Hi held her skirt in one fist, hiding behind her, unsure of what was happening around him.

There, in Eulalie's lap: a blanketed wriggling bundle. Shine crept closer. Large slate-blue eyes, delicate rosebud of a mouth. A halo of golden fuzz on her head. A furrow in her creamy brow, as if she were puzzling things out. Where was she? Who were these people?

"Shine, meet Wren," Flanagan said. "Birdie's baby girl."

She immediately stretched out her arms and Eulalie rose, placing the infant gently in the crook of Shine's elbow.

"I didn't trust myself to deliver her safe and sound to you," Flanagan said. "But fortunately, I knew someone who could ride shotgun. *And* keep a baby happy. We picked up Elsie and Hi when we got to town."

Eulalie looked around the room uncertainly. But every pair of eyes she met was welcoming. Grateful. Rebecca patted the chair seat and Eulalie returned to her perch, relieved.

"Thank you, Eulalie."

"Miz Shine, you know I've been wanting to see where you Strong women come from," she said with a pointed look at Rebecca. "What kind of land this must be to grow the biggest crop of stubborn I ever seen."

"She is . . ." Shine searched the infant's frowning face, amazed the way the worry lines smoothed away. Relaxed. And those curious eyes, her mother's eyes—innocent, trusting—closing once, snapping back open. And then closing again, asleep. "A miracle."

But a babe without her mama this far away from home could only mean one thing.

Shine wept.

Later, over a batch of turnip greens and pot likker—soaked up with a batch of Elsie's cornbread—Flanagan recounted his many exploits. Shine's tip-off. The capture of the criminal Nash. The terror of the massacre. How he had flattened himself to his lap as the barrage of bullets from the two tommy guns found their marks in every other passenger. Rising in the deathly quiet afterward, covered in blood and Nash's brain matter.

"Oh my goodness!" Elsie exclaimed. "This is the supper table! And there are children in the room!"

Everyone knew she was the one who couldn't stomach the gory details, since neither Hi nor Wren was old enough to understand.

"Sorry." Flanagan colored. "Didn't mean to offend. One tends to get callous in that line of work. And needless death and suffering is not something I ever want to get used to."

"Amen," Elsie said. "Thank you."

"Anyway, after my partner got out of the hospital and I exhausted my months of paid leave, I quit. Headed down to Hot Springs to find Shine. She was gone, but Merle was still hot over holding the last of her debt. And stealing his pants and hat to boot!"

"And a bit of black shoe polish for my hair," Shine added. "I looked better in his duds than he did!"

Everyone laughed.

"I paid him off and told him in no uncertain terms that I'd come after him if he dared look you up," Flanagan said. "So you're all square."

"Hmmph." Shine didn't like being beholden to anyone, even John Flanagan. "Thanks. I'll be paying you back."

"No need," Flanagan said. "It wasn't much. I think he was angrier that you'd gotten away. Made him look bad with the mayor.

"Anyway, I headed to the boardinghouse to see if Bernyce Ward might have a spare room for the night," he went on. "That's when I learned that Birdie had given birth . . . but didn't survive it."

All the forks and knives stopped, the chewing and swallowing, too. Elsie wiped a tear from the corner of her eye with a napkin.

"That is the saddest thing I've ever heard," she said. "And that's saying something."

"Yes, but Miss Ward was thrilled to see me." Here, Shine smirked. The old woman had been sweet on Flanagan forever.

"She knew I could track down Shine—and she believed in her heart of hearts this child belonged with Birdie's only real friend. She had no family. And Miss Ward said she was too old, tired and set in her ways to raise a child, as fond as she had grown of Wren in the weeks she cared for her."

"But . . . what do *I* know about babies or children?" Shine's heart seized. This wasn't about holding a child on her lap for an evening; this was forever. And she was completely unprepared, unqualified.

"Aw, Shine," said Rebecca. "Since when did you become a scaredy cat? You don't need to *know* anything."

"She's right," said Elsie. "You need love, courage and a good sense of humor. Besides, you've got family to help you figure it out."

Can I do this?

Shine looked down at the sleeping infant in her lap, long fringed eyelashes against the pale cheek. Almost as if she were mirroring Shine's anxiety, Wren's face darkened, eyes squeezing more tightly shut. Then: a single whole-body squirm and she relaxed into her baby dream state once more.

"I'm glad you're offering, Else. Because I think the first thing I'm going to need help with is a diaper."

John

He couldn't fall asleep on the wooden cot in the second bedroom, his feet hanging off the end like in a cartoon. The quilt couldn't cover his entire body at once, so he alternated between warming his toes and then his neck and shoulders.

But that wasn't what was keeping him awake.

He couldn't stop thinking about Shine. The way her face had lit up when she saw him. Maybe it was only that she had thought he was dead. But it made him happier than he could account for, the way she had leaped into his arms.

He would leave tomorrow, though. There was no excuse to stay, now that he had delivered his precious cargo. While the Strongs assured him that the new cabin was roomier than the original, it was still a hardship, all this company crammed into every corner. After everyone had a belly full of apple crisp topped with fresh cream and talked themselves hoarse, it was decided John would take one room and Eulalie and Wren could sleep in the other. She had insisted: "It's my last night with this angel."

Elsie made a small pallet on the floor for Hi; then a larger one between him and the woodstove for the three sisters.

"It's like old times!" Shine was delighted, crawling right between Elsie and Rebecca.

"Good God, I hope you don't still kick and wiggle like you did back then," Elsie sighed.

"And I hope you don't still kiss your pillow like you're practicing for your prince," shot back Shine.

"And I hope the two of you will keep your traps from flapping long enough for me to get some shut-eye," said Rebecca.

Flanagan had protested, offering to sleep in the barn, but the sisters wouldn't hear of it. And now he was inhaling the sweet smell of freshly hewn cedar planks and planning his goodbye.

He had brought something to give to Shine.

He thought she might get a kick out of it.

Rebecca

She waited until her sisters' giggles, poking and whispers had ceased, giving way to gentle, even breathing before she rose. It had felt good to be cocooned in the warmth of these women she had loved so fiercely for so long. It *was* like old times. And if someone had asked her a few years earlier, this very scene is the one she would have described as her idea of contentment; what would make her the happiest.

But life is nothing but continuous change—both expected and unexpected. Of the three of them, she probably understood this best. Like the seasons here on her mountain. How warm tender drops of an April rain readied the soil for the imminent miracle of seeds and sunlight; the hot beating summer sun turned the early neon greens to tones that were deeper, more substantial, while blackberries plumped every pillow of their being with sweet purply juice. Then: the fire on the mountain that was fall, burning oranges, crimsons, golds; and finally winter, edging brown leaves with frost, blanketing the hillsides in cotton-white quiet.

She had changed, too. Now her idea of happiness included something more. The unexpected. And she had not thought to have another chance at it.

A large December moon hung like a china plate in the sky, casting a cool white beam through the window of the room she had given up to the guests. Wren's basket beside the single bed was still. But Eulalie's eyes were open, dark pools reflecting the moonlight, when Rebecca had pushed aside the curtain that served as a door.

She stood uncertainly. Finally, she climbed over the foot of the bed and slid in behind her, beneath the quilt, bending around Eulalie's body like a bow. Gently, she reached over Eulalie's side and placed her hand across her lover's heart.

Rebecca finally knew what she wanted. Was she brave enough to ask for it?

A soft whisper: "*Stay with me.*"

Eulalie covered Rebecca's hand with one of her own.

Shine

She was up early. Not as early as Rebecca. Her place on the pallet was cold. But Elsie still slept, her mouth open slightly, one arm flung above her head as if she were being dramatic.

Shine stepped softly around the edge of the makeshift bed, admiring handsome Hi, eyes closed and body similarly slung across his blanket, legs and arms akimbo. No sound out of Flanagan yet. She tiptoed to Rebecca's room to peek in on Wren. Part of her couldn't believe the girl was real, that anything that had happened yesterday was real.

But there she was, nestled in the curve made by Eulalie's chest and drawn-up knees. The woman slept on her side, her bottom arm safeguarding Wren from the edge of the bed. And behind them both: Rebecca, arm draped over Eulalie. Nesting dolls. Large to so very wee.

Surprising . . . but then, not. Shine considered the two women, fitted closer than a hand in a favorite glove. Her shy, gentle sister had had a secret, too. Smiling, Shine pulled the curtain closed behind her. Likely the baby would wake everyone soon. Best let them enjoy their peace while they could.

Out in the barnyard, Shine shivered in the brittle morning light. The temperature was a few ticks above freezing but still bit into her bones. She relit the fire that had died out yesterday in all the excitement. She needed to finish her task.

And she had some thinking to do.

Wren. How perfect she had looked, curled into Eulalie's arm. Natural. Shine could picture her growing up here, with Rebecca and Eulalie to love her. Surrounded by these hills and hollers, she could splash in Kinney Creek, explore the woods and wilds with her cousin. But Shine didn't want to stay on the farm. She wanted a new adventure; to see what was next. She still had Capone's card scribbled with the contact in St. Louis, creased in two places and worn to roundness at the edges from the many times Shine had slid it from her pouch to look at it. To dream.

And who knew? Maybe she would even venture to Kentucky, look up a Mr. Robert Smythe. Just out of curiosity. Find out where she got her fire—inside *and* out. Not because she needed a daddy. She had already had the best. Imperfect, but perfect for her. He had taught her so well. Loved her so much.

I wish you were here, Daddy. You'd know what I should do.

Shine looked at all the parts of the old still—the coils and kettles, jars and jugs—and righted the mash barrel that lay on its side. She remembered how they had measured the dry kernels of yellow corn and grains of barley, round and dusty brown. The way she had sprinkled in the yeast from her open palm; a fistful always the exact right amount. Plus the unknown, the part left to chance; the little "somethin'-somethin'" Gran or Daddy tossed in that made the mash special and slightly different every time.

She submerged the dusty mason jars in the kettle, where the water was beginning to form the minute bubbles that preceded a rolling boil. Added another log to the fire beneath.

Fire.

No good batch of mash happened without it. The heat raising the temperature of the mixture until it boiled. Then weeks of fermenting, until the time came to unseal the barrel.

"Use that nose now, girl." Shine could almost hear her daddy's voice in her ear. Smell the rush of sweet fruit all the way up to the top of her head.

Pineapples.

"That's right."

Then cooking that fermented mash, collecting the vapors. Distilling it all down until the clear, pure liquid dripped—slowly at first, then faster—into the jug.

"Taste it now, girl," she heard Hiram say. "Let's see if you know your heads from your hearts."

Of course. Shine beamed, alone in the barnyard. *Thank you, Daddy.*

She had always been the best at discerning the heads from the hearts, that subtle shift when the batch of shine hits that sweet, smooth center. It was time for the hearts—*her* heart—to take over.

Shine would raise the baby. For Birdie. Even if she had to learn on the job. She'd done that before, hadn't she? She would make a family like she and her daddy had made moonshine, putting together a bunch of unlikely ingredients, things that didn't come from the same place, or naturally go together. Stir it all up and see what happened. Test it. *Taste* it.

And then crank up the heat. Because that was life, wasn't it? The fire that you couldn't always control. But what you made of it, what you *did* with it . . . that could be something special.

Something you could see *through*—stunningly clear and shining and powerful.

The Strong stuff. A family. *A life.*

She was ready to get to the good part. The *best* part.

Shine wiped the last of the jars dry, placing them in a wooden crate to store in the barn. Then she dried her hands on her dress.

"Good morning, sun!" She heard John's voice from the front porch and looked up to see him stretching his arms wide, greeting the day. "And good morning, Shine."

But before she could return his greeting, he was hurrying across the barnyard toward her, practically running. He held his hands behind his back, awkwardly, as if he was trying to hide something.

He stopped right before he reached her, dropping down to one knee in the dry dirt, meeting her astonished face with a hopeful grin.

Tails

June 1941

Wren

"Are we there yet?"

She poked her curly blond head through the space between the front seats.

"Wren, if you ask one more time, I swear we will stop this car right now and I'll turn you over my knee!"

Wren chortled with delight. Her mama would do no such thing. She flounced back into her seat and watched the Ozarks scenery go by: pastures chock-full of cud-chewing cattle, sturdy hardwood forests, thick fields of fescue and sleepy towns. The occasional bump in the road bounced her so high her blond ringlets nearly touched the ceiling.

It was her favorite time of the year.

Summer.

Everyone loved being set loose from the confines of the classroom. Freedom from the tedious days of lessons, tests, recitations and homework. And how the city neighborhoods would swell with the metallic musical tenor of ice-cream trucks on their rounds, promising Popsicles and chocolate-covered ice-cream drumsticks in exchange for a warm, closely held nickel. A short streetcar ride to an aquamarine gem of a public pool for relief from the heat, radiating from the cement sidewalks and redbrick buildings.

But Wren loved summer because it meant going to the farm. It meant cousins. Aunts who spoiled her with love and attention. Magnificent meals made with vegetables picked by her and Aunt Eulalie from the garden of a morning. Adventures she could never have in St. Louis—like blackberry picking, trying to sneak a warm fresh egg from beneath a sharp-beaked hen or wading in the freezing creek water until her feet and ankles grew numb. Not to mention using an outhouse to do her business instead of a flushing toilet!

Aunt Elsie always let her pick out a flowery fabric from the store and helped her sew a frilly dress—something her mother had no interest in or patience for. Aunt Becks took her hunting, although she rarely brought a gun along these days. Her gentle aunt liked long winding hikes up the mountain and through the woods, showing her how to track animals, recognize different bird songs and tell a persimmon tree from a pawpaw. But best of all was sharing this special time with her mama; how heading to the Ozark Mountains put her in a good mood. And if her mama was happy, well . . . her daddy was, too.

She confirmed that with a glance in the rearview mirror. She couldn't see his mouth, but her daddy's blue eyes were smiling.

He loved her mama like crazy. And Wren loved them both.

She'd always known he wasn't her real father. But her mama had told her she had both as well: a father *and* a daddy, just like Wren. "Any man can be a father, but being a daddy is a choice. That's something special. Mine sure was. All I got from my father was flaming orange hair. And a hair trigger."

Her mama loved saying that.

Wren would never know what part of her was from her father. But her mama made sure to tell her about the mother who birthed her and loved her to the moon: Birdie. Wren had her long corn-silk yellow curls and big violet eyes. Her pluck and her sass. Plus her tendency to talk your ear off.

Like now.

"Daddy, tell the story about asking Mama to marry you." Wren never tired of the tale, had it more or less memorized. "Please?"

"Not *that* old chestnut." Her mama sounded annoyed—but also pleased.

"Well, the first time I ever saw your mother, she was running down the side of a mountain like her hair was on fire. In fact, I thought her hair might *be* on fire, it was such a shock of orange," he said.

"Not like now," Wren interjected.

"Nope," her mama replied. "After I cut my hair off, it grew back dark red."

"That happened the *second* time you were running from the law," her father said, feigning a frown. "But that day, I was searching for an illegal moonshine still on a rocky Ozark mountainside. Didn't find the still, but I did find a shoe."

"A *strange* shoe!" Wren loved this part. How her daddy discovered the boot with cow hooves on the sole, chasing her mama on a game trail through the thick woods. She didn't have any trouble imagining what it looked like; that very shoe had a place of honor atop the fireplace mantel in their home in St. Louis. Her mama kept threatening to take it to work, set it on the bar at her tavern for a conversation piece: Shine's in South City.

"Finally, I came upon a cabin and barn. There was a family there with three girls," her daddy went on.

"Rebecca, Elsie and Shine!"

"Yes," he laughed. "I felt like Prince Charming, trying to see which of the sisters belonged to that ugly slipper. I didn't find out that day, although . . ." Here he gave a sly glance toward the passenger seat. "I had a pretty good idea.

"I kept that shoe—half hoof, half boot—for a long time," her daddy said. "And when I realized I didn't want to live anymore without your mama, well . . . I brought it with me to the farm. The same day I brought you and Eulalie there."

Wren clapped her hands. This was the best part!

"You found Cinderella!"

"Now, hold on a minute," her mama said. "I was *not* a princess."

"Neither was Cinderella—before she met her prince," her daddy said. "That's part of your charm."

"Anyway. Then what happened?" Wren was getting impatient.

"I knew I couldn't stay on the farm. But I didn't want to leave her, either. So I mustered up my courage and met your mother coming across the barnyard. Before she could even say 'How do?' I got down on one knee in the dirt and manure. Then I pulled that shoe out from behind my back and asked if the owner might consider saying '*I* do.'

"And she said 'John Flanagan, I *might* . . .' "

Wren jumped in: " 'But you gotta know you can't marry the Strong out of me.' "

Her parents shared a sidelong glance. Grinned.

" 'I wouldn't dream of trying,' I told her. And that was that."

"Well, if the shoe *fits* . . ." Her mama shrugged and poked her daddy in the ribs.

Wren settled into her seat once more, hugging her knees. She couldn't wait to get to the farm.

"How much longer?" she wanted to ask.

But thought the better of it.

Author's Note

I grew up on a farm about ten miles south of West Plains, Missouri, just a few miles from the Arkansas line. It's beautiful country—hills of dense woods and pastureland, cut through with creeks and rivers lined with steep limestone bluffs and caves. But making a living on this land has never been easy. As John Flanagan puts it in the novel, "one could argue that rocks were a cover crop in these parts."

But Ozarkians are a notoriously creative bunch. And while the making of moonshine whiskey had long been a folk tradition of these people of predominantly Scotch-Irish descent, the start of Prohibition and the subsequent Great Depression caused the illicit industry to explode in those hills and hollers. Suddenly, corn was worth more by the gallon than the bushel.

And women were a big part of the business—particularly in transporting the goods—since in many states it was illegal for law officers to search a woman. At one point, the government feared that female bootleggers outnumbered their male counterparts five to one!

The idea of a woman-run moonshine operation in the hardscrabble Ozark mountains piqued my imagination—and this book is the result. I read extensively about the temperance movement and Prohibition, learned how moonshine was made, and immersed myself in the culture and customs of my beloved Ozarks. I especially enjoyed *Queen of the Hillbillies: The Writings of May Kennedy McCord*, which informed the character of Lidy, with her colorful language (words like "whangleathery"), "granny cures" and superstitions. And McConnell and Flanagan take their inspiration from the famous pair of New York City prohibition officers, Isadore "Izzy" Einstein and Moe Smith.

An adventure to Hot Springs, Arkansas—that "loose buckle on the Bible Belt"—gave me the chance to stay at Al Capone's favored and still grand Arlington Hotel. From there, I wandered "Bathhouse Row" and explored the Fordyce Bathhouse/Visitor Center in Hot Springs National Park, took a soak in the thermal spring waters of the Buckstaff Bathhouse, visited the Gangster Museum of America and peeked into the Southern Club—now home to Josephine Tussaud's Wax Museum! I also took the train to Union Station in Kansas City, where lore has it that marks on the stones at the eastern entrance are bullet holes from the Kansas City Massacre.

Kinney Creek doesn't exist, except as a montage in my mind of all the glorious cold-water creeks and rivers I waded, swam, fished and floated growing up. And the fictitious town of Kinney owes a nod to Dora, Missouri—for the stories my grandad used to tell of his family taking eggs to the general store on a Saturday to sell or trade . . . and of course, the joy of a penny candy in a pocket afterward.

The moonshiner's craft requires the mixing together of disparate ingredients, adding heat at just the right times to ferment and distill them into something that's pure, refreshing and packs a punch. I hope I've managed to do something similar in these pages.

I hope you enjoyed this shot of "the Strong stuff."

Sources

Blumenthal, Karen. *Bootleg: Murder, Moonshine, and the Lawless Years of Prohibition*. Square Fish, 2013.

Clayton, Merle. *Union Station Massacre: The Shootout That Started the FBI's War on Crime*. Bobbs-Merrill, 1975.

Courtaway, Robbi. *Wetter than the Mississippi: Prohibition in St. Louis and Beyond*. Reedy Press, 2008.

Hanley, Ray, and Steven G. Hanley. *Hot Springs, Arkansas*. Arcadia, 2000.

Lugo, Catherine. "Hooch and Hell Raisin': Women Bootleggers." *Homestead.org*, 22 Feb. 2024, www.homestead.org/homesteading-history/women-bootleggers/#maggie-bailey8220queen-of-the-mountain-bootleggers8221.

McCord, May K., et al. *Queen of the Hillbillies: Writings of May Kennedy McCord*. The University of Arkansas Press, 2022.

Ostmeyer, Andy. "Old-Timers Recall Days When Hills Were Flowing with . . . Moonshine." *OzarksWatch Magazine-* Missouri State, 1991, cdm17307.contentdm.oclc.org/digital/collection/p17307coll1/id/242/rec/11.

Poindexter, Jennifer. "How to Make Moonshine the Old-Fashioned Way in 6 Easy Steps." *Morning Chores*, 3 Nov. 2023, morningchores.com/how-to-make-moonshine/.

"Prohibition Agents Lacked Training, Numbers to Battle Bootleggers." *Prohibition*, 28 Feb. 2024, prohibition.themobmuseum.org/the-history/enforcing-the-prohibition-laws/lawenforcement-during-prohibition/.

Raines, Robert K. *Hot Springs: From Capone to Costello*. Arcadia Publishing, 2013.

Randolph, Vance. *Ozark Superstitions*. Read Books, 2008.

Sholtis, Elizabeth. "Shaking Things Up: The Influence of Women on the American Cocktail." *Virginia Tech Undergraduate Historical Review*, 23 July 2020, vtuhr.org/articles/10.21061/vtuhr.v9i0.4.

ACKNOWLEDGMENTS

This book has been a crazier ride than a tricked-out 1928 Model A Ford coupe with a load of hidden hooch on a moonless Ozarks backroad at midnight!

Thank you so much to everyone who made it possible for me to write it (and arrive at the end in essentially one piece). Especially my husband, Clay, who picked up the slack when deadlines loomed—whether watering my beloved flowers and garden or fixing a fabulous meal. You are my best cheerleader, and I love you.

To my three amazing kids: Benjamin, Levi and Vivian. I am so fortunate to be your mom; it has been the privilege of my life. You have encouraged me every step of the way on this writing adventure and that has made it especially sweet. And Ben . . . you are a website master/technical consultant extraordinaire! Shout-out to KitKat, Twix and Finn, my furry, four-legged support group. I always have the best inspirations when I'm walking my pup!

A special thank-you to all the Benson, Collins and Anderson family members—I love you so dearly. Your support and enthusiasm have been incredible. Dad, I appreciate you hounding your local librarians with my business card . . . it paid off! That goes for you, too, Uncle Bill! And my siblings, Kevin and Dacia: you two are something special; I love being in St. Louis where I can spend more time with you! Of course, I couldn't have done any of this without my mom, Maureen: I love and miss you every single day.

I have so many people to thank for their help in making *The Moonshine Women* into a book. First and foremost, my agent, Marlene Stringer, for believing in me, these characters and this story. And John Scognamiglio, my editor, for his enthusiasm and excellent suggestions—I'm so proud to publish under your imprint! Special gratitude for gifted Kensington creative director Kristine Mills for another gorgeous cover! Likewise a huge thanks to the entire team at Kensington, especially Jackie Dinas, Vida Engstrand, Matt Johnson, Alexandra Nicolajsen, Andi Paris, Lauren Jernigan, Carly Sommerstein, and freelance copy editor Gary Sunshine. And the talented Kim Wade, for the author photo . . . you are *so* good!

Thank you to my beloved Warren Wilson College community, particularly David Haynes, an extraordinary mentor who continues to encourage me as a friend and neighbor here in St. Louis, and the talented Dominic Smith, a smart and generous teacher. I'm beholden to many Warren Wilson colleagues and friends—especially my first reader, pep-talk-giver and super-duper writer Katie Runde: would not have made it through book two without you! I'm also grateful for the thoughtful suggestions from dear Wallies and beta readers Lynette D'Amico and Leslie Koffler. And Elisabeth Hamilton and Virginia Borges who—along with Katie—create the most amusing (and thought-provoking!) writer–friend text chains ever.

And friends: so many! Elaine Johnson, Catey Terry and Judith DelPorto: truest friends from the trenches of motherhood. My Theta sisters everywhere—I have been astounded and touched by how you have shown up for me and my novel! Especially Mary Rudder, Shari Johnson, Leslie Hutter, Janis Jones, Tina Schnelle, and Ann Walters. And high school friends, too: Carla Smith, Sonya McDonald, Michelle Moody, Teresa Durham, Jill Brooks, Janice Redburn and Zizzer-supreme Amber Redburn.

Thanks to all the tremendous book groups I've been able to participate in—via Zoom or in person—from the UK to CA and even Mexico (MO!), and everywhere in between. Sharing my book with readers is the best part of this whole journey. And I've been lucky to be a part of several exceptional book groups myself: the Red Tent Women of Calvary Episcopal Church in Columbia, MO, and the Liberal Ladies of Liberty, MO. Love you all!

And to all the wonderful booksellers, reviewers and librarians who have taken a chance on and championed my books: you are the best! Love my local indies: Left Bank Books, The Novel Neighbor, The Book House, Main Street Books, Dunaway Books, Leviathan Bookstore and Spine—plus Skylark in Columbia, MO. And last—but far from least—the St. Louis Public Library–Carpenter branch: my office-away-from-home. Every single soul there is a gem.

A READING GROUP GUIDE

ABOUT THIS GUIDE

The suggested questions are included to enhance your group's reading of Michelle Collins Anderson's *The Moonshine Women*!

Discussion Questions

1. In the prologue of *The Moonshine Women*, the premature baby is supposed be—according to an array of old wives' tale tests and superstitions—a boy. When a disappointed Hiram Strong holds his third daughter in his hands instead, he christens her "Jace," which means "the Lord is salvation" and declares that she will save the family. Does she?

2. A colt's tongue cooked in cast iron to cure epilepsy; a potato carried in a pocket to ward off rheumatism. Lidy Strong is full of what people in the Ozark hills call "granny cures." Which one did you find the most interesting or surprising? Can you share one from your own culture or upbringing?

3. Alcohol—particularly "moonshine"—is problematic for the Strong family. Both Hiram and his abusive father were alcoholics; Jed's drinking dramatically changes his personality for the worse. Yet it becomes the family's livelihood during Prohibition. Shine even ends up slinging drinks at the Southern Club in Hot Springs to pay off a debt. How do they survive with this cognitive dissonance? And what does it say that none of the Strong daughters drink except for what the job requires?

4. The one "Strong woman" we don't hear from directly in the novel is Alta. Hiram worships and grieves her; a put-upon Lidy resents her. Rebecca and Elsie crave her softness and stories—while Shine has no memories of her at all. How do you feel about this complicated voiceless character? Do you believe—as Shine comes to—that she shouldn't be judged too harshly for her worst transgression or mistake?

5. There are many motherless daughters in *The Moonshine Women*, from the three Strong daughters to Birdie and little Wren. How do the women mother each other? Do sisterhood

and female friendship become even more important when our mother figures are unavailable or gone?

6. Hiram calls Shine his "daughter of the spirit." He wishes he could take credit for her fire, but "he knew it was not his. Yet he protected it, nourished it, tried his best to temper it. She would be the strongest Strong, the best of the batch. This Shine honored him most of all, carrying his name along with his know-how." What does he mean? How does Hiram's love and acceptance play a part in Shine's later decision to form and embrace her own unconventional family bonds? In the end, who do you think is the "strongest Strong"?

7. The "cow shoes" that Shine wore to cover her tracks were just one creative way that moonshiners and bootleggers kept their operations clandestine during Prohibition. The novel mentions tricked-out cars with hidden compartments and specially crafted garments and containers worn to conceal liquor on the human body. Have you heard of others that you found particularly clever?

8. Elsie is a storyteller like her mother; a young woman who desperately wants to believe in "happily ever after." How does that outlook affect her choices about motherhood and marriage? Eventually she comes to understand that "the most important stories are the ones we tell to—and about—ourselves," and that she is stronger than she (or anyone else) knew. Do you agree that sometimes we just need to "rescue [our] own damn self"?

9. Throughout most of the novel, Shine is bent on revenge—first for Hiram's death and later for her friend Birdie's rape—and continually thwarted. But when she finally has a chance to exact some justice in the barn loft, Shine balks. Later, she muses that revenge had seemed "satisfying. And if not easy, at least straightforward: an eye for an eye, a tooth for a tooth. But mercy? Forgiveness? That was tougher. More compli-

cated. Meandering. Certainly not achieved in one hotheaded instant." How does this shift in her understanding allow Shine to move forward instead of being mired in the past?

10. Rebecca is not much of a conversationalist—except for one-sided talks she has with the farm animals and the wild creatures of their land. How does her reluctance to speak up about Jed cause trouble? And later, with Eulalie? Discuss some of the complicating factors in her romantic relationship. What finally pushes her to risk giving voice to her own wants and desires?

11. As Lidy dies, she welcomes the transformation of her ruined earthly body into a "clear burning spirit with an unexpected kick." If Lidy is moonshine, what spirit or drink best describes you and why?

12. Two devastating crashes in the novel happen almost simultaneously: Jed and Rebecca's car accident as they are pursued by the law and the stock market crash of October 1929. How does the aftermath of the wreck affect the Strong family? How does it mirror what happens to their community, Hot Springs and the country at large as the Great Depression takes hold?

13. When Shine begins her bartending gig at the Southern Club, she is both starry-eyed and fearful of her first famous customer, Al Capone. She believes they are "the same on some level, willing to do whatever it took to survive and to keep their families safe and cared for." Do you agree? Or does Shine discover a line she won't or can't cross?

14. Lidy believes "the lot of women [isn't] right"—specifically that an undesired pregnancy disproportionately affects the female who will be "saddled with their mistake for the rest of her life." This situation plays out repeatedly over the course of the novel, from Alta and Elsie to, perhaps most heartbreakingly, Birdie. Do you agree with Lidy? Or is hers a sentiment

and symptom of the era? What about her tongue-in-cheek assertion that "There'd be no babies if it were up to men to carry and birth them. The end of the human race"?

15. Jed is trouble from the beginning, and he causes headaches, heartache and even a couple of broken bones for various Strong women throughout the book. At his core, he longs to be a part of the Strong family and the moonshine business. When circumstances create the opportunity for him to join in at last, how does he handle it? Do you feel sorry for him? Are his feelings of being used and discarded valid? Or is the world—at least the Strongs' world—truly better off without him?

16. John Flanagan is an idealist whose experience as a "prohi" reflects the arc of the temperance movement and failed Prohibition experiment—as he goes from passionate believer to an increasingly skeptical and finally disillusioned veteran. How does this "rule follower" fare with a rogue partner, armed mountain moonshiners and well-connected criminals? What finally jolts him out of his passivity to pursue what he really wants?

17. Of Lidy, Elsie says, "Right or wrong, but never indifferent. She was a Strong, through and through." Did you agree with the steely matriarch's decisions to do what she thought best—whether keeping a painful secret or ending a life prematurely?

18. Making moonshine requires careful identification of the different parts of the distillate: the poisonous "foreshots," the "heads" (which still contain too much methanol for human consumption), and the coveted "hearts," the smooth sweet middle before the final slick stuff of the "tails." While Shine becomes an expert at discerning the difference at an early age, she is far less adept at handling matters of her own head and heart—until it's almost too late. Are you glad she gets a second chance with John?

19. Shine decides "she would make a family like she and her daddy had made moonshine, putting together a bunch of unlikely ingredients, things that didn't come from the same place, or naturally go together. Stir it all up and see what happened. Test it. *Taste* it. And then crank up the heat. Because that was life, wasn't it? The fire that you couldn't always control. But what you made of it, what you *did* with it . . . that could be something special. Something you could see *through*—stunningly clear and shining and powerful. The Strong stuff." This metaphor for the complicated ways in which families are created, tested and constantly changed seems appropriate for most of our families. Do you agree?

Visit our website at
KensingtonBooks.com
to sign up for our newsletters, read more from your favorite authors, see books by series, view reading group guides, and more!

Become a Part of Our
Between the Chapters Book Club
Community and Join the Conversation

Betweenthechapters.net

Submit your book review for a chance to win exclusive Between the Chapters swag you can't get anywhere else!
https://www.kensingtonbooks.com/pages/review/